PRAISE FOR MICHELLE BRAFMAN'S

SWIMMING WITH GHOSTS

"I really enjoyed *Swimming with Ghosts*, for the excellent characters, unusual plot inside the world of local competitive swimming, the fine writing, and the frequent insights and humor. I raced right through it."

—**ANNE LAMOTT**

"Lurking beneath the seemingly mundane surface of swim clubs and pasta parties and petty squabbles are dark secrets. Best friends who have much to hide, marriages that are not what they seem. In this page-turner of a tale, Michelle Brafman leads the reader into the deeper waters of deception, loss, and self-destructive obsession. This is a story that creeps up on you and then holds fast. It will stay with me for a long time to come."

—**MARY MORRIS**, author of *The Jazz Palace* and *Gateway to the Moon*

"*Swimming with Ghosts* dives into the world of children's competitive swimming with sharp observations and an abundance of empathy. I was thrilled to spend time at the picture-perfect River Run swim club, caught in the swirl of family secrets and friendship. Moving perfectly between humor and darkness, Michelle Brafman delivers a delicious and compelling book about jealousy, addiction, and legacy."

—**JENNIFER CLOSE**, bestselling author of *Girls in White Dresses* and *Marrying the Ketchups*

"Who knows when a perfect life might be ripped out by the roots? It's summer, and as closest friendships go under and family secrets surface, a storm may be coming for Gillian Cloud and her picture-perfect swim club community. Michelle Brafman is such a sharp observer of suburban life, and Gillian and #bestie Kristy are a deliciously written female friendship. So compelling, I snuck out of bed at night to finish it. Dive in!"

—**HELEN SIMONSON**, author of *Major Pettigrew's Last Stand* and *The Summer Before the War*

"Beneath the surface of Michelle Brafman's propulsive *Swimming with Ghosts*, with its delightful humor and sharp observations of suburban mores, swirl dark undercurrents. Riptides that threaten two families lurk behind the luaus stalwart Gillian Cloud organizes at the community swimming club and her whitewashed Facebook posts. With open eyes and extraordinary compassion, Brafman tackles the shame of love addiction, illuminating its links to other addictions and what true recovery entails."

—**LISA GORNICK**, author of *The Peacock Feast* and *Louisa Meets Bear*

"I devoured *Swimming with Ghosts* in a single day, tearing through one unputdownable chapter to the next. A perfect book club pick, Brafman writes with loving sensitivity and humor about two close friends, their families, and the secrets that join them together."

—**BETHANY BALL**, author of *The Pessimists* and *What to Do About the Solomons*

"Swimmers and readers rejoice! Michelle Brafman's *Swimming with Ghosts* is proof that the most important events in life happen at the pool. Fast-paced and frequently hilarious, we unsuspectingly float on the novel's wry, quirky humor until we're suddenly over deep water, gazing into the depths of our need for purpose, friendship, and love. Anyone heading to a pool or beach this summer should have a copy of *Swimming with Ghosts* in their swim bag."

—**DAVID MCGLYNN**, author of *A Door in the Ocean*

"Michelle Brafman deftly peels back the layers of suburbia, revealing an unforgettable summer that's part *Peyton Place*, part *American Beauty*, with a hint of David Lynch. As she knows, competitive youth sports is a world that drives some of the best over the edge. Yet it can also heal so many of us."

—**TIM WENDEL**, author of *Escape from Castro's Club*

SWIMMING WITH GHOSTS

ALSO BY MICHELLE BRAFMAN

Washing the Dead

Bertrand Court

SWIMMING WITH GHOSTS

A NOVEL

MICHELLE BRAFMAN

KEYLIGHT
BOOKS
AN IMPRINT
OF TURNER
PUBLISHING

Keylight Books
an imprint of Turner Publishing Company
Nashville, Tennessee
www.turnerpublishing.com

Swimming with Ghosts

Cover and book design by William Ruoto

Library of Congress Cataloging-in-Publication Data
Names: Brafman, Michelle, author.
Title: Swimming with ghosts : a novel / Michelle Brafman.
Description: First edition. | Nashville, Tennessee : Turner Publishing Company, [2023]
Identifiers: LCCN 2022037218 (print) | LCCN 2022037219 (ebook) | ISBN 9781684429547 (hardcover) | ISBN 9781684429554 (paperback) | ISBN 9781684429561 (epub)
Subjects: LCGFT: Novels.
Classification: LCC PS3602.R344415 S95 2023 (print) | LCC PS3602.R344415 (ebook) | DDC 813/.6—dc23/eng/20220805
LC record available at https://lccn.loc.gov/2022037218
LC ebook record available at https://lccn.loc.gov/2022037219

Printed in the United States of America

With love,
this book is for
my mother, father, brother,
and all who came before
and after.

If you surrendered to the air, you could ride it.

—**TONI MORRISON**, *Song of Solomon*

JUNE 2011

1

CHARLIE

It's Pasta Pep Rally Night at River Run, the local pool, and Charlie Cloud shows up for three reasons: he wants any excuse to escape the prison of his office on a sweltering Northern Virginia Friday, he gets a charge out of watching his son lead the team in cheers, and he loves the bejesus out of his wife, Gillian, who's addicted to "the magic of summer swimming," so why not show up at an event once in a while and make her happy? Charlie's not entirely sure, though, that sitting at a picnic table in his business-casual khakis with a plate of lasagna and two brownies is accomplishing anything more than adding volume to the flesh hanging over his belt. He wipes his forehead with a tomato-stained napkin. Christ, it's hot.

"Give me an M!" Charlie's son, Justin, also the assistant coach, yells to the dozens of kids huddled in the shallow end of the pool. "M!" they shout back in unison, so loud that they drown out the thrum of a typical June Friday night: lifeguard whistles, ice cream truck music, and the occasional "My turn next!" from a kid waiting in line at the diving board. Justin and the swimmers continue the call-and-response until they've spelled out Manta Rays, the team's name. The Cloud family knows every single cheer ever composed for the River Run Manta Rays. How could they not? Gillian put both of their boys on the team when they were six, and before then, during family road trips to Nags Head, she taught them the cheers she learned while growing up at River Run. Charlie grew up swimming too, even competed during his freshman year at Colby and coached a bit, but none of his experiences matched the intensity of this low-stakes summer community pool scene. Such a curious phenomenon.

Between bites of pasta, Charlie chats with the old guard, the few parents he still knows, as they file in with platters of homemade mac and cheese, ziti, orzo smothered in pesto, garlic bread, salad, and cookies. Major carb loading. They place their offerings on the assigned picnic tables Gillian and her best friend, Kristy Weinstein, have set up beside the clubhouse, a few yards from the pool. On the fence behind the tables hangs a "Let's Go, Mighty, Mighty Manta Rays!" cardboard sign, its corners curling from the humidity.

The newer parents smile at Charlie, but only because he belongs to Gillian, River Run queen, and Justin, River Run royalty and a coach to boot. Mainly, he's invisible, but that's okay. Back in the day, Gillian's dad was a legend at the pool, and Gillian proved it by hanging pictures of him in the clubhouse and even in the foyer of their home. Good ole Sebastian Norton is everywhere. Even though Charlie didn't meet him before he died, he knew the type: a little too handsome, massive charisma, big drinker, and a real Don Draper with the ladies. Of course, he'd never mention any of this to Gillian. To her, Sebastian Norton is the stuff of fairy tales.

Charlie is full, but he goes in for seconds of lasagna. He promised himself he'd stop eating big meals, but here he is, mopping up meat sauce with his second piece of garlic bread and eyeing another brownie. He promised himself he'd start swimming again this summer, but here he is, mid-June and he's yet to buy himself a bathing suit that fits. And he promised himself he'd pick up his guitar again, but his Squier Telecaster sits in the basement, badly in need of new strings.

Time to make himself useful. He heaves himself up from the picnic table to help Kristy and Gillian feed the swarm of guppies who have just hopped out of the pool. As he approaches the buffet, he catches one of the swim dads sneaking a peek down Kristy's bikini top.

"Thanks for helping out, Charlie," Kristy says without looking up from the foil she's unpeeling from a bowl of salad.

"Isn't he a sweetheart?" Gillian hands him a pair of plastic gloves.

"No charge." He pulls the gloves onto his sweaty hands and dishes out two helpings of orzo for the next swimmer in line, a long stringy kid who looks like he's mid-growth-spurt.

"Thank you, sir."

Nice manners. "You're welcome. I'm Justin's dad, by the way."

The boy's eyes, indented with red goggle marks, light up. "That's so cool."

Gillian nudges him gently with her elbow. "You're a real celebrity, Justin's dad."

The moms line up after the kids are seated, and as Charlie doles out more salad than pasta, Gillian personally greets each one of them. She inquires about a mother-in-law's hip replacement, a kid's new asthma medication, and a rescue dog's surprise surges of aggression. Gillian treats every Manta Ray mom and dad as a guest in her home.

Gillian and Kristy are leaning into each other as if chatting in the quiet section of the library, likely whispering about who's going to bring the cases of water or the Manta Rays' tent to the meet tomorrow. For the past ten summers, Gillian and Kristy have cohabitated the ten-week-long, adrenaline-saturated cocoon that is community summer swimming. They were friends for only a year when Gillian shared this precious slice of her childhood with Kristy, who scarfed it down without chewing. Then, when the "Brangelina" craze hit, a River Run parent nicknamed Kristy and Gillian "Krillian." It stuck. They live in their own world, those two. Sure, at first Charlie felt like the odd man out, but he's gotten used to it over the years. Besides, Kristy's the best friend Gillian has ever had.

Kristy takes a bite of a pecan bar, then runs her tongue over her gums to remove any nut detritus before giving Gillian her "Do I have anything unsightly caught in my teeth?" smile.

Gillian takes a good look. "All clear."

"Thanks, girl."

The line has dwindled down to a few stragglers and some of the older swimmers going back for seconds, so Charlie clears the dirty plates from the empty picnic tables. After he's filled a few garbage bags, he takes them outside the fence to the trash bins. When he lifts up the lids, the stench of old watermelon rinds, discarded swim diapers, and stale beer makes his eyebrows wilt. He'll go back inside to the pool and say goodbye to Gillian and Justin and then head home, change into his shorts, and catch a new episode of *Breaking Bad*.

While Charlie is standing outside the fence, all of his senses awaken, and the scene in front of him appears in Technicolor: the stringy boy trying out a card trick on Justin, the hive of parents rounding up their empty platters and sugared-up kids, and the yellow sun setting over the water. The soft wind that rustles the backstroke flags feels like a fingertip crawling up his bare arm. He has the hearing of a dolphin or a bat, and the sound of Kristy and Gillian's giggling pierces the low hum of the pool. Something draws his gaze up toward the diving board, where Gillian's dad used to perform his famous swan dives. A chill overtakes him even though he's sweating his boxers. And then poof. Everything looks, feels, and sounds normal again. Spooked, he hurries away from the pool and drives home without saying goodbye to anyone. A few scenes into his TV show, he forgets all about that creepy alertness and the chill that followed.

ONE SUMMER LATER

JUNE 2012

2

KRISTY

Kristy texts her two children from the driveway. *Come out here and help me with the groceries, darling spawn.* In seconds, Kristy's daughter, Mia, comes barreling out of the back door. The light catches her blond hair as it bounces against her shoulders, broad and tanned like Kristy's.

"OMG, Mom! Did you hear the breaking news about the pool?"

"OMG, how did you hear already, Bob Woodward?" Kristy asks, always amused by Mia's exuberance over a good scoop, particularly if it relates to the River Run pool. Both Mia and Kristy had caught Gillian's River Run obsession like it was a fly ball at a Nats game.

"We are officially without a head coach. Aunt Gillian texted all of us coaches." Mia and her brother call Gillian and Charlie aunt and uncle because Mr. and Mrs. Cloud seems too formal and calling an adult by his or her first name doesn't fly with either Kristy or Gillian.

"I can't believe Zeke quit." Mia hoists four bags from the car with ease. "I mean, practice has started."

"We're up a creek," Kristy says.

"Pool drah-ma!" Isaac strolls out of the house, still sliding one foot into a flip-flop. Not an athlete of any kind, Isaac couldn't give a hoot about the River Run coaching crisis. Slight, like his father, he struggles to lift the remaining bags from the car.

As Mia opens the door to the house, she says, "Spill, Mom!"

Kristy tells the kids everything she knows, that Zeke has jumped at the opportunity to work for a start-up in Hong Kong.

"Aunt Gillian must be flipping out." Mia removes an oversized honeydew from one of the bags.

"She'll figure out something," Kristy assures Mia. Zeke had been a serviceable if uninspiring head coach they'd never had reason to fire, so it isn't a huge loss. The timing is awful, though. Who will they find to step in so late?

"Aunt Gillian to the rescue," Mia says. "As always."

"Yup. And she called an emergency meeting for tonight, so guess who's in charge of dinner?"

"Chipotle?" Isaac asks.

"Nope, you and your sister," Kristy says. "Roasted chicken thighs. All you have to do is stick them in the oven and make some rice and a salad."

"Did you use that marinade stuff from one of Dad's angsty pregnant lady patients who named their baby after him?" Isaac had taken on the mantle of the family wiseass last year when he started high school.

Mia pokes Isaac in the ribs. "That joke's kind of old, dude." She wants to become a high-risk OB, just like her dad. And yes, there are quite a few babies in Northern Virginia named David or even Davida.

"Mom, your phone." Isaac points to Kristy's vibrating iPhone on the counter.

"I bet it's Aunt Gillian," Mia says with conviction.

It's not Gillian. It's Travis, Kristy's stepdad. Kristy picks up right away, because Travis never phones on Thursdays. After her mother died, Kristy and Travis maintained the family phone ritual: every other Sunday afternoon, for eight to ten minutes. No more, no less.

"Hiya, Kristy." The combination of the cigarette smoke Travis has drawn into his lungs for decades and his Virginia twang makes him sound like the actor Sam Elliott.

"Hi, Daddy." She goes into her bedroom. "You okay?"

"Helluva mess," Travis says after he tells her about a pipe that burst and wreaked havoc on the basement of her childhood home, twenty-seven miles out I-66 and a universe away from the Arlington McMansion she shares with David and the kids.

"Sorry that happened, Daddy." Not that she has a fondness for her old house, but Travis sounds overwhelmed.

"Thanks, sweetheart."

"I can come over to help." Her neck muscles tighten, as they always do at the thought of returning home, so she uses the ritual she and her ex-sponsor once devised to ground herself in the present. With intention, she taps the gold Star of David pendant her husband gave her after her conversion to Judaism.

"Kris, that's not why I called. I just wanted to know if you want me to save a box of yours that I found."

Kristy has no interest in preserving anything from her past, but something in her father's voice makes her blurt, "I'll be over after my meeting tonight."

After they say their goodbyes, she goes to her closet to change for the meeting, and just like that, a lens clicks and she sees the room through her mom's eyes. Yes, it dwarfs the childhood bedroom she shared with her sister; yes, she can fill up three shoe racks; yes, she owns more than thirty pairs of yoga pants with matching tops; yes, she paid Gillian, a professional clutterbuster, to organize her excess. And yes, Gillian featured Kristy's closet on her website. When Kristy's mother was alive, she took note of David's BMW, their second dishwasher, and the mezuzah hanging on their doorframe. "Please be careful," Flo whispered as she gave Kristy a hug the morning she married David. Her mother didn't have to finish her sentence.

Kristy picks a skinny mid-rise cut of jeans that few other women her age can pull off, a sleeveless shirt that shows off the cleavage David purchased for her fortieth birthday, and a pair of wedge sandals that David says makes her legs stretch on forever. She spritzes herself with Velvet Haze. Although she rocks the athleisure wear, thanks to hours of spinning and sculpting, she likes to look good when she knows that other women are either checking her out or keeping an eye on their husbands who are doing the same. It thrills her to win the night. Gillian is her first friend whom she's never viewed as a competitor, which perplexed Kristy at first. Then she decided not to question her good luck in finding someone who made her feel so warm and relaxed. Gillian feels like home.

"Hey, baby," David calls from the hallway outside their bedroom.

Kristy is brushing her lashes with mascara. "In here."

"Someone smells delicious." Still in his scrubs, David stands behind her and wraps his arms around her waist.

She turns around and gives him a quick hug.

"Mia reported on the emergency meeting tonight."

"Yeah, and I have to stop at my dad's afterwards." She sighs.

David listens carefully while she tells him about Travis's flood. She returns the mascara wand to the tube. "I'm off, then."

"Okay, um. Be careful," he says. They rarely discuss Travis, but David once commented on how long it takes for her to return to his Kristy, Kristy Weinstein, after visiting her family. The pre-David Kristy, Kristy Frick, was one hot mess.

3

GILLIAN

Gillian is filling bowls with her designated swim-team committee snacks, trying to swat away an uneasy feeling about tonight's meeting. She knows she's being silly; during her tenure as team rep, she once broke up a parent brawl about a relay spot and stepped up to host a divisionals championship meet at River Run with ten days' notice. What's a little coaching crisis? Easy peasy.

She looks up when Kristy lets herself in through the back door. My gosh, is she happy to see her friend. "Hola!" Kristy slings an arm around Gillian's shoulders and draws her in for a hug. The familiar scent of Kristy—her musky perfume and peppermint from the Altoids she pops constantly—soothes her. After Kristy releases her, Gillian, whom her two boys call "the human lint roller," reaches up to pluck one of Kristy's blond hairs from her shoulder. "I'm glad you're here."

"Oh, come on! Where else would I be?"

"You're a tonic, Kristy Weinstein."

Kristy pinches a couple of grapes from a bowl and tosses them into her mouth. "You've got this, Gil."

Gillian arranges five Mason jars so that they are equidistant from one another. "We've got to move fast. Ready or not, the first A meet is happening a week from tomorrow."

"You're really worried?"

"You know I've got a love–hate relationship with surprises." Gillian fidgets with the collar of her Manta Rays polo, embroidered with "Gillian Cloud, Team Representative" a few inches above her heart.

"Look, any other rep in the county would be shitting pineapples right now, but we all know you'll figure this out."

Kristy's profanity used to shock Gillian, but now it makes her laugh. "Thanks for the vote of confidence," she says, but Kristy's reassurances fail to soothe her like they usually do.

Kristy walks over to the pantry for a bottle of lime-flavored seltzer and a jar of pomegranate syrup. "I'll make us our drink."

Charlie enters the kitchen, freshly showered and shaved. "One lemon heading your way." He grabs a lemon from the fruit bowl on the kitchen table and tosses it to Kristy.

Gillian is taken aback by Charlie's playfulness and his knowledge of the official swim-team committee meeting beverage. But then again, Charlie has been full of surprises since he stopped working. It's been six months since he was let go, and he hasn't come close to landing a job. He's clearly lost his already-weak taste for developing real estate. She bit her tongue instead of inquiring about his last two interviews, though she's growing nervous as heck about how they'll cover the boys' college tuitions. Not Charlie: his "sabbatical" is treating him well. He's tan and taut from working out like a fiend, and there is something else different about him, the way he moves his body, a subtle new confidence in his simple "Hey there, Kristy. How ya been?"

"No complaints, Charlie."

"Kind of a bummer about the coaching situation, huh?" He smiles, exposing the dimple that caught her eye at that bar in Waterville decades ago. Golly, it's possible that he is now even better-looking than he was when they first met.

"Not worried." Kristy points to Gillian with her thumb. "Not with your better half at the helm."

Charlie nods and fills the Mason jars with ice while Kristy slices the lemon, pours seltzer and a shot of syrup into the jars, and hands one of them to Gillian, who immediately wipes down the counter. Charlie opens a beer, but Gillian rarely drinks alcohol because she doesn't like to lose control of any situation. Ever.

The doorbell rings, and Charlie jumps up from his chair to answer it. Bizarre. He usually avoids swim-team people. Once he even called them "the River Run cult." The remaining three committee members arrive in tandem. These women, together with Kristy, carry most of the volunteering load for the team, and Gillian handpicked them all. She stands in front of the framed photo of her father's swan dive in the foyer and greets each one. Although she'll deny it to Charlie, she does love the way her attention makes them purr. She leads the women downstairs, to the rec room which Charlie converted from a family TV room to a man cave after Justin and Sebby went off to college.

When Charlie follows and settles into Gillian's chair, helping himself to a handful of Trek Mix, Gillian shoots him a look as if to say "That's my seat and you're excused now," but he continues to chomp away. Odd. They're typically excellent at communicating nonverbally about when it's time to leave a party or how to weave a sensitive topic into a conversation with one of the boys.

"Thanks for coming on such short notice, ladies." Gillian talks through the smile that she knows makes people trust her to fix whatever is broken, be it a pace clock at the pool or a team without a coach. "As you know, we need to find a replacement for Zeke."

"Stat," Kristy chimes in. "By Monday anyway."

"We're only one week out from our first meet, but let's not panic." Gillian lowers her hands as if she's a conductor cuing her symphony to lessen their instruments' volume. "And one week from the pre-meet tie-dye pep rally, which I will take care of."

"That makes me think of . . ." One of the women launches into the tired story about their last coach, who didn't grow up as a Manta Ray. Mr. Purkman, an elementary school math teacher who gave brilliant stroke advice, went under when they pushed him into the pool after they won their first meet. It turned out he didn't know how to swim, and after a few seconds of mouth-to-mouth he spouted water like Shamu. He was now working summers at a Home Depot in Seven Corners, which was a darned shame. The kids adored him.

The digression is making Gillian feel antsy. She keeps glancing over at Charlie, willing him to leave, but he is listening too intently to notice her. Since when is Manta Rays history so compelling to him?

"Beloved committee members, let's not lose our focus." Gillian claps her hands together sharply. "Any practical ideas?"

The food-sales chair sits up straight and fidgets with an earring while she offers up her son for the job. "I'll put Liam's name in the ring. We could bump him up to head coach."

"Pool bylaws," Gillian says delicately. Both Liam and Justin are rising college sophomores, one year too young to assume the job of head coach. Not that Gillian is objective, but Justin is a hit with the parents and kids, and Liam Port—well, let's say he's never put a kickboard away in his life. "Let's brainstorm a bit more here." A germ of an idea is trying to sprout in Gillian's mind, but Charlie is distracting her by bouncing his leg up and down. She wishes he would take his Trek Mix and shaking leg and head upstairs.

Gillian is about to try again to dismiss Charlie when Kristy turns to him and says, "You look like you're going to erupt over there." She adds with her snorty laugh, "Do you have restless leg syndrome or something, Charlie?"

4

CHARLIE

Charlie always bounces his leg when he's about to make a bold move. Charlie hasn't bounced his leg in a very long time. He grasps his knee to stop himself from thumping his heel against the carpet while Gillian lets the committee members serve up one rotten idea after another. Her bright blue eyes blaze, and her elfin features morph into her pixie warrior vibe, a hundred and ten pounds of spunk. He can tell she's cooking up a solution to the crisis, but his idea is so much better. Gillian has no clue about his scheme, glorious in its perfection: Charlie Cloud as head coach of the Manta Rays.

Charlie has suppressed his talents for years. He was never going to bring in enough money to suit Oliver Quinn, whom he himself had hired and mentored. After eighteen years of service to the firm, that double-crossing prick "restructured" Charlie's department and gave him a four-month severance package, now expired. Enough. It's Charlie's turn to grab the brass ring, especially after the decades of afternoons, nights, and weekends he spent shackled to his desk, crunching numbers for the rainmakers to secure their deals. He sat and sat until he grew a belly and a lard ass. He wants more than anything to molt that Charlie Cloud. Fuck, yeah.

Wait a minute. Maybe his idea isn't feasible. He needs to make real money. The boys' tuition installments are coming due next month, and they're still paying off Sebby's wisdom teeth extraction from last winter break, which Gillian has reminded him of twice this week. He's been too chicken to tell her that he blew off his last job interview, a referral from one of her clutterbuster clients, or worse, that he opened two new credit cards to cover the bills. Gillian hates carrying debt.

Does he even have the cojones to go through with his plan? Could he pull off coaching a team? It's been years since he swam or coached, but he was good at both, something he and Gillian had bonded over on their first real date in their junior year of college. Greasy cheese pizza, two pitchers of beer, and a night of everything-but sex. They fell hard.

Gillian shoots him a glance, and he knows from the way she's maneuvering her pretty lips into a broader smile that he's annoyed her, that she wants him to scram. Nobody knows better than Charlie what River Run means to his wife. She blew a gasket when he suggested that they move the photo of her dad's swan dive an inch up the wall after they repainted the foyer. One inch. Charlie isn't looking to mess with her treasured family history with the pool; he only wants to find a way to rehabilitate his life. He'll get his mojo back this summer and then figure out his next professional move. Afterwards, he'll go back to not giving a shit about the River Run pool.

Go with your instincts, he reminds himself, from that place deep inside him. Maybe the whole thing even started last summer at the pep rally pasta party when he caught that weird chill. Back then he was so lethargic he could barely move. None of that matters now. His plan is fucking brilliant.

He is running out of time. Gillian is squaring her shoulders, ready to make her big announcement. A lock of her inky black hair has escaped from her ponytail, and she brushes it away from her cheek. She looks radiant tonight. Nothing makes his wife come alive like fixing a problem. She clears her throat.

It's your time, Charlie. Let's go. Before she can open her mouth, Charlie sits up straight. "I have a solution to our crisis."

The women turn and wait for him to speak. Gulp. The tips of his ears warm.

"What is it, Charlie?" Gillian asks sweetly, but he knows she's poised to swoop in and save the day with one of her sensible ideas.

"I'd like to be considered for the coaching job." His words hold the consistency of a brown banana.

Gillian burrows her eyes into his and examines him for what seems like ten minutes. This is the take-charge gaze that first attracted Charlie when he was her R.A. and led their dorm floor on a hike in Acadia National Park. He was so taken with her beautiful calves that he missed a key turn. Gillian looked right into his soul before reaching into her backpack, whipping out a trail map, and redirecting them to their path. Following Gillian has always felt as natural as walking or breathing. For now, though, his very vitality rests on his ability to tuck his Gillian feelings away.

Gillian bursts into her infectious giggle. "He's joking, but I actually do have a super idea for a head coach."

He turns toward the committee. "I'm not kidding, folks."

"Oh, honey." Gillian is still grinning, but the rosy flush crawling up her neck telegraphs her thoughts: *What in tarnation are you doing, Charlie Cloud?*

"Little-known fact, folks. I used to coach in the summers when I was in college, and truth be told, I'm a more accomplished competitive swimmer than anyone you've ever hired. I can do a better job than all the coaches you've spent the better part of this hour complaining about." He speaks with perfect elocution.

They stare at him.

"I can do a meet lineup in my sleep, and I know what it means to make a deadline. Look no further, because I'm your best bet." He pauses for effect. "And you know it."

He has them. If he'd allowed himself to dream during those years of corporate drudgery, he would have come up with this very plan. He believes every syllable of the stump speech he's just delivered to the committee. Yes, everything in his life has led him up to this moment. *His* moment. Finally.

"And who else are you going to find who can start on Monday?" There, he's played his trump card. If he looks his wife's way, he'll catch a glimpse of that little girl who clung to her River Run pool to keep her safe from god knows what was going on in her house. So he doesn't look.

He scans the room, and though the members are quiet, he can hear the gears turning inside their heads. Kristy shifts in her seat. He loves the hell out of his wife, but she's had full access to the team for years. Now it's his turn. They'll figure out the money thing.

The other members are low-hanging fruit, thanks to Gillian, who selects people who are hardworking and easily swayed by someone with a sense of purpose.

"Aye," says the first member.

Boom. Boom. Boom. The rest follow, except for Kristy.

Gillian looks at Kristy, who glances back at her.

"I—" Kristy swallows hard. "Um, I think we should think this through a bit more carefully."

"No time," Gillian says through a smile that now looks like it will break her face.

Kristy smooths an eyebrow with her pointer finger.

"Aye!" Gillian says with great enthusiasm, and Kristy follows suit, like she always does.

He won. Holy shit, he won.

5

GILLIAN

What. The. Heck. Gillian is clapping so hard over Charlie's coup that her palms sting, but there are so many things wrong with what he's just done. How could he act so irresponsibly? Her business is thriving, but they've been digging into their savings because she barely earns enough to cover their monthly nut, not to mention other mounting expenses. Plus, the very public nature of Charlie's surprise move embarrasses her.

She gauges the response from the committee. Her committee. Her pool, for that matter.

Quick, Gillian, think. You can do this. Think back to the barbecue fundraiser for an Arlington County adult literacy program, when you spun the calamity of serving up fifty pounds of *E. coli*. You've got this under control.

She waits for the calm, the moment of clarity that always shows up in time for her to weave the facts of a crisis into the fabric of a new truth. Without a second to spare, a plan for the reframing arrives. She has to pretend that she's been in on this all along, or the committee will feel sorry for her. She loathes being pitied.

Gillian walks over to Charlie, rests her fingers on his shoulders, and turns to the group. "Congratulations, babe." She removes her hands from his body. "Coaching has been on Charlie's bucket list for years." Usually if she says something with enough conviction, she believes it. Tonight her words feel cottony in her mouth.

Charlie's new grin, borderline cocky but inviting too, makes her feel simultaneously furious and turned on. He pumps his fist in the air. "Go, Manta Rays!"

Honestly, what's left to say?

Of course Kristy stays after everyone else leaves, but Gillian can't help but notice that she keeps looking at her watch.

"Let me walk you out." Gillian guides Kristy toward the front door, away from the kitchen, away from Charlie.

The sun has just set. Gillian loves when the June days stretch out. She waves at her neighbor, out for his nightly smoke.

"That Charlie," Gillian says as if her husband were some irascible little boy who got into trouble for goofing off in class.

"Didn't see that one coming." Kristy presses a button on her car key to unlock the door.

Gillian had seen something coming, but then again she'd been feeling that old pit in her belly for months. If Gillian were to confide in anyone about the pit that returned to her stomach after Charlie was fired, it would be Kristy. The pit had made its debut after her father lost his job and Gillian assumed they'd move out of their house into the shelter where she volunteered with their church every Thanksgiving. That was where drunks and their families ended up, she'd thought to herself as she ladled mashed potatoes onto the residents' plates. The pit faded slightly when her mother conquered her fear of driving over bridges so that she could cross the Potomac River to work fifty-hour weeks in Woodward & Lothrop's alterations department. Her mother said she was proud of Gillian for babysitting every day after school and weekend nights, but she said nothing about how Gillian hid her earnings in her mom's makeup kit so her father wouldn't swipe the cash to buy vodka. That spring, her mother talked the pool treasurer into waiving the Nortons' fees, and by June a less prestigious private school out in Maryland hired Sebastian to step in for their headmaster, an older gentleman who had died in his sleep. Gillian's childhood was bifurcated into two distinct periods: the times she felt the pit and the times she didn't. Now she's even angrier with Charlie for dredging all this up and turning her into her younger brother Patrick, a chronic navel-gazer who blames all his woes on their father. Makes her batty.

Gillian chooses not to reveal any of this to Kristy, because Gillian is a fixer, not a fixee, and relishes her role as Kristy's guardian angel. Gillian and Kristy met shortly after their mothers died, and although they weren't exactly each other's type, both commented on how they were drawn together like positive and negative ions. Kristy made Gillian laugh and loosen up a bit, and Gillian taught Kristy how to swim, dress for a charity gala, interview caterers for her kids' bar and bat mitzvahs, along with myriad basic skills she lacked. Gillian needs to be that person, especially now.

Kristy breaks the silence. "I guess we didn't have much of a choice. Who else could step in so fast?"

Gillian slaps a mosquito that has landed on her shoulder.

"We'll just do our thing, like we always do," Kristy says with an earnestness that makes Gillian want to cry, like the time she appointed Kristy to help out with scoring and compiling the team results, and Kristy hugged her so hard that Gillian thought she'd crack a rib. Gillian had been waiting her whole life for the perfect friend with whom she could share River Run. Kristy, with her sexiness and money, is an object of envy, but nobody understands Kristy's core like Gillian does.

"You're right, Kristy."

"You up for a one o'clock spin tomorrow?" Kristy asks while they stand in front of her car. Gillian can tell by Kristy's question and the clip in her voice that she's ready to finish up the evening, and Gillian also wants to be alone with her thoughts.

"That's a terrific idea." Gillian wraps her arms around her friend for a few seconds before Kristy's cell phone vibrates inside that new Kate Spade bag she loves showing off.

"Everything will be all right, Gil."

"Go take your call. Could be one of the kids." Gillian releases Kristy into the night.

6
KRISTY

After Kristy arrives at her childhood home, she pauses before she gets out of the car. She's come a hell of a long way from this little house, and she's come even further from the pathetic love addict she was before she met David. She doesn't believe that adage "once an addict, always an addict," because she has this thing licked.

There's a note from Travis taped to the front door, saying that he darted out to borrow a Wet Vac from Mr. Peterson up the street, so she sticks her hand into the planter box for the spare key and lets herself in through the back.

The air in the kitchen feels moist against her skin. Her eye catches the red vinyl chairs that her mother bought at a garage sale. "You can't believe what rich people throw away," Flo had said on their drive to a church rummage sale in South Arlington when Kristy was nine. Kristy loved their trips to this part of Virginia. The view of the tip-top of the Washington Monument practically touching the clouds made her feel like anything was possible. That morning, she and her mother returned to Manassas with the chairs and a pair of patent leather party shoes for Kristy to wear to her brand-new half-sister's christening. Size ten and a half, and only one size too big.

A couple of old chairs is all it takes to pull Kristy back to the morning her mother brought baby Nora home from the hospital.

Before Travis left to pick up Flo and Nora, he had made Kristy, just Kristy, French toast on the griddle. "Thanks, Daddy." She cracked a smile inside every time she said that word aloud, even though she'd been saying it for a year and a half. Until third grade, it had been just Kristy and Flo, who told anyone who got nosy about Kristy's real dad, "He isn't with us anymore." Nobody ever asked where he was.

When Travis finally came home with Mom and Nora, Kristy sprang up from the lookout chair in the living room and opened the front door. The four of them stood in the hallway, Travis holding baby Nora so that Kristy could see her pointy head, about the size of a grapefruit.

"This is your sister." Flo stroked Kristy's hair. "Nora, meet Kristy," her mother cooed.

"She's so cute." She was actually kind of ugly, which made Kristy feel relieved in a weird way.

"You're tired, Flo, go get yourself a little shuteye," Travis said, not taking his eyes off the baby. "I'll feed Nora." Travis was the oldest of eleven children, so he knew all about feeding babies. And making the best French toast ever.

"Let me make a bottle first, honey," Flo said, real sweet. Purple moons encircled her eyes, and she still looked pregnant.

Kristy followed her mother into the kitchen and watched her fill a pot with water and turn on the stove to warm it up. She mixed the formula and gave the bottle a good shake before dunking it into the pot. After a minute or two, she removed the bottle and squeezed a drop of formula on her wrist. Had Flo gone to all this trouble to feed Kristy?

Flo handed the bottle to Kristy, and the two headed out to the living room. Flo went on upstairs while Kristy gave Travis the formula and sat down on the chair across from the couch, where he slung one of those brand-new pink JCPenney burp cloths over his shoulder.

Travis wore a smile Kristy had never seen before as he watched his baby's lips slurp on the warm bottle. Kristy tasted a bitterness in her mouth. She wanted him to stop feeding Nora. Now. After Nora finished part of the liquid, he placed her little body over his shoulder and patted her back. "Attagirl," he chuckled after she burped. He brought her grapefruit head to his bristly cheek. Eyes closed, he drank in her smell. He looked like he was praying. When Kristy offered to take Nora's near-empty bottle into the kitchen, Travis complimented her on being a good big sister. Standing in front of the griddle drying on the rack, she brought Nora's bottle to her lips and sucked until the milky sweetness coated her tongue. She wanted more. She was considering making herself a little formula when Flo appeared out of nowhere and yanked the bottle from her hand.

"Kristy, what in God's name are you doing?" Flo scream-whispered so Travis wouldn't hear.

Kristy's cheeks burned with shame. "I don't know." She looked down. Even her big, clumsy feet felt hot.

"No drinking your sister's milk." Flo tapped the bottle with her fingernail. "This is for Nora."

Kristy cried into her pillow that night and lots of nights after. Her parents only cared about Nora. She felt like she had before Travis showed up, like that dresser Mom bought at a garage sale and then got mad because it took up too much space in her bedroom. She was as invisible as air. She'd rather cut summer vacation short, even if it meant sitting through a boring social studies class, than spend one more minute as the big-sister helper. On Nora's one-month birthday, she told her mother that she was going over to her friend Mandy's house to play. Instead, she biked two miles to visit Travis at his auto repair shop. She knew lying was wrong, but for crying out loud, she just wanted a minute without her sister gobbling up all the love.

The dryer buzzer rings, pulling Kristy back to the here and now. She deposits her purse on one of the chairs and ventures downstairs to tend to the laundry. Her feet remember to tiptoe down the steps, as she did during those high school years when she snuck boys—always the ones with the serious girlfriends—through the basement window, to the ratty old couch Travis had brought home from the shop. After she sprouted breasts, she figured out how to arch her back and hold a boy's gaze that extra second. "This slutty business isn't cute," Flo fumed after she caught thirteen-year-old Kristy on the couch, straddling the teenager who cut their neighbor Mrs. O'Connor's lawn every Wednesday afternoon. Kristy quit bringing boys home, for a few months anyway, but she couldn't wean herself from the high of prying them away from their girlfriends, even if it meant doing things she didn't like. So she got smarter about sneaking them inside.

Kristy hesitates at the foot of the steps before kicking off her sandals and hopping a puddle to reach the cement floor, away from the semifinished section where pencils and laundry clips raft on the water pooling over the dingy green carpet. The floor is slick against her soles, and she steadies herself by grasping the side of the ping-pong table, laden with a record player, fishing gear, and boxes of files that her father must have rescued from the flood.

Travis's laundry room smells like dirty rainwater and Downy. She removes the warm towels from the dryer and places them atop the machine. She'll fold them upstairs so she can get the hell out of this cricket factory. She scoops the wet linens out of the washing-machine basin and loads them into the dryer. A heap of Travis's sleeveless undershirts, which he wears beneath his short-sleeved button-up shirts, even on the hottest of days, lies in a basket on the floor. She's putting them in the washing machine when she hears Travis call her name. She startles. "Jeez, I didn't even hear you come down."

Travis bends over to pick up a frayed hand towel and throws it into the load. "Good to see you, Kris."

She pours detergent into the basin and starts the machine. "Let's go upstairs."

"I'll get your box." He walks to the far end of the ping-pong table and retrieves a worn box, her name scrawled on the top with a Sharpie. "Here we go."

She follows him up to the kitchen and sets the clean towels on the chair next to the one with her purse.

Still carrying the box, Travis says, "It's a little wet, but it should be fine if you take everything out and let it air-dry right away."

"I can fold the laundry before I leave."

"Better go dry this thing out." Travis pats the box.

Both relieved and aching for him to insist that she stay, she pecks him on his leathery cheek. "I'll be back tomorrow with our dehumidifier."

He glances at her with that old apology in his eyes. None of that "slutty business" was his fault, she always wants to say, but she never has. Not even after her ex-sponsor told her that she would never fully recover from her addiction until she and Travis laid out their moldy history on his rickety kitchen table.

"Night, Daddy." She holds the box as far away from her body as she can as she walks back to her car.

Kristy pulls up to her house, built on the site of a cute postwar prairie teardown. Their three-car garage only fits two cars because it overflows with bikes, golf clubs, snow skis, and other sporting goods. "Crap," she mutters to herself, removing the box from the trunk and making some space next to her mountain bike. She'll deal with it tomorrow.

It's almost ten o'clock, and David, Mia, and Isaac are sprawled out on the plump leather couches in their family room, watching an Orioles game on the obscenely large flat-screen TV David purchased for the family last Hanukkah. Now Kristy wants a bigger one. Isaac is wearing his O's hat backwards, and David is sitting next to Mia, her Mac open in her lap, her fingers working through a knot in her hair. The house smells like garlic and chicken, like nourishment.

"Mom!" Mia leans into her phone. "More breaking news."

"River Run alert," Isaac mocks. In a week, he will leave for a trip to Israel with David's parents, and he won't give the pool a thought.

Mia makes a swatting motion at him. "Aunt Gillian just posted that Uncle Charlie is going to coach the Manta Rays. Mom, is it true?"

"Like that's going to happen." Isaac pretends to swat Mia back. "The pool is all Aunt Gillian, all the time."

"Charlie doesn't seem the type to lead a team," David adds in that superior tone that both annoys her and makes her feel safe.

"Mia's right." Kristy recaps Charlie's winning sales pitch for the Weinstein family.

"Why didn't they hire Liam?" Mia asks too casually.

"Too young." Kristy is grateful to have a ready-made response. Mia has it bad for that entitled jerk.

Mia isn't going to let this go. "We've got a meet in a week, and Liam could so totally step in."

"He's a power tool." Isaac speaks the truth for Kristy.

"What's wrong with Liam?" David looks up from the game.

"Let's not go there," Mia says. "That's going to be really weird for Justin, having your mom like basically run the pool and having your *dad* as your boss."

"Weird to work for your father," Isaac agrees. "No offense, Dad."

"None taken."

"How's Aunt Gillian?" Mia gets the whole River Run thing.

"She's putting up a good front," Kristy says as if Gillian just had to put down her dog.

"Kris, don't get in the middle of this. It's between Charlie and Gillian." David looks at her for a second before he turns his attention back to the television. "Besides, nothing gets Gillian Cloud down for long."

"True, but Aunt Gillian is River Run dynasty!" Mia pipes up. "This is different."

David, like Isaac, doesn't invest his energy in the River Run cult, as Charlie calls it. David prefers to spend his leisure time at his parents' exclusive golf club in Bethesda instead of the bare-bones community pool. The golf club reminds Kristy that despite her shopping habits and new Land Rover, she doesn't have the right pedigree or religion to fit in with his crew. Come to think of it, she only fits into the River Run crowd because Gillian made it so.

"My loyalty is to Gillian," Kristy announces. "Always."

"Sure is! You're Krillian!" Mia says before heading up to her bedroom, electronic devices in tow.

"Come here." David reaches out his arm, and Kristy cuddles up next to him.

"Who's gonna win?"

"The O's if they keep at it." Isaac places his palms together in prayer. "Let's watch another inning, Dad."

Kristy rises from the couch and makes her way to the kitchen, which she can tell Mia and David cleaned. Isaac never remembers to close the cabinets. She removes a jar of Jif Extra Crunchy from the pantry and a spoon from the silverware drawer and digs in hard. David detests this habit, but he is otherwise occupied until the commercial; by the time he comes into the kitchen, she's devoured a half-dozen spoonfuls of peanut butter. She puts the jar away and sits on a kitchen stool with a glass of water.

"How are you, love?" He leans over and wraps his arms around her shoulders.

"You know." This is all she needs to say to convey her usual disorientation and clinginess after a visit to Manassas and the accompanying stroll down memory lane.

He kisses her on the top of the head and releases her. "How's Travis?"

Kristy shrugs. "He's Travis."

"And the basement?"

"Soggy." She runs her finger over her lip to remove traces of peanut butter. "The box is soggy too, so I left it in the garage."

"What's in it?"

Kristy is afraid to open it. "No idea."

"I'll go get it."

"Leave it, honey." She doesn't want David touching that wet old thing, and she doesn't want it in the house either. "I'll air it out on the porch tomorrow."

He caresses her chin with his strong, slender surgeon's hand before he tilts her head to the side and studies her carefully, as if he's never seen her before. He eyes her lip. "Jif?"

She grabs his finger. "Not saying."

They laugh, and she kisses him. He always smells clean. The commercial is over and it's time for David to laser-focus his attention back on the game. She's long since accepted that she is the commercial break from his regular programming: his work, his parents, his beloved sports teams, the kids. Never another woman, though. She knows this. It's all good. The ads are of Super Bowl quality and predictably timed.

"I'm beat." She craves a hot shower and some quiet.

"Be up soon."

"Good night, Isaac," she calls out to the den.

Later that night, when David comes to bed, she pulls the sheets back and he climbs in beside her. With the precision of a man who understands the female anatomy, he touches her in all the right places. She reciprocates, and for a good five minutes afterwards her limbs feel heavy. They lie quietly. David rolls away from her and gets up to pee. Walking to the bathroom, he throws back his shoulders, packed with muscle he and his personal trainer have worked so hard to build. When he returns to bed, she says, "Turn onto your stomach," and he does and then groans when she kneads out the knots from his lower back. Her hands travel up and down his spine until he falls asleep. All night she spoons him tightly.

7

GILLIAN

Gillian wakes up early and angry the morning after Charlie seizes the swim team. While he's out exercising, she flips on the light and checks the status of her latest Facebook post: "You'll never guess who's coaching the Manta Rays this summer." Whoa, #crossthisoffcharliesbucketlist has scored 581 likes overnight, one of her top-rated posts. What the heck? Instead of reading the 106 comments, she scrolls through her feed. One of Gillian's clients tagged her in a picture of "a new spectacularly organized mudroom, compliments of Gillian Cloud." This makes her feel a little better. The housewives and working mothers of Northern Virginia, particularly the ones with executive functioning issues, pay Gillian handsomely to make order out of their mudrooms, closets, kitchens, and home offices. Lord knows, she needs the free PR. She's going to have to work her tail off this summer. Oh, and here is yet another post of her college roommate Vickie's family trip to Spain. They made it to Sevilla without a hitch: "Sangrias for all!" Only a few months ago, Vickie had claimed she was too low on cash to contribute to the Colby College alumni campaign. Counting other people's money is a tacky habit Gillian picked up after Charlie lost his job. That isn't quite true. The first holiday season after Sebastian was fired, her mother declared a "homemade-gift Christmas," and Gillian coveted the pretty sweaters and Bonne Bell Lip Smackers her friends found under their trees and in their stockings, and the out-of-season suntans they acquired on Florida beaches.

Charlie bounds up the steps into their bedroom, and she pretends she's still asleep.

"Gil." He reeks of chlorine.

"I'm sleeping."

"No, you're not." He strokes her shoulder. "Come on, hon."

Gillian throws back the covers and sits up. "How long have you been plotting your big move?"

"Since an hour before the meeting."

"I don't believe you." His pitch had been so well calculated.

"How was I to know we'd need a coach?"

We? This is new. Charlie has always referred to the Manta Rays as either "her team" or "your mother's team." She scowls at him. "You blindsided me."

"I didn't mean to."

"Did you ever think it might be a good idea for us to discuss this first?"

"What's eight more weeks of unemployment in the grand scheme of things?"

Because Charlie has an MBA, Gillian had always left him in charge of their finances and set aside the bills and credit card statements for him to open. But ever since he was let go, she's been carefully reviewing every piece of mail that falls through the slot. "We're going to have to dip into our 401(k)s to cover our expenses."

Charlie traces a vein in her forearm with his index finger. "I'll make it back, Gil."

How many times had she heard her father make this promise to her mother? *I'll make it back, May. I'll find something soon, May.* She blinks away these thoughts. "And did you for a second think about how this decision would affect our son?"

"Did you?"

"You're invading Justin's space."

Charlie answers with a pleasant, "I don't think you want to go there, sweetheart."

"Wow, Charlie." Is he really going to bring up what happened with their eldest? "So you think I chased Sebby from the pool?"

He looks sheepish. "That was a cheap shot," he mutters.

It's more than a cheap shot. He's picked at a scar that she worries will never fully heal for Sebby. Or for her.

"I'm sorry." He moves toward her.

She inches away from him. "Are you?" The old Charlie would have been sorry, and he never would have brought up one of her most shameful parenting moments ever.

"Gil, Justin texted from the beach last night." He holds the screen in front of her eyes.

She waves away the phone. "I'm sure he and Jack are having a ball." Jack Johnson is a sweet kid. Oh, the Johnsons with their beachfront property and family Honda business and well-documented ski trips to Breckenridge every December. Good lord, she's got to shake off this bitterness. It just doesn't suit her.

Charlie breaks her trance. "After I messaged him about the big news."

Gillian takes the phone from Charlie and reads Justin's text. "Cool, Dad. Congrats." Does Justin really think this news is cool? He won't tell them if the news bothers him; unlike Sebby, he's a pleaser. Charlie maneuvers himself on the bed so that both their backs are resting against the headboard, and they stew in cold married silence.

"Why did you do this, Charlie?"

"Not to upset you." He kisses her bare shoulder. "It seemed like an obvious solution."

"Obvious?"

"I can't explain it, but I need to do this before I figure out my next move."

She lets him drape his arm over her shoulder.

"It feels weirdly right."

"To you, maybe."

"There's more than enough River Run left for you." Charlie caresses the top of her arm. "And Kristy."

"That's not the point. Aside from making a financially irresponsible decision, you bulldozed your way into the meeting and snatched . . ." He swiped her family heirloom right from under her nose. And that hurts even more.

Gillian turns to study his profile in the morning light. Sebby and Justin inherited Charlie's high forehead and long eyelashes. Charlie's dirty blond hair is thinning, so he's been cutting it shorter and shorter. His face was sheathed in a layer of pudge for so many years that she forgot about his nice cheekbones, a contrast to his amoeba-shaped nose, which he'd broken three times playing water polo. She always thought water polo too rough a sport for her mild-mannered husband. Well, as her father always said, when you assume, you make an "ass" out of "u" and "me." Ha! She banks on the fact that Charlie is still Charlie—steady, reliable, and dry. At least Kristy is very much still very much Kristy.

Charlie presses his index finger and thumb together. "Can you loosen your grip on the pool a wee bit?"

"I'll try." She wants to hold on to the pool tighter than ever.

Gillian awakes in the middle of the night after a vivid dream about her father. She hasn't dreamed much about either parent since their respective deaths, but this one beckons her back in time, to the summer of 1973, to a home swim meet at the pool and a Manta Ray victory.

When the announcer recited the score after the meet, Gillian felt a warm, sticky hand pushing her into the bright blue water. Soon, the whole team was splashing around the shallow end hooting and hollering. Everyone laughed when her father jumped into the pool in his starter's uniform, white shorts and a polo shirt, which Gillian's mom let her iron and starch, even though she was only eleven. Gillian's whole body swelled with pride whenever he led the team in a fierce game of Sharks and Manta Rays. The River Run lifeguards, moms, dads, and kids were a little bit in love with this version of her father. He brought the magic to the pool. Gillian used to wish she could freeze these moments in time. Starting every September, she would cross off the days on her calendar until the next swim season began.

Dad hopped out of the pool in one easy motion and approached the clubhouse, a cozy converted Sears Catalog home tucked behind a line of oak trees. A bunch of swim moms—timers, ribbon writers, bake-sale workers—allowed him to cut through their circle as if he were Moses parting the Red Sea. Gillian once overheard one of the moms comment on "Sebastian Norton's shock of blond hair and Robert Redford jawline and big brown eyes," but that wasn't the only reason people liked her father. He knew just what to say to light someone up from the inside out.

Sharks and Manta Rays was not as fun without Dad leading it, and Gillian was hungry, so she signaled her pals: time to get out. Mom had nicknamed Gillian and her three friends the River Rats. Debbie and Linda poured Dixie cups of Hawaiian Punch for the group and stood in line for the sandwiches Gillian's mom had made the night before. Fran snagged the last ham and cheese and a seat next to Gillian.

"Let's have a sleepover!" Debbie said. She had a faceful of freckles and a grayish tint to her blond hair. The first week the pool was open, the operator messed up the chlorine levels, and now the River Rats wore their ashy hair and greenish teeth as a badge of honor.

"My parents don't let me do sleepovers," she lied. In truth, she didn't want to invite the girls back to her house, not for a sleepover, not ever. And she wanted to stick close to home, just in case.

"Gillian, look who's calling you!" Fran pointed to the guard station and nudged her with her toe.

"Come on over here, Gillian Norton," bellowed Scott, the head guard, a ponytailed college boy who had swum for the River Run Manta Rays and now helped coach the team. "I've got good news for you."

She bolted up from the picnic table. She felt her friends' eyes on her back as she walked as fast as she could, without running of course, to the guard station. Maybe they were going to let her blow the whistle for adult swim this afternoon! Who needed a sleepover, anyway?

Scott tugged one of her pigtails. "Look, we're down two guards. We need all hands on deck today." He wheeled a swivel chair up to the lifeguard counter toward Gillian. "All yours."

"Mine?" Gillian had been dreaming of checking in members in the lifeguard office, but she didn't think it would happen until she turned twelve, at the earliest. She touched the Bic pen wrapped in masking tape etched with "Property of River Run Pool" in red letters. No pen was going to disappear on her watch. Today she would be the one writing the dates down on the families' assigned index cards and—oh, my gosh—keeping track of guest passes!

One hour into the job, Gillian's parents and brother came to say hi. Dad's new camera dangled from his neck as he raised a cigarette to his lips. He leaned toward Gillian and whispered, "I'm proud of you." To her relief, his breath smelled like cigarette smoke and plain coffee.

Gillian melted into her father's praise, proud that she knew how to make him happy, even if not for long. "Thanks."

"Look who's here," Dad said, and he and Mom ran off to snag chairs right next to Mr. and Mrs. Spillman. Gillian watched Mr. Spillman reach into his cooler and hand Dad a bottle of beer. She stuck her hand in her pocket and felt for the rabbit's foot she'd won last summer for making every single swim practice. If she stroked the fur fifteen times, maybe she could make Dad stop at one beer.

A few hours later, she heard voices swell from the pool area. Kids were chanting. "Mis-ter. Nor-ton. Mis-ter. Nor-ton."

"Go out and look," Scott said. "Your dad is the man, you know that, right?"

Gillian stepped away from the desk and passed her buddies on the way to her family's spot at the far end of the diving well. The sun had eaten up most of the early-afternoon shade. Gillian stood between her brother and her mom, who was chewing on a nail she'd polished pastel pink only yesterday. Gillian picked up her father's camera and pressed the viewfinder to her eye, tracking Sebastian Norton as he rose from his seat. He took a long drag on his cigarette, picked up a stray beer bottle, and jammed the butt into its mouth. He tightened the tie of his trunks and winked at the swimmers chanting his name.

Dad approached the diving board and started his climb. The chanting grew to a roar, "Swan-dive. Swan-dive." When he reached the last rung, Gillian held both her and her mother's breath as his foot wobbled.

Even the loudest little kids quieted down. He stood on the rear of the board and gazed past Patrick to Gillian. For a second, she thought she'd get in trouble for using his camera without his permission, but instead he yelled, "Get this, baby girl," his faint slur likely unnoticeable to anyone but a Norton. "I will," she mouthed.

Gillian prayed. She asked God to wrap his arms around Sebastian and guide him into the water so he wouldn't hit his head on the board and die. She prayed for Mr. Spillman to run out of beer, for the family to head home before her father started wanting something stronger, and for her mom to designate tonight Jiffy Pop Saturday, where they would eat popcorn and then play Monopoly.

She pushed the camera harder into her eye socket, trying to sense when Dad would start his dive. The sun beat down on his broad brown shoulders as he strode across the board with great purpose. Gillian's heart pounded so hard, she thought it might rattle the River Run pen she'd tied on a string around her neck. He jumped, once, twice, three times, and on the fourth bounce he raised his hands over his head and leaped into the air. In that split second, Gillian moved back far enough to capture him in his glory—his long arms spread like Jesus on the cross and his lips split open into a grin practically spanning the width of the pool—but she stood close enough to edit out the beer bottles around his empty chair.

Click.

Dad's entry was perfect. God had listened to her.

8

CHARLIE

One bold move begets another, and a few minutes after Gillian takes off for her spin class with Kristy, Charlie makes a decision. He trots into the kids' bathroom and hunts down the electric razor he gave Justin when he first started to shave. He flicks the switch with his thumb. *Bzzzz.* The old razor has plenty of juice. He looks at himself in the mirror, at the wimpy hairs that grow thinner every day, at the faint goggle-strap tan on the sides of his face. He turns his head to the left and mows the hair as he does his lawn, in neat rows. Stubble falls to his shoulders like snow. The vibration against his scalp starts his blood flowing, and he hums an old Eagles tune as he shaves the right side, the back, and then the top of his head. His scalp tingles. His new baldness makes him look like a badass mofo. Kojak, eat your heart out.

Charlie's ready for his first practice.

He throws his shirt into the hamper, showers, and Dustbusters the bathroom floor. He's found his bliss. After years of loitering on the margins of his life, he's discovered what he is meant to do—coach swimming. He was never cut out for the boardroom. He hated the political jockeying, and the actual real estate development work bored the crap out of him. If Gillian didn't wake him up with one of her pep talks, he had to set two alarms to get his ass out of bed. This morning, Charlie sprang out of the sack at five-thirty, ran six miles, shaved, showered, and donned his new uni: shorts and a T-shirt. Now he's in line waiting to order an Americano at Starbucks. He used to rely on two or three coffees to get himself through the day and then grab a bottle of Coke before he trudged to the Metro to go home from D.C.

The air-conditioning blows cold on his scalp, which he can't stop touching.

9

GILLIAN

Per usual, Gillian is the first to show up at the fancy spinning club that she, card-carrying member of the National Association of Productivity and Organizing, writes off as a business expense. Yes, a hiatus from the class would save them a hundred and fifty dollars a month, but let Charlie quit his gym to cut down their overhead. Besides, she's recruited some of her best clients from these forty-five-minute mind, body, and spirit sessions.

Gillian selects two bikes in the first row and positions herself between the cycle she's saving for Kristy and the one occupied by a Lulu, Kristy and Gillian's nickname for a certain kind of woman whose daytime wardrobe consists exclusively of Lululemon exercise attire. Kristy is technically a Lulu too, but part of her charm is that she can poke fun at her obsession with acquiring name-brand items. Gillian is about to chat up the Lulu when the class starts.

"Okay, ladies. Let's get to work." Paige, their beloved instructor with purple-streaked hair and a shoulder full of tattoos, adjusts her headset and leads the class through a warm-up. Gillian pedals hard right away, her body releasing pent-up stress.

Paige points toward Gillian. "Well, someone's on fire today."

Gillian picks up the pace, as if she can cycle away from the panicky child inside her. She is riding a stationary bike, though, and therefore fails to gain any distance from the weakest parts of herself.

"Okay now, ladies. Let's attack our first incline. Show me what you've got." Paige's raspy voice projects a calm urgency.

Gillian's thighs burn, but the tempo of the music has picked up, and soon she's one with the pulsing bass line. As she ascends the hill, she stands up and leans further over the handlebars, ignoring the two women clamoring for the bike she's saved for Kristy.

"I'm your sherpa, people. Hand over what is weighing you down and fly up this hill!" Paige lowers her voice, amplifying its authority, leaving Gillian no choice but to surrender her body and then her brain. And that's when she fully embraces the reframe she gave lip service to the night before. Thank goodness for endorphins! First, Justin will continue to establish himself as a leader of the River Run team. He'll teach swim lessons to baby Manta Rays in the afternoons, and when he's free, he'll fill the house with his summer swim friends, for whom Gillian will prepare copious amounts of pasta and blueberry muffins and Trader Joe's burritos. She'll run the laundry line on the back porch, where the kids will hang up their wet towels. The house will reek of chlorine! And why hasn't it occurred to her that Charlie will need her to help him figure out how to handle the many moving parts of serving as head coach of the Manta Rays? She'll provide useful pointers on how to work with the parents, handle the entries, and organize his coaching staff. The worry from the past months will magically dissipate at River Run. She can be a part of the summer and take on enough new clients to prevent running up the credit cards Charlie has opened to pay the bills. Last year she pledged to take on the responsibilities of social director in addition to her position as team rep, but she'll have to find someone else to fill in. Maybe Charlie is right, coaching is just what the doctor ordered to get him back on track. She and Charlie will work as a team! Charlie's move is a blessing, not a curse! Her old love for him fills her pumping heart.

"Awesome job, warriors! Now you can coast down what we climbed. Feel how much lighter you are," Paige tells them.

Gillian feels the best kind of woozy as she tilts her head back.

Kristy bursts into the room, hijacking every biker's attention because they all covet her body. And she knows it. And loves it.

"Let's get back to it. This next hill is going. To. Burn," Paige calls.

Kristy hops on the bike Gillian saved and they pedal together, their legs in sync for the remaining twenty minutes of the class. After Paige finishes leading the group in a warm-down, Kristy puts her hands on her hips and leans back. "I needed that."

"Same here."

The Lulu turns to Gillian. "Hey, aren't you the woman who clears clutter?"

"That's me."

The fit thirty-something prattles on about her disorderly closets.

Gillian listens as she, the Lulu, and Kristy dismount their bikes and walk over to the rack where they left their gym bags. Gillian unzips the side pocket of her bag, reaches in, and hands the Lulu a card with her contact information on one side and her slogan on the other: *Let Go or Be Dragged.* Zen Proverb

"Looks like you caught a live one," Kristy says after the woman thanks Gillian and walks away. "Definitely the type to hold on to her old homecoming corsages."

"You're terrible."

"Let go or be dragged." Kristy takes a swig from her water bottle, shooting Gillian a sidelong glance. "You feeling any better about things?"

"Yes, I am." Telling Kristy her new plan to become Charlie's right hand makes Gillian feel giddy.

"Good, you're not going to step back from the team."

"No need!"

Kristy gives her one of her "Oh, Lucy" looks, which only makes Gillian more certain that her plan will work.

"Do you want to grab a quick latte?" Gillian is eager to unveil the finer points of her scheme to her friend.

Kristy flings her bag over her shoulder. "Love to, but I have a couple of errands I need to run."

Kristy would typically give more details, but Gillian knows when to give Kristy her privacy. Besides, they'll likely talk at least two or three more times before the day ends.

10

KRISTY

Gillian was a maniac on the bike this morning. Jesus, twenty minutes after the workout Kristy is still dripping. She does crave an iced latte, but she wants to get home and pick up the dehumidifier for her dad. And she wants to get that damn box out of her garage. Then she'll call Gillian and listen more attentively to the details of her new River Run plan. David was right about nothing keeping Gillian down for long. She's like that old Timex ad, "Takes a licking and keeps on ticking."

Kristy thinks about everything else on her docket for today. Shit. She's almost forgotten that she's supposed to work her hotline shift. She enjoys feeling like an authority when she responds to calls about baby fevers, constipation, and ear pain. David never pressured her to work, but she kept up with her nursing because Flo made her swear that she would never let her credentials go. "David could leave you for a woman of the Jewish persuasion, you know," Flo commented the week before Kristy and David wed. One trip to Travis's is all it takes for Flo to get back into her head.

As Kristy approaches their designated Starbucks, located halfway between their houses and seconds away from River Run, she can practically taste the milky, ice-cold coffee on her tongue. Travis can wait. She turns on her blinker, pulls into the strip mall, and parks her car. She's about to get out when through her rearview mirror she spots a fit man with a shaved head and a laptop tucked under his bicep. There's something familiar about his gait. Charlie?

She backs out of her spot before he sees her. If he tells Gillian that he bumped into Kristy at their Starbucks, she might think that Kristy has blown her off.

Oh, sweet David. He lugged their old dehumidifier from the basement into the garage before leaving for work this morning. She stares at the wilting cardboard box Travis gave her, tempted to heave it into the trash. What good could come from rooting around in her past? From going through old yearbooks signed by her only friend and finding the senior photo with her Farrah Fawcett hairdo? Or the letters Nora wrote her when Kristy was sent away to Bible camp?

Nora. Thinking about her sister feels like having a root canal without Novocain. Thank God Nora and her husband live in Lynchburg; Princess Nora wasn't of much use when she lived in town. Throughout Flo's quick decline, Kristy took on her care, and it wasn't just because she was an RN. Nora only showed up once every few weeks for ten-minute visits, which Kristy knew hurt Flo. The night the will was read, Kristy found out that to Nora, her mother had bequeathed her grandmother's diamond brooch and an unremarkable stock portfolio she'd hidden from Travis. To Kristy, nothing. Zilch. Zero. Not so much as a bobby pin. Kristy finally had enough of feeling like the ugly bastard child, and she cut Nora from her life. No regrets.

Kristy picks up the box, carries it from the garage to the back porch, and sets it down in a sunny spot next to one of the wicker chairs. She bends over and shimmies off its mildewy top to find labeled and stacked memorabilia from her childhood. The sight of her mother's handwriting jolts her. She tweezes each item: a ridiculously ugly potholder Kristy wove at Sunday School (the day Mrs. Bowles exiled her to the hallway for handing out pieces of Bazooka to the boys); report cards (all As); letters Kristy wrote to Flo from Bible camp (before Kristy was caught giving her best friend's boyfriend a hand job); Kristy's acceptance into

Virginia Commonwealth's nursing program (with a hefty scholarship); Kristy and David's wedding announcement from the *Washington Post* (the first and last Weinstein family event Travis and Flo ever attended); baby photos of Mia and Isaac (that never made it to her parents' fireplace mantel, blanketed with pictures of Nora's kids); an article about love addiction that Kristy sent Flo after Mia was born (Flo dismissed the article and the disease that brought the family so much shame). She shivers in the hot sun. If the filthy part of her resurfaces, if she relapses, she'll lose everything. Only a moron would risk blowing up this beautiful life she worked so hard to create, but then again, her ex-sponsor always said that relapsing has nothing to do with intelligence.

Mia's arrival into the world poked the ravenous bear that had been hibernating inside Kristy, and she relapsed when David's accountant, a beet-faced man with black curly hairs growing out of his ears, came on to her at a holiday party. David thought it was cute, and so did Kristy, until two days later when the accountant called looking for David and she started phone-flirting with him. Kristy said that she was way too fat and postnatal for this, but the accountant said she'd be even sexier with "big milky tits," and for days afterwards Kristy waited for him to call again so that they could talk more about what he liked about her body. Anticipating the accountant's phone calls and fantasizing about meet-ups offered her a divine release. For a full month she succumbed to the urge to track down every bit of information about his life, especially his wife. Mia was a terrible sleeper who could only nap while Kristy or David drove her in their van, and every time Kristy buckled Mia into her car seat, she swore that she wouldn't drive by his house hoping to catch a glimpse of his horsey-looking wife loading their kids into a minivan adorned with decals of soccer teams. But she did. Even if she got lucky, her stalking filled her with self-disgust.

The next week, while she was having a pedi, she picked up a magazine with an article about love addiction. Kristy snorted to herself, thinking about that Robert Palmer song "Addicted to Love." What was she, some kind of sex addict? She read on. A love addict receives a dopamine hit from the chase, and a sex addict gets high from the actual orgasm. She thought about the thrill she felt when the accountant first called or when a man held her gaze. She shut the magazine. "That's me," she said aloud. "Oh, my God."

Kristy spent the next week rationalizing her shenanigans with men. She was simply a flirt. Only a week later, after she sleuthed out the Safeway where the accountant's wife did her shopping and stole the woman's full cart of groceries, did she call David's mom to babysit Mia, pump the milk out of her breasts, and attend her first Sex and Love Addicts Anonymous meeting. She breathed ten sighs of relief after each addict's share, feeling less alone about "intriguing," surprised that the thing she did when she caught a man's attention had a name. Even if she didn't cop a buzz from having sex, she'd sleep with a man if it meant more "love." So fucking true. Everyone in the rooms understood the lure of the call, and nobody judged or shamed you for showing up at a man's house because you couldn't stop yourself even though you knew better. Like Kristy, these women grew consumed with men who treated them as if they were invisible, or worse, but the feeling that she could give them what their girlfriends or wives couldn't was like shooting heroin. They'd chosen her, if only for a fleeting moment.

After Kristy's second meeting, she approached Beverly, an earth-motherish woman in her late forties who dyed her curls bright red and spoke in a thick Boston accent. She wore long dangly earrings that sounded like wind chimes when she moved her head, and the kind of funky, shapeless dresses you find at museum gift shops. Beverly had what Kristy wanted—freedom from both chasing the high and suffering the degradation of love addiction—so she mustered up the courage to ask Beverly to become her sponsor. Talking to Beverly felt like treating herself to a warm bowl of soup on a cold day. After months of long phone calls Kristy made while Mia napped, Beverly delicately suggested that Mia's arrival had sparked old feelings about Kristy's competition with Nora. Ridiculous. She loved Mia with everything she had, and then some. Once Kristy started feeling stronger, she quit the meetings, and a year later she quit Beverly, who had told her dozens of times that addiction was a progressive disease.

Okay, exhuming these memories is about as much fun as having a Pap smear. Enough. The only thing Kristy wants to hang on to from this little time capsule is the potholder.

Her knees crack when she stands up and goes inside for a Hefty bag. After she scoops the curated souvenirs of her life into it, she notices a legal-sized ivory envelope in the bottom of the box. No label. She picks it up and peeks inside.

A newspaper clipping? What had Flo been saving? Kristy's every instinct screams at her to toss the envelope in the trash bag, and Beverly advised her to heed her intuitions, big and small. But how can she not open this? Maybe Flo wrote her a letter explaining why she left her out of the will? Or how she really did love Kristy as much as Nora? Pathetic. No, Kristy is way too old to entertain this tired bullshit.

Kristy tears open the envelope.

She removes the yellowed newspaper clipping. The paper feels flimsy against her two fingers. "What the . . ." Her mouth gapes as she glimpses the photo she's seen hundreds of times on the wall of the River Run clubhouse and in Gillian's foyer. Kristy can recite in her sleep the story of the famous *Washington Post* contest-winning photo of Sebastian Norton's swan dive, taken in 1973, ten years before his death.

Why would Flo keep a copy of the article? Yes, the photo was a big deal at the time, but likely only to members of the River Run pool. This made absolutely no sense.

Kristy extracts another item from the envelope. A birth certificate. This document is a different shape and color from the one she used when she took her driver's test and applied for her first passport. She combs the parchment-like paper with the pad of her finger. No need to be so jittery, she tells herself aloud. She taps her Star of David. Sweat beads on her upper lip.

She reads the information aloud.

"'Female.' Check. 'Birthdate: 2/13/64.' Check. 'Prince William County, Virginia.' Check. Check. Check." She knows all this already. "Kristine Anne Blackwell." Wait. Ever since she could remember, the name on her birth certificate was Kristine Anne Frick. She reads on, her eyes falling hard on the listing of her parents' names.

"Mother: Florence Blackwell."

"Father: Sebastian Norton."

11

CHARLIE

Charlie thanks the barista for his coffee and sets up camp at a corner table. He reaches into his backpack and exhumes old meet results, blowing into his hands as if he were holding dice.

Charlie lost his job the week he turned fifty, a milestone birthday that had hit him hard. "You're dead weight, Cloud," fucking Oliver had told him before offering a borderline crappy severance package. "We pay you a lot, and you just don't hustle."

He's going to hustle plenty at the River Run pool, in the form of winning divisionals and racking up All-Star times. Under Charlie's stewardship, the Manta Rays are going to bust right out of their sorry little Division 14. A week from today, Charlie will be coaching his first meet. Now all he has to do is figure out a winning lineup.

The moms and dads are the gateway to the swimmers he needs to recruit to the team, and he's observed enough of his kids' sports scenes to figure out that there are four kinds of parents: those who want their children to receive special attention from the coaches and will stop at nothing to get it; those who advocate equal treatment for all kids because favoritism will tank any community; those who swear that they belong to the second category when they really belong to the first; and those who are too preoccupied or too wise to get into their kids' shit.

Charlie will first go after the easiest marks, the parents who want special treatment for their children.

"Boy, we'd sure love to have Brendan back this year," he says to the first mom who answers his call.

"You know, I don't think Zeke even knew Brendan's name," she says.

"I remember Brendan's dolphin kick."

"His father swam the butterfly," she replies breathlessly. "For UVA."

"Tell you what, why don't you, Brendan, and Dad too, if he's free, come by after practice Monday night, say hello, and chat for a bit. No commitment."

She does not pause for a second. "Yes, we'll do that."

After a few more calls, he discovers that if he can talk to these parents on the phone and ask them a few questions about their kids, he's got them. He barely touches his Americano.

12

KRISTY

Sebastiannorton. The words bleed into each other. No, it's impossible. She touches the birth certificate again, expecting one of those winter shocks that come from rubbing her socked feet against the carpet.

She picks up the document and the clipping. No shock. She places both items flat on the table and sits still, eavesdropping on a loud conversation between the starlings who shit on her fence every morning. They can't drown out her mother's voice in her head. "Kristy's father is not with us anymore," Flo responded demurely when someone asked. "Nosy parker," her mother muttered after the person was well out of earshot. When Kristy was twelve, she mustered up the nerve to press Flo for more details about her bio-dad. "Motorcycle accident," was all she said before snapping at Kristy for leaving her sneakers in the front hallway. Kristy sensed that her mother wasn't telling her the entire story, that something about Kristy's coming into being embarrassed her. She'd known it in her cells and tissues, and when she felt most apart from the Fricks, she fantasized about her handsome dad, who had been mistaken for dead, banging on the door and begging to whisk her away to a house with a daughter whom he loved way less than Kristy. In this imaginary house, Kristy would be the Nora, the princess.

Kristy dials Travis, not having a clue as to what she will say when he answers. The phone rings for what seems like an hour before his machine picks up. She pictures him outside taking apart their ancient lawnmower, one of his favorite pastimes. She imagines him through new eyes. Travis is a small man, half the size of Sebastian Norton, and his teeth are nicotine-stained and disorderly, unlike Sebastian's Kennedyesque white choppers, which are on full display in the many photos that she and the rest of the River Run community regularly admire. Travis's narrow shoulders slope; and Sebastian and Kristy's broad backs taper down to their slim hips like a V.

The sound of Travis's voice makes her jump. "Travis Frick here, leave me a message if you like. [Pause.] Thank you, then."

"Dad, I'm sorry, but I can't stop by today with the dehumidifier. I'll call you." Her voice shakes harder than her hands.

She rests her palms on the documents for one or twenty minutes, she can't tell.

Why didn't her mother tell her about Sebastian? She thinks back to the long drives to the rummage sales, only blocks from River Run. Her mother radiated longing. Had she been a love addict too? Impossible.

Kristy never said aloud that she wanted to live in a nice home close to the Potomac River one day, but when she and David put a deposit down on their house, practically walking distance from the pool, Flo fell silent on the other end of the phone. She died six months later.

Had her mother placed her in Gillian's path?

Holy shit.

Gillian.

Aunt Gillian.

Krillian.

13

JUSTIN

The Clouds' house smells like butter when Justin comes home from his week at the beach. Mom must be making her Manta Ray cookies. When Justin and Sebby were little, she took them to the Torpedo Factory, a cool building filled with art studios over in Alexandria, and commissioned a sculptor to design a Manta Ray–shaped cookie cutter. Totally over the top, but that's Mom.

She greets Justin at the door and hugs him before shooing him back to the porch to remove any excess sand from his body. If he wants to tease her, he'll take his towel and jammers out of his duffel and watch her sprint to the cleaning supplies closet and whip out her Dustbuster. That's the kind of thing Justin's brother would do, just to push Mom's buttons. Now Sebby makes it a point to go AWOL during the swim season. This year he's tending bar up in New York and studying for the LSATs, not that he needs to prepare. He nails standardized tests and swim races; it's the daily grind—doing his homework and showing up for class or swim practice back in the day—that screws him up.

Justin showers quickly and wipes a thin layer of sand from the tub. When his ex-girlfriend Tiff dumped him, she called him an anal-retentive mama's boy. Maybe if he'd agreed to take a trip with her this summer instead of coaching the Manta Rays, they'd still be together. Justin didn't have the balls to tell his mom that he wanted to spend the summer with Tiff or to tell Tiff that he wanted to travel with her but only after the swim season ended. Now he's glad she's transferring to UCLA next year. The mere sight of her makes him hurt.

"Sit, sit, honey." Mom sets a plate with two cookies at his place. "Careful, the frosting hasn't quite gelled yet."

He takes a bite of cookie. "Mom, these are so good."

"Wanted to help make your dad's first coaching day memorable." She gives him that goofy grin that makes everyone love her and then picks up her phone from the kitchen table and stands.

"He'll dig that," Justin says.

"Say cheese, Justin."

He dutifully smiles and raises the cookie to his mouth for the picture.

"There we go." She clicks and uploads the image to Facebook. "Mind if I tag you, cutie?"

"Go ahead." Justin doesn't mind all the Facebooking. He's grown up with it.

After she finishes hashtagging, she sits back down and says, "Tell me about the beach."

"The waves were like bizarrely huge for this time of year."

"Almost forgot." She bolts up for the milk carton in the fridge and pours him a glass. "Did you remember to give Mrs. Johnson our hospitality gift?"

"Yes, she loved it." He takes a big gulp of milk.

Mom rambles on about how she couldn't decide between chocolates or the basil-flavored olive oil until it's time to name the elephant hanging out in the kitchen, practically helping himself to a Manta Ray cookie. "What do you think of your dad coaching the team?"

"I'm okay with it, Mom."

"Good," she says so cheerfully that he wonders if it was her idea to have Dad coach. He can't imagine his father making this move without her blessing. Mom owns the team. Parents swarm around her because she's the party, always, and they want to be invited. Countless times his mother has told Justin and Sebby that the pool is their legacy, that everyone idolized their grandfather, Sebastian Norton. Justin wishes he could have met the legend.

"Your dad's going to need our help."

"*Our* help?"

"Justin." She jumps out of her chair again for a napkin, hands it to him, and dabs her upper lip to signal that he should do the same. "Granted, your father has coached swimming before, but that was eons ago, and he knows nothing about the *dynamics* of the River Run family."

Justin wipes crumbs from his stubbly lip and listens to Mom map out her plan. She, Dad, and Justin will partner up to run the team.

"And speak of the devil," Mom says.

Dad bounds through the back door. "Hey, what's up?"

Mom turns around in her seat. "Charlie?" She points to her head.

Justin turns around to find his father standing in the kitchen, bald as a baby. "Dad . . ."

"What do you guys think?" he asks, but Justin can tell by the way he's grinning that he really doesn't care what he and Mom think.

"Well, aren't you full of surprises?" Mom walks up to him and inspects his entire scalp with her hands. "Let me touch up the back."

"Does that mean you like it, Gil?" Dad sounds like a little kid.

She caresses the hairy spot on the back of his head that she will fix. "You know, I don't hate it."

"It looks cool, Dad." What happened to his tired-looking father who used to fall asleep in front of the television every night?

"My God, this kitchen smells good," Dad says. "Look at those!"

"Mom made Manta Ray cookies for your first practice."

Dad puts his arm around Mom and leans down to kiss the top of her head. "That was awfully nice of you, Gil."

"Have one, you'll need your energy so the mapping out of the season can officially begin." Mom pours Dad a glass of milk.

She walks over to her little desk in the kitchen, loads her arms with a neat stack of files, and sets them down on the table. "I took the liberty of organizing Zeke's old papers." Mom's cheeks flush as she shows them each labeled tab: Past Rosters, Entry Forms, Swim League Handbooks.

"Gil, you didn't have to do this for me."

"Oh, come on, honey. I did this for us, for River Run." Mom smooths her shirt over her skirt. "I mean, for heaven's sake, we have our first Saturday meet in a matter of days."

"Yeah, like your first practice with the team is the day after tomorrow, Dad," Justin says.

"He's ready, don't you worry." Mom squeezes Dad's shoulder.

"Thanks, Gil." Dad shoves the last bite of cookie into his mouth and makes a big show of patting his abs before scooping the files up in his arms.

"Let's get to work!" Mom says.

"I got this, babe. You do so much for the pool."

"Charlie, honey, there's some . . ." She looks up at the ceiling, searching for the perfect word to make her point. ". . . *nuance* to dealing with the River Run community."

"I'll call you if I need any help." He holds the files to his chest. "Thanks for these!"

"I'm here if you need me," Mom says in the singsongy voice she uses when she's hurt.

"Hey, Justin. Come on downstairs with me. I've been going through last week's time trials and other old meet results, and I have some ideas for the season. I'd love your input."

Justin stands in the middle of the kitchen, equidistant from his parents: Dad facing in the direction of the basement steps, Mom concentrating hard on dotting cookie crumbs with her finger and placing them on a napkin. She looks as sad as she did during Justin's last dual meet as a Manta Ray, when the announcer made a little speech during the break about Justin's college plans, the points he'd scored for the team, and his cheering skills. Afterwards, a dozen younger swimmers charged at him with hugs, balloons, and baggies Mom had filled with her Manta Ray cookies and tied with green and white ribbons. When the kids released

Justin from their clutches, he caught a glimpse of Mom shoving on a pair of Aunt Kristy's sunglasses so nobody could see her eyes well up. But Justin had seen. Mom didn't cry or pout. It wasn't her thing.

Justin turns away from Mom, toward Dad, tanned, bald, and reborn.

He walks toward his father, who likely isn't trying to be a douche by not inviting Mom to join them; he's just not thinking about his coaching as one of Mom's River Run jobs. Dad needs him, and Justin likes that. Anyway, Mom will be fine; she has Aunt Kristy.

14

KRISTY

Kristy never should have opened that box. Now she feels her mother and Travis watching Kristine Blackwell Norton Frick Weinstein host David's parents for Shabbat dinner, shop with Isaac to pick up supplies for his trip, spin with Gillian, bumble through her hotline shift. She can't turn down the volume of the recording playing over and over in her mind. It goes like this: No way are she and Gillian siblings. They're polar opposites. Gillian is a coupon cutter, and Kristy spends money with reckless abandon. Gillian's bladder is the size of a macadamia nut, and Kristy's is as big as a camel's. Gillian loves Madonna and bubblegum music, while Billie Holiday and Amy Winehouse pierce Kristy's soul. Gillian often forgets to eat. Kristy, always hungry or thirsty, is never without a snack and a water bottle or a Starbucks Venti iced latte with whole milk, which she sips through a straw. On the other hand, both Kristy and Gillian have flat feet and wide hands with long phalanges and small nail beds.

But what if the birth certificate isn't a mistake? What if she could swap Nora out for Gillian? She hates the envy and bitterness that bubbles up inside her at the mere mention of Nora's name, and Gillian—well, being with her feels like a hug. Now Kristy's thought wheel always includes the burning question of how in God's name Flo Blackwell and Sebastian Norton could ever have found each other.

Kristy tries Travis again, and this time he answers. Her voice sounds as high-pitched as that recorder Mia and Isaac learned to play in fourth-grade music class. "Hey there, Dad. You still need that dehumidifier?"

"Don't you worry about it, Kris. All taken care of."

"Sorry I didn't get it out to you sooner." She shoots up from her chair and paces around the first floor of her house. "Did you look inside the box, Dad?"

"How about that potholder?" He chuckles.

"How about that birth certificate?" Now she's whispering, like Nicole Kidman delivering the money line of a climax scene.

"Oh, Kris." She can hear the static of him rubbing his palm against his whiskered jaw.

"Oh, Kris, what?"

"When the time is right," he says softly.

Kristy is touched by the tremor of emotion in his voice. "When the time is right? What does that even mean?"

"It means that your mom insisted you would come upon this information when you were ready for it."

"So she had some kind of psychic powers? She knew that your pipe would burst and that you'd summon me to take the box. Did you even know what was in it?"

"No, or I would have approached things differently."

"Yeah, it kind of sucks."

"I want you to remember this." He sighs heavily. "The day your mom came into my shop with you was one of the luckiest days of my life."

Travis had told her this once before, after Flo told Kristy the fake story about her real father.

"Did you know it was him?" Kristy starts pacing up and down the deck. "You know, Sebastian Norton."

"Never a need for me to know the name."

Travis is not the type to pry, and Flo did die before Kristy found Gillian and in turn the River Run pool.

"But how?" It was impossible that her mother and Sebastian could have occupied the same zip code, much less—well, she didn't want to think about that either.

"I only know that he was the headmaster at some boys' prep school, and that she worked for him in the office, that type of thing."

She paces faster. This is starting to make sense. Flo's clerical skills were excellent; she'd worked her way up from secretary to office manager at the local Allstate Insurance branch that employed her right until the month before she passed. She also made Kristy learn how to type sixty words per minute and familiarize herself with the workings of a computer.

"None of this matters, Kris."

"It matters."

"I'm your dad, always will be." Each word comes out of his mouth like it's a separate sentence.

"I know, but do you know who Sebastian's other daughter is?"

"No. Have I met her?"

He knows nothing about her life. How could he? She'd kept her parents at arm's length from the world she built with David. "No."

"Should I?" he asks gently.

"I guess," Kristy responds bitterly. "She's my BFFL."

"Your baffle?"

"BFFL. Best friend for life." Kristy used to think that grown women who used this term were ridiculous, but that was before she scored a BFFL for herself. Gillian is Kristy's person, the Ethel to her Lucy, the Louise to her Thelma, the Cristina Yang to her Meredith Grey. The only female, other than Mia, with whom she's never felt an ounce of competition.

"What are the chances you two would find each other?" She can picture Travis opening his frog-like eyes wide.

You can't believe what the rich people throw away. She can practically hear her mother's voice, tainted with longing, while they used to drive through Gillian's childhood neighborhood on their way to a church rummage sale. Shit. Was Flo hoping to spot Sebastian Norton? Kristy shudders as if she herself were in the midst of a stalking episode. She stops pacing. "Oh, my God."

"What, honey?"

Kristy feels ill. "Do you think Gillian could know?"

"Don't think so."

"How can you be sure?"

"Your mom never even told me anything about Sebastian Norton."

"What?"

"What would have been the point? I knew enough."

Now Kristy understands why she and Gillian were so ferociously drawn to each other that morning at the playground. Five minutes after they met, Kristy handed Gillian infant Isaac so she could tie Mia's shoe. Babies love Gillian, and he cooed happily in her arms while she and Kristy started talking like they were continuing a conversation they'd begun years ago. Their deep connection had everything and nothing to do with their recently losing their mothers. Holy paradigm shift, Batman.

Kristy says a weak goodbye to Travis and walks outside. She sits down on the Adirondack chair on the far side of the deck, tucking her feet under her legs. She rests her head on her hand, closes her eyes, and leans her ear toward her heart. The birds have taken off for someone else's yard, and in the quiet she knows what is true. She believes the birth certificate. A torrent of love for Gillian overtakes her. Exhilarated and exhausted from the emotions of the day, she rises from the chair. She's late to meet Gillian. It's time to share the news with her sister.

15

CHARLIE

Gillian is organizing the gear closet when Charlie arrives at River Run for his first day of practice. Part of him appreciates her sincere desire to help him locate the pace clocks, kickboards, and pull buoys, but another part feels that new twinge of annoyance at her efforts to team up with him this summer.

Charlie and Justin sit together at a picnic table, waiting for Liam and Mia to arrive. Where the hell are they? Charlie had asked the coaches to show up a half hour before practice.

Charlie knows Liam will be a challenge. When he snuck into the pool last summer to smoke pot, River Run turned a blind eye because he's the son of a committee member, Trish Port, an expert at roping parents in to sweat their asses off over a grill and churn out dozens of dogs and burgers at five dollars a pop (with a bag of potato chips and a can of soda thrown in). Liam reminds Charlie of the kind of frat boy he loathed at Colby. Right name. Right pedigree. Treated women like crap.

And then there's Mia. She inherited Kristy's long graceful arms and blond hair and David's curls and strong nose, and she can look beautiful or ugly, depending on if she smiles. She smiles a lot. She's engaged with life and all things River Run. Mia is the only one of the coaches who's young enough to compete this summer, so she'll be both his swimmer and his employee. She inherited some of David's hubris, yet she's also vulnerable to a kid like Liam. Team romances never end well.

Mia and Liam stroll in together, twenty minutes late. "Hi, Unc . . . I mean, Coach Charlie." Mia grins at him, flashing her big white teeth.

"Mia." He nods. He will not be her Uncle Charlie at River Run. He needs to wipe that smirk off of Liam's face and assert himself as the boss right away. Otherwise they'll own him. He hates conflict. He reminds himself of that fucking Oliver. Just do it; they're teenagers, for God's sake. "Guys, first, three-thirty means three-thirty. Not three thirty-four or three thirty- five." There, that wasn't so bad.

Mia apologizes, Liam says nothing, and Justin nods as if to say "my dad can be a hard-ass," which isn't really true, but Charlie appreciates the support.

"Second." Charlie's voice travels down a chunk of an octave. "We're going to win our division this year."

"Really?" Mia looks at him intently.

"We finished fourth last year." Liam sounds like he's correcting Charlie's math.

Charlie tells them about his research and Justin's stats, and by the time he finishes making his case, all three of them look, if not entirely convinced, open to the idea of the Manta Rays becoming contenders for the crown.

He removes his Ray-Bans, looks each of them in the eye, and says in an even deeper voice, "Let's evolve!"

They laugh, but he can tell that he's moved them. Gillian was so wise all these years. If you have a plan, people will follow you. Well, unless someone comes along with a better one.

16

GILLIAN

A familiar rush of adrenaline pumps through Gillian as she stacks up the kickboards in neat piles. The pool's a drug to her: the aroma of chlorine and sunscreen, the thick awning of trees that shades the water when the sun starts to retire, the swimmers answering the call of the ice cream truck. The pool holds a charge even on a quiet day like today. Later this week, though, after school lets out, River Run will be officially open at this time of day. A retired gym teacher whom Krillian nicknamed Jane Fonda will be leading a dozen of her admirably fit contemporaries in a feisty water-aerobics class. The lifeguards will endure Gloria Gaynor and Diana Ross blaring from a boom box perched on a lounge chair, and later in the afternoon they'll watch over the hordes of children, nannies, and moms looking for relief from the D.C. area humidity.

Gillian threads her ponytail through the hole of her River Run Manta Rays baseball cap, which combined with her clipboard makes her look like *The Love Boat*'s cruise director, Julie McCoy, according to Charlie. He has an encyclopedic knowledge of the cast and plotlines of dozens of 1970s television shows that Gillian's father never allowed the Norton children to watch. In one of his drunken rages he tossed the family's "idiot box" out the den window. A few days later, he retrieved the set to watch the Watergate hearings.

Kristy pokes her head in the door of the gear room and surveys the neat piles Gillian has made out of the mess. "This project must have been catnip for you."

"Don't make fun of me." Gillian giggles, and when she doesn't hear Kristy respond with her irresistible belly laugh, she looks up at her friend.

Kristy stands in the doorway, her head resting against the frame, her hands folded in front of her. She gazes at Gillian lovingly, yet with a furrowed brow.

"Whatcha looking at?" Gillian adjusts her cap.

"Just you."

Gillian springs to her feet. "My work is done here. Let's go outside."

Kristy strokes Gillian's arm with a tenderness that takes Gillian's breath away.

17

CHARLIE

The swimmers arrive at four o'clock in a herd. They've already been practicing with Zeke, so they sort themselves into lanes. Once again, Charlie knows he must convey his authority immediately, or he'll be toast.

"Good afternoon, all. Before you jump in the water, let me introduce myself."

One of the boys is about to push his buddy into the pool, but Mia intervenes. "Listen up, dudes."

"I'm Coach Charlie. Can everyone say hello?"

They mumble a hello.

"I didn't hear you say, 'HI, COACH CHARLIE.'"

"HI, COACH CHARLIE."

He puts his hand to his ear. "I can't hear you." Christ, he sounds like Sergeant Carter from *Gomer Pyle*. Nobody ever gave Sergeant Carter shit.

They scream. "HI, COACH CHARLIE."

"That's better. Now, we're going to have a heck of a good time this summer. And." He pauses for dramatic effect. "*And* you guys are going to work hard and swim fast. How does that sound?"

Silence.

He opens his arms wide. "SOUNDS AWESOME, COACH CHARLIE!"

"SOUNDS AWESOME, COACH CHARLIE," they respond.

Charlie gives them a thumbs-up. He takes a lane for himself, and gives Justin and Mia cards with the set he wrote for their assigned lanes. Liam hangs back and takes his phone out of his pocket. No coach of Charlie's is going to whip out an iPhone or goof off on the diving board or flirt with the lifeguards on his watch.

Charlie holds out his hand and stares Liam straight in the eye. "Hand it over."

Liam looks around to see if anyone's watching. "Seriously?" He shrugs and surrenders the phone.

"Go help Mia, Liam."

Charlie gives the kids a 300-meter warm-up and watches them closely while they swim, taking note of the ones with a lot of strength and no technique, and vice versa.

"Sydney," he calls out to a tall, athletic-looking twelve-year-old girl. "Come here for a second."

She climbs out of the pool, giggling from the extra attention.

"You're so strong. You must play a winter sport."

Sydney blushes, but she looks happy. "Basketball."

"Okay, Sydney-LeBron, do you want to swim faster?"

She nods her head up and down rapidly.

"What happens when you're trying for a rebound? What do you do?"

"Um, jump?"

"Exactly. Now when you push off the wall, pretend you're jumping for that ball and see what happens."

"Okay, Coach C."

He shows her where to position her arms to streamline her body, and the next time she pushes off the wall she flies by the older kids one lane over. Beautiful. He picks three more kids, intuitively knowing which pointers they need and how to convey them clearly. Nothing about real estate development felt this natural. Or fun.

18

GILLIAN

Gillian bounces from chaise lounge to chaise lounge, making herself available to the newer moms, who always need her guidance. She's ready to field their questions about Zeke's abrupt departure, but nobody cares about Zeke. "Charlie's so into this," a second-season mom comments as she offers Gillian a carrot dipped in hummus. Charlie's a natural. Who knew? He couldn't organize a simple game of touch football at the boys' birthday parties, but today he's a veritable E. F. Hutton. Instead of responding to the mom's observation, Gillian accepts the carrot and chomps on it, even though she hates hummus.

She looks over and sees Kristy deeply engaged in conversation with Liam's mom, Trish, whom Krillian definitively does not like. Mia and Liam will be a couple soon, if they aren't already. Behind the two women, a line of minivans and SUVs are streaming into the River Run parking lot. Families who previously quit the team are arriving on deck: the little sister of a girl whom Mia excluded from one of the many clubs she formed in middle school, a mom who'd signed up to write ribbons for every single meet and never once showed up, the crazy-talented ten-year-old breaststroker who now, as a teen, towers over his tall mother, and the dad who complained that his twins didn't receive enough attention from Zeke.

"Good Lord, Charlie's been recruiting," Gillian says. Odd. Charlie never reached his potential in the business world because he's a great numbers guy but completely inept at making rain. But here he is engaged in animated conversations with swimmer after swimmer, parent after parent. Maybe he does need this experience to give him the confidence to find his next job.

"He sure has, Gil. I ran into Adrienne Mills at the grocery, and she said Charlie had called her," one of the mothers offers.

"Like, on the phone?" Gillian's shocked, but she looks over at him, and sure enough he's chatting up a family with nine-year-old fraternal twins.

"And a follow-up email," whistles a mom who reminds Gillian of her childhood pool friend Linda. Linda, Fran, and Debbie all moved away, and Gillian has replaced her River Rat posse three times since she joined the pool as an adult. The only constant has been Kristy, but Gillian wouldn't categorize her as a regular old member of the squad. Kristy falls into a different category completely.

"Time to pass out treats." Gillian reaches under the chair for a Tupperware container full of her Manta Ray cookies.

"Gillian's cookies!" one of the moms cries out.

"A little something special for Coach Charlie's first day." Gillian waves the Manta Rays napkins she ordered for last year's banquet.

Leaving the Tupperware for the moms, Gillian heads over to the lifeguard station with a half-dozen cookies. On her way she passes the extremely tanned older gentleman who on roasting-hot days like today fills his water pistol with ice cold water and squirts children as they go by. He's been coming to the pool since the boys were babies. "Hi, Mr. Delfor. Can I interest you in a cookie?"

"Gotta watch my girlish figure, but thanks for the offer." He squirts her bare legs.

Gillian laughs, although she finds his habit more than a little obnoxious.

"Hi, Mrs. C," says a young guard whose father taught biology to both Sebby and Justin at the local high school. "Mr. Delfor get you?"

"Sure did." Gillian extends the cookies to him. "Here you go, Teddy."

"Thank you!" He plucks a frosted Manta Ray from the stack. The guards have been a ravenous crew since back in the Sebastian Norton era when River Run decided against a snack bar. No snack bar. No tennis courts. "Too bougie," as Justin and Sebby would say.

"Take the rest for Sarah and Aubrey." She points her thumb toward the guards sitting in the chairs in their red shorts and white tank tops, their skin just starting to brown.

After her cookie delivery, Gillian positions herself on the deck, adjacent to the pace clock, and waits for the kids to finish practice. A couple of times she feels Kristy's eyes on her, all the way from across the pool. One of the returning swimmers spots Gillian, and as soon as the others see him munching on a sugar cookie, they swarm around her. "Let's form a line, Manta Rays." And they oblige her.

"Thank you, Mrs. Coach C," says a ten-year-old girl, her lips smothered in green frosting.

Mrs. Coach C? "Nice manners, cutie pie."

Gillian's grateful for a task to help her pass the time while Charlie talks with the parents. This must have been how he felt all those years while Gillian wrapped up her business at the pool. It doesn't matter, she'll catch up with Kristy. They didn't talk much over the weekend. She scans the deck, but her friend is gone.

19

KRISTY

Kristy was all set to share the big news with Gillian, but when she watched her friend greet every parent and swimmer like she owned the place, something inside her twitched, like a muscle that hadn't fired in a long time.

She needs to splash cold water on her face. Reboot. On her way to the women's locker room she stops in front of the Sebastian Norton shrine. Kristy faces the framed photo of Gillian standing next to their big, handsome father, a camera slung around her neck as she holds the newspaper clipping featuring the swan dive photo.

Hi there, Dad. Now that Kristy knows the truth, she can only see the features she shares with Sebastian. How did she not notice the similarities before? Kristy touches the frame. Gillian once said that her father was the most charming man on the planet. No wonder Flo fell for him. Could her mother have acted so impulsively? Impossible, Flo despised this trait in Kristy. Flo likely viewed Sebastian as a ticket out of the sad, impoverished life she shared with her alcoholic father.

"There you are!" Gillian's voice is like a shrill alarm interrupting a dream.

Kristy hones in on a smaller image in the shrine. "I never noticed how much you look like your mom, Gillian."

"Everyone tells me that," Gillian replies.

Now is the time to inform Gillian that they are related. Not just related—they are real sisters. Gillian will have a field day on Facebook:

Gillian and Kristy posing in front of the Sebastian photo, grinning, arms around each other's shoulders, #longlostsisters, #bloodisthickerthanwater, #krillian. See, Kristy knows her sister so well she can craft her beloved hashtags.

"Charlie might be a while. Let's go talk in our place." Gillian turns on her heel and walks out toward the pool.

What if Kristy decides not to follow for once? She steals another glance at the photo of her father, and before she peels her eyes away from the glass she catches sight of her reflection, of the old greedy look on her face, of Sebastian hovering above her hairline. Her heart rams against her chest as she turns away from her father and exits the clubhouse.

Gillian is waiting for Kristy at the huge oak shading the water. Kristy will tell her while they're sitting on the swing, leg to leg, rib to rib, as they rock back and forth on the ancient plank of wood, etched with the names of dozens of kids who made River Run their summer sanctuary. The first time Gillian invited her to share this private ritual, Kristy felt as if her whole body was being held.

Kristy perches herself atop the swing, on the spot where Gillian and Patrick scrawled their names so many years ago. Wait a second, Kristy's name should appear on that swing too. River Run is her birthright. She paid attention during Bible camp after all.

That pulsating muscle inside her hardens, curling in on itself like a fist. For now, the Sebastian secret belongs to her and no other sibling. She needs time alone—with her father. She manages to turn her attention back to Gillian, who's prattling on about the pool board's proposal to cut down the oak tree.

"Why do they want to do that?" Kristy asks as they pump their legs.

"Because it's old," Gillian answers with disgust. She pauses, likely waiting for Kristy to say that the board is just being difficult, that Gillian is in the right. Kristy says nothing.

"I'm going to meet with an arborist." Gillian aims her iPhone at the empty pool midair. They descend and stop the swing in unison, and seconds later Gillian uploads the photo to her Facebook page with the caption "Manta Rays 2012. Calm before the storm."

20

GILLIAN

Charlie walks to the swing, his eyes radiating a light that Gillian has to admit is sexy. He slides one of the deck chairs over.

"How many of the new kids signed up?" Gillian asks, fully expecting him to say half or less.

Charlie wipes his brow and grins. "All of them."

Impossible. He must be teasing.

"You rallied that many people over a weekend?" Kristy slaps her thigh.

Gillian's annoyed. Why didn't he tell her he'd been recruiting? Now she feels foolish for presenting him with Zeke's old files when he'd clearly already located these swimmers on his own.

"And I have another idea, now that I have Krillian here." Charlie raises his brows and widens his eyes. "What do you say we automate?"

Charlie lists the advantages of the automated system, all of which Gillian understands perfectly well. Parents can sign up for their kids' meets online, they can post results more easily at swim meets. Blah, blah, blah.

"No, honey, too soon." Gillian speaks slowly as she explains that the Manta Rays have always handled meet entries and results manually.

Kristy looks at both Charlie and Gillian. Kristy would be most affected by the change since she handles the mechanics of the meet: generating entry cards, tallying results at the competitions, keeping the records current. After she took the job, she started following summer league swimming results like some people track batting averages, and she can call up almost every Manta Ray's best time in all five events.

She waits for what feels like a whole minute before she says, "It's doable."

Gillian expected Kristy to side with her as she always does. "By Saturday?"

"If I hustle," Kristy says, "I can do it."

"I'm not doubting your ability." Gillian doesn't know many people who are as intuitive about numbers and computers as Kristy, except for her brother Patrick, who works as an IT specialist when he's sober enough to hold down a job. It's a little aggressive, though, to switch the whole entry system five days before the first meet.

"It's time, Gil," Charlie says too sweetly.

Gillian gets what Charlie's been trying to tell her since he took over. She has no vote. The committee will give him free rein over the team because he's a trusted adult.

"It's getting late. I've got to drop something off to a client in McLean tonight." Gillian faces Kristy, sticks her pinky and thumb out, and holds them to her cheek. "I'll call you."

Kristy returns the phone gesture. They'll talk later about Charlie's newest move.

Gillian pats Charlie's knee. Coaching is a lot more complicated than digging up a few names or running one practice. Or even automating. Charlie will need her soon. Just wait.

21

KRISTY

Maybe Kristy could have distracted herself from the urge to touch Charlie's freshly shaven head if they weren't walking out to the parking lot together. During the conversation about automation, she could think of nothing else. It's the type of gesture a love addict avoids, like an alcoholic would steer clear of a wine-tasting party. When they reach her car, she asks Charlie, "Can I touch your head?"

He half-laughs and then tucks his chin to his chest. "Go for it."

She inches toward him, and a whiff of his chlorine-scented sweat overpowers her. Don't do this, Kristy. Bad idea. Bad idea. Bad idea.

He waits patiently for her to follow through on her request.

Stop it now, Kristy. Turn the fuck around. She can hear Beverly, her ex-sponsor, in her mind. This is your first compulsive taste. You'll be toast if you don't walk back to the pool or call Gillian or touch your Star of David.

"Were you just busting my chops?" Charlie says, but keeps his head bowed. Had he picked up his chin, she would have walked away.

She raises her fingers to her gold charm, but they continue toward him on their own. She presses her palm against the smooth, warm skin of his scalp and rests it on his crown as if she were a priest giving him a blessing. A current zaps every single finger.

Charlie lets Kristy's hand linger for a second longer than appropriate before laughing nervously and retreating from her touch.

Now she wants more.

One touch. Boom. That's all it takes. Shit. She'd better get home. Fast.

Kristy cobbles together dinner: a quinoa dish made up of leftover roasted vegetables, a can of chickpeas, and fresh basil from Gillian's garden. She half-listens to Mia, Isaac, and David discuss Isaac's Israel itinerary and Mia's year-end chemistry project and David's obsession with the Olympic track and field trials. David ran track in high school until he blew out his knee.

During a pause in the conversation, Kristy considers casually mentioning her news. *Hey, guess what, kids? Sebastian Norton is your grandfather.* The Weinsteins will start spending Christmas morning at the Clouds' house, sipping hot cocoa, exchanging gifts marked "Aunt Gillian" and "Uncle Charlie," but now for real. Kristy will reclaim Christmas! She'll have to tell them sometime, and maybe she can defuse this whole stupid encounter with Charlie by sharing the news. No, she has to talk to Gillian first.

Instead, she asks, "How do you think practice went today, Mi?"

"Like, awesome." She describes the parents fighting for Charlie's attention and the kids who had quit in past seasons showing up for practice and how great the team is going to swim this year. "I never knew Uncle Charlie was such a badass."

"Always thought Gillian wore the pants in the family," David says with a snarky look on his face. Kristy doesn't laugh at his old joke; she prefers to think about Charlie's badassery.

22

CHARLIE

Charlie drives home from River Run with one hand on the steering wheel and the other stroking the top of his head. He's like the Biblical character Samson in reverse; his baldness is giving him super strength. After a first practice that could not have gone any better, Kristy was game for automating the team. And did she really ask to touch his scalp?

By the time Charlie gets home, five more parents have responded to his email messages. They've heard terrific things about the new coach and hope they're not too late to sign up their kids, some of whom are fast. He didn't even need to try to impress any of these parents.

He shudders at the memory of his misguided efforts to earn his former work colleagues' respect: the phony chortling at their sexist and racist jokes, the time they flew him up to a strip club in Manhattan for a client outing. "Don't be such a wuss, Cloud," Oliver hissed as he shoved a ten-spot into a stripper's G-string. "Come on, Cloud," one of the firm's biggest clients said, and Charlie plastered a smile on his face, reached into his pocket, and shoved a bill inside the G-string of a girl who looked like one of their old babysitters. He guffawed appropriately, to be one of the boys.

Normally Charlie would share any stroke of professional luck with Gillian, his best friend, but she's still out. He thinks more about the way Kristy took his side about automating. That was a surprise. He's always thought Kristy viewed him as an appendage of Gillian's, and he's always thought of her merely as the other half of Krillian. Yeah, he's aware that Kristy's a knockout and that when she walks into River Run, men and women take notice of the way she can still sport a skimpy bikini. Her short blond hair, slender nose, and strong jaw make her look like a more athletic version of Josie Bissett from *Melrose Place*. You can tell she's the kind of woman who likes the attention, and her asshat husband, David, is the kind of man who likes to be married to the kind of woman guys salivate over. Although Charlie is not oblivious to Kristy's looks, he never was one of those guys. Gillian is more his type.

On impulse, he dials Kristy's number.

23

KRISTY

Kristy spits a mouthful of toothpaste into the sink before picking up her ringing phone and checking the caller ID. Charlie! Ignore the call. Get a grip, girl. She answers it.

"I think I know why I'm hearing from you." Her tone is flirty.

"I can't believe we're going to automate," Charlie says with a smile leaking out of his voice.

Kristy should speak to Gillian further about this move. At the end of last summer, the committee decided to wait another year until they computerized all aspects of the meet. Gillian is still the team rep, so she should have some say.

"Who's on the phone?" David asks as he enters the bathroom. He's on call, and within minutes, he'll be out the door.

"Charlie, can we talk later?"

"Of course. Sure. Talk later." Charlie hangs up.

"Good ole Chuckles," David sniggers.

Good ole Chuckles is taking ownership of his job and his body. His baldness makes him look sexy. Did she just think that? Never imagined she'd place the words "sexy" and "Charlie" in the same thought bubble.

"When will you be home?" She dabs the new cream her dermatologist prescribed around her eyes.

"We're going to try to do a VBAC." He kisses her. "Don't wait up."

"When are you going to hire another doctor?" She clips her bangs back from her forehead and applies a different cream to the worry lines that the same dermatologist routinely Botoxes away. "You're working too hard."

"We might have found our guy," he assures her. "Fingers crossed."

"Wake me up when you get home." She draws him to her and kisses him hard.

"Now, that's an offer I can't refuse."

"Go, you." She wants to tell him that they need to talk about something big and messy, that she's feeling shaky, that the beast inside her is stirring after a deep slumber. She knows to wait until after his shift. Even then, there's only so much she can share. She never corrected him when he attributed her erratic behavior after Mia was born to postpartum issues; she only revealed that she'd struggled with moods in the past.

She sits on her bed, staring at her phone, deliberating about whether to call Charlie back. Maybe she should talk to Beverly. No, she doesn't need her sponsor. Although, if this is true, why is she Googling her?

She hears a knock on her bedroom door. Beverly would say that Kristy's Higher Power has intervened by sending Isaac to her at this particular moment. She'd call it a Godshot.

Isaac appears with a stack of cards in his hand. "Wanna test me?" He desperately wants to make his high school's competitive Quiz Bowl team next year and for his last birthday asked for boxes and boxes of cards with questions about every topic under the sun.

"What's on the docket for tonight?"

"U.S. History."

She pats her bed. "Have a seat, mister."

"Thanks, Mom," Isaac says after he answers the final question about the first Clinton administration with effortless precision. Kristy was never great at history.

"Keep this up, and you're going to make the team, no problem." Kristy rubs his forearm.

"Thanks, Mom," he says again, bopping up from the bed. "Hope so."

She wants him to stay and answer more questions. Eventually they'd get to President Clinton's impeachment. Oh, the Monica months. Oh, the blue dress. She understood their dance well.

Kristy can spot a love addict a mile away. She recognizes that girl who cops a buzz from winning the affection of her friends' boyfriends and husbands, settling into the role as the other woman because she doesn't think she deserves more. That girl does her friend's nails, listens to her problems, helps her with her math, and takes her to Planned Parenthood for birth control or an abortion. But that doesn't mean that same girl won't steal a friend's man if he's there for the taking. And it doesn't mean that while she's at it, she won't take as much from the friend as she can carry in her arms.

Kristy was that girl. A long time ago. Not now. Not ever again.

Oh, hell.

She picks up her phone and dials Charlie's number, and when he answers, she says, "Let's figure out how we're going to automate."

24

GILLIAN

As the Manta Rays team rep, it's Gillian's duty to oversee the coaching transition. She's scheduled her work so she can attend Charlie's entire first week as head coach. At the end of his third practice an unfamiliar young mom breezes onto the deck area with her daughter and son and walks toward Gillian and Charlie, who have just begun discussing dinner plans.

"Sorry to interrupt," she says. "Are you Coach Cloud?"

"I am." He gives the smile that's taking up permanent residence on his face.

"I hope we're not too late to join the team." The woman explains that they've just moved to Arlington from Pittsburgh and their neighbors told them to come by the pool tonight to meet the new coach.

"No, not at all." Charlie introduces Gillian as his better half, failing to mention her position with the team.

"I'm Shannon O'Leary." She extends her hand to Charlie and then Gillian. "And this is Riley and Sean."

Shannon wears the kind of cutoff shorts Gillian wore before she decided she was too old to show so much leg and started wearing L.L. Bean skorts exclusively. Shannon and Gillian even share hyperextended knees, breaststroker knees.

"Your kids look the same age as mine were when they started swimming." Gillian high-fives them. "I'm the Manta Rays rep."

"Oh, hi!" Shannon's face lights up. "Lot of work running this team, huh?"

"Labor of love." She likes this Shannon person. "Welcome."

"Thank you." Shannon puts both hands on the small of her back and describes to an attentive Charlie the minutiae of Riley's swimming experience. This is the man whose eyes used to glaze over like he was a Krispy Kreme donut the minute Gillian started talking about anything concerning River Run.

Kristy appears, and Gillian excuses herself to greet her. She hugs her friend hello because she wants Kristy to know that she is here to talk about whatever has been distracting her. Kristy wears a pretty white sundress and smells different. New perfume? Weird, she usually arrives at the pool in her workout clothes, looking fantastic but not caring if she's had a chance to shower after her run or spin class or workout with her trainer.

"Hey, can I ask you something, Kris?"

"Is it about automating?" Kristy jokes.

"No way." Gillian pretends she isn't slightly miffed that Kristy was so quick to approve Charlie's absurd request to automate. "What do you think of Shannon O'Leary?"

"Who is Shannon O'Leary, may I ask?" Kristy's tone is downright jovial.

Gillian discreetly motions toward the woman talking to Charlie.

"Still don't know Shannon O'Leary."

"Okay, I just met her too. But . . ." She laughs. "But she reminds me of someone."

Kristy glances over at Shannon and Charlie. "You?"

"Sort of."

Kristy keeps staring in their direction. "Are you thinking of her for social director?" She's read Gillian's mind.

"I mean, I'll do the tie-dye T-shirt pep rally because it's coming up on Friday, but Shannon can handle everything else, the luau and all."

Kristy turns her attention back to her friend. "Gil, are you really going to hand over this job?"

"I don't have a choice." *Charlie's little move gave me no choice. I need to work as many hours as I can.* Gillian fights the resentment that has been burrowing into her thoughts lately, mainly at night when she falls into bed exhausted from seeing so many clients. She reaches into her purse for her phone and in a second is perusing Shannon's Facebook page.

Social-media stalking is something you do in private, like picking your nose, and this intimacy she can only share with Kristy. "Well, then, let's check out Shannon. What have we got here?" Gillian clicks on the video from Shannon's goodbye party. The Pittsburgh community clearly adored Shannon and her sporty, handsome husband, Gray, to judge from their tearful reminiscences about cookouts, Steelers games, and Shannon's famous whoopie pies. Gillian points to a photo of the mutant Oreos. "I know you don't like chocolate, but those look yummy."

"I think Shannon would be fanfuckingtastic." Kristy's looking toward Shannon and Charlie again. "Be back in a sec." She practically skips toward the clubhouse, her cotton dress swaying against her body. Kristy is emitting a familiar energy that unnerves Gillian. She's acting as though she has secret good news that she isn't yet ready to share. Gillian hates secrets.

25

KRISTY

When Charlie calls a second time, David is delivering another baby, and Mia and Isaac are asleep. It's dark in her bedroom, and she's lying under the sheets in a camisole and panties—she would never succumb to the frumpy sweats women her age wear as pj's.

"How's it going with the automating?" Charlie asks.

"I figured out how to do it."

"So fast?"

"Not a prob. I'm David's IT bitch." Kristy laughs and updates Charlie on the details of the new software she's purchased. Flo was right about the value of learning computer skills, which are intuitive for Kristy. She acquainted herself with David's operating systems for his practice, and troubleshooting gives her an excuse to shine around the office in her Manolos and tailored pants and make sure the girls know that David is off-limits. Whisk his tenderness with a dollop of borderline arrogance, and voilà, any gestating woman will fall madly in love with him. That she accepts, but a colleague or employee who has designs on her husband demands that, like a dog, Kristy pee on her man.

"Geez, Kristy. David's lucky to have you."

Kristy tumbles into his warm words, and they chat about the pool, never mentioning Gillian once. David's patients love him because he's so responsive, but often by the time he gets home from work, he's talked out. Charlie has always been an attentive listener, but Kristy assumed it was because he didn't have anything to say. Charlie now has plenty to say about the team and his ideas for growing it and winning the season, and Kristy wants to hear it all.

"Thanks for indulging me," Charlie says. "I'm rambling."

"You're not. So, you've really been studying every single meet result from the past five years?"

"I know, I'm a geek."

"True confession." She tells him about her Saturday-afternoon ritual of jumping on the NVSL website and looking up the results of each meet in the league.

"You do NOT do this."

"Do too."

"Prove it."

"Fine," she says. "Joey Jefferson."

"The backstroker?"

"Yup, he's going to be the top dog in the 11–12 age group this summer."

"I saw that too. He went a 32.6 last summer." They laugh together. "Holy shit."

"It's late," Kristy says almost in a whisper.

"Sorry to keep you. I really appreciate you handling this computer thing." Charlie's voice shifts to a businesslike tone.

"Not a big deal," Kristy says. "You're going to take the Manta Rays to a new level."

"Thank you," he responds gruffly, as if she's embarrassed him.

After a pause, they both say good night. Charlie's shift in tone incites a minute response in what Beverly called Kristy's addict brain. The withdrawal from their intimacy, maybe only imagined, is twice as addictive as his making her feel heard and seen. Without an invitation, Donny Everson visits her memory. She was barely fifteen when she became addicted to Donny, the manager of the high school football team. She counted the seconds between their meetings. When he pulled up to the gas station a few blocks from her house, she'd walk to him real slow, dizzy from that eager look in his eyes. She'd have been happy to stop things right there, but he drove her to the parking lot at Burger King, where she blew him while he downed the bulk of an order of onion rings and a strawberry milkshake. When she was done, he gave her the rest of the rings. The cold grease coated her tongue, and for hours afterwards she tasted onions and Donny Everson's stuff. One time he didn't show, and she called him and hung up when he answered. And then she switched lunch periods and sat alone staring at him and Nancy Deblitz sharing her egg salad sandwiches (gross). Nancy tripped her twice in the hallway and wrote "slut" on her locker, so the guidance counselor made sure that they didn't have any of the same classes or lunch periods. It didn't matter. Donny still pulled into that gas station once a week for Kristy. To this day, she can't look at an onion ring without gloating about her win.

Donny was her first share with her SLAA group, and she drank up the hugs from Beverly and the other members of the fellowship after detailing her desperate quests for love. She described how her mother had monitored Kristy's appetites even before she became a slut. If Mia and Isaac inquired about Flo, Kristy never mentioned their grandmother's pursed lips whenever Kristy took an extra helping of potatoes. Instead, she told them that her mother had proofed Kristy's nursing school applications and taught her how to bake a pie crust from scratch and change the ribbon in a typewriter, which was true. Flo wanted a good life for Kristy. The day Kristy befriended Gillian, her mother must have been tickled, as she watched from her perch in heaven. Kristy supposed she could thank Flo for pushing her out of her nest, because otherwise she would never have met David. Or Gillian. Or Charlie.

The next afternoon, Travis shows up at Kristy's house unannounced an hour before the Friday night tie-dye T-shirt pep rally is supposed to start. He rings the front doorbell, which only strangers use. David's parents, who live across the river in a Maryland suburb, have their own set of keys to the house.

She looks through the peephole and opens the door. "Dad!"

"I wanted to make sure you were okay," he says tentatively.

"I'm sorry I worried you." Travis, not the kind of father to stop by for a cup of coffee, only visits when he's invited. He comes over three times a year: autumn to watch a Redskins game with Isaac, winter for a chili dinner, his favorite, and late spring for a cookout. He never visits in the summer, because the hot months are reserved for River Run and he always spends half of August with Nora and her family.

"Come in, come in," Kristy says.

Isaac and Mia appear as Travis stands in the enormous foyer with the high ceilings. With his slicked-back hair and short-sleeved button-down shirt, he resembles one of those men whom the Weinsteins hire to service their lawn or HVAC system. Thinking of Travis in this way fills her with shame.

"Hi, Grandpa." Isaac and Mia greet Travis, embracing him stiffly. What else? Were they supposed to jump up and down and scream "Grandpa Travis is here! Yay!!!" They barely know him.

"Mia, you keep getting prettier." Travis chuckles. "And Isaac, when did you start towering over your old granddad?"

Mia's phone buzzes in the pocket of her jeans, and Kristy can tell that she wants to take the call. "I've got to turn in my paper online before tie-dye night."

Travis smiles. "Don't let me get in the way of your schoolwork."

"Grandpa, you should come tonight. You've never even been to River Run." Isaac tosses a tennis ball in the air.

"Isaac, can you give your grandpa and me a minute?"

Isaac trudges upstairs, still playing catch with the ball.

"And could you please not do that on the steps?"

"I was the same way when I was Isaac's age." Not exactly. Travis was an all-state baseball star who played a year in the minor leagues. He follows Kristy to her kitchen, which seems too large and overly applianced in her father's presence and too small and antiquated in the presence of David's friends. She pours two tall glasses of ice water and motions Travis to sit down at the round kitchen table.

"How are you?" He lowers his voice. "You know, after . . ."

"Oh, not great." She sips her water. She wants to tell him that she's off her rocker, that she's teetering on the edge of a relapse, that she's having unholy thoughts about Charlie Cloud, her fucking brother-in-law. Travis would understand. He caught her in the basement enough times.

"I'll bet." He cups the glass with his gnarled hand.

"This is all surreal." More than once, Kristy had wished she had a sibling who needed her or a father who was important and powerful. And glamorous. Gillian depended on Kristy's dependence on her, and here was Travis checking on her, and all she could do was pine for Charlie. "Come to the tie-dye night, Dad."

"You sure?"

"It will be fun." Maybe having Travis around will protect her from further flirtations with Charlie. She has to stop.

26

JUSTIN

Aunt Kristy asks Justin to show her father around River Run while she trots off to talk to Dad. He likes giving the tour, and Mr. Frick seems like a cool dude. The skin on his neck looks like an alligator's, and he carries Slim Jims in his front shirt pocket. Unlike Aunt Kristy, he speaks with a thick Southern drawl, and he looks nothing like her, or Mia or Isaac either.

Justin walks Mr. Frick around the circumference of the pool, first to the side where Mom and Mrs. O'Leary are busy making a vat of soda ash to treat the tie-dye water, then to the diving board, storage shed, big oak tree with the swing, and locker rooms. Mr. Frick nods politely, but pools aren't his scene, Justin can tell. Maybe he can't even swim.

As they head toward the pool house, Justin serves up the stories he's heard Mom tell over and over, how River Run purchased the property back in the '50s, how they razed the small homes on the land but kept this cozy little bungalow. He leads Mr. Frick inside to the former living room. "Kind of weird to have a fireplace in a swimming-pool clubhouse," Justin says.

"Does anyone ever use it?"

"No. But they probably did back when it was a house."

Mr. Frick unsticks his shirt from his skin. "I suppose a fire would be overkill."

Justin walks Mr. Frick past the trophy cases and record board. Uncle Patrick still holds the 10 & Under record for the 25-meter butterfly. Sebby almost broke it before going on to smash a bunch of other River Run records, before that weird thing happened with Mom. Mr. Frick's interest perks up at the wall of photos. He reaches into his shirt pocket for his reading glasses and puts them on, lasering in on an ancient framed newspaper clipping. This is the point where, if Mom were here, she'd proudly explain every picture that features the Nortons.

"My mom took that photo of her dad," Justin explains. "It won some prize and was featured in the *Washington Post.*"

"I see that."

"My dad calls it Mom's first post." Stupid joke to share with Mr. Frick, who is likely not a Facebooker.

Mr. Frick doesn't appear to be listening, so enamored is he with the photos.

"Yeah, because my mom is always posting on Facebook."

Mr. Frick studies a different photo, this one of a high-school-aged Mom holding a clipboard. "That your mom?"

"Good eye!"

He points to the caption. "I cheated a little bit."

"My mom grew up here. Like, at River Run," Justin says with more than a little pride in his voice.

Mr. Frick scrutinizes the images of the Nortons for what seems like a really long time. "Uh-huh."

Aunt Kristy and Dad appear with their arms full of pizza boxes. "There you are," she says to Mr. Frick, like she's way excited about having her dad here or something. Justin wonders why Mr. Frick has never visited before.

"Dad, this is Charlie Cloud, Gillian's husband and now head coach of the Manta Rays." Aunt Kristy is amped up tonight.

"Nice to meet you, Mr. Frick." Dad extends his hand as he taught Sebby and Justin to do when they were kids.

"Call me Travis." Mr. Frick looks Dad right in the eye, another thing Dad taught Sebby and Justin.

"Travis it is." Dad smiles. "If you'll excuse me, duty calls." He walks out to the pool.

"Your dad's catching up on some Manta Ray history," Justin says to Aunt Kristy.

Mr. Frick's big eyes travel between his daughter and a group photo and Dad.

Justin points out Mom and Aunt Kristy in the photo. "They call them Krillian. Kristy plus Gillian."

Aunt Kristy laughs nervously.

"'Preciate the tour, Justin." Mr. Frick reaches into his pocket and hands him a Slim Jim as they walk toward the clubhouse door.

"Oh, cool. I love these. Thank you!" Justin's passion for dried beef product comes from hanging around 7-Elevens with Tiff, who smokes a lot of weed and craves Slim Jims and Slurpees when she's high.

Outside, kids are swarming the table to receive their free Manta Rays T-shirts. Parents are jockeying to talk to Dad, who's tousling boys' hair, shaking dads' hands, and smiling confidently at mothers. "It's going to be a summer to remember, Mr. Frick," Justin says, not knowing exactly why.

Mr. Frick stays quiet while he takes a last long look at the swan-dive picture of Sebastian Norton.

27

CHARLIE

Charlie's attending his very first Manta Rays tie-dye pep rally, years after his kids have grown out of the activity. He doesn't need any kind of rally to get fired up for tomorrow's meet. He's more excited than he ever was for one of his own races, but a little nervous too. He walks out to the parking lot to say hello to a group of swimmers he hasn't yet greeted.

"Hi, Coach Charlie!" calls Katie, one of the thirteen-year-old girls, waving a neon green car-window marker she's using to decorate her parents' minivan.

"Hey, ladies." He walks over to her and a few friends who are all deeply engaged in making car art. It's only a matter of time until the Clouds' vehicles will be adorned with Manta Rays hype scrawled in a rainbow variety of colors.

"Hey, Coach Charlie." They look up and smile.

"What have we got here?" He circles the van and examines their work. "'13–14 Girls ROCK.' I like it."

"Thanks." Katie looks pleased.

"Oh, and 'Eat my bubbles!'" He points to the slogan and the picture they've drawn of bubbles. "Come on in when you're finished. There are T-shirts to be dyed."

"We're almost done!" one of the girls calls after Charlie, who is heading back to the pool.

The pool typically quiets down in the evening, but it's humid, so the place is still hopping. It's almost seven, and the gold June light dapples the water. Adult swimmers crawl up and down the length of the pool, loud children toss a Frisbee that keeps ending up in the lane of two lap swimmers, a couple of middle-schoolers practice their handstands in the shallow end, and families barbecue while their toddlers run around in swimming diapers.

Gillian and Shannon are still fiddling with the soda ash. Gillian's arms are strong, and she looks good in sleeveless shirts. She keeps fit, partially because she's always moving, cleaning, fixing. She also carries herself like a woman who knows her body, which Charlie has always found sexy. He plops down with Mia and a group of ten-year-old girls and fastens rubber bands around bunches of cotton. The girls belt out the lyrics to "Call Me Maybe," a catchy little pop ditty. They know every word.

It seems like Kristy shows up wherever he goes, or maybe he's just growing more conscious of her presence. This time she appears along with her father to tell Charlie she forgot a box of T-shirts in her garage. "I'm going to run home and pick them up. Be back in ten." She grazes Charlie's shoulder with hers. Is he imagining it, or is Kristy touching him more? He feels Travis watching them like a lifeguard scanning a pool.

"I'll chat with your dad," Charlie says.

"Dad, you're in good hands here." Kristy holds Charlie's eyes in hers. Travis is watching her closely, as if she's a kid who has a sugar buzz from eating too much cake at a birthday party. Sebby is that kid, Charlie thinks, and his crashes are ugly.

"Be right back," she says.

Both men settle into lounge chairs while Kristy walks past a peripatetic Gillian who is now straightening up the tables and sorting rubber bands. Shannon collects the bands Gillian drops on the grass, almost before they fall.

"Funny name." Travis looks in their direction. "Krillian."

"Yup." Charlie chuckles. "They met at a park up the road."

"That so? Right up the road?"

"Legend is that they felt like they knew each other." Charlie snaps his fingers. "Right from the get-go."

Travis looks at him with interest. Strange. Travis seems like the kind of guy who would sidle up to a bar and watch a Redskins game with a cold one and an order of Buffalo wings, not the type to bother himself about two middle-aged women's friendship, even if one of them is his daughter.

Charlie touches the tips of his fingers together. "They were like magnets."

Travis strokes his chin. "Hmm . . ."

Charlie now remembers wondering why Kristy's dad hadn't shown up for Isaac's or Mia's bar and bat mitzvahs, but he didn't care enough to ask Gillian about it, or if he did, he can't remember what she said. He never used to pay much attention to a mention of Kristy.

Travis looks like he's going to ask a question. He tugs on the bill of his cap, like he must have when he played in the minor leagues, and Charlie only knows this fact because Isaac told him. Just as Travis opens his mouth, a screech erupts from across the pool. One of the eight-year-old girls has kicked over a container of red dye, and it's spilling into the water. The rest happens in slow motion. Shannon sprints from the shed toward the bucket to prevent the remaining contents from emptying into the pool. She trips over a lounge chair and lands right on her elbow. River Run is silent, save for the vroom of an airplane making its way to Reagan National and the sound of bone meeting cement. Shannon clutches her elbow close to her body. "Oh. This is not good. Not good at all. Oh. Oh. Oh. I think I broke it."

Charlie bolts over to Shannon, but Gillian has already assumed control of the situation. "Okay, let's give Mrs. O'Leary some space, guys." Gillian pauses for a second. "We'll be just fine. Everything is going to be fine, Shannon. Justin, can you go get some ice?"

Shannon's eyes water as she rocks back and forth.

"Mommy, you look like you're going to cry." Riley's little body shakes with fear.

Gillian motions Charlie to take care of Riley and Sean. "Your mom's going to be fine."

Charlie puts his arms around their shoulders.

"Can you straighten your elbow?" Gillian asks gently.

Shannon starts to extend her arm but then yanks it back to her body.

"Charlie, will you call Shannon's husband to pick up the kids? His cell should be on the roster, Gray O'Leary." Gillian watches Shannon with concern. "We'll get you to the emergency room. Let's clear a path here."

Gillian parts the crowd with her old authority, leaving Charlie in the background watching his wife take charge, the O'Leary children at his side. Charlie misses the old Gillian, even if she's not simpatico with the new Charlie.

"Look, Coach C." Riley points to the pool.

The red dye has trickled into the water. It looks like blood.

28

GILLIAN

"Oh, hon. Does it hurt like a mother you-know-what?" Gillian asks Shannon, who, now safely in the car and out of her kids' earshot, releases a gusher of tears.

"Yes." She wipes her cheek with her good arm. "Fuck, yes."

"That's right, hon. Keep the f-bombs a-flying."

"Fuck, fuck, fuck, fuck!" Shannon shouts.

"Yes, fuck, fuck, fuck!" Gillian repeats with gusto. No wonder Kristy swears so often. It feels good.

"Thanks, Gillian," Shannon says gratefully.

"Glad to help." Gillian means it even though she hates hospitals so much that she delivered both of her children at a midwives' center. When Charlie had his gall bladder removed, she forced herself to sit with him. But she'll be fine now; she suspects Kristy will show up because she knows how to handle any medical situation and always senses when Gillian needs her.

"Hang tight. We're almost there." Gillian pulls up to the emergency room of Virginia Hospital Center and stops right outside the entrance, her heart beating in her throat. She knows this spot well. "Come on now," Gillian says to Shannon, and runs around to the passenger side to help her from the car, as she did for Sebastian so many times.

"Oops. Sorry." Gillian sees that Shannon is fully capable of extricating herself from the car. "I'm going to park. I'll be back in a second."

After Gillian parks, she darts to the hospital entrance like she's just been caught in the rain, running from the force of the bad Sebastian memories that have been needling her lately. She'll focus all her thoughts on tending to Shannon.

Not to be. Sebastian's ghost attacks her without mercy. Breathe, Gillian. Breathe.

Gillian was sixteen the first time she drove her father to the hospital. This was the day she quit asking God for favors. It was a rainy late August afternoon, the only time Sebastian had ever broken his River Run beer-only rule and brought a large flask to the pool. Gillian sat spine-straight in the lifeguard chair, eyes on her father, praying for bad weather. When the dark sky released four successive bolts of lightning, Gillian blasted her whistle and yelled, "Everyone out!" to the one hearty swimmer left. There was always one who stayed well past the time it was sensible to go home. "Get my camera, Gil," Sebastian barked at her from the far side of the pool, making a swan dive motion with his arms. Gillian jumped down from the guard chair, twisting her ankle as she landed. A searing pain shot up her leg as she hobbled over to intercept Sebastian before he reached the diving board. His thick hair was matted against his forehead, his eyes were red and milky, and his whole body stank of alcohol. "Time to go home, Dad," she told him, sliding her arm through his, and by some miracle he agreed. She didn't bother fighting him for the car keys. Nobody took the wheel of Sebastian's prized Mustang. Her ankle swelled as he drove them home. He brought the flask to his lips, removing his free hand from the steering wheel to tap the bottom. Gillian steered the car while Sebastian drained the last few drops. No wonder he hadn't put up a fuss about leaving River Run. He was out of booze.

Gillian finds a ladies' room before tracking Shannon down. The woman in the next stall is peeing with great force. Gillian calls Kristy. Maybe her friend can stop the home movies from unspooling on the projector inside of her head. Maybe Kristy is on her way to the hospital. It would be like her to show up without making a fuss. Kristy doesn't pick up.

When Gillian and Sebastian got home, May did not help take care of her drunk husband, because she was furious about her discovery of yet another one of his girlfriends, this time a neighbor who lived two houses down. Nor did she tend to Gillian's ankle. May stayed locked in her room while Sebastian spent the remnants of the afternoon sprawled out on a lawn chair in the backyard in the warm rain, emptying and refilling his flask with the jug of Jim Beam at his feet. Gillian sat at the kitchen table, icing her ankle, lifeguarding her father. She longed for the high-functioning Sebastian who neatly stashed the flask in his old army trunk in the garage, the Sebastian who insisted on walking Patrick and Gillian's beloved basset hound Homer at night and returned liquidy and calm. Eight and a half months ago, after he'd run over Homer with his prized Mustang, he'd started to get sloppy with his drinking and his women. Drinking whiskey at River Run, though, that was a new low.

Gillian dials Charlie and then Kristy. Come on, one of you, please pick up.

At dinnertime May emerged from her room, weary and swollen-eyed. She kissed Gillian and Patrick and made them English muffins and eggs and jelly, their designated drunk Sebastian meal. The three of them picked at their food, trying not to look out the window at him. They said nothing when he rose from his chair, stumbled across the lawn, and burst through the door. Gillian tried to make eye contact with Patrick to tell him to go to his room, but Patrick cast his eyes down at the runny mixture on his plate. "Finish your eggs, Patrick," Sebastian ordered, dripping rain over the dry floor. Patrick shoveled the last few bites of cold eggs into his mouth. "Lick the plate, Patrick." Patrick dragged his tongue along the pretty blue bone china May's mother had willed her and placed the clean plate in the sink. Pinkish slime coated his chin, and Gillian wanted to wipe her brother's face with her hand. "Sorry, Dad," he mumbled. "Sorry, Dad," Sebastian mimicked, and went on to lecture Patrick about how he was a waste of free tuition at Sebastian's current boys' academy. "You sound like your father," May whispered harshly, further infuriating Sebastian, who reached into the sink and cracked the plate in two. "That's enough," May said, and walked over to the basin to retrieve the porcelain pieces. Patrick scampered up the stairs, and minutes later Gillian found him curled up on the floor of her closet. The two huddled together until they heard their mother climb the steps. Gillian's ankle throbbed, so when the house was quiet, she went back downstairs for ice and she found Sebastian lying in a pool of vomit on the kitchen floor. She didn't run for her mother. She was a lifeguard, strong enough to clean Sebastian up by herself, with a little help from Patrick. Gillian drove her mother's Buick to the Virginia Hospital Center, the car reeking of alcohol and throw-up. "He stinks," Patrick said, pinching his nose until Gillian stopped the car in front of the emergency entrance. "He's just a little—" Gillian started to make an excuse for Sebastian, but Patrick cut her off. "Don't, Gil. Not today." The two of them dragged their father out of the back seat. Gillian limped through the emergency-room door, the weight of Sebastian bearing down on her ankle so hard that she feared it would go the way of Patrick's plate.

A line is forming for Gillian's stall, and her legs feel too gummy to walk. Before she exits the bathroom, she fixes her hair and washes her hands through two cycles of the automated sink.

When she emerges, she finds Shannon sitting in the waiting room, her jaw clenched in pain. "Can I get you something to eat or drink?"

"No, thank you, just catching up on *The Suite Life on Deck*." Shannon nods toward the television.

Gillian sits in a hard green chair and watches the insipid show that used to make Sebby and Justin howl.

~~~

The night Gillian brought Sebastian to the hospital, she sat next to Patrick in the waiting area, watching reruns of *Hogan's Heroes* while the doctors pumped their father's stomach. A nurse with a blond perm noticed Gillian's limp and brought her an ice pack, which Gillian held to her ankle as she imitated Colonel Klink's thick German accent to make Patrick laugh. Patrick asked if the stomach pump resembled Gillian's bike pump or a gas pump or the old well pump at their dad's family farm in Illinois. Growing up, Sebastian told them, he used to pump water from deep down that tasted cold and clean, just like water should.

The next day, Gillian purchased industrial glue with her lifeguarding money and painstakingly cemented the blue plate back together, stuffing the bad Sebastian into the crack. He'd remain sealed inside of those fissures as long as she didn't venture into her scary places: hospitals, his old school, the road where he died, drunk and with a woman half his age. See, that was Patrick's problem, he dwelled in the cracks. May always called this kind of navel-gazing a waste of energy.

~~~

Gillian picks up her iPhone to see if Kristy has texted. Nope, not yet, so she checks her Facebook page, pinging each photo with a like.

"Do you like everything on Facebook?" Shannon asks.

"What's not to like?"

They giggle together.

A nurse calls Shannon's name and escorts her to the X-ray room. Gillian starts to get up, but Shannon motions her to sit down. "I'm just going for an X-ray," Shannon says weakly. "You've been so helpful already."

Yes, she's very helpful. She likes to help. That's what she does. It makes her feel good. It makes her forget. The helper of the past and the helper of the present are merging, and she's trapped between the lost Gillian of her late teens and the lost Gillian of middle age. Trapped. And there isn't one thing she can do to reach a safe shore, except maybe to engage in more helping.

"Call if you need me." She pops a piece of Trident spearmint gum in her mouth and snaps a photo of the television screen with the hospital sign behind. "Bucket of dye + a heroic effort by our very own Shannon O'Leary to spare the River Run pool from a Valdez-like spill = one hurt elbow." #ZackandCodystillbigtroublemakers.

The gum loses its flavor quickly, so Gillian wraps it in a tissue and hunts down a trash can. Thirty people have already liked her *Suite Life* post. Not bad. It feels good to stretch her legs, and she finds herself walking toward the wing that housed her father and his freshly pumped stomach. He stayed sober for five months and twenty-one days after that episode. He never apologized to Gillian, Patrick, or May. Six years later Gillian broke the same ankle while ice-skating with Charlie; that's the reason she offers when the threat of rain makes her ankle murmur.

Shannon's nurse approaches Gillian. "I'll take you to your friend. The doctor just finished up."

Shannon's elbow is lounging in a sling and her eyes are half-closed when Gillian enters the room. "Hey there," Gillian says.

Shannon opens her eyes and smiles. "Hey."

"Let's get you home to your kids."

"I just talked to them, and they're a little freaked out." Shannon sounds exhausted and doped up. "Thank you so much."

"When you're feeling better, we'll do your orientation at the pool." Gillian taps Shannon's shoulder a little too hard. "And figure out the luau, of course. It's going to be here in one week!"

Shannon nods her head. Gillian picks up Shannon's purse from the chair.

"Thanks, Gillian." Shannon rises gingerly.

"No problem." Gillian slings Shannon's purse over her own shoulder. "You know, we should have dinner, with Kristy too, all three families."

"I'd love that."

"Maybe tomorrow? To celebrate our first meet?"

"Yes! Let's do it!" Shannon says.

"Spare you a night of cooking, and I know for a fact that Kristy doesn't have any plans." Gillian is now her old self, not the play-acting version. "She'll definitely want in."

29

KRISTY

Kristy's temples are throbbing when she and Travis get home from the tie-dye pep rally.

"What can I get you to drink?" Kristy asks. "Water? Seltzer? Coke? Juice? Beer?"

"A glass of juice would be real nice," Travis says.

"Orange? Cranberry? Guava?"

"Orange," he says. "If you please."

She pours his juice, hands it to him, and then fixes herself a glass of seltzer and downs three Tylenol.

Travis sits down. "That Shannon took quite a spill."

"The dye, not Shannon," Kristy jokes. "Big spill."

Travis is usually her best audience, but tonight he offers a courtesy laugh.

"Gillian's probably wigging out right now." Kristy takes another sip of seltzer. "She hates hospitals. Actually, she's terrified of them."

"Let me get out of your hair then. Go to her."

"I have a minute." She should have let Mia drive Travis home and followed Gillian and Shannon to the hospital, but how often did her father visit the pool? Come on, Kristy, be honest, Beverly would have said, you couldn't rip yourself away from Charlie.

He stares down at the fractured terra-cotta tile under his foot. "I'm going to come back and fix that," he says.

"You don't have to, Dad."

"No bother at all."

"These McMansions are all coming apart at the seams." She surprises herself by disparaging the home that has made her feel superior to Travis, Nora, and Flo.

"It sure is a nice place." Travis is too gracious to comment on the speed with which Kristy and David built the house.

"Maybe you can fix the tile when you come back to say goodbye to Isaac before his trip." First the pep rally, now a special goodbye for a six-week trip, when Travis habitually goes months without laying eyes on Isaac.

"I'd like that."

Kristy is going to miss Isaac terribly. He's big-hearted and wickedly funny too and has always been content with what life offers him. Kristy feels annoyed. "Why do Jews have a compulsion to travel to one of the most dangerous countries in the world? Do they not watch CNN?"

Travis shifts in his seat. "I can't answer that, Kris."

Of course he can't, he knows nothing of the life she's built, the culture she's adopted. Her bad. She wants to burst into tears, the way she did when she was a kid and trying like hell to hold it together and then someone nice and concerned asked her what was wrong and she totally lost it. "I wish Isaac weren't going away."

"He'll be back before you know it."

Yes, she's upset about Isaac leaving, but that's not what's bothering her at the core.

"I'm glad I got to meet Gillian," he says.

"My sister!"

"And Charlie," he says quietly.

He knows. She could tell by the way he was watching them tonight.

"Be careful, Kristy." This is the most he's ever said about her slutty business.

Her body burns as if she's experiencing an epic hot flash, of which she's only had a few so far, and sweat streams down the back of her neck, dampening her hair. "I will."

"He's your brother-in-law." Travis has never spoken directly about Kristy's love addiction, even after he caught her with boys.

Kristy feels as though her shame might make her whole body go up in flames. "I know."

"Gillian hasn't had it easy." Travis produces an envelope from his pants pocket. "I found this in one of your mom's files." He hands Kristy an old newspaper article: "Headmaster Asked to Resign from Northern Virginia High School." Sebastian posed for the photo in a suit, his hands crossed over one another. He looks older and puffier than he was in the shot that hung in the pool clubhouse. Kristy reads the article slowly, folds the brittle paper, and holds it in her lap. Instead of feeling repulsed by his inappropriate behavior, though, she feels as though she knows him, as though he would understand her.

"I guess I'm not surprised." She glances down at her big Sebastian Norton feet. She needs a pedi. "His indiscretion is how I got here, right?"

Travis gives her that sad look again.

She's feeling entirely unhinged. "Gillian must know the truth about Sebastian if stories like this ran in the paper."

Travis shrugs. "Suppose you're right."

"She's a pro at stuffing unpleasantness under the rug." Kristy knows that Charlie's coaching bothers Gillian, who is so cheerful about it that she's practically convinced the team that it was her idea. And she knows that Gillian is fretting about their lack of income too.

"People do what they have to do to get by," Travis states simply.

She hands him back the article. "Here."

"You should have it," he says.

"As a reminder of who I am, huh?"

"That's not what I meant."

But she knows on some level this is exactly why he gave her the clipping, maybe not initially, but after he observed her with Charlie. Kristy yearns for him to ask her if she wants to talk, and when she can't bear waiting another minute, she downs the last of her seltzer. "I should go to the hospital."

"Okay, Kris." He gets up to leave.

That old want rumbles. "Dad!"

"What? You just said you had to go," he says.

"But I didn't mean it."

"I'm not a mind reader, sweetheart."

"Can't you treat me like her?" She lets out a thin laugh. "Nora?"

Travis does not join her. "Kris, you're not Nora."

"You've always made that clear." Kristy studies the orange liquid in Travis's glass. She never even tasted real orange juice until David's parents invited her for a bagel brunch one Sunday morning. Sunday was the only day Travis closed his shop. On church mornings, Kristy toasted slices of Wonder Bread and smothered them with butter, cinnamon, and sugar for her father and Nora. After they went upstairs to join Flo in dressing for church, Kristy mopped up the sugar and cinnamon from their plates with her forefinger and licked it.

"I meant that you're you, and I like you just fine." He stands next to his chair, not staying, not going.

The thought of him leaving makes her ache.

"It seems like I keep putting my foot in it, don't I?"

She's losing herself to that fucking girl again. The fucking girl. The pathetic, half-naked girl in the back seat of some boy's car, offering her body, her tongue, her hands, over and over so he wouldn't zip up. She never picked the kind of guy who liked pillow talk. Once they zipped, they were gone and she felt exactly as she does right now. Ill. Hollow. Feral.

Do not ask. Do not ask. Do not ask. Kristy, for Christ's sake, do NOT ask. You know better.

Kristy can't help it. "Do you love me as much as you love her?"

He looks right at her. She thinks he might cry. "How can you ask me that?"

She swallows air, since the saliva in her mouth has dried up. "How can I not?"

She lunges at him for a hug. Now she's done it. She's pushed too far. Asked for more than he has to give. Chased him away for good. She was acting like Eleanor, a love addict and alcoholic she met in the rooms. Once, Eleanor described taking a sip from a margarita at a work happy hour and then unsuccessfully batting away her compulsion to sneak out of the bar and find a bottle of tequila she wouldn't have to share. Kristy wants to gulp down the whole bottle: Travis, Sebastian, and Charlie too.

30

CHARLIE

"I made oatmeal, people," Charlie says to Gillian and Justin the morning after the tie-dye fiasco, the first Saturday dual meet of the season. Oatmeal is the Clouds' official good-luck food, and the Manta Rays will need it to beat the Mighty Sharks, the toughest team in their division.

"Thanks, Dad." Justin slides into his seat at the kitchen table. "So, how is Mrs. O'Leary?"

Gillian points to her elbow. "She cracked her radial head. Long evening, but she'll be fine."

Last night, Gillian was quiet after she returned from the hospital, and when Charlie asked her if she was okay, she said, "I hate hospitals." He tried to hold her, but she wriggled away. He wanted to know if Kristy had showed, but he suspected not. By the time she left the pool with Travis it was late, and Charlie now assumes that Kristy's absence might have something to do with Gillian's mood. After he turned in, he heard her downstairs in her office, assembling boxes for her Monday client. This morning he notices that she has pruned their cookbook collection, stacking the outdated books in a neat pile she labeled "Arlington Library."

"That's good to hear." Justin hands Charlie a bag from a costume store up on Leesburg Pike. "Mia and I picked this out for you, Dad."

Charlie retrieves a Superman cape from the sack.

"Superheroes!" Gillian puts her palms on her cheeks. "My favorite theme."

"Let me." Justin ties the red strings of the cape around Charlie's neck. "There you go, Superman."

The best part about taking this coaching job has been the chance to get closer to Justin. Charlie always found it easier to connect with Sebby, maybe because they were less involved with River Run. He's grateful for the recent hours he's spent with Justin, geeking out on swim stats. They were up late every night this week, researching the results from last year, figuring out how the Manta Rays could best exploit the Sharks' weaknesses. He ran his lineup by Kristy, and they agreed that the meet would probably come down to the last relay. He'll make sure it will be a good day no matter who wins.

"What are you two grinning about over there?" Gillian sprinkles flaxseed over her oatmeal.

"Big day, that's all." Justin excuses himself.

Gillian takes a bite of the oatmeal. "Perfection, Charlie." She starts going on about a Facebook photo of Shannon O'Leary making whoopie pies. "She must have made them yesterday before her tie-dye injury."

"And what, pray tell, is a whoopie pie?" Charlie teases.

"A mutant Oreo." Gillian shows him the photo of Shannon slathering frosting between two cakes the size of coasters. She titled the post, "Making whoopie (pies)." "She'll bring them to dinner tonight, I bet."

It hasn't taken Gillian much time to shift her energies toward tonight's dinner party. The beauty of Gillian is that she never lingers on a negative emotion for long. "You're obsessed," Charlie says.

"You're a little obsessed too." She raises an eyebrow as she glances toward the Superman cape fastened around his neck.

Charlie adjusts it. "What? The theme is Superheroes."

Gillian tugs gently on the string.

"We've gotta blast." Justin appears in the kitchen in a Spider-man body suit, a drawstring bag slung over his shoulder. "The caravan's leaving soon."

"We're ready." Gillian clears the plates and soaks the oatmeal bowls in warm water. Ten minutes later, minivans and SUVs form a line behind the Clouds' car in the River Run parking lot. Charlie gets out and poses with the team while Gillian snaps away. When Sebby and Justin were younger, Charlie always stayed in the car reading the *Post*, not paying much attention to the kids preening in their costumes. Today, he wants his presence noted. The air damn near crackles.

After Gillian takes the last group photo and the kids return to their cars, Shannon drives up in her Manta Rays T-shirt, arm in a sling. The moms gather around her, and she assures them that she's fine, thanks to Gillian.

"Hi, Coach C," Riley says with more poise and confidence than any ten-year-old Charlie has ever met. Right then his intuition tells him that she'll find her way onto the mixed-age relay, the last event of the meet.

"Wonder Woman, right?" The kid looks like a mini version of Lynda Carter. "You've got Super Shero powers." Charlie fist-bumps Riley. He's been doing a lot of fist-bumping lately.

Riley beams. "Yeah, I'm a Super Shero."

Gillian orders Charlie to pose with Riley and little Sean, who's wearing a Buzz Lightyear costume and bright green rain boots. Charlie lets her take one picture before he cuts her off.

"We best get moving." He gives Riley a fake salute and watches Justin climb into Mia's car. Where's Kristy?

31

KRISTY

Kristy begs off joining the caravan, using the excuse that she needs to arrive early to the meet to set up the computer. Not true. She can set up a computer in the time it takes a grown man to shave half his face. Travis was smart to use the clipping of Sebastian's fall from grace as a reminder of what Kristy stands to lose if she keeps pursuing Charlie. A thick, cold slime of remorse coats her insides all the way to her mouth as she imagines the young Gillian reading that article about Sebastian. Kristy slides the article into the pocket of her shorts to remind herself what happens to people who can't control their cravings. She can't fathom a life without David.

Kristy enters the Mighty Sharks' deck through the women's locker room, where two prepubescent girls wait in line for the stalls to change into their bathing suits. She goes outside and greets Lizbeth Clark, the opposing team's automation representative, who is sitting on a folding chair in front of her computer.

"Hot as balls." Lizbeth sticks a towel down her shirt, beneath her bra. "The girls are already soaked."

Over the years, Kristy and Gillian have exchanged dozens of glances prompted by Lizbeth's oversharing about the aesthetician who singed her vajayjay while waxing her bikini line, or her naughty Yorkie, Dennis, who showed up at her block party with her diaphragm between his teeth.

Kristy is almost finished double-checking her file when Gillian sneaks up behind her and presses a cold soda can against her neck. She thrusts her shoulders back and lets out a yelp.

Gillian giggles. "I didn't mean to startle you. You look like you need a little cooling down."

Kristy taught Gillian this trick back when they used to hang out on Kristy's porch, rocking on wicker chairs and sipping the seltzer drink they'd invented while the kids played and Kristy nursed Isaac. Gillian showed up regularly with Tupperwared meals, nursing pads, toys for Mia, and anything she eerily intuited Kristy needed. She organized Kristy's nursery and kitchen just for fun. David's mother had also cooked and babysat for the Weinsteins, but this was different. Gillian showed up for Kristy first and foremost.

Kristy feels a surge of gratitude and shame as she leaps from her seat, startling Lizbeth, and hugs Gillian hard. "I'm sorry I didn't show up at the hospital last night," she whispers into Gillian's ear.

"Oh, it's perfectly fine. You had your dad and all," Gillian says, and squeezes her too hard.

"No, I should have come," Kristy murmurs, feeling worse that Gillian is being so understanding.

"Don't give it a second thought." Gillian clicks her pen. "So, is everything okay in automation-land?" As team rep, it's Gillian's job to make sure that the meets run smoothly.

"All systems go." Kristy wants to be rid of Gillian. "I only need to check on a few things."

"I'll leave you to your few things, but first I wanted to see if you'll come for dinner tonight with the O'Learys."

Oh God no. That's a horrible idea. Kristy reminds herself of the article in her pocket. "Sure," she says to buy herself some time to come up with a lie. "Talk later?"

"Of course I'm going to check in on my superhero over there." Gillian switches her gaze to the far end of the pool, to Charlie, his cape waving in the balmy breeze.

Kristy's Charlie lust has bitten her like the radioactive spider who dug into Peter Parker's flesh and turned him into Spider-man. To hell with the clipping; she wants Charlie, and she wants him to herself.

Gillian starts to walk toward Charlie when Shannon approaches her. "Oh, my God! This team spirit is AWESOME!"

"The kids have a ball. My boys did." Gillian won't say anything else specifically about Sebby. Everyone knows to avoid the topic of Gillian's "epic fail," one of Mia's terms, with her eldest son. Kristy has always taken Gillian's side, even though she knows deep down that Gillian fucked up.

"Uh-huh." With her good arm Shannon takes a selfie.

"Let's do another one." Kristy steps into the shot and mugs for the camera.

Shannon posts the picture of Kristy, Gillian, and herself with the hashtag #swimmoms. "How's this?"

"Nice!" Gillian gushes. "Don't forget to tag me."

Kristy puts her hand on Gillian's arm. "Do you mind if I borrow Shannon?"

Shannon looks pleased. "Me?"

"We could really use someone to help out with automation, to verify that the kids' times match up with the results."

"I don't really know much about swimming, but I'd be happy to help." Shannon slips her phone into the pocket of her shorts.

"Shannon." Gillian strokes Shannon's good wrist. "Riley's event is soon after the meet starts. You're going to miss her race."

Kristy suppresses a frown. "We won't let Shannon miss a swim, right, Lizbeth?"

"Not a one," Lizbeth answers.

"Well, it looks like you've got everything under control here," Gillian says.

"Kristy and Charlie did a bang-up job of getting us what we need." Lizbeth grabs a pencil from behind her ear.

"You've been talking to Charlie this week?" Gillian looks surprised.

Kristy has been wowing him with her texts about random swim stats. "Little bit."

Gillian looks confused, and Kristy can't blame her. One minute they're hugging, and the next Kristy is diverting people's attention from Gillian just for sport. She needs to call Beverly, right now, before she takes more from Gillian, who has done nothing to deserve this treatment. Neither had the other wives or girlfriends or fiancées.

32

CHARLIE

After the kids have warmed up, Gillian touches the sleeve of Charlie's shirt. "Do you guys need anything?"

"Thanks, Gil, but we've got it all under control." Charlie jerks his head toward Liam, who's standing a few feet away with a stopwatch in his hand. "We figured out a system to take splits!"

"Good on you, Charlie," she says brightly, and trots off to make her rounds, checking items off the list on her clipboard: timers in place, tents pitched, coolers filled with icy water, and programs distributed to coaches and the Clerk of Course. She picked and groomed such competent people that she only needs to oversee the meet and solve any crises that arise. Charlie can now grasp the magnitude of her organizational prowess. She's something.

The announcer, a Mighty Sharks dad with excellent pipes, opens the mic and says, "This is the moment you've been waiting for, sports fans." Clearly the man studied broadcasting in college. He introduces three adorable eight-year-old girls who proceed to sing the National Anthem off-key. Charlie takes off his hat and places it over his heart. Thankfully, he's wearing sunglasses, because his eyes well when the girls randomly hit the high note. He's one lucky bastard to be able to coach these kids, to feel a part of something bigger and better than a stupid real estate development firm. His next gig absolutely has to make him feel this powerful.

It's showtime.

The Sharks' 8 & Under swimmers nose out the Manta Rays in the first two events. "It's okay, it's okay," Charlie reassures Justin and himself. When the starter calls Riley's heat to the blocks, Charlie knows the meet is going to turn around. Riley's start is rough, and even though Charlie has been working with her on her stroke, her left arm still swings around wildly. She's strong and swims with heart, though, and makes her move after the turn.

"Go, Riley, go!" Charlie, Liam, and Justin scream in unison as Riley gains on the two girls next to her.

Justin cranes his neck so that he can see the wall. "She's got it. She's going to win."

"Come on," Charlie shouts. "Bring it home, girl!"

Riley finishes first.

"Yes!" Charlie raises his fist in the air. The first upset of the meet. Watch out, Mighty Sharks. By the end of the backstroke events, the score's even. Gillian approaches him. "Good job, coach!" Then she natters on about the Sharks' impressive spread for the volunteers: breakfast sandwiches, quiche, and yogurt parfaits stacked with granola and perfectly ripe strawberries. He couldn't give a shit about yogurt parfaits right now, and Gillian couldn't care less about winning the meet. That's not what summer swimming is about for his wife.

"Justin, let's get everyone fired up. We could win this thing."

Justin follows Charlie to the shallow end, where the kids are standing together for their cheers. With their heads sheathed in green bathing caps, they look like a bouquet of balloons. Mia hoists Riley into the air as if her shoulders have been waiting their entire existence for this little girl's arrival.

"We are the Manta Rays," Justin hollers, waving his ropy arms in the air.

"Mighty, mighty Manta Rays." Mia leads the response.

"Are we the best?" Justin yells, a vein in his neck popping out.

Charlie joins in, his cheers releasing tension.

"Of course we're the best." They laugh when Sean jumps up and down on the pool deck in his boots.

Mia adjusts her bathing cap, and even with that latex smothering her hair, she projects Kristy's aura of beauty. Luckily, Justin and Sebby have remained immune to her charms.

"Come here, Riley." Riley emerges from the pool and runs up to Charlie.

"You were the fastest 10 & Under freestyle swimmer this week. You up for swimming on the mixed relay?"

Riley looks up at Charlie as he explains that this relay consists of the fastest swimmer in four different age groups. "And the meet just might come down to that last relay."

"Coach C, I can do it." She sprint-walks over to the automation tent to tell Shannon.

Kristy approaches as the kids gather behind the blocks for the final relay. "Charlie." She leans into him, turning her face toward his ear. "We need to win this relay to win the meet." Her breath smells like peppermint. "Thanks for telling me," he says, his nerve endings dancing the flamenco. He wants to win. Badly. Let nobody doubt that he's qualified for the coaching job. "Mia, make sure to help Riley with her start," he says as Mia leads the relay swimmers to their lane. "It needs to be legal, even if she's slow off the blocks."

"Got it," Mia says. "Let's go get this, girl." Riley trots after her like a puppy.

At the sound of the official's beep Riley dives into the water. The race is neck and neck. Come on, Riley. Come on. Riley puts her head down for the last ten meters, and Charlie wants to jump right into the pool and pull her to the wall for the finish. No need, Riley reaches out her arm and wins her leg of the relay. The next two swimmers hold Riley's small lead. Margo Miller, the Manta Rays anchor, has enough of a kick to stave off the fast swimmer catching her one lane over. That speedy Shark is gaining on Margo, however, and by the time they pass the flags and approach the wall they're dead even. Charlie can't yell he's so nervous.

Both girls touch at almost the same time.

"Too close to tell," Liam says.

Charlie watches the timers from both lanes huddle together, and seconds later he and Mia and Justin are jumping up and down as if they've just won the Super Bowl. Gillian is clapping hard too.

"We did it." Justin hugs Charlie. "The whole enchilada."

"Let's wait until it's official," Charlie says through a grin that splits his face open.

Shannon runs over to Charlie. "This is amazing. Amazing. Amazing. They were amazing." She puts Sean down and gives Gillian a one-armed bear hug, and the two rock back and forth before Shannon returns to her post. She's hooked. After today, she'll be an indentured servant of the River Run pool.

Gillian shushes everyone when the announcer clears his mic. "The Manta Rays will be heading to Panera for lunch, and stick around, Sharks, we're firing up the grill." He teases. "But you probably want to know the score, don't you?"

"Give us the score!" the crowd roars.

"Mighty Sharks 209. Manta Rays 211. Congratulations to our guests."

Charlie tilts his head back and closes his eyes with the joy of a swimmer who has just learned that he set a world record.

"Not bad for your first meet." Gillian gives Charlie a thumbs-up.

Mia and Justin take Charlie's hands and lead him to the side of the pool. The entire team encircles him. Justin, Liam, and Mia lead the team in a sportsmanship cheer: "Two, four, six, eight, who do we appreciate? Three, five, seven, nine, who do we think is mighty fine? The SHARKS!" He wants to remain in this circle for longer, his entire being enveloped by the Manta Rays.

33

GILLIAN

Sweat rolls over the seal of the no-nonsense sunscreen Gillian wears to protect her freckled skin from further damage. There's Charlie, surrounded by his adoring swimmers. He's so present. So handsome.

Charlie looks happier than she's seen him in years, maybe ever. A hum of success emanates from his every pore as they walk to the car. "If we keep this up, we'll score the best record this season," Charlie says as he slides into the driver's seat and starts the engine.

"Unbelievable." Gillian adjusts the vent so that the cold air will dry her face. "Last season we finished second to last."

"Justin's a huge help."

Gillian never tires of hearing nice things about her sons, even if their own dad is handing out the compliments. She loves watching how the kids respond to Justin's gentle enthusiasm. Her love for both of the boys leaves her breathless.

Charlie puts his hand on her leg. "Gil, I'm having a lot of fun with the team."

Fun. She hasn't had much fun today at all. It took her until the break to remember the last time she'd felt lonely at a River Run meet: the July her father went to Boston for his first rehab stint. May instructed Gillian and Patrick to tell the folks at the pool that their father was up in Cambridge, code word for Harvard, taking a special summer course for headmasters. Gillian was thirteen. She was terrified that her father would never get better, or worse, that he'd never come home, her fears a lead ball rolling around in her stomach. They evaporated after Sebastian returned from rehab, clear-eyed and calm-fun. This morning Gillian felt the pit that had been coming and going lately, but it was as strong as it had been when she was a kid. Ridiculous. There was no Sebastian to leave or return. She couldn't lose somebody who had been dead for years. Darn that hospital visit last night. Darn their money worries.

Gillian turns her attention to posting a picture on Facebook of Mia and Charlie smiling. While she is cropping the photo to perfection, Kristy texts. *I'm so sorry, Gil, but we can't make it tonight. David forgot to write his partners' potluck on the family calendar, and we have to go.*

"That's strange," Gillian says.

"What?"

"Kristy texted. Let me just reply real quick." The annual partners' potluck always takes place in late July, which Gillian knows because she and Kristy always scour *Bon Appetit*'s June issue to pick a unique recipe that Kristy can pull off. Kristy sends another message. *Early this year. Too many people are traveling this July.* Kristy lies often and easily, mostly over stupid things. Gillian accepts this trait because Kristy's mostly straight with her. She gulps down a throatful of hurt and texts Kristy back. *What are you bringing?* Kristy responds immediately. *Picking up Georgetown Cupcakes this afternoon. Lame, I know, but everyone loves them.*

Gillian punctuates her message to have fun with three tiny pink hearts. Kristy's been acting so strangely, manically happy and then distracted, or both at the same time. Maybe she feels "triggered," as the kids would say. Sometimes Kristy needs space. That's probably all it is.

"Everything okay?" asks Charlie.

"Kristy and David aren't coming tonight," she tells him.

"She's not?"

"I said *they're* not, and since when are you and Kristy so buddy-buddy?"

"Buddy-buddy?"

"I understand you've been talking all week."

Charlie's doing that thing where he chews on the inside of his cheek, like he's both pleased and embarrassed about something.

"Charlie, you're not acting like yourself either."

"You know Kristy follows the stats closely, right?"

"'Closely' is a bit of an understatement." Kristy checks her phone for the meet results on Saturday afternoons and then plunges into the NVSL website to inhale the times of children she will never meet and teams the Manta Rays will never race.

"Just taking advantage of her database, Gil."

"I have a database you could take advantage of too." Gillian's trying her hardest not to sound petty. "Just about other River Run matters. Like our traditions!"

"You've been great."

Gillian switches subjects. "I'm going to marinate the lamb when we get home."

According to Shannon's Facebook feed, she went through a phase where she posted her nightly menus, and apparently lamb kebabs were a big hit with her kids.

Back at home, Gillian showers and puts on dry clothes before marinating five pounds of lamb that they can't afford. She sets the table and Charlie mows the lawn. At three o'clock the thermometer outside their bedroom window reads ninety-five degrees. River Run will be packed. She picks up the phone and texts Kristy. No response. She wants Kristy to call and tell her that she's okay, that Krillian's okay. Maybe they could laze around the pool for an hour. No doubt Diet Cokes and gossip are flowing freely; Riley and Sean, like Justin and Sebby and Gillian and Patrick before them, are likely lining up in front of the ice cream truck, palming plastic baggies filled with quarters. Riley will be ordering for Sean as Sebby did for Justin and Gillian did for Patrick. Shannon's husband and a fresh crop of dads will be playing Sharks and Minnows with their children, swatting away mosquitoes and speculating on who will make it to the World Cup finals. Gosh, Gillian hasn't spent a weekend day at the pool yet this summer.

At five o'clock Gillian locates a bin of Justin's Pokémon books for Sean. The cute little fella adores Justin. She prepares her tried-and-true green bean and basil recipe, then washes a mélange of red and orange raspberries, which along with the gallon of vanilla ice cream she bought at the Safeway will augment Shannon's whoopie pies beautifully.

Gillian picks up her phone and dives headfirst into her Facebook feed as she's been doing regularly in the afternoons when the house grows too quiet. Shannon has tagged Gillian in two shots! Gillian scans her feed, prolonging the deliciousness of flipping over to Shannon's page. She reads Charlie's former colleague Mitzy Macken's post about how she managed to work a seventy-hour week, sew costumes for the entire cast of her daughter's summer theater group, and cook a week's worth of chicken dishes for her dear friend who is recovering from bunion surgery. Gillian starts tallying her own weekly work hours and accomplishments, but gives up and hops onto Shannon's page.

"Riley's First Saturday Meet," Shannon has titled her album, which features an image of Riley beaming at Gillian, with the caption "Riley befriends the Manta Ray moms." Gillian's earlier malaise lifts. She signs off to dry her berries. The heck with Mitzy Macken.

Justin texts that he's on his way home from the pool. She plucks Charlie's favorite Talking Heads CD from their collection and hums along while David Byrne sings about a 7-Eleven, which reminds her of college, when Charlie was falling in love with her, when she was the RA to a floor of co-eds who worshiped her (their word, not Gillian's), when she was the queen of fun with a capital F.

"Someone's feeling festive." Charlie takes her hands in his and twirls her around.

She kisses him hard and they want to keep going, but she whispers, "The O'Learys will be here any second."

Charlie runs his hands up her arms, but her mood is passing.

"It's almost five forty-five. They should be here by now." She backs away, reaching for her phone. Out of habit she clicks on Facebook, where Kristy has tagged Shannon in a post. Kristy never posts. Gillian stares at her screen for a few seconds and blinks. She enlarges the photo of Shannon, lounging in the wicker chair, Gillian's wicker chair, on Kristy's back porch. In the next image white frosting sticks to Kristy's lips like Elmer's Glue as she holds a bare chocolate whoopie pie cake in each hand.

34

KRISTY

Kristy has gone too far. Her Facebook post of the photo of her and Shannon and the whoopie pies will crush Gillian. Shannon planted the idea in Kristy's mind after the meet when she said she'd baked whoopie pies for Charlie and Gillian to thank them for taking such good care of her and her kids last night. That spidery part of Kristy hissed. Despite evidence to the contrary, though, she wasn't trying to hurt Gillian when at 4:30 she'd used Mia, Riley's new idol, to lure Shannon to her porch, knowing the O'Learys were expected at Gillian's at 5:30, or when she'd eyed the plate of whoopie pies Shannon brought inside so they wouldn't melt in the car and asked, "Hey, can I try one of those?" or when she'd snagged four pies for her family, or when she'd separated the two chocolate orbs, licked the center, and said, "God, these are good," even though chocolate tastes like chalk to her. And once Kristy started, she couldn't keep herself from grabbing her iPhone and asking Shannon to take a photo of her holding the dismantled pie.

Shannon's likely arriving at Gillian's about now. "Do you want to order Lebanese Taverna tonight?" David calls out from the great room. "Lamb would be heavenly," Kristy responds, aware that Gillian has made this exact dish to serve the O'Learys.

Kristy goes upstairs to brush the taste of chocolate from her mouth. She gargles with Listerine and then sits down on the thick carpet on the bathroom floor.

Fuck, she has lost all control.

It takes her two seconds to re-Google Beverly, thanks to her ex-sponsor's website advertising her jewelry-making business. She cradles the phone in her palm and examines the pewter pendants Beverly has inscribed with various slogans such as "Progress not perfection," "No better, no worse," or "Easy does it." One touch will connect her to Beverly's earthy voice. Her index finger trembles slightly because the last time they spoke Kristy hung up on her, annoyed with Beverly for urging her to work her program.

Beverly answers on the second ring, and Kristy doesn't hesitate before mumbling into the phone, "It's Kristy, do you remember me?" Of course she remembers Kristy, she says. No, she's not angry, quite the opposite. Kristy unloads her story about Sebastian and Gillian onto Beverly.

"Now, that's a trigger." Beverly's voice brims with compassion.

"There's more." Kristy hears footsteps outside the bathroom.

"Kris?" David knocks. "You okay in there?"

"Fine. Be down soon, babe."

He says through the door, "We're going to pick up dinner now."

"Thank you!" Phew. Kristy wants the house to herself for the duration of this conversation, although she has no plans to get up from the bathroom floor or stop whispering.

"What else is going on, Kristy?" Beverly asks with more kindness than Kristy deserves.

"I've been sorta intriguing with Charlie." Beverly taught her this term for finding a man fix. "Um, Gillian's, you know, husband."

Beverly sighs. "Yeah, that makes sense."

"It makes no sense, actually. Why Charlie? Why now?"

"That's what we do."

"What do you mean?"

"Kristy, we had so many talks about your stepfather. Travis, right?"

"Good memory."

"You felt that he gave all his love to your sister, Nancy."

"Nora."

"Nora, right, sorry." Beverly's Boston accent has thickened. "Now you find out that you weren't seen, much less loved, by your bio-dad."

"Okay, okay." The truth stings like hell.

"You were primed to relapse, and given what you said about Charlie's life, it makes sense that you found each other."

"You think he likes me?" Kristy's heart leaps with hope and plummets with shame over the way she's been flirting with him.

"Kristy, that's not the point."

Man, she's a goner. "I've been such a shit to Gillian too."

"You're trying to win again. You want Charlie to pick you, not your sister."

"Yeah. You're smart."

"It's your pattern."

"Okay, okay." She closes her eyes. "It all came on in a nanosecond."

"This disease will keep doing pushups inside you, getting stronger and stronger, so if you relapse just a little bit . . . wham! It will take you out."

"Consider me taken out." Kristy's heard all this before, but now it makes sense, and getting help makes her feel slightly better. "So, what do you suggest I do?"

"There's a meeting not far from your house tomorrow at four." Beverly gives her the address.

"I'll go." She commits before she loses her gumption. "I'm such a loser."

"Shaming isn't going to help. But you know what will."

"Using the tools of the program."

"Yes. Go to a meeting. Keep calling me. And for God's sake stay away from Charlie, and probably Gillian for a while." Beverly pauses for emphasis. "At all costs."

"I will." And in that moment Kristy intends to attend the four o'clock SLAA meeting tomorrow and ask someone to take over as automation chair so she can stay the hell away from Charlie, Gillian, and the River Run pool. She will make an amend to Gillian and David and do service and call Beverly every day and find a therapist who can help her sort out her feelings about Sebastian and figure out a way to tell Gillian that they are sisters. Swear to God she will.

35

JUSTIN

Dinner with the O'Learys is an epic clusterfuck. They arrive almost an hour late with half a plate of oversized Oreo-like thingies and five pints of Ben and Jerry's: Cherry Garcia, Coffee, Phish Food, Vanilla Bean, and Chunky Monkey. Mrs. O'Leary makes a huge deal out of telling everyone how much she appreciated Mom taking her to the hospital. Mom makes a huge deal out of the ice cream, but Justin can tell she's pissed about something.

Mom is in some mood; she posts six pictures by the time everyone sits down to eat their lamb. Dad compliments Riley on her awesome swims. Mom's a good cook, so everyone chows down. But Justin wishes that they'd stop talking about the luau this Friday. Mrs. O'Leary's super psyched about her plans: rum punch instead of beer, which Mom hates because drunk people make her edgy; a new band, which Mom hates because she already put down a deposit on the band she's been hiring every year since he was born; catered food, which Mom hates for no other reason than the luau has been a potluck since she was a kid. Dad tries to intervene before Mom can shut Mrs. O'Leary down at another new twist, "Honey, Shannon's going to do a bang-up job." He spears a green bean with his fork. "We're lucky to have her aboard." Mom smiles really big, but Justin can tell it's killing her to let go of planning this event.

Dad switches the conversation to the Olympics and describes how Ryan Lochte flips tractor tires as part of his training, claiming that

Lochte is going to beat Phelps in London next month. After dinner Justin takes the kids outside to play a little hoop. Sean still hasn't taken off his rain boots. He's a funny kid.

When Justin brings Riley and Sean back inside for dessert, everyone seems more chill, but then things get even more fucked up fast.

"Thanks for the whoopie pies, Shannon. They look sensational," Mom says.

"Sorry we couldn't bring more. Kristy invited us over for a quick drink and . . . well, let's just say she loves her chocolate."

Mom frowns and Dad takes everyone's ice cream orders. Even Justin and Dad know that Aunt Kristy hates chocolate. They've eaten like a million desserts together, and Mom is always coming up with new "Aunt Kristy desserts," which means chocolate-free.

"Let's take a few pics." Mom pulls out her trusty phone. "You don't mind?"

Here we go.

Dad tries to stop her. "Gil, they look tired."

"This will just take a second, honey."

She smiles at Mrs. O'Leary. "One or two before you put these little ones to sleep."

"Come on, kids." Shannon tries to herd her children. "One photo and then we'll hit the road."

Justin cringes when Mom gets all bossy about their Facebook fun, and this time it's no fun at all. He hates when she gets all intense and weird.

Mr. O'Leary cajoles the kids to pose, but he looks like Mom's holding him hostage.

"Hold on a second." Mom bounds over to the drawer. "Let me get my selfie stick!" She returns with the gift Charlie gave her last Mother's Day. "I'm not that bad," she said, but took the joke well. Here she is, though, stick in hand, moving everyone around like they're pieces of furniture. Sean and Riley sit on Dad's lap, and everyone else gathers around them. Mom takes a few shots before she emancipates the

O'Learys. By the time they drive off, Mom has already edited, posted, and hashtagged a photo that makes it look like everyone had a blast at the dinner from hell.

Justin's happy to escape to his room, even though his air-conditioning doesn't work that well and it's still hot as hell outside. He's jonesing for a Slurpee. He's jonesing for Tiff. Slurpees were his thing with her, and she only drank grape. "Hey," he texts her, knowing it's a really bad idea.

Mom said that even if he and Tiff got married—like, who was talking about marriage anyway?—time apart was good. She said they needed to individuate, not the kind of word she usually used. Justin didn't get it; Mom and Dad met in college, and they've been together ever since. Besides, the purple 7-Eleven logo he's tattooed on his ass makes it pretty hard to forget about Tiff. And he wishes that she hadn't chosen to individuate with a guy named Dill. "Like in the pickle?" he said when he found a text from Dill while Tiff was in the shower. "No, like in *To Kill a Mockingbird*, asshole, and stop reading my texts," she said, and didn't even apologize for ending a year of a pretty good thing in thirty seconds.

No response from Tiff. He knows he shouldn't, but he checks her Instagram feed. Looks like she's "on holiday" in Iceland with Dill's family. Here they are, arms wrapped around one another in their big fucking sweaters. Social media lies anyway. He comforts himself by imagining they're as miserable as the O'Learys were while Mom documented their heinous dinner.

He wishes he'd taken Sebby up on his invitation to spend the summer in New York. Sebby offered up his couch and a gig busing tables at a restaurant down the block from his apartment. Justin was tempted but couldn't let Mom down by not coaching, and if he could have manned up, he would have traveled with Tiff and she wouldn't be snapping selfies with Dill.

He tosses his torture device on the bed and heads into the bathroom to splash cold water on his face. The thermostat reads eighty-five degrees. According to the *Post*, this summer is slated to be the second hottest in D.C. metro history. He needs air.

All is quiet, save for the sound of the television blaring from the great room, the coldest spot in the house. His parents are lounging together on the sofa, watching an episode of *Downton Abbey*. Mom started the series because people tell her that she looks like Elizabeth McGovern. Justin looks like Elizabeth McGovern too, same lips and small nose and skinny body, unless he lifts weights for hours a day, which he does, because what guy wants to be skinny? It's worse than having Elizabeth McGovern as your biopic.

"Heading out for a bit," Justin says as he walks toward the back door. "Mind if I take the car?"

"Go ahead." Mom puts the show on pause. She seems like she's returned to her regular self. "You going to catch up with some of your old squad?"

Justin lies and says yes, and his parents wish him a good night, and that's that. They never question him about his whereabouts like they did with Sebby. Justin's a rule-follower even when he doesn't want to be.

Justin drives to the 7-Eleven, buys himself a large grape Slurpee, and brings it with him to River Run. He punches in the code on the keypad adjacent to the clubhouse door and lets himself into the pool, illuminated by underwater lights and a damn near full moon. He slides off his flip-flops and sits down, dangling his toes in lane six. The heat wave makes the pool feel like a bath.

Mom's intensity with the O'Learys reminds him of that Monday night meet when she took things too far. Nobody in the family ever talks about that night. Justin was eleven and Sebby fourteen, and they were screwing around in the shallow end of the pool, waiting for Mom to finish sorting ribbons. It took forever because she corrected either the alphabetization or the spelling of the swimmers' names on the folders, and she wouldn't accept their offers of help with the sorting. When she was finally done, she walked over to Justin and Sebby, who were inside the clubhouse, standing right in front of the record board. All the swim-team boys, including the ones who had no chance of breaking records, memorized the stats. Between them, Sebby and Uncle Patrick, they owned all the boys' 14 & Under Manta Ray records.

Sebby held every pool record for his age group except in the 100-meter individual medley, thanks to a nationally ranked swimmer from another team who had smashed the record back when Sebby was still an 8 & Under. "You're gonna get that last one this summer." Mom put down her ribbon file-folder and pressed her hand to the glass. Her voice was filled with fire, which was weird because she wasn't the kind of over-the-top swim mom who took her kids' splits or bugged coaches about lineups and relay spots. She never cared who won the meets, even. Sure, she protected her traditions, like the luau and preserving the swing and the sketchy tree from which it hung, but this record rant was not her.

She used the bottom of her shirt to clean the smudge her palm had made on the glass. "I like seeing the Nortons own all the records." Mom did not sound like herself.

"I'm a Cloud." Sebby failed at his attempt at humor. Justin laughed, but Mom looked at him blankly.

"And I'll get it, Mom. I'm close."

"Like a tenth, right, Sebby? You did a 1:04.6 last year." Justin was one of those boys who studied records instead of breaking them. "I bet you get it before this season."

"Well, I bet he can swim under a 1:04 right now." Mom snatched a watch from the box sitting on the bench. At first she sounded like she was kidding.

"Funny, Mom," Sebby said.

"Let's have a go at it." Now she sounded like Mom, always coming up with some kind of plan for them to clean out their sock drawers or picnic at the Tidal Basin during cherry blossom season or wash the family cars.

Justin laughed at this crazy idea; Mom must be yanking their chain. They made jokes about parents who pulled shit like this.

"Laugh all you want, but I mean it." Mom lowered her voice, which was now soft and totally creepy.

"It's dark." Even though Sebby towered over Mom, he looked like a little kid next to her.

"Make you swim faster." She twirled the watch string around her finger.

"Mom." Sebby looked toward the locker rooms, where the guards had retreated to scour away a day's worth of grime with their sponges and bottles of Lysol. They could emerge any second. "This is a little bizarre."

She twirled the watch faster, looking right at Sebby. She looked possessed.

Justin considered going into the locker rooms to distract the guards so they wouldn't come out on deck, but he couldn't bring himself to move.

Sebby followed Justin and Mom out to the pool, took off his shirt, and slid off his shorts quickly. The sky was black and the air oppressive for nighttime. Justin removed a pair of goggles from his bag and tossed them to Sebby, who caught them and put them on. He stood on the ledge of the pool and shook out his arms.

Mom positioned herself where the starter always stood, the moonlight shining upon the Manta Rays T-shirt she wore to all the meets. "Take your mark," she said, but not so loud as to lure the guards out of the locker rooms. Maybe nobody would ever find out about what they were doing.

Sebby curled his body into a C, his fingers grasping the ledge of the pool, the moon shimmering down his back.

"Go," Mom whisper-barked.

Sebby exploded off the ledge and entered the water cleanly, cupping his hands over his head, dolphin-kicking almost half the length of the pool. He emerged into the effortless butterfly that every Manta Ray tried to copy. When he switched to backstroke, Mom ran over to the flags and shone her iPhone flashlight on the pool to signal that the wall was only a few meters away. Sebby was cutting through the water like a steak knife through a stick of soft butter. After he hit the wall, Mom took his 50-meter split. "He's going to break this record," she said to herself, almost as if she'd forgotten that Justin was standing within earshot. Justin chewed a nail off during Sebby's breaststroke and freestyle legs. But not Mom. She was focused on Sebby. "Come on, come on." She sounded mad or something. During the last lap she got in his face. When he took a breath, she waved her hand like she could hasten him to the finish line, as if something—but what?—was riding on his breaking the record. It wouldn't even count if he did because this wasn't a real competition. With ten meters left, Mom ran over to the end of his lane and crouched down so low that Justin thought she might fall into the water. When Sebby touched the wall, she punched the button on the watch with her thumb.

"You went under a 1:04." She frothed. "1:03.8."

Sebby's chest heaved. He took off his goggles. "Who are you?"

"I'm your mom, and I'll tell you who you are." Her nostrils flared. "You're . . ."

Holy shit. She was going to say Sebastian Norton. Out of the corner of his eye, Justin spotted the two lifeguards staring at this spectacle, mops in hand.

"Mom," Sebby said calmly, nodding toward them. "It's time to go."

Mom glanced at the guards and then at the watch in her hand and then at Sebby. She looked as if someone had just caught her shoplifting or something. In a quick second, she returned to normal, as if she had shaken herself out of a trance. "I don't know what got into me," she murmured, and walked away toward the darkest corner of the pool.

Sebby hopped out of the water. The guards said nothing as Justin followed him out to the overly lit parking lot. Barefoot, dry clothes in hand, Sebby was still winded from the swim.

Sebby never broke that pool record; he didn't even come close to his best time that season, and afterwards he quit swimming for good. Justin never saw Mom freak out like she had that night, and as with any other embarrassment in their lives, they pretended it never happened. The guards kept quiet about it too. Justin sometimes wondered if he'd imagined the whole thing.

He snaps a picture of the dark pool and sends the image to Sebby. Two seconds later his phone buzzes.

"'Sup?" Sebby speaks over the bar noise in the background.

"'Sup with you, dude?"

Sebby's practically shouting. "What are you doing at the pool?"

"Do you remember that night you broke the IM record?"

"You're calling me about that? Shit. I thought something was up with the parents."

"Did that really happen, or was it one fucked-up dream?" Justin's voice shakes.

Sebby pauses, his silence giving way to the clanking of glasses, laughter, and a throbbing bassline. "It was one fucked-up dream that really happened."

"Yeah, I thought so." Justin tells Sebby that the most haunting part of that night was that he wanted Sebby to break the record too. While Sebby was booking through that second 50, Justin forgot about the lifeguards and how horrible this might be for his brother. Mom has a way of making you want what she wants, and then when things don't work out, making you deny you ever wanted it in the first place.

"Justin, what's going on with you?"

"Mom went a little loco tonight." Justin tells Sebby about Aunt Kristy and the whoopie pies and the Facebooking on steroids.

"That's rough," Sebby says. "Sheesh."

"What should I do?"

Sebby is quiet.

"You still there?" Justin's worried that he's scared Sebby off.

"You should call Uncle Patrick."

"What? Uncle Patrick?" He's the family screwup.

"Yeah, definitely call him."

"You talk to him?"

"All the time. He's real."

"Really?" Mom and Dad are either sending him money, or Mom's making fun of his "AA mumbo jumbo."

"My boss is giving me the stink eye. I'll be home by midnight. Call me back."

Justin hugs his knees to his chest and feels the bones in his lower spine pop as he rocks back and forth on the cement. Sebby and Uncle Patrick talk? When Justin was younger, their uncle took them to see one of the *Toy Story* movies and bought so much popcorn, Milk Duds, and Coke that Sebby puked. Mom scolded Uncle Patrick about his repulsive excesses. When he was sober, Uncle Patrick looked like Justin's grandfather and Sebby: tall and jacked with enormous hands and feet and blasts of blond hair. When Uncle Patrick's drinking, he's puffy, greasy-haired, and grainy-smelling. Justin's afraid to talk to his uncle. It's a hell of a lot easier to act like Mom and pretend that bad shit like the night she made Sebby swim in the dark, empty pool is all in his head.

36

GILLIAN

Gillian confirms that Kristy lied about why she had to miss the dinner with the O'Learys. It was ridiculously easy to find the alleged hosts of David's office potluck, Ellen and Jay Miller, on Facebook. Last night, Ellen Miller posted photos of themselves vacationing in Bethany Beach, enjoying a carafe of chilled white wine with their crab cakes. Thinking about Kristy's lie beckons the image of Kristy wolfing down one of Shannon's whoopie pies. One minute she's hugging the dickens out of Gillian, and the next she's lying and stealing dessert. It makes no sense, but then on some level it kind of does. Well, Gillian certainly isn't going to wallow in hurt feelings or her embarrassment over her behavior with the O'Learys or her sadness while sitting in a hospital with her Sebastian memories. She has a plan, simple and foolproof. Keep busy, useful, and lucrative. See, that's her brother's problem; despite Patrick's meetings or his amend making or his one-, two-, three-year chips, he doesn't understand that if you believe that life is looking up, then it most certainly will.

Pat Benatar serenades her on her way to visit one of her favorite clients, Belinda Boyd, a junkerboo (junk room client) who lives in a \$2.5 million home in McLean. Gillian has been working with Belinda over the course of a dozen Sunday mornings, not because Belinda's schedule is busy, but because setting Belinda, or any other client, free from clutter requires an intuitive understanding of their readiness to let go and pacing them accordingly. Gillian has been invited to speak to numerous women's groups about this very topic, which was how Belinda found her.

Belinda's house smells like freshly brewed coffee and the gorgeous stargazer lilies she arranged in a Kosta Boda vase in the foyer. Gillian needs to ask Belinda to settle up with her, a conversation she dreads. Why is it that the wealthiest clients are the slowest to pay? She chases down her bitterness with a sip of Belinda's sweet fresh-squeezed orange juice. Belinda has also garnished a plate of cranberry date bread for Gillian with a curled orange peel. They sit in Belinda's sunny gourmet kitchen, sipping and nibbling for twenty minutes while thoughts of Kristy's stunt and Shannon's trapped expression the other night and Belinda's near six-hundred-dollar balance float away.

When Belinda's ready, she leads Gillian to the junk room, which they are now calling "an evolving work space." There's nothing as invigorating as making order out of a junk room, typically a spare bedroom operating under the guise of a home office, where a client has been stowing dead mail, children's art projects, speeding tickets, and other more emotionally laden items. Together Gillian and Belinda shed garbage bags full of refuse, and now they're down to the closet, which Gillian guesses stores the most difficult junk to sort.

Gillian opens the French doors, scanning the contents of the closet for the items that Belinda has been cocooning. There it is. Top right shelf.

"Come here, stand beside me." Gillian holds out her hand.

Belinda, a regal woman, walks toward Gillian. Gillian puts her arm around Belinda's shoulders, which are arranged in an apology. They both stare up at the shelf.

Gillian lowers her voice. "Are you ready for this today?"

Belinda looks down at her leather sandals with the gold-bejeweled straps. "I know, I know. 'Let go or be dragged.'"

Gillian squeezes Belinda's shoulder. "That's right."

"Go ahead."

Gillian climbs on the stepstool, removes a dust cloth from her pocket, and wipes the surface of the tattered box before setting it down on Belinda's Oriental rug. Belinda sits cross-legged and opens the box, her lower lip trembling as she retrieves a bundle of old letters. "She wrote me every day."

Gillian knows that whatever Belinda is shrouding with junk has something to do with her beloved cousin.

"When did she pass on, hon?" Gillian clucks.

"She didn't." Belinda blinks hard. "That's the worst part."

"What do you mean?"

"She just stopped talking to me, and I never knew why."

Belinda's comment slices deep into Gillian. Is this the direction Kristy is heading? No, Kristy must have had a darned good reason for what she did Saturday night.

"She ghosted me."

Ghosted? Gillian has never heard this term, but it's easy enough to figure out from the context. Would Kristy ever ghost Gillian? Impossible.

Gillian places a box of Kleenex next to Belinda. "I'm going to give you some time with these." She leaves the room quietly. Belinda's basset hound escorts her to the front door, and she scratches him under his chin longingly. Homer was a basset hound. She needs to collect herself: quit longing for the dog her dad ran over and worrying about Kristy's mood.

She retrieves some storage boxes from her car, and when she returns, Belinda is sitting on the floor amidst a sea of used tissues. Gillian eases down beside her.

Belinda clutches a red envelope with a photo taped to the cover.

"May I, Belinda?"

Belinda hands her the envelope and Gillian examines the photo: Belinda and her cousin standing on top of a mountain that Gillian recognizes as Sugar Loaf, wearing matching gap-toothed grins, Mickey Mouse T-shirts, and cutoff shorts.

Gillian takes in the image. "A picture paints a thousand words. You can make this one your reality."

"What do you mean?"

"You and your cousin were happy here. If you frame this, you can remember yourselves that way. Happy. You two were happy." Gillian pictures one of the dozens of photos she posted of her and Kristy at the pool, on the swing, flipping pancakes. Krillian could not be undone. "If you look at this photo enough and stow the sad letters away, you can be HAPPY."

"Gillian?" Belinda looks concerned.

"Sorry, I got a little carried away."

Belinda tenderly removes the photo from the envelope, turns it over, and sets it on the floor.

"Good girl." Gillian uses her hypnotic tone, which Sebby and Justin call her "you're scaring the children" voice. "Here is the box for the letters." The lid's sturdy and will seal tightly enough to preserve the paper. "You know what to do."

Belinda removes the letters from the old box and dutifully tosses them into the container, and Gillian burps the lid.

"See, if you select the proper storage bin, these letters won't bother you or your family." As she speaks, it becomes clear to Gillian that she needs to re-stow her Sebastian memories and hide them away as neatly as Sebastian had the whiskey flasks in his army trunks. Since Charlie lost his job, she's been playing a good game of whack-a-mole, tamping one memory down as another springs up. Until the hospital visit, anyway.

"And this"—she waves the photo—"I will take to my personal framer, and when you're ready, we'll hang it up."

"You're really something special, Gillian."

"You are too." Gillian means it. Yet she also realizes that she can't ask Belinda for the money now. She'll have to follow up with an email about the overdue payment. Is Charlie even worrying about paying their bills?

Typically, her clients' gratitude for her help feeds her, but today she feels unusually exhausted from guiding Belinda through the final phase of her junkerboo journey. She's working too many hours, with the help of the Coke Zeroes she keeps in the cooler in her front seat. She downs half a can before navigating her way to the home of the Lulu she and Kristy met at their spinning class last week. She tries Kristy again, but no answer, and then Sebby calls when she's a few miles from her next appointment.

"How's the Big Apple treating you, honey?"

They chat for a few minutes, careful to veer away from the topic of the Manta Rays. Sebby will never come back to the pool. The night she made him swim that IM in the dark she pulled what Patrick would call "a real Sebastian." She still didn't know what had come over her or how that Sebastian part of herself had appeared with no warning. Throughout her school years, she and her father sat at the kitchen table while he retaught her the geometry she couldn't grasp the first go-around in class. He was an excellent teacher. When she scored her first B, he showed up at school, semi-liquored up, and argued for an A. Gillian thought her cheeks would incinerate as she watched Mr. Rand, her favorite teacher ever, glance at her with the same expression the lifeguards gave Sebby that horrid night. To Mr. Rand's credit, he did not change the grade.

Best to stick to safer subjects. They have plenty to talk about, from Sebby's job to politics to their shared love of action films (they'd watched *The Terminator* together four times). When Gillian arrives at her new client's home, she and Sebby hang up with their typical "I love you."

This client, a harried young mom, answers the door in stained athleisure wear. "Thank God you're here, Gillian."

"Happy to help." Gillian walks through the large kitchen, past a pot on the stove, its sides encrusted with hardened orange macaroni, to the mudroom. She takes in the dirty socks, Bakugan balls, library books, wet bathing suits, and soccer balls—and then waits for the surge of energy that accompanies her confrontation with other people's messes. "Always happy to help," she repeats.

37

KRISTY

Kristy promises herself she'll return Gillian's texts after Isaac leaves for his trip to Israel. She feels rotten about hurting Gillian, but she's trying to stick to Beverly's edict to steer clear of the Clouds. She's even stopped texting Charlie with her swimming-stats missives, for one day anyway.

During their car ride to Dulles, Isaac inserts his earbuds, leaving Kristy and David to listen to NPR in silence. Kristy wishes Mia had come with them, but she was called to sub for a lifeguard who was sick, and weren't they trying to teach her a strong work ethic? When Mia and Isaac hugged goodbye this morning, for a second Kristy felt rays of sunlight shine into her being.

When they arrive at the airport, Kristy's in-laws, Marlene and Herb, are waiting at the check-in counter. Kristy offered to drive out to Potomac to pick them up, but they declined. "No use in you schlepping out to Maryland, and we like to leave earlier and give ourselves a little more wiggle room," Marlene said, admonishing Kristy in her Marlene way for her habitual tardiness. Herb and Marlene look like the kind of couple who would produce a son like David: Herb with his scrubbed surgeon's nails and tidy Ralph Lauren polo shirts and Marlene with her travel-friendly Chico's outfits and Hadassah life membership, which she gifted Kristy after her conversion.

After Isaac checks in he walks over to Kristy, shiny new passport in tow, and puts his hands on her shoulders. "Mom, I'm going to be fine."

She strokes his cheek. He inherited David's and Herb's weak chin and heavy beard. They all started shaving when they were twelve. Isaac is all Weinstein.

"I'm just going to miss you, that's all." She clutches him until he gasps.

"You giving me the Heimlich, Mom?"

They all laugh, and then David embraces Isaac and says into his hair, "I love you," which Kristy hears because she's standing too close to both of them.

"We better get going, dear. We'll miss our flight," Marlene says.

Kristy kisses Marlene on the cheek. "Be safe." She blinks back the tears as she watches Isaac take a place in the security line, flanked by David's parents.

On the drive home, Kristy says one thing to David. "Is this trip really necessary?"

"More people get killed driving on the highway than they do traveling in Israel, honey. He'll be fine."

Unlike David, Charlie wouldn't have dismissed her concerns, but then again, Charlie doesn't have parents like Marlene and Herb, but then again, Charlie's dad is super critical according to Gillian, but then again, she needs to stop thinking about Charlie. "Forget it."

"Forget what?" He's losing patience with her.

"Nothing." She rarely regrets her choice to convert to Judaism. She hungered for the security of David's family and the fortress he helped her build between the Fricks and her new self. It was her idea to study with that rabbi who guided her deep into the psyches of Adam, Eve, Cain, and Abel, her idea to dunk in that holy pool of water so she'd be considered kosher. She mirrors the way Herb and Marlene practice their Judaism: she reads books by Jewish authors, writes big checks to the Jewish Federation, and hosts Break Fasts on Yom Kippur. She even fasts. She let Marlene pick out the party planner for the kids' b'nai mitzvah to make up for the huge disappointment over Kristy and David's elopement. Kristy never agreed, though, to put Isaac in jeopardy, and she's angry with David for not standing up to his parents. It was the least he could do after all the accommodations she's made over the years. But he won't. He'll never confront his parents directly. Marrying Kristy was a kind of passive-aggressive fuck-you to Herb and Marlene; Herb, who called all the shots in David's life, and Marlene, who needed her children to need her. He made the cut neatly by leaving Mindy Rothenstein at the altar to pursue Kristy.

"Sorry, I know this is hard." He reaches for her hand, and she gives it to him.

When Kristy and David get home from the airport, she lets him seduce her, but their lovemaking feels different to her, like it isn't enough, like he's a sub for Charlie.

"You hungry?" she asks.

"For you." He reaches for her again.

She feels restless. "Let's eat carbs."

"I'll make us a grilled cheese."

Wow, he never eats fried carbs; he must really be feeling guilty over sending Isaac to a perpetual war zone. "That would hit the spot."

Kristy slathers the bread with butter, and David fries the sandwiches. The smell of melting cheese reminds her of how Travis cooked on Sunday nights (chef's night out, Flo called it), and she gobbled up his offerings despite the big lunch they'd eaten after church. She and David dig into the food, chewing methodically until they clean their plates. Kristy wants another sandwich, but David clears their dishes and puts them in the sink.

David wraps his arms around Kristy's waist as she soaps the griddle. "I'm going to hit some golf balls," he says.

She should ask him to stay, curl up with him on their oversized couch and tell him all about Sebastian. But then she'll have to reveal every detail in order for him to understand the full scope of why this news has knocked her so wildly off balance. Isaac's trip is freaking her out too.

She opens her mouth to ask him to stay, but instead she says, "I bought you a new tube of sunscreen."

Kristy wipes down the counter while he lets himself out the back door. She sits at her kitchen table in the big house, silent save for the beep of another text from Gillian.

38

GILLIAN

Gillian vows to stop texting Kristy, but it's hard. It's time to focus her energies elsewhere, like on taking as many spinning classes as possible at the gym so that she can recruit more Lulus or showing Shannon where to find what she needs for the luau and other social events.

Today is the first morning practice of the season, and Charlie scooted out of the house early to hit Dunkin' Donuts for boxes of jelly, chocolate, glazed, Bavarian cream, and his favorite, French crullers. Of course Gillian had planned to do that, in keeping with the River Run tradition of the team rep providing the first round of donuts, but she has to pick her battles. She's not going to die on the donut hill when there are so many other important events to plan, like the luau for starters.

When Gillian arrives at the pool, she finds Shannon helping Riley adjust her goggles before practice.

"Hello, O'Leary family."

Sean rubs a streak of white cream into his nose. "Are you going to take our pictures, Mrs. Coach?"

Gillian winces at the memory of the night they came over for dinner. "That's funny, Sean."

Shannon laughs. "No, bug. Mrs. Cloud and I are going to talk about arranging fun parties for the team."

"I'm going to help Coach Justin." Sean folds his arms across his bony little chest.

"You sure that's okay with Justin?" Shannon asks.

"Oh, sure. He'll love it." Justin has been a little quiet since the O'Leary dinner, but last night he offered to watch Sean while Gillian met with Shannon.

Sean and Riley grab their swim gear and run off to say hello to Charlie and Justin. A lifeguard blows his whistle and reminds them to walk.

"Thanks again for inviting us to dinner." Shannon puts the caps back on her tubes of sunscreen and tosses them into her oversized pool bag. "You've been so nice to us."

"It was great fun. Wasn't it?" Gillian wants Shannon to corroborate the Facebook pictures.

Shannon comments on the Virginia heat instead.

"How's your elbow feeling?"

Shannon extends her arm and draws her hand to her body. "I'm starting to get more mobility."

"That's terrific news."

Shannon looks at her watch and says with good humor, "So, what have I gotten myself into here?"

Gillian hands Shannon a draft of the social calendar. "Might make the most sense if I show you where we keep everything you'll need for our various events."

Shannon pecks a quick text with her good hand. "Um. Okay."

"Let's start with the clubhouse, then." As they enter the homey building, Gillian leads Shannon to the former living room. Her legs ache from this morning's class as she walks Shannon past the trophy cases and lingers in front of the wall of photos. Every single person Gillian has recruited to the swim team committee, especially Kristy, stopped to examine these framed black-and-whites. They each commented on the young Gillian and the swan-diving Sebastian. Every single one. Shannon, however, appears more interested in eavesdropping on a lifeguard's conversation with a member who'd lost his nose plugs at Early Bird lap swim this morning.

Gillian puffs out her chest. "That's my family."

"Yeah, I saw that photo of your dad in your house." Shannon shifts her weight onto her other leg.

"The Nortons." She beckons Shannon to admire the glow of Sebastian and his children.

"Right, yeah. I've heard about your family." Shannon is still more interested in the nose plug situation a few feet to the left.

"Let me show you where we store things." Gillian guides Shannon to the small kitchen. "Hokay. Let's start with the pasta parties. Technically they're potlucks, but we need to fill in because some families show up empty-handed—week after week, but let's not get catty—and expect to be fed. We, and by 'we' I mean myself and the last few social directors, always make a lasagna or a big vat of spaghetti, store-bought sauce is fine, to fill out the spread. But anyhoo, we also stock extra drinks, because, well, the aforementioned folks don't bring drinks either, best to buy Coke, Sprite, and Pepsi—caffeinated and decaf—but the big bottles, not cans. The cans tend to . . ." Gillian lowers her voice, looks toward the lifeguard desk, places her hand on the counter, and makes a creeping gesture with her middle finger and forefinger. "Walk away, if you know what I'm saying. Same goes for any kind of food, really. We've got some rather large but entirely lovable mice who dress in red bathing suits and carry whistles." Gillian winks. This is all good-natured swim-team committee fun, joking about the guards. Shannon isn't laughing, though. Gillian opens a closet. "Tables and plastic cloths are in here, along with pitchers for lemonade and iced tea, in case you do run out of soda. Here's the powder for each. And that's about it. Any questions?"

Shannon furrows her brow. "Would it be possible to simply order pizzas and drinks for the pasta nights?" She raves about the fabulous New York–style pizza she ordered from the Italian Store over on Washington Boulevard.

Gillian adjusts her visor. "As you noticed . . ." Gillian fake-frowns and taps her own elbow. "We do order pizzas for tie-dye night, but otherwise we do pasta."

Shannon fake-smiles.

"I think the team would be a little disappointed if all of a sudden we up and ordered pizza every Friday, even as fabulously as the Italian Store makes it!"

"That way nobody would have to make lasagnas, and we could order the drinks with the pizzas. And no m-i-c-e." Shannon fake-cackles at their new inside joke.

"That's an idea, Shan." The last three social directors never suggested such a thing. "Maybe we should keep things as they are for at least the next few pasta parties . . . since the sign-up sheets are all taken care of, and then go from there? Let me walk you outside."

Shannon drops the subject and follows Gillian down the path past the big oak tree and the swing, toward the shed. Gillian doesn't bother telling Shannon about the history of the swing. She stops at the door to the ancient shed. "Don't be afraid if a few crickets jump out at you. This is prime breeding ground."

"Uh-huh. Uh-huh." Shannon peeks at her beeping phone.

Now Gillian is feeling rushed. Any minute, Shannon and her text messages could disappear. She opens the creaky door, and sure enough, two or three crickets greet them.

Shannon jumps. "You weren't kidding. These are creepy."

"Don't worry. You get used to them." Gillian remembers the first time she was accosted by a cricket in this very spot, about forty years ago. Yesterday she'd wiped down the boxes of kickboards, stopwatches, and theme decorations for the meets, so the closet sparkles, but it still smells like gasoline from the lawnmower.

"What a job you did organizing this space!" Shannon whistles. "You're a pro."

"Flattery will get you everywhere, Shan." Gillian proudly acknowledges her handiwork.

"What's up there?" Shannon points to the top shelf.

"Those are the Christmas lights for the luau."

"Oh?"

"We climb up on that ladder over there and drape the trees in lights. It's gorgeous."

Shannon pulls out her phone and starts typing away. "I bet. I already ordered tiki torches, though. We had them for our pool fundraiser last year in Pittsburgh, and they make everything so summery."

First the catered dinner, then the new band, and now this? My goodness, Shannon works fast. Gillian supposes that she had to; the luau is only days away! "Let's walk to the other side of the pool and I'll show you where we've traditionally set things up."

Gillian walks the length of the pool alongside the lap lane, where a triathlete is mowing down a feeble older swimmer. The rest of the lanes are jam-packed with Manta Rays. At the end of the pool, Gillian and Shannon turn and walk behind Charlie and the other coaches, who are still trying to impart practice etiquette to the new swimmers, like how to swim on the correct side of the lane so they don't concuss one another. Sean stands next to Justin with his hands on his hips.

"Hi, Mommy!" Riley lifts her body out of the water and shouts to Shannon, who waves back.

"Such a cutie, that Riley, and Charlie says she's going to be fast." Gillian plays the Charlie card.

"She's having a lot of fun." Shannon looks at her watch for the tenth time.

Gillian picks up the pace as they walk over to the patch of grass near the diving board. "Okay, so here is where we hold the luau. We move the round picnic tables and use the oblong ones for food."

"Can't we set up closer to the pool?"

Shannon is exhausting Gillian.

"Could you set up closer to the clubhouse? That way we'd be stationed nearer to the fridge."

Gillian is relieved to see Sean head toward them. "Hi, Coach Sean. I think you have a visitor there."

Sean wraps his little arms around Shannon's knees. "There you are, bug. Did you have fun helping Coach Justin?"

Sean nods his head vigorously.

"Looks like our time is up." Gillian flashes her "big bad selfie smile," as Kristy calls it.

"Thanks so much, Gillian! We're in great shape for the luau." Shannon dislodges Sean from herself and laces her long fingers through his pudgy ones, the rising summer sun at their backs as they walk in the direction of Shannon's chair. Gillian watches them, remembering when Sebby and Justin were small enough to hold in her arms.

39

KRISTY

Two days after Isaac takes off for Israel, Kristy feels worse than ever. And even though Beverly explained why she was craving Charlie and what pursuing him would do to her marriage and her home, their talk couldn't stave off her impulses for long.

Exercise helps, so here she is at the crack of dawn, hiding out at David's gym so she won't risk running into Gillian, her half-sister, at spin class. She'll never get used to calling her that. She climbs on the treadmill, the one closest to the window, and inserts her earbuds so nobody will approach her. She's headed ninety miles an hour, no brakes, right off a great cliff. She knows what she has to do to stop herself from careening into the air. She dismounts the bike and dries the sweat from her hands on a thick white towel.

Reaching inside her bag for her phone, Kristy walks out into the bitch-slapping heat in order to talk to Beverly in private. She never makes the call. She doesn't need Beverly to remind her to stay away from Charlie. Kristy will do the right thing on her own. Her resolve lasts until she drives out of the parking lot of David's gym. What would it hurt to stop by the pool and see if Gillian's swimming Early Bird today? Make an amend for the whoopie pie incident? What would she say? *We're actually sisters, and my love-addiction sponsor told me that finding out about our dad triggered me, and I've been lusting after your husband. Sorry about the pies!*

Maybe she's gotten over Charlie. What would it hurt to see him and test her feelings?

A deep instinct that Beverly would call her Higher Power implores her to hang a U-ey and drive in the opposite direction from the River Run pool. Fast. Step away from the pool, from Charlie and Gillian and the wild feelings. She slows down and veers to one side of the road, contemplating the turn. Her foot betrays her. She's that dog who broke through the invisible fence, nerve endings ablaze, running, running leashless into speeding traffic.

There's a nice-sized crowd for Early Bird this morning. "Oh, what the hell." Kristy lets herself out of her car. The clubhouse is closed during morning swims, but the locker room is open, and Kristy sits down on one of the benches. The air smells like antiseptic. Mia complains about having to clean the bathrooms, and Gillian goes on about her love of the smell of Pine-Sol. Who loves the smell of Pine-Sol? For Kristy, cleaning meant working her way out of Flo's house.

The summers between her college years, Kristy worked the morning and afternoon shifts in a nursing home, mainly cleaning up old people, wading in their shit and pee. It was good money. When her last shift was over, she disinfected herself, teased her hair, made up her face, squeezed her boobs into a push-up bra that left marks on her back, and slid on her waitressing uniform. The first time she came downstairs in her outfit, Flo pursed her lips, Travis looked away, and Kristy shrank in their disapproval. Prim, churchgoing Flo asked her the same question over and over: "Why can't you work an extra shift at the nursing home?" "This pays more, Mom," she said, and eventually started changing in the restaurant bathroom. When she wore the push-up bra, she earned twice as much in tips. The bartender, Bob, gave her long hugs where he ran his hands up and down her back and around to her front. She kissed him once, but he pushed her away, which made her want to do more things to Bob, with his adult acne and big butt. Rumor had it that Bob's girlfriend, the assistant manager, threatened to cut off his balls if he ever had sex with one of the waitresses. Kristy would have taken the risk.

Kristy's proud that she married well and found a way to spare her daughter these indignities. Growing up, Mia's biggest concern was that she'd miss the ice cream truck. Isn't this what parenting is all about? To want your children to have a better life?

When she gets up from the bench, a lava-like hunger foams inside her, so explosive that it makes her feel light-headed. She washes her face with cold water, and in the mirror she notices Gillian's bra hanging in a cubby. She walks over and rubs the cotton blend between her fingers, remembering their bra-shopping expedition. Renee, the Nordstrom intimates expert, wrapped her tape measure around Gillian's torso. "Thirty-four D. Women would kill for your endowments." Renee winked and gave them both a tutorial on placing their breasts properly in the cups, then handed Gillian a fitted T-shirt she pulled off the rack and told her to put it on. "My God, they're so big," Gillian murmured. Renee shook her head. "You're just not used to them standing at attention." Kristy's D cups had to be purchased.

Kristy faces the cubby, attuned to the sound of the splashing outside and the lifeguard giving the Early Birders a five-minute warning. She stuffs the bra into the waistband of her biking shorts. The room starts to spin.

She needs to put that bra back and phone Beverly, like right now. Instead she tugs down her shirt to conceal the bulge and escapes to her car. Kristy backs out of the lot so quickly that she almost hits the smelly garbage bin behind her. Only when she's home in her bedroom does she remove the stolen bra from her waistband. She slides off her shirt and exercise bra, stands in front of the mirror, and examines herself. And then she fastens Gillian's bra around her rib cage, carefully adjusting each hook. She hikes the lacy straps up over her shoulders. Her lats are bigger than Gillian's; the hooks will leave familiar marks on her back, but her breasts fit perfectly into Gillian's cups. So much for the amend making.

40

JUSTIN

During afternoon practice, Justin is unable to focus on his lane of hyperactive thirteen-year-old boys who are supposed to be swimming hard but instead are passing one another by diving under the water and yanking each other's feet and toes. He's too distracted by what he saw: Aunt Kristy meeting with a smiling Mrs. O'Leary and then walking over to Dad to talk into his ear.

Sebby's right about Justin needing to get away from his parents' drama. Liam invited him to see *The Avengers*, and Justin wonders if he can stomach him for a whole night. He only agreed to go because he has to find something to like about the kid since they're working together all summer. Plus, Justin is always down for a Marvel flick.

A couple of hours later, Justin's sitting in the front seat of Liam's moody old Volvo.

"Let's go get a Slurpee." Drinking Slurpees makes Justin feel closer to Tiff.

"What are you, like nine?"

"Liam. It's baking out there." Liam's AC blasts warm air onto his face. "And in here too."

"I've got something else in mind to cool you down."

"Whatever. Let's just stop by the 7-Eleven. It's right there."

"Dude, you're obsessed."

Maybe Liam saw the tattoo on his ass. "It will only take a few seconds." Justin makes a show of unsticking his sweaty back from the seat.

"You're whining like a little girl." Liam pulls into a liquor store. "No Slurpee tonight. What I have planned is way better. Totally sick. Trust me."

Justin follows Liam into the store only so he can open one of those big honking fridges and stick his head inside. Liam uses his fake ID to buy a pint of vodka and two six-packs of Corona Lite, chick-brew, he calls it. When they get back into the car, Liam cranks The Black Keys, a band emblazoned on every T-shirt he owns. His plan becomes clear to Justin as they head in the direction of River Run. Crap.

Justin's nocturnal visits to the pool are something he does alone, or did with Sebby way back when. To make matters worse, the white Honda CRV parked in the River Run lot belongs to Mia, whom Liam has been talking about banging for the past week. It feels wrong to talk about any girl this way, especially Mia; Justin's known her since she was in preschool. Besides, she's too good to fall prey to Liam's bullshit.

"Dude, Mia is still in high school."

Liam ignores Justin and gets out of the car. Justin wants to bolt, but he stays put out of his protectiveness toward Mia and the pool. He feels as he did his senior year, when he invited a few friends over while his parents were out of town and a car full of drunk girls showed up thanks to Instagram. Justin found two of them in Mom's closet, trying on her scarves and laughing their asses off. The next morning, Justin tried to re-file the scarves by color and size, but he hung a purple one on the blue peg, which was his undoing. For the first time ever, Mom took away his phone. The drinking had ticked her off, but she was more upset that these girls had defiled her closet. When it came to Mom, there were certain things you didn't mess with.

Liam parks next to Mia's car, and they walk down the path to the pool, Liam's arms full of booze. The weather app on Justin's iPhone reads ninety degrees. Mia has brought her friend Amber, a lifeguard who quit the team a few years ago and crushed on Justin last summer. The girls stand at the entrance to the clubhouse, Amber smiling at

Justin as if she's been waiting for this night her whole life. Liam kisses Mia on the shoulder. "Let's go get wet." He smiles, exposing his freakishly long eyeteeth. In the moonlight he looks like a vampire.

Liam and Justin know the code to the pool, and Liam punches it in and opens the door to the clubhouse, which always smells like wet dog. The water's smooth and dark. A rabbit darts across the grass in front of them, and Amber takes Justin's arm. He pulls away. Amber used to brag about blowing off her cleaning duties and swiping six-packs of Diet Coke from the fridge; Mia doesn't hesitate to plunge the toilets when some chick flushes down a tampon. Justin wants to drag both girls back to Mia's car and tell them to go home. The bottom will drop out if he gets caught here; he'll lose his job, or worse, disappoint Dad. He's afraid to leave, afraid to stay.

The girls sit on the edge of the pool and dangle their bare feet in the water while Justin hovers behind them, as if he were the lifeguard. Liam pops open two Coronas and hands one to each girl. Amber guzzles the brew down, chasing a buzz hard, while Liam takes the bottle of vodka from the bag and chugs it like lemonade.

Amber and Liam are getting loud. "Hey, pipe down," Justin tells them. There's an old couple who live in a cul-de-sac that butts up against River Run, and apparently the acoustics enable them to hear everything. Once the old man came over to the pool and told Sebby and Justin that he'd call the cops the next time he caught them there.

Mia and Amber wiggle their T-shirts over their heads, revealing their matching red bras, and slip into the deep end. Justin's so hot that he dives into the pool in his boxers. He floats for a second on top of the water, face up, savoring the weightlessness and the break from Liam's and Amber's voices. When he emerges, Amber shrieks as if he's just tickled her armpits. Justin decides that this is the worst sound he's ever heard in his entire life.

Liam has stripped and is jumping on the board naked, vodka bottle in hand.

"Get down, you idiot," Justin whispers as loudly as he can.

"You're such a pussy, Justin. Can't you just have some fun?" Liam jumps up again.

Justin deliberates over whether he should get out of the deep end and climb up on the board to grab the bottle or wait for Liam to jump in the water so he can save him if he hits his head. "I'm going to do the Sebastian Norton swan dive." Liam raises his arms. Trying to pull off the dive is an activity that belongs to Justin and especially Sebby, the only one who has ever mastered it. Who is this asshole even to attempt to imitate Sebastian Norton? The sight of a drunk Liam jumping on the diving board pisses Justin off. "Get the fuck down," he screams from someplace deep, not caring about the neighbors, not caring about what getting caught might cost him.

"Dude." Liam looks angry and embarrassed. "Mellow the fuck out."

"Put the bottle down, Liam." Justin's voice is still raised.

"Will do." Liam sets the bottle on the board.

"Good. Now get down," Justin says.

"Nope. Not until I do my Sebastian."

"You're being a douche."

Liam taunts Justin. "Girls, go get your iPhones, we can post my picture in the clubhouse. And on Facebook."

Justin wants to punch the shit out of him.

Liam kicks the vodka bottle off the board, and the clear glass shatters, spraying shards on the deck. Mia gasps. Liam's so wasted that he could drown. He jumps three times and performs the sorriest excuse for a swan dive Justin has ever seen. He enters the water, a few inches from Justin, who waits for him to emerge for what feels like five minutes. He's just about to dive underwater to look for Liam when a swirl of water rustles the hairs on his calves. Liam pops up, shaking his bangs from his face. "Gotcha." He throws back his head and cackles.

Justin glances at Mia, who looks torn between common sense and the thrill of Liam, and then at Liam's smug face, which only makes him madder. Justin gets out of the pool and puts on his shorts.

"Just admit that I got you," Liam taunts.

The weak pool light casts a glow on Liam's skin. "Clean up the glass from the bottle you broke."

"You going to tell Coach C?" Spittle flies from Liam's lips.

"Liam," Mia says. "Let's go find a broom."

"Yeah, go tell your dad what I did, and I'll tell him you were here, watching." Liam's fangs glisten.

"Just go." Justin waves his hand in the air. "Mia, you drive." His harsh tone works. They leave, and by the sound of the compliant engine they're taking Mia's car. Justin is on guard duty the next morning, so he'll arrive early for his shift and clean up the glass in the sunlight.

Fucking Liam could have killed himself tonight on that board. Justin shoves his feet into his flip-flops so he won't cut them on the glass and walks to the diving board. He leaves the flip-flops at the bottom of the ladder and climbs to the top. Before walking the five steps to the edge of the plank, he draws the warm air into his body. He exhales as he jumps off the board, spreading his arms out to his sides. As he flies into the air, he moves his head up and then down. In the seconds before he brings his hands together for his swan dive, he feels an energy bearing down on his feet, pushing him toward the water. He fears the force will jam his head into the bottom of the pool, crushing his skull like an aluminum can. He yanks his feet under his body to slow himself down, and his breath comes out of his lungs in clumps as he enters the water. He swims to the side of the pool as quickly as he can, as if he's seen a ghost.

As Justin walks home, a memory sideswipes him out of nowhere. He was seven and Sebby was ten. Mom was cleaning out the swim-team shelves in the shed, and Dad was reading the Sunday *New York Times*. It was late August, and everyone was out of town. Justin was waiting for a turn on the diving board, holding the ladder, the metal almost too hot to touch. Mom emerged from the shed while Sebby was midair, arms outstretched, his chin tilted toward the sky. Justin assumed that Mom would send him to the car to retrieve a throwaway camera she kept in case life presented her with a moment like this one. She'd ask Sebby to repeat the dive for sure. Instead, she turned her back on Sebby, and when Justin caught a glimpse of her face, it revealed a grief so raw that he buried the image deep inside himself. Would Sebby remember the dive? Mom's face?

He dials his brother, but the call goes straight to voicemail. On impulse, he scrolls through Sebby's text messages and finds the one he sent with Uncle Patrick's number. Maybe Uncle Patrick stayed away from the pool because he encountered that force Justin had just felt pressing on his feet. Justin isn't ready to find out.

He walks to the 7-Eleven. When he opens the familiar door, the fluorescent lights and shriveled breakfast sausages, lonely in their glass case, comfort him. He helps himself to a large cup and plastic cover and walks over to milk the Slurpee cow, as Tiff used to say. He palms the black udder and pushes down, enthralled with the torrent of purple slush gushing through the plastic hole. He pays for the drink with the last three dollars in his wallet.

He sits on the bike rack to drink his Slurpee in peace, unwrapping the straw and stuffing the flimsy paper in his pocket. The red plastic feels smooth against his lips, and he chews on it for a second before taking a big sip of the drink. He's so thirsty that he gulps down the soupy ice, chugging it like Liam chugged the vodka. This is no way to drink a Slurpee, Tiff told him the first time she saw him attack the ice like a rookie. He stops. Too late. The cold freezes his brain, and there's nothing he can do but wait for it to thaw.

The next morning, Justin shows up at Early Bird a half hour before it starts so he can clean up the broken glass. He hunts down the slivers of Liam's vodka bottle, trying not to freak himself out about the ghost he felt the night before.

Luckily, he finishes by the time the first swimmers, his parents, arrive at the pool. Dad has to go downtown to his old office to pick up a box of his stuff, so Justin will coach the morning practice that follows Early Bird swim. Mom and Dad are standing side by side, putting on their goggles. Mom has been even more off since the dinner on Saturday night. He can tell she's sad. Mia said that Mom's swim-team crew got together on Sunday night for margaritas. Mom usually organizes these gatherings, but Justin's pretty sure that she didn't know anything about this one.

It's only a little after seven but already so humid that the clubhouse windows are beading up. Mom straightens out the lounge chairs—she can't help herself—before she and Dad dive in. They split a lane and swim long today, no stopping, no sets, no kickboards. Dad swims ahead of Mom, but she picks up the pace so she can draft off him, for a few hundred meters anyway. Her face and chest are bright red when they stop, and she lunges out of the pool and wraps a towel around herself. When she rubs her hands on the terrycloth and reaches into her backpack, Justin knows what's coming next: the Gillian Cloud selfie. She's trained all the Clouds to seamlessly interrupt a conversation to pose, as if they lived under a flight path and have grown accustomed to pausing for a loud airplane.

She types away and then shows Dad her post. "You'll like this one, Charlie."

"That's a good one, Gil." Justin can't tell if he really means it, though. He kisses Mom's cheek, gives Justin a few instructions for the practice, and heads into the locker room.

"You were up and out early this morning," Mom says.

Justin jumps at the feel of her cool hand on his shoulder. "Went for a little run first." He hates lying and does so now without taking his eyes off the dozen swimmers who have filled out the lanes.

"Dad told me that you two think we can beat the Sea Lions on Saturday?"

Justin loves figuring out lineup possibilities with Dad. Zeke couldn't put a decent lineup together to save his life, but Dad's a pro at placing his pawns on the chessboard. "We really could."

"He says you're doing a bang-up job." Gillian walks over to the side of the pool, retrieves a chair, and sits down next to Justin.

"Thanks," he says, his voice full of pride.

Mom's lips are bluish; she's the type who's always cold in the water, regardless of the temperature. "I've been meaning to ask you. Have you seen anyone suspicious around the pool?"

Her question gives him a start. She must have found out about last night. "Not really. Why?"

"Someone stole my bra. Right out of the locker room."

Justin bursts out laughing in relief. "Actually?"

"Yes. Actually! During lap swim yesterday." Mom play-punches his arm. "It's not funny."

"I'll keep my eye out for anyone who looks sketchy."

"Why would anyone steal someone else's bra?"

"No idea."

"Such a violation." She starts shivering. "You don't just take things that aren't yours," she hisses.

"Sorry, Mom." Justin doesn't know what else to say. It doesn't matter, though, she isn't really listening.

"Well, whoever took it better look both ways before she crosses the street."

Mom's way overreacting. "Why?"

"Karma bus." She laughs, but Justin can tell that she doesn't find anything about her stolen bra the slightest bit amusing.

"Hey, Justin." Mr. Graves, a ninety-year-old man who has not missed a day of summer lap swimming in fifty years, pops his head over the side of the pool and eyes a stack of kickboards.

"Here you go, Mr. Graves." Gillian bounces up and hands the old man a board.

"Thank you, Gillian Norton!" Mr. Graves is one of a handful of old-timers who still call Mom by her maiden name.

"Thanks for doing that, Mom."

"I've been fetching Mr. Graves his kickboard since well before you were born." Gillian's eyes traverse the lanes of the pool. "What do you think of the changes to the luau?"

"Um . . ." He doesn't want to go there.

"There's nothing I can do to stop it, but I have a bad feeling."

"What kind of bad feeling?" Justin doesn't tell Mom that he has an odd feeling about the luau too, but he can't name it. Maybe he's still bugged out from last night.

She fixes her gaze on the pool. "Justin, promise me you'll work on Friday night and keep an eye on the drunks."

"Promise."

41

CHARLIE

Before Charlie leaves the pool, Gillian straightens his collar. "Go get 'em." For a second, he and Gillian are back to who they used to be. Then, as he's driving over the Key Bridge to his swank former Pennsylvania Avenue office, he thinks how much he doesn't want Gillian's pep talks or her cold hands on his neck. He wanted to grab his morning swim alone, but Gillian wasn't having it. She's determined to catch the bra thief, but Charlie knows she'll make any excuse to spend time at River Run, because it's slipping through her fingers like water. Between her efforts to pump up her business and tend to myriad pool responsibilities, she isn't sleeping, and the bags under her eyes make him feel guilty.

Conversely, Charlie's "at the height of his powers," a stale line from the book reviews he reads religiously. He's always wondered what that would feel like. Now he knows. He's building something. The Manta Rays are 1–0 with every chance of creaming the Sea Lions this Saturday. If they can beat the top two teams in the league, they're golden. As far as the family's growing Visa bill and pending tuition payments, he and Gillian agreed that she'll make as much money as she can this summer and they'll figure the rest out after the season. He would feel less like a shit about all this if Gillian weren't trying so hard to be helpful, or if thoughts of Kristy weren't popping into his head like the boners that launched surprise attacks back in junior high. Or if hiding these Kristy thoughts from Gillian were as easy as hiding the fact that he'd opened another new credit card last week.

This morning, for the last time, he'll make that miserable commute downtown to pick up some personal items—his framed diploma, a few photos, a spare dress shirt and tie—that he couldn't bring himself to collect on his last day at the firm. The HR director is in a meeting, so Charlie takes a seat in the lobby. He pulls out his phone and glances at Gillian's morning Facebook post. The light is perfect, and he barely recognizes his new body. He winces at Gillian's hashtags: #summerbliss #hottie #couplethatswimstogetherstaystogether. He wants her to stop posting about the Clouds' perfect life. Stop micromanaging Shannon O'Leary. Stop chasing after Kristy. Stop trying to fix and control. Just stop.

Christ, he can't stand this lobby. Hates the bad art and phony mission statement and fake plants. He wants to draw mustaches on the framed photos of the partners, who've perfected the quintessential facial expression: three parts earnest to one part fun and inviting. They've already removed his photo from the wall.

"Well, if it isn't Charlie Cloud." Oliver Quinn emerges from his office, scanning Charlie, from his newly bald head to his toes.

"Good morning, Oliver."

"Holy shit, Cloud. This life agrees with you, doesn't it?"

Oliver's fake joviality doesn't fool Charlie. "Sure does." He imitates Gillian's selfie smile.

"So where did you land?" Oliver smirks.

"You've never heard of this outfit, I assure you." Charlie will make ninety-five hundred dollars coaching this summer if he earns a bonus. He considers telling Oliver that he never oversleeps, that he's his own boss, that people line up along the side of the pool to talk to him, and that he has no tolerance for jerks like Oliver. He regularly admonishes Liam for his dick-like moves. Maybe he'll save the business world from the likes of another Oliver. No. Oliver will never understand. He'll only think Charlie pathetic and defensive.

"You going to make me guess?" Irritation creeps into Oliver's voice.

Charlie isn't going to sully his sense of well-being by exposing his new life to Oliver's cynicism, and he doesn't have to because the receptionist, younger and prettier than the one he remembers, summons him.

"That's me, Oliver," he says in the tone Oliver used when he climbed up the corporate ladder, using Charlie's back as a rung. He's tempted to pat Oliver's puffy cheek, but instead he looks at him with indifference.

Charlie approaches the desk, and the receptionist picks up his box from the floor. "Funny, your things were right here all along."

"Thank you." Charlie takes the box with a corner of his diploma sticking out of the top. "Take care, Oliver."

On the way down in the elevator, Charlie considers Oliver's day unfolding, the daily circle jerk of a meeting, the midday crash after too many morning donuts and too much bread from the basket of some trendy D.C. restaurant, the late nights to catch up on the real work.

Sayonara, suckers.

Sebby calls while Charlie's negotiating Pennsylvania Avenue traffic. When Sebby ended his swim career, they started spending more time together during the summer season. Sebby never liked to get near Gillian while she was, as he put it, "under the influence of the Manta Rays."

"Sebby!"

"Coach Cloud! Master of the Manta Rays!"

"Ha-ha. How's life?"

Sebby updates him on the job, the studying. They discuss Mitt Romney clinching the Republican nomination and his chances of beating President Obama the whole way home: back along Pennsylvania Avenue, through Georgetown, across the Key Bridge over the grayish-green Potomac water, and back up Lee Highway.

"Kind of nice to be talking about politics again," Charlie laughs. In the fall, Gillian will be driving south to knock on doors for President Obama, but now she clearly has no bandwidth for much of anything except River Run and busting clutter.

"Yes, there is a world outside of the River Run bubble," Sebby says knowingly.

"You're right, Seb." Although just now, Charlie's pretty content residing in the bubble.

"One last thing, Dad."

"What's that?"

"Everything okay down there?"

"It's different, that's for sure. Why do you ask?"

Sebby pauses. "I've been talking to Justin."

"He's doing a great job." Charlie's careful not to sound too enthusiastic about the team. He doesn't want Sebby to feel that he's ditched him.

"I'm sure he is. He's really into it."

"What's going on, Seb?"

"Sounds like Mom's having a tough time." Silence, except for the Manhattan street sounds and faint noise of his son's breath.

"Talk to me."

"I'm going to be late for my shift."

"Seb?"

"Yeah?" Sebby isn't going to tell him anything else.

"Let me worry about Mom."

The call leaves a bitter aftertaste in Charlie's mouth, as if he's brushed his teeth with the toothbrush Gillian uses to clean the bathroom fixtures. He's a jerk for the way he was thinking about Gillian only a half hour ago. A part of him blames her for his feeling like crap about himself for all those years he worked at the firm, and an even uglier part of him wants to punish her for it. And what about Justin? Has Charlie's happiness blinded him to the stress his son is clearly picking up? The kid absorbs everything.

He'll sort all this out later, after he accomplishes his agenda for the day. He'll stop at Whole Foods and pick up a nice piece of swordfish, and they'll grill and have a quiet dinner and discuss Sebby's summer job or the financial crisis in Greece. Anything but the Manta Rays. And Kristy.

42

GILLIAN

Gillian's exhausted from exhausting herself to distraction with the things she prefers not to think about, primarily Kristy. While Charlie's picking up his personal effects at his old office, she texts her and asks to meet at Starbucks. It's time. Kristy texts back that coffee is a fantastic idea. The possibility of their resuming their normal stride makes Gillian want to cry tears of relief.

An hour later, Gillian pulls into a space in the strip mall a few slots over from Kristy's SUV. She opens the door to the Starbucks, shivering at the blast of air-conditioning. Kristy's standing in line with her back to Gillian. She traces the hem of Kristy's new brown exercise shirt. "Is this from Lucy?"

"Sale," Kristy answers. "What do you think of the color?" Yes, this is Krillian, engaged in a constant conversation. No pleasantries needed. Phew.

"Matches your eyes."

"Thanks."

"Thanks for coming." Gillian hasn't realized how much they've been avoiding eye contact until they're looking right at each other.

"Of course, Gil. Coffee's on me."

"The next one's on me, then." Are they going to become coffee buddies now? Whatever works, as long as she doesn't lose Kristy.

"I'll get you your French Roast." Kristy reaches inside her enormous bag for her wallet and places their orders.

"I'll grab us a place to sit." Gillian finds an empty table and watches Kristy walk over to the pickup line. Her gait looks different; she sticks out her chest and cocks her head to one side, and well, she's kind of shaking it, as Kristy would say. It takes forever for the barista to make their drinks, and the sound of the milk steamer grates on Gillian.

"There you go, one French Roast and one Iced Venti Skim Latte." Kristy carries the cups to the table and sits down.

"Do we need to talk?" Gillian says.

Krillian always made fun of these kinds of chats. "Too much drama," they'd say with disgust, reveling in their effortless friendship.

"About what?" Kristy wipes foam from her lip.

"Really?"

"Look, I'm so sorry about bailing on your dinner. Total calendar mess-up, and then I told Shannon we'd lend her our air mattress, so she came over with the kids, and that's how the whoopie pie thing happened, which I never should have posted. But I was going to tell you about everything before you saw the post, and then David had some issue with his computer, and I got all distracted. I should have been in touch sooner." She takes a gulp of air and puts her hand on Gillian's forearm. "I'm so glad we're doing this. I've been feeling like crap."

Gillian badly wants to believe Kristy's story. She's constructed a beautiful tale, the cadence, delivery, and timbre resembling the story she told about not showing up at the hospital after Shannon fell. Gillian's familiar with this type of tale, she heard it her entire childhood, from her father.

Gillian chooses to believe Kristy because it will hurt too much not to. "I've missed you."

Kristy looks up from her cup, and she's the Kristy who adores Gillian. "I'm sorry."

"I'm just glad we're talking," Gillian says.

"Me too. Forgot your sugar. Hold on." Kristy stands up suddenly, knocking Gillian's drink over. The scalding liquid puddles on the table and spills over onto Gillian's bare thigh.

"Shit." Gillian rarely cusses, but the pain surprises her with its sharpness.

"God, I'm so sorry. I'm so sorry." Kristy retrieves some stray napkins from the next table.

Gillian mops the liquid from her freckled leg while Kristy marches behind the counter and flags the young manager. She asks him for some ice, leaning over so he can sneak a glance at her breasts before filling a baggie with ice cubes. Gillian's seen Kristy play the beauty card dozens of times, but she can't blame her friend for the way men respond to her. Today, though, Kristy is definitely more aggressive with the card. What's going on with her? Gillian takes the bag from Kristy and mutters a thank-you. Her leg is bright red. She bites her quivering lower lip hard so she won't shed her stockpiled tears.

"Yeesh. Does it hurt?" Kristy asks.

"Yeah." Gillian doesn't look up. "It hurts."

Kristy allows the comment to hang in the air and grow so weighty that neither one of them can pick it up alone. Gillian tosses the wadded-up napkins on the table.

"I'm sorry," Kristy mutters.

"Please stop apologizing."

"Sorry," Kristy says coyly. "You know, for apologizing too much."

Gillian can't help but laugh.

In a too-chipper tone, Kristy says, "Shannon's excited about the luau."

"It's going to be an interesting one." Gillian invites Kristy to slip back into their River Run mode.

"Gil, I have to go. My day to help David out."

Kristy's lying. Again. Kristy helps David on Fridays, and today is Wednesday. If Gillian challenges her, she'll make up a new story, brilliant fibber that she is, and what would be the point? Gillian rises from her chair, her leg now a deeper shade of red from the cold.

"Keep some ice on that, okay?" Kristy recommends as they walk out to their cars. She gives Gillian an awkward hug before they part.

Gillian opens her car door and rests her foot on the seat for a good angle on her burn. It takes two shots to get the pic right, and then she posts it: #icedcoffeenexttime #morningjoewithmybestie #krillian.

43

CHARLIE

Neither Gillian nor Justin is home when Charlie returns from picking up his things at the office. He tosses his box in the basement and heads upstairs to take off his khakis and one of the many sage-green shirts Gillian bought him because she says that color brings out the green in his eyes. He heads back to River Run to give three private lessons, leaves the pool briefly for an hour to pump iron at the gym, and returns to coach afternoon practice. The kids are looking good. They just might win the meet on Saturday.

A group of mothers clamors to talk to him after he finishes his lessons. Last summer if Charlie showed up at a practice and sat in the lounge chairs close to some of these very same women, clad in their yoga gear and chatting easily while arranging carpools, tennis games, and Peapod deliveries on their iPads, he would have been invisible. He could have peeled off his trunks and taken a dump on the pool deck, and they still wouldn't have looked up from their screens. Once, he eavesdropped on the yoga lionesses gossiping about a new mom who was timing her daughter's workout swims with the stopwatch function on her iPhone. This summer he will tell such a mom or dad to please put the stopwatch away. "I've got this," he will say, and they will comply. And this afternoon the lionesses are not ordering groceries off Peapod or reading their book-club novels, they're mesmerized by Charlie Cloud. Charlie has captured the attention of the occupants of twenty lounge chairs. He is seen.

Keys in hand, Charlie texts Gillian to tell her that he's going to pick up some swordfish for dinner. This is his plan, but then Kristy shows up as he's finishing his text, and before he knows it he's sitting at a picnic table with Kristy and Shannon going over last-minute arrangements for Friday's luau. Gillian only gave up this event for a good reason, to be of service to Charlie and the family. Still, she's been stalking Shannon since the O'Learys showed up late for dinner with an anemic plate of whoopie pies, an obscene amount of apology ice cream, and one too many observations on how Riley has taken to Mia.

Charlie's back in seventh grade and has been asked to abandon his best friend to sit at the popular table. He doesn't even ask if they've invited Gillian, who for the past fifteen years has planned the event.

Shannon sets down a legal pad. "Okay, let's just go through the details."

"Sounds good." Kristy smiles at both of them.

"The food will be delivered at six sharp."

Gillian has been going on and on about the travesty of catered food and how this year Krillian will not be making their big run to Costco for drinks and paper goods.

"The band will start playing at about seven." Shannon scribbles on her pad. "And Justin will set up the tiki torches when it gets dark. Love that kid."

"Thanks. Me too." Charlie winks.

Gillian insisted that the tiki torches were unsafe. She'd purchased regular lights years ago when she took over planning the luau. She made a good case for protecting the drunk parents from knocking over these skinny fire posts, but Charlie knew that all her changes were really intended to make the luau more like it had been when she was growing up. Christmas lights. Limbo contests. A potluck. It's obvious why Gillian has not been invited to this meeting; Kristy knows how much Gillian would resist the new plan. But why is Kristy defecting so easily? And why doesn't that stop Charlie from wanting to be around her?

"Okay, looks like you have everything under control." It's almost seven, and Gillian's waiting for him at home.

"Charlie?" Shannon bites the tip of her pencil. "Is Gillian going to be okay with all this?"

"Likely not," he answers without hesitation.

"Bummer." Shannon picks at the eraser. "I'm not trying to upset her."

"Shannon, you're a good egg, and trust me, nobody wants to upset Gillian, but you're the social director, so you have to make your own decisions," Kristy assures her.

Kristy folds her arms across her breasts, drawing her workout shirt down enough to expose her cleavage. When she catches Charlie's eyes roving toward her top, he pivots his head toward Shannon.

"I guess." Shannon picks up her phone from the table. "You know what, guys? The sitter just texted me. I better scram."

Charlie watches Shannon exit the pool. She doesn't seem like the kind of person who would thrive on drama, either creating it or convincing herself that it isn't there. "Looks like it's time for all of us to take off," he says.

"Before we leave, Charlie, could you please help me bring in the new tent?" Kristy asks. All week she's been coaxing him to stay at the pool, to be late for Gillian. Charlie, can you check this revised set of meet results? Charlie, can you bring in the case of soda . . . extra copy paper . . . the printer from my car?

Kristy's legs are as long as Charlie's, and he falls in step with her easily. Occasionally she walks into him, brushing her side against his, and he surprises himself with an urge to drape his arm around her shoulder.

"Here we go." She opens the back of her car and reaches for the tent that Gillian ordered for the team. He tries not to check out her ass. "One. Two. Three," she says, and they pick up both sides of the heavy bag, hoist it out of the car, and carry it to the supply shed behind the oak tree with Gillian's swing. His breath quickens as he opens the door with one hand and holds on to the tent with the other.

"Look at that bicep, Charlie Cloud." Kristy's been using this girlish voice with him when they're alone.

They walk the bag to the back of the dark, sticky shed and lean it against the wall. Kristy turns around to face him. He's never noticed the gold flecks in her irises before. Her forehead is starting to sweat, and he imagines her lying next to him, wet and spent. They stand like this for a few seconds.

Charlie hears Justin outside talking to one of the lifeguards. What if he'd walked into the shed? Charlie's being paranoid. What's there to see? It isn't like Charlie and Kristy are touching each other. But that's not true. They're touching without touching, and there's enough electricity in that shed to light up the entire Arlington power grid. They wait until Justin's voice fades before Kristy exits the shed, Charlie following in the wake of her musky scent.

"Where'd the time go?" He looks at his watch.

"Bye, Charlie." Kristy gives a little wave. "Thanks for your help."

He feels her gaze on his back as he walks toward the parking lot, straightening his shoulders to make them look broader, buoyed by seeing himself through Oliver's and Kristy's eyes. Hell, the photo Gillian snapped this morning launched this glorious day. Or was it so glorious? That chemical taste returns to his tongue. He gets into his car and zooms off, putting as much distance as possible between himself, Kristy, and the pool. Otherwise, he might fall in.

44

JUSTIN

After Dad and Aunt Kristy leave the pool, Justin finishes up his shift and takes off. He finds himself at the 7-Eleven, confronting the Slurpee machine. "Fuck this." He returns the plastic cup to the stack. He's done mourning Tiff, one Slurpee at a time. He's done worrying about Dad's male menopause and Mom's control freakdom. He isn't going to go all *CSI* on her stolen bra or make himself responsible for every adult who throws back one too many mai tais at the luau. Not his job. He will, however, force himself to unsee the whacked vibe he picked up between Aunt Kristy and Dad coming out of the shed. And who's he kidding? He'll get caught up in all the rest of it too.

He drives away from the 7-Eleven, away from River Run. He doesn't know where he's going, but then again, he kind of does. Soon he's sitting at a booth at Bob & Edith's, ordering himself waffles with no syrup, extra butter, and a side of bacon. Uncle Patrick used to bring him and Sebby here on weekends, before Mom made excuses for them to cancel their get-togethers. "Patrick is a bad influence," Justin overheard her tell Dad.

Justin peruses the songs on the mini-jukebox at his table, but they no longer feature Uncle Patrick's favorite, "You've Lost That Lovin' Feelin'." The Righteous Brothers sang in the background while Uncle Patrick explained how hard drives and soft drives worked in a way that Justin could grasp. It was awesome. He and Sebby were sure their uncle would invent some new computer technology that was smarter than

Google. He would accept his Nobel Prize, and the video would run over and over on CNN's news reel. Some reporter would ask him if he had kids, and he'd reply, "No, only two nephews." The reporter would ask "What do your nephews think?" He wouldn't have anything to say because he wouldn't know.

The waitress sets down a plate of waffles drenched in syrup. Justin doesn't want to make a fuss about the syrup, so he takes a bite of waffle, the clot of gooey flour catching in his throat. Too sugary. He tosses a ten-dollar bill on the table and heads home, hoping he'll find his parents cuddled together on the couch watching more *Downton*.

The house is dark. He goes to sleep, but not before checking his Instagram for Tiff's updates.

45

KRISTY

The day before the luau, Kristy calls Beverly to confess the bra heist and her luring Charlie into the shed, and they agree that Kristy must get to a meeting as soon as possible. Too afraid she'll wimp out, she asks Beverly to accompany her to an evening meeting that begins in an hour. Kristy almost turns her car around twice on her way to the church, located only 4.6 miles from her house according to Google Maps. The building is so close to Chain Bridge that she also considers crossing the Potomac and hiding out in a Bethesda strip mall off MacArthur Boulevard, at that little French bakery started by two former White House pastry chefs. She'll pick up a rainbow assortment of Parisian macarons and bring them home for the kids.

Instead, she pulls into the church parking lot, sits in her car, and peels off four fingernails' worth of unchipped polish while she waits for Beverly to arrive. An old minivan drives up, and Beverly gets out. She looks the same, except that she's let her auburn hair go gray, and wiry curls frame her face, which is a bit fuller. Kristy stoops over and rests her head against Beverly's bony shoulder, and Beverly turns toward her and holds on tight. She forgot about Beverly's superior hugging skills and how she always smells like the woods. Beverly waits until Kristy's ready to end the embrace before handing her a jewelry box.

Kristy opens the box, which contains a pewter necklace with "One Day at a Time" inscribed on the plate. She wants to cry. "This is so nice of you."

Beverly strokes Kristy's arm. "Let's do this, girl."

They enter the musty basement of the church. We come in all shapes and sizes, Kristy thinks as she examines the women sitting in folding chairs in a circle, cupping their various containers of coffee and tea. The assigned speaker tells her story, which replicates one—no, three—of Kristy's misadventures with attached men. But this woman also talks about her strength and hope, neither of which Kristy thinks she'll ever have.

"Any newcomers who would like to share?" asks a pale woman with uneven bangs.

Kristy glances at Beverly, who radiates the kind of pure, unadulterated maternal-style love she's only ever received from Gillian. "I'll go." It takes a few seconds for the words to make their way out of her mouth. "I'm not a newcomer, although I've been away from the program for a while. My name is Kristy, and I'm a love addict."

"Hi, Kristy," the roomful of sex and love addicts greets her cheerily.

Beverly hands her a bottle of cold Dasani from her bag, and Kristy takes a sip. She assumes she will begin by describing how finding out about Sebastian triggered her, how she's been intriguing with Charlie, but she uses her three minutes to tell the story of having sex with the boyfriend of her college roommate. Debbie Wright. Late-night gab sessions and donut runs be damned. She even wore Debbie's favorite sweater the night she seduced her boyfriend. Every boy in his hall thought that Debbie was the shit, and it gave Kristy enormous pleasure to sneak into his single when Debbie went home to her perfect family on weekends. And then she grew obsessed and got sloppy and got caught. And cast out. Debbie forgave her boyfriend, but Kristy had to find another room. The RA arranged a single for her.

By the time she finishes her story, she's sobbing. Chasing after Charlie's attentions could cast her out for life. You'd think that would be enough to make her stop this nonsense. Beverly and the four women who line up to hug her know that it isn't. They hold her, like a baby.

46

GILLIAN

The morning of the luau, Charlie asks Gillian to shave his scalp. He perches himself on a chair facing the bathroom mirror while Gillian stands behind him and mows his head with his brand-new electric razor.

"Put your chin down so I can get your whole neck."

Charlie complies. "You and Shannon have everything all set for tonight?" he asks into his shirt.

"This is Shannon's night." She focuses intently on making clean rows on his tanned scalp. "Not mine."

"Really?" Charlie yanks up his head.

"Be still. You want to lose an eyebrow?"

She can't blame Shannon for not wanting her to hover. Gillian felt the same way when she took over planning the luau so many years ago, when she turned it into a family-friendly event similar to the luaus of her youth.

"Um, okay. I thought you were bent out of shape about the tiki torches."

Why is he stirring up trouble? Besides, it isn't the torches that are making her crazy. She doesn't like drunk, out-of-control behavior at the pool, and Charlie knows it. "Charlie, do we really have to discuss this?"

"Sorry. Do you have any clients today?"

All of a sudden he's concerned about their income?

"Sadly, no." Gillian wishes she were busier today; she's waiting to hear from four potential clients who all need her more than they care to admit. Their closets are a sight, and let's not even talk about the photos weeping from their sorry albums. Gillian threw in album-organizing as value added because family photos inspire some of the best poses for her own Facebook posts.

"Smooth." Charlie rubs his head. "You do good work, Gil."

She puts her fingers over his. "Shaving is kind of satisfying."

"You're welcome to scalp me any time."

"Besides, I'm sure Shannon and Kristy have everything under control." She tries to sound upbeat.

Charlie removes the cutter head of the razor.

"Let me do that." She reaches for the little brush and rubbing alcohol and scrubs Charlie's skin cells and whiskers away from the razor parts.

"Thank you." He hugs her.

"Of course, Charlie." Her voice sounds just like her mother's. *The Norton children are gracious, Gillian. No matter what.* Charlie has made it clear that he doesn't need her help, and the gals at the pool treat her like she's yesterday's news. And this is why Charlie's encroachment upon her River Run world reminds her of the time a family set up camp too close to the Clouds on their long-awaited trip to the beach. She wanted to bark, "Rehoboth is a big stretch of sand, you space invaders!" But a woman raised by May Norton would never behave in such a manner, so she smiled instead and made small talk. Thank God, because she ran into that family four more times at Funland. She doesn't want her husband to move too far away from her metaphorical towel, she just wants Coach Charlie to find his groove a bit further down the shoreline. She's relieved when he takes off for the gym.

Gillian's closet is a work of art, a daily inspiration for her in helping the most organizationally challenged clients achieve perfection. Her Hawaiian number for the luau hangs with her "almost never" clothing, which includes the little black dress she wore for Charlie's annual Christmas party, the mauve gown she wore to a Kennedy Center gala, and her ski pants, pressed and cleaned for next winter. She unwraps the dry-cleaning plastic from the Hawaiian uniform she bought the summer she worked at the Chart House in Old Town. She was a top-notch waitress. The very best. Not only was she attentive, but she knew how to convince a customer that he needed that slice of Mud Pie for dessert or that the expensive scallops were more delicious than the modestly priced roast chicken. She takes pride in the fact that twenty-some years later, she still fits into the dress and has worn it to every River Run luau. She removes it from the hanger and tries it on. It bags around the waist, thanks to her incessant spinning and her stress level, and without her super bra her breasts droop. This won't do. Who in God's name stole her bra?

She changes quickly and takes off for Tysons Corner. Gillian doesn't mind the crowded parking lot and incessant construction like Kristy does. Her first stop is Nordstrom, where she looks for the enthusiastic and skilled salesperson with the tape measure, but she is nowhere to be found. What was her name? Randi? Renee?

She finds the bra on her own. Initially, she purchased one in beige and washed it in Woolite every other night; today she plunks down her credit card and buys three, in beige, pale pink, and black. To heck with their budget. Whoever designed this baby knew what she was doing. Unlike the breastplates made for women her size, this bra has soft cups and delicate lacy straps. A nice saleslady—aren't they all at Nordstrom?—escorts her to the changing room, where she abandons her stretched-out Maidenform and tears the tag off the shiny pink bra. She smooths her T-shirt over the new piece of intimate wear and examines her reflection. Much, much better. The girls, as Kristy calls them, have been badly in need of some sturdier scaffolding.

She meanders through the mall. After purchasing a Diet Coke from the pretzel stand, she sits down on a bench and watches an Israeli man emerge from his kiosk to accost women with sun-damaged skin. They aren't buying his Dead Sea tonic, but he's so handsome that they let him rub the lotion on their wrists and necks.

The caffeine gives her a jolt, and she continues her mall-cruising. She remembers the swimsuit store that carries Hawaiian dresses. The music is loud, and she can barely hear the salesperson direct her to a rounder of Aloha wear. She locates a nice blue dress that would bring out her eyes and takes two different sizes into the dressing room. The size four lingers above her knees, but she still has nice legs, and it looks good. She's about to open the door to track down the salesperson and ask her opinion when the woman a dressing room over answers her cell phone. "Hey." Gillian recognizes the voice right away. She squats down and examines the feet of the speaker. These gunboats belong to Kristy. Long tapered toes, a bunion, and flat arches that match her own. These feet that belong to a tall person like Kristy had also landed on Gillian's body, like two alien spaceships.

Gillian listens. "Shannon, can I call you in ten? I'm trying on a dress for tonight, and I'm in a changing room." Silence. She watches Kristy slide on her sandals. She's painted her toes a new shade of teenybopper pink. "I'll totally bring you here next year." Kristy's giggle, which Gillian knows to be contrived, nevertheless suggests an easy intimacy.

Gillian flees her changing room so she won't get caught eavesdropping. Kristy has moved on. Now she's Krannon. Gillian blinks hard to prevent her tears from falling as she walks out to the sales floor, where Kristy, in a flowy Hawaiian dress with thick straps, is standing at a rounder, two more dresses slung over her forearm.

"Nice dress, Kristy," Gillian says in her honeyed May Norton tone.

For as long as Gillian lives, she will never forget the look Kristy gives her, a mix of surprise and "Why are you here?" disdain, as if Gillian were the girl in high school with the noxious BO and hairy legs whose proximity could wreck your social standing but whom you let sit next to you at the school assembly because you don't want to look mean to the teachers who are watching the interaction. "Um, thanks."

Gillian touches the blue dress on Kristy's arm. "I'm going to buy that one, and I can't imagine that you would want to be twins."

Kristy puts the blue one back on the rounder.

"What's up with you?" Gillian blurts.

"So much." Kristy looks impossibly sad.

Gillian softens. "Are you okay?"

"I'm fine, Gil. I was going to call you to come out here with me, but—"

"It's okay, Kristy." Gillian can't stand to hear one more lie.

Kristy's purse slides down her shoulder, dragging the strap of her dress. And there in the light of day is the pretty bra strap that belongs to Gillian, who recognizes the tiny rip in the lace instantly. She pinches the fabric between her thumb and index finger. "Is this my bra?"

"No, it's not. I have one like it. I meant to tell you that."

Gillian has not been imagining things. Kristy has in fact been helping herself to Gillian's life: her friends, River Run, whoopie pies, and her bra. Red spots sprout on Gillian's chest and snake up her collarbones and neck.

Gillian doesn't know what else to do but to take her iPhone out of her purse, heave her arm around Kristy, her fingers resting atop the bra strap, and snap a selfie: #dresscheck #luaumantaraystyle #krillian.

47

KRISTY

While Gillian updates her Facebook post, Kristy slaps a hundred-dollar bill on the counter and dashes out of the store. She almost trips as she walks as fast as she can to the food court, clutching the bag with the blue dress that will look much better on her than it will on Gillian. She'll go to the party tonight in Gillian's chosen dress and bra. Kristy's desire for Charlie and whatever belongs to her half-sister grows inside her, like a fetus, every day becoming bigger, hairier, more mature, kicking her in the ribs with the full force of its tiny feet.

A determined Chinese woman in a red apron and an eager smile thrusts a toothpick speared with a piece of poultry at Kristy. "Thank you," Kristy says, and pops the ginger-flavored meat into her mouth. She seats herself at a two-top close to the bathroom where nobody will bother her, because who wants to sit next to a public bathroom while they're eating? Definitely not Gillian. She settles in and arranges her shopping bags around her feet. *Chill the fuck out.* She tries to drink up the frigid mall air, but a heaviness in her chest restricts the flow.

Kristy wants to take flight off that cliff with Charlie more than she wants Beverly to stop her from landing hard and breaking every bone. She touches her phone and calls up Beverly's contact information.

"Call Mona," she instructs Siri instead.

"Hey there, Mona. You have time for me?" Mona, her aesthetician, is normally booked up weeks in advance, but today she has a cancellation, so Kristy lucks out. As she walks quickly to her car, she looks up at the clouds, hoping it won't rain. Her body senses a storm coming. The air is as thick as meatloaf.

Twenty minutes later, she's lying on Mona's table, naked from the waist down, inhaling the scent of lavender and wax. "You're an angel, Mona."

"Don't I have you down for next week?"

"You do, but I have a special event tonight."

Mona raises one of her beautifully shaped eyebrows. "Okay, so what would you like?"

Kristy smiles naughtily. "Brazilian."

Mona whistles. "David's birthday?"

"Hmmm . . ."

Mona studies Kristy. "I'm not going to ask."

"Nothing like that. Just a little midlife crisis."

"Got it." Mona dips her cardboard stick into the pink wax and spreads it over the insides of Kristy's thighs.

Legs splayed, Kristy doesn't flinch when Mona tears the adhesive strip off the tender spots.

"You're one cool customer," Mona remarks. "Let me clean you up." She wipes away the wax with a warm oiled washcloth. Thelma, Kristy's old boss at the nursing home, used to touch Kristy's thighs. Her body betrayed her every time Thelma stroked her with her fat fingers. For a quick second, Thelma made her feel special. In exchange for access to Kristy, Thelma assigned her the easiest ward: no biters, patients who were still with it enough to shit in a toilet, and holiday shifts where she made triple time.

Kristy told David about Thelma once when they were both drunk. He thought it was hot that Kristy had been with women and asked her if she and Gillian were attracted to each other. No way, Kristy said. She couldn't imagine having sex with Gillian. It violated a taboo she could now name.

"Mia?" Kristy calls when she arrives home.

"Up here, Mom," Mia shouts from her bathroom. She's going

to work the luau and is sitting on the lip of the tub, neon-orange nail polish in hand. "Come here and help me." She drapes her calf over Kristy's lap and hands Kristy the bottle. Kristy unscrews the top and drags the brush over her daughter's toenails. After she finishes, she blows on Mia's polish slightly, knowing that this will send her ticklish girl into a fit of laughter, which it does. Mia's laugh always makes Kristy giggle.

"My work here is done," Kristy says. "You look pretty, sweetie." Mia's browned skin glows. Kristy's aware of the source of her daughter's radiance. She sees Mia alternately flirt with and ignore Liam. Kristy hopes he's just a rite-of-passage asshole, as opposed to the kind of man Mia will be drawn to in the future.

"Do you want to drive together, sweetie?"

"Sure. Leave a little before six?" Mia's fanning her toes with her hands.

Kristy leaves Mia to her primping and retreats to her room to stretch out on her bed. She falls into a deep, short slumber, and when she wakes up, perspiration drips down her back. When the heat index climbs over a hundred degrees, the upstairs air-conditioning unit will only cool down to seventy-eight or so. David insisted on installing a window unit, but she always forgets to turn it on. She showers, careful not to make the water too hot, soaping every inch of herself, her hand lingering on her slippery hairlessness. She turns around to face the stream as the water tingles against her bare skin. She only indulges herself for a few seconds before turning off the shower. Standing naked and damp in her bathroom, she dabs drops of Michael Kors Wonderlust behind her ears and knees and on the insides of her wrists. Last Hanukkah, David bought her this perfume because he liked the way it smelled on one of his patients. Kristy likes its spiciness. Too hot to blow-dry her hair, so she slicks it back and fishes around her jewelry box for the pair of big gold hoops she bought last winter in Aruba. Too hot for makeup, so she only applies a coat of lipstick, two coats of mascara, and some concealer under her eyes. Too hot for panties, so she doesn't wear any.

She steps into her new Hawaiian dress, blasts the window unit on, and sits down on the end of the bed to cool off. She hears David and Mia talking. Has David decided to join her? Not possible. He always excuses himself from luau night. But what if he's changed his mind? David would be even more effective than Beverly in protecting her from herself.

He walks into the bedroom in his dress shirt, a suit jacket slung over his arm. He reeks of success. A woman with looks comparable to David's would not be blessed with so much attention from the opposite sex, Kristy thinks as he makes hula-dancer motions.

"Are you coming?" She opens her eyes wide to convey a hopefulness she doesn't feel.

"You'll have more fun without me."

Too much fun. "That's not true."

"I took a shift tonight."

"Okay." She pretends to pout.

"I didn't have much of a choice."

"David, you've got to find someone. You're working around the clock."

"It shouldn't be this hard, but it is." He sits on the bed next to her. "You smell really good. Stay here, and I'll see that you get lei-ed."

They share a long kiss. "All right, Dr. Weinstein. We'll finish this later."

He cups her breast with one hand and hikes her dress up over her knee with the other. She covers his wrist and whispers into his ear, "I've got a surprise for you for later." Liar, liar.

"You ready, Mom?" Mia calls from downstairs.

"Later, David." Kristy pats the mattress. "Right here."

"Let's take my car." Mia dangles her keys. "I'll chauffeur you, and we can reminisce about me learning to drive."

"I can't believe Isaac's going to get his permit soon." Kristy misses Isaac so much it hurts inside.

"Then you won't have to cart anyone around."

Mia's most forthcoming with news about her life, her friends, her schoolwork when she's sitting in the passenger seat and Kristy's eyes are affixed to the road. During the years when Kristy drove Mia to swim practice, she knew all the details about Mia's friends, who'd started dating or menstruating or fighting with their mom. Not so much since Mia started driving.

As soon as Kristy walks out the back door, sweat runs down the backs of her legs. "Let's crank up that A/C," she says, as they get into Mia's brand-new 2012 Honda SUV, a gift from David's parents. Kristy told them that a Civic was plenty of car for a teenager, but they sprang for the SUV because they insisted that it was safer. Kristy wanted Mia to contribute to the monthly payments, but she backed down. She had to pick her battles with David's parents.

"So, what do *you* think of the tiki torches, Mom?" Mia asks.

"I'm fine with them." The people at the pool must be talking, which makes her feel protective of the woman/sister whose husband she's after.

"Look at the sun."

Kristy looks up. "Blazing orange."

"The air is stultifying."

"Nice SAT word."

"The air is as humid as it can possibly be without raining." Mia adjusts her visor.

"It's going to rain, honey. Trust me."

"Did you know that today is the hottest day ever in the D.C. area?"

"I believe it." Kristy detaches her back from the seat.

"Seriously, it was a hundred and four degrees at four o'clock."

"A hundred and four?"

"Yeah, the old record was a hundred and two, set back in 1874." If Kristy wants to know any factoid, she asks Mia.

Mia fans her chest with the collar of her shirt as she pulls into the pool parking lot. The two let themselves out of the car.

"Be good tonight, Mia," Kristy says. She watches her daughter walk toward Liam, who's looking Mia up and down, licking his chops. Creep.

Charlie's standing with his hands on his hips, staring up at the bombastic sun. Kristy approaches him, a raw energy clawing its way out of her gut, not the least bit thwarted by Gillian darting into the frame.

"You two match," Charlie says. "Do you want me to take a photo?"

"Why not?" Kristy stands next to Gillian, and they squint into the sun and smile in a Pavlovian kind of way.

"Do you want me to send you this twins shot, Gil?" Charlie asks.

Not twins, just sisters, Kristy could blurt, but she won't reveal their relationship to Gillian yet, not until she's ready, not until she's done, though she's not sure what "done" means.

"The dress looks terrific on both of you," Charlie says. "I'm going to chat up the band." He walks away.

"New band," Gillian says.

"The dress really does look great on you, Gil." Kristy holds out an olive branch.

"Not compared to you," Gillian says without malice. It's true. Kristy's taller, with narrow hips, and the material would billow if there were any wind. Kristy considers apologizing for the bra, but now isn't the time.

Gillian smiles extra-brightly at Kristy, who mumbles a few polite words before walking away. She feels Charlie glance at her as she heads toward the pool where Shannon, with her good arm, is trying to recover an unlit tiki torch that is lying on the grass. The torch has toppled onto its side. Shannon's cheeks are flushed, but she isn't perspiring. "These things are a little unstable."

Kristy leans her weight on the stick, driving it into the ground. "They're okay, as long as we don't get a strong wind."

"A strong wind would feel fabo right now." Shannon fans herself with her free hand. "This sling is so hot."

"Oh, I'll bet." Kristy pushes the torch further into the ground. "We should be fine. Let's just make sure all of them are planted firmly."

"I'll help." Gillian turns up again, like a piece of gum stuck to the bottom of Kristy's shoe.

"Really, Gillian?" asks Shannon. "That's so nice of you."

"It's the River Run way. We all pitch in."

"You're sure?" Kristy asks. Gillian's acquiescence to the torches signals a weakness that only makes Kristy want to take more from her and then feel sick about it. Rinse and repeat.

"Yes. Hard job to do with one arm." Gillian touches Shannon's sling gently with her finger.

"You got that right." Shannon divvies up the torches between Gillian and Kristy. "You two are the best. I'm going to check in on our grillers." She walks off to the four Weber grills Kristy talked her into lining up near the clubhouse. The catering company has provided sides and three men in Hawaiian shirts to work the grills. Sweat bleeds from her scalp and runs down her neck.

Gillian and Kristy tend to their assigned torches. Kristy is standing near the oak tree, planting the last pole, when Charlie approaches her with two mai tais in hand.

"Do you smell that?" Charlie asks.

"I know. One of our grill masters spilled lighter fluid." Kristy pinches her nose. "It stinks."

"Good thing it's going to rain," Charlie says.

"Yeah, but hopefully not too soon."

"Here." Charlie hands Kristy a mai tai.

Alcohol will only loosen her inhibitions. She should refuse. "Why not?" She accepts the mai tai, and when Charlie touches her wrist while handing her the drink, a current races up her arm.

Just because she takes the cup doesn't mean she has to sip from it. She encircles the cool plastic with her fingers. She's thirsty. She holds the rim against her lips. Just because she takes a sip doesn't mean she has to drink the entire thing. The liquid honeys her tongue.

She follows Charlie to the food line, and they fill their plates with ears of corn and swordfish kebabs fresh off the grill. While the other men look dorky in Hawaiian shirts, the rayon tenting over their bellies, Charlie's shirt fits nicely, and the soft green in the floral pattern brings out his eyes. Kristy puts her hand on Charlie's waist. "You look terrific too." She makes both of them blush.

After Kristy downs her third mai tai, she goes to the bathroom to freshen up and runs into Mia washing her hands.

"Did you hear the band, Mia?" Talking about the band at a party, like complimenting someone on a haircut or neckwear, is that thing people do when they either don't have anything to say to one another or want to avoid a real conversation.

"You're slurring." Mia rips off a paper towel from the dispenser and dries her hands.

"Must be the heat." Kristy has warned Mia numerous times against the demon rum, and now Mia witnesses her downing too many mai tais. "Went right to my head."

"Be careful, Mom," Mia says softly as she walks out of the bathroom. Then she stops and turns around, like soap-opera characters do after a hard talk. "Easy on the mai tais, please."

"Oh, honey. I'm careful, you know that," Kristy calls after her.

"One drink is too many and one hundred is not enough." This inscription is one of the most popular AA sayings featured on Beverly's pewter dog tags, like the one Beverly just gave her, the one she'd shoved into a drawer. Oh, and then there was the talk about cross-addiction, when Beverly told her that addicts rarely have one vice. Kristy isn't a drunk, but she's eyeing a full mai tai one of the partygoers has left in a cubby. She downs it while the owner pees.

48

JUSTIN

Justin volunteers to head-guard at the luau only because he promised Mom he'd keep an eye on things. Torches burn brightly around the pool, and the air fills up with water and a static spark while the middle-aged garage band, which does not suck, plays surf music. The bass player has taken off his shirt, and it's not pretty. And there's fucking Liam, yukking it up with Mia, who's loitering around his chair. Come on, Mia. He shouldn't have to nag her to report to her post. He walks over to them.

"My mom's wasted." Mia rolls her eyes.

"They all are, which is why we need to do our jobs." Justin gives Liam the stink eye.

Liam glares back. "Can you not be a buzzkill pussy for one night, Cloud?"

"Maybe one night, but not this night."

"Whatever." Liam returns his attention to the pool.

Justin looks at Mia. "You good?"

"Yeah, I'm good." Mia glances over at the stage and the band and then averts her eyes. Aunt Kristy's chatting up the lead singer, throwing her head back with a phony giggle.

"Jesus Christ." Justin turns his back on Mia and returns to his chair, smack dab in the middle of the pool deck, where he can see everything.

49

GILLIAN

Shannon positions herself next to one of the tiki torches, microphone in her good hand, orchid in her hair, firelight on her face, and belts out one of the best versions of "The Rose" Gillian has ever heard. Gillian has traveled far enough back into Shannon's Facebook feed to find footage of her starring in a community theater performance of *Hello, Dolly!* Shannon's no Barbra Streisand or Bette Midler, but she can sing.

One of the dads is prodding Charlie to get up on the stage and play a song. Charlie shakes his head bashfully, but he did spend the entire spring honing his guitar chops. He's ready.

"Char-lie. Char-lie. Char-lie," Kristy chants and claps her hands, and soon a circle of people clad in their Hawaiian garb and leis join in until the sound swells into a roar. Gillian shuts her eyes. *Mis-ter. Nor-ton.* She needs to get away from this noise. She needs some cold water. She makes her way to a patch of grass adjacent to the diving board, where buckets have been filled with bottled water and ice. The wind's picking up, and another tiki torch starts to sway. "I've got this," Gillian calls to no one in particular, and runs to the torch. A shard of glass refracts a sliver of light. After she fixes the torch, she picks up the glass and studies the blue letters that spell "odka."

Gillian stands still on the spot where Sebastian Norton discarded the beer bottles she edited out of the frame of the famous photo.

The chanting stops, and Charlie's singing "The Gambler." Gillian dumps the glass into the trash can and forgets all about the water bottles as she turns her attention to him. He's sitting on a stool, a guitar strap around his neck, the small muscles in his forearms fluttering as he strums. Kenny Rogers and Charlie sing in the same register, and Charlie knows all the words to this tired song. It works. Just before he takes his bow, Gillian whips her phone out of the pocket of her dress and captures her husband waving at his minions.

They lock eyes, and she mouths, "You were fantastic."

He smiles back, and all is forgiven.

50

KRISTY

The band can't match Charlie's or Shannon's performances, and their music becomes a noise to shout over while everyone continues to drink and sweat. Kristy's the first to jump into the pool, lit only by the tiki torches and the underwater lights. She floats on her back, her dress ballooning out around her as she stares up at the starless sky.

Soon the shallow end fills with women in their dresses or the bathing suits they're wearing underneath or some combination of both. Kristy dunks her head back into the pool, and ripples wash up against her newly waxed skin. The water, tepid as it is, feels divine. She dives under and escapes the sounds of the swimmers splashing and squealing and the band's Beach Boys medley. She opens her eyes and, through the wavy blur, makes out Charlie's shorts, his legs within her grasp. She swims closer to him. When her lungs feel as though they'll burst, she surfaces. His hand grazes her breast during her ascent from the water. It can't be an accident. Hot damn.

She hopes Mia hasn't seen anything. Mia's standing by the diving board chewing her lip while Liam and Justin sit in their chairs, watching the adults swim. A tipsy Todd Barry, his bare chest draped with several leis, bumps into one of the torches and almost knocks it over.

Gillian, the only adult still dry, marches over to Shannon, who is sitting on the edge of the pool, her toes dangling in the water. Strands of hair have escaped from Gillian's ponytail and are plastered to the side of her head as she points to the torches and Todd. Shannon looks at her blankly.

Gillian huffs over to the guard station and snatches the five-gallon Deer Park jug from its dispenser. The container's huge, and she waddles around the pool, holding it to her belly, only stopping to heave it into the air and douse every torch.

Kristy floats over to Shannon. "What's going on?"

Shannon puts down her cup. "She wants to avoid a situation." She gets up to help Gillian.

Kristy steals a gulp of Shannon's drink. "Please, one clumsy move isn't going to create any situation."

Charlie gets out of the pool and helps Gillian extinguish the last few torches. Kristy hopes they'll start quarreling so Gillian will go home. They won't. Gillian would never make a scene in public. Even now, her tantrum disguises itself as yet another act of service to River Run. *Stay, Charlie, just stay.*

Charlie allows Gillian to lead him out of the pool. Kristy suspected that Gillian would go home early, but she hadn't calculated that Charlie would go with her. Sick with disappointment, she finishes Shannon's drink.

51

GILLIAN

"You can stay," Gillian says to Charlie as they walk to the car. "I know you want to." She feels like ripping his beautiful bald head off his shoulders and "shitting down his neck," as her father would say in a moment of anger. She's sick and tired of his popularity and ever-expanding reign over the pool. Why can't he go back to being out of shape and unhappy?

"I'm fine leaving." His patience makes her feel more pathetic.

"No, you're not, but give me the keys. You're not driving."

"Gillian, you're too angry."

Gillian curls her lip in disgust. "You're too drunk."

Charlie relents and hands her the keys.

Gillian starts the car and backs out of the lot slowly. "Well, I'm not going to say I told you so."

Charlie looks at her.

"About the torches, the stupidity and danger of the whole idea."

Charlie says nothing.

"I know you think I'm overreacting, but I'm not."

"Let's let this go, Gil."

"Do you think I was going to leave those torches to the discretion of a bunch of drunk people?"

"Do you ever leave anything to the discretion of anyone?"

"Nice, Charlie."

They say nothing more until she reaches their driveway and hits the brakes too hard, sending both of them lurching forward.

"What I said before." Charlie furrows his brow. "That wasn't kind. I'm sorry."

"Charlie, I'm not going to let this go. And I'm not going to let the pool go. You ride in here on your white horse, and you're a magician with the kids, and the parents and coaching staff love you, and we're even winning, like who the heck ever cared about winning? We're in Division 14! It's never been about winning." Gillian feels like *she's* the drunk one, not Kristy, who was strutting around guzzling mai tais.

Charlie puts his hand on her leg. "I know it's been a hard start to the summer."

"Not for you," she snaps.

He strokes her damp skin.

She removes his hand. "Or Kristy, who was in rare form tonight."

"Everyone was drinking, Gil."

"Kristy doesn't drink hard liquor," she spits. "Ever."

"It's hot."

"You don't get it. My Kristy doesn't drink mai tais or steal bras or lie to me or blow me off like a junior-high-schooler or take your side on everything."

"Come on. You think she stole your bra?"

"I know so. She was wearing it."

"Let's go inside. It's baking out here."

"I'm not finished. My Kristy returns my texts and calls."

"You're not rational." Charlie opens the door and gets out of the car.

"Go ahead, just give me a minute."

Gillian leans her warm arms over the steering wheel and stares at the white-painted colonial, such a close replica of her childhood home that Patrick makes every excuse not to visit. On nights when the Norton house was too hot, Gillian and Patrick filled glasses with ice cubes and sucked on them outside on the screened-in porch, and on cold nights when Sebastian was drinking, they snuck out to the porch and huddled together for warmth. The Cloud house doesn't have a screened-in porch.

She takes her phone from her purse and posts a picture of Charlie holding his mic, crooning on about a train bound for nowhere. She uploads the caption, typing furiously with one hand. "One of the hottest nights in D.C. history. The hubby giving Kenny Rogers a run for his money." #smokin'.

She walks into the house, the rush of an air-conditioned breeze kissing her flesh. She climbs the steps to the upstairs bathroom and stands next to Charlie, who's naked in front of the mirror, a dry pair of boxers and shorts in his hand. She needs a night apart from Charlie, a little time to regain her bearings. Mascara rings her eyes, but she doesn't bother to remove either the dark smudges or her dress before crawling into Sebby's bed and passing out.

52

JUSTIN

Everything gets real quiet after Mom and Dad leave, and people empty out one by one. Justin hopes they're sober enough to drive, but really what's he going to do about it if they aren't? Take away their keys? He wishes he could. And holy fuck, it's hot.

When Mr. O'Leary asks Justin to help break down the tables and return them to the church, he jumps at the request. Get him out of here so he can breathe for a few seconds.

Mr. O'Leary's fielding a work call from some guy in Istanbul, so Justin doesn't have to make small talk with him during the ride or the twenty minutes he sits in the car waiting for the call to end. "Thanks for your patience, Justin," Mr. O'Leary says after he hangs up. Justin feels as if he's watching himself unload the tables from Mr. O'Leary's SUV, watching himself watch Mr. O'Leary struggle with the key to the church basement door, watching them carry the tables down the steps and stack them against the wall.

The pool's empty now, the drunks have gone home, but that only solves part of the problem. Something bigger is brewing with Mom and Dad, and it's making him feel sick.

53

CHARLIE

While Gillian sleeps in Sebby's bed, Charlie watches a DVD of *Breaking Bad*, trying to quell his fierce urge to drive right back to the pool. Gillian won't even know he's gone. He can think of nothing else but finding his way back to Kristy Weinstein's breasts.

Halfway through the second episode, he convinces himself that he should return to the pool to help the guards clean up and manage any drunk adults. He shouldn't have bailed on Justin, either.

When he arrives at River Run, the band members are loading amps and instruments into their respective cars.

"You sounded great, guys," he says.

The lead guitar player salutes him. "Not a bad Kenny Rogers, man."

Three lone cars are parked in the lot: Justin's, Mia's, and Shannon's. Damn. He missed Kristy. Mia and Justin are probably helping Shannon clean up. It's dark, close to ten thirty, so he can't see much without the torches. He hears voices and then recognizes Kristy's laugh. The sound fills him up, from his toes to the top of his head. Kristy, Shannon, and Mia are on the far side of the pool, picking up cups and plates and stuffing them into trash bags. Of course Liam is nowhere to be found. Prick.

"Hope I'm not too late to help," Charlie says.

Shannon speaks first. "Is Gillian furious with us?"

"She'll be fine," Charlie assures them. "Where's Justin?"

"With my husband. They're returning the tables to our church."

"And Liam?" Charlie can't help asking. He doesn't want to see Mia get hurt.

"He met up with his college friends tonight," Mia says, so softly Charlie can barely hear her.

Charlie looks at Mia and Kristy. "You guys go. I'll finish up."

"No, Charlie, I'll do it," Shannon says, but she's holding her bad arm, and Charlie can see that she's uncomfortable and exhausted.

Kristy bites her lip hard. "Shannon, you need to give that arm a rest. I'll help. How about you drive Mia home and call it a night?"

Mia gives Kristy a look. "Mom, you're going to drive?"

"You're a worrywart. I'll be fine by the time we finish cleaning up," Kristy says.

This isn't cool. Charlie knows that Kristy and Gillian made a rule that if their respective kids consume even one drink, the car is off limits. Kristy shouldn't be driving tonight, but he says nothing.

"Why don't you have Charlie drive you home?" says Shannon, the only adult in the room.

"Will do." The idea thrills Charlie, who can't wait another second to be alone with Kristy. He feels like he did when he first met Gillian, when he tried to send telepathic messages to her friend Henrietta to leave the bar so he could have Gillian to himself. He'd just had another one of his excruciating dinners with his father, and Gillian had made him forget all about what a loser he was in his dad's eyes.

Shannon turns to Mia. "Let's get you home. It's awful out here. Even in the water."

Kristy kisses Mia. "Write a note for Dad, he should be home soon. I won't be late."

The mention of David gives Charlie pause and maybe even an ugly glee, but not for long. "Let's get the rest of this stuff," he says.

Kristy and Charlie busy themselves stuffing plastic bags with party trash and an occasional abandoned cob of corn. He does not look in Kristy's direction once during the ten minutes it takes them to finish cleaning up. They don't touch, either.

"We should pick these up." Kristy points to the long train of plastic green leis leading from the grill to the clubhouse. "They really stink of lighter fluid."

"In a sec." He stares up at the moon, takes off his shirt and shorts.

Kristy steps over the string of leis and walks toward the water. "I suppose we can clean these up later."

Charlie jumps into the pool in his boxers. The water feels milky. He moves his torso like a dolphin. In an effort to crush his desire for Kristy, he reminds himself of how he's always wanted Gillian, to devour her, to bite into her neck and feast on her relentlessly cheerful marrow.

He dives under the water, and when he surfaces Kristy's sitting on the ledge, her calves submerged in the pool. He yanks playfully on one of her toes. "Come on in."

She lowers her body into the pool, barely making a crease in the water. She tilts her neck back, strands of hair encircling her head like a crown. They tread water, inches apart but still not touching. The corner of her dress caresses his belly.

"And to think you used to dread seeing me," Kristy teases. As close as Kristy and Gillian are, the two families rarely got together, and when they did, Charlie counted the seconds until the gathering was over.

"It was more David." David, aka God, made Charlie feel the same way he felt about himself at the firm, that maybe his dad had been right. He was nothing.

He is Charlie Cloud, dammit.

"Be back in a minute." He hoists himself out of the pool and walks over to the shed, where Shannon stored the tiki torches Gillian had so dramatically doused with that water jug. A naughty thrill seizes him as he pinches a bamboo pole. He plucks a box of matches from the shelf and exits the shed. He plants the torch next to Gillian's oak, then retrieves two more and places them next to the barbecues. He lights them all. This pool doesn't belong to Gillian. *He* doesn't belong to Gillian. He winks as he walks back to Kristy.

"You're a little crazy tonight, Charlie," she says.

"Tonight we're all a little crazy." He jumps back into the pool and swims toward the shallow end. Kristy takes hold of his ankles and kicks her feet.

"I've always wanted to do that," she says.

"Do what?"

"Um, swim with a partner."

They're standing in three feet of water, facing each other. She's shorter than Charlie, but only by an inch or two. He reaches around her, lets his hands wander down her back before unhooking her bra. He's so sick of hearing about this fucking bra. She wriggles out of the garment so that it floats between them, cups down, the straps like arms. Her dress gathers around her waist, and he reaches under the balloon of fabric and runs his palms up her muscular thighs. She throws her head back as his hands rove upward. Jesus, she isn't wearing panties. And she's had a Brazilian. He strokes her bare skin and takes her cheeks in his hands for a few seconds before he peels off her dress and kisses her. She tastes like alcohol and pineapple. Sweet, but with a graininess to her, and something else too, something familiar.

He does none of the things he's fantasized about doing to her. He can't wait to get inside her. She climbs on his back and wraps her arms around his neck as he walks her over to the stairs on the side of the pool. He sits on the ledge, and she yanks down his boxers and straddles him. He kisses her on the mouth and shoulder, then takes one of her nipples in his mouth and sucks, almost biting her. She moans. They are fucking something out of their system, and when they're done, they sit side by side, naked and stupefied.

54

JUSTIN

"I think there's some mean weather brewing," Mr. O'Leary says as he nears the River Run lot. "Get home quickly, okay?"

Justin feels a storm in the air too, so he thanks Mr. O'Leary and walks briskly to his car. What is Mia's Honda still doing here? He looks toward the pool, where light flutters from tiki torches. Liam must have come back to be with Mia. Idiots.

Out of nowhere, a gust of wind like Justin's never felt before in his life nearly knocks him sideways. A loud pop sounds in the distance. The pool lights go out. What the fuck? The wind's too strong for these little fires. He breaks into a jog, intending to extinguish the torches and tell Mia and Liam to go home. By the time he reaches the fence, an even fiercer wind howls. This must be a tornado. He will die right here, right now. The gale rocks the big oak tree and sends the attached swing twirling wildly in the sky. Pool chairs and chaise lounges cartwheel across the deck. A man springs up from the side of the pool, pulling up his boxers in one fluid motion. Fucking Liam. Justin looks more closely. The man is bald.

Dad?

The woman struggling to yank on her dress is not Mia. He recognizes the pattern from earlier in the evening. Mom? Did they make up?

This woman is not his mother. The woman covering herself is Aunt Kristy. Oh no, no, no.

Dad runs over to the tiki torches. He's too late. The wind thrusts two of them into the air. Thick orange ribbons stripe the black sky. As soon as the flames land on the leis, they explode into an orange ball. Fuck. The lighter fluid. Justin gasps. He told Liam to hose down that patch of grass, but he should have taken care of it himself.

Before Justin can make a move, the turbulent air lets out a giant yelp and yanks the enormous tree from its roots, sending it crashing down to the ground with a boom, knocking over the third torch. A fresh strand of leis ferries the fire to the clubhouse. It's happening so fast, and so very slowly.

"Dad!" Justin screams. "Get away from the fire."

"Get Kristy out of here," Dad yells back.

She stands frozen at the edge of the pool watching it all, her dress on backwards. Justin runs to her. He can only think about getting her out of the fire's way as fast as he can, so he picks her up and swings her wet body over his shoulder in a fireman's carry. The broken branches kindle the lei fire, and soon the entire side of the clubhouse erupts into flames.

"Put me down, Justin." She turns around and screams, "Charlie!"

Dad sprints toward them, flames in his wake, his eyes filled with terror. And shame.

Justin releases Aunt Kristy carefully, and the three of them puff hard while Justin dials 911 on his cell phone. He can barely touch the keypad his fingers are shaking so badly. By the time he finishes dialing, the wind has passed and there's rain. Sheets of it, but not enough to put out the flames licking the clubhouse.

"You should put yourselves together," Justin says to Dad and Aunt Kristy with a mixture of sternness and shock.

She adjusts her dress while Dad scurries to his car and fishes out a pair of gym shorts and a "Go Manta Rays" T-shirt.

The three of them stand side by side, drenched, watching the ravenous fire wolf down the River Run clubhouse.

55

CHARLIE

Charlie's the first of the three to move. He runs toward the clubhouse. There must be a fire extinguisher. He can put out the fire by himself. He can save the photos of Gillian's family. He can rescue the piece of Gillian he's been destroying all summer. He's made her irrelevant. Obsolete.

He can redeem himself to his son. Who knows how much Justin saw? Justin follows him and grabs his elbow. "No, Dad," he says firmly. "The fire truck will be here any second." He puts his arm around Charlie, and Charlie melts into Justin's narrow chest.

56

KRISTY

The parking-lot lights are out. No power. Off in the distance, sirens blare. Smoke invades Kristy's lungs as she watches Justin cradle his father. She's played the perfect Eve, luring Charlie to bite the forbidden fruit, destroying Gillian's Garden of Eden. Justin will never look at his father in the same way. Walls are smoldering, walls decorated with photos of Gillian's delicate mother, of their handsome father swan-diving into the pool.

She's done it. No more pool house, no more family legacy for Gillian. No more legacy at all. Charlie turns around to face her, but he can't look her in the eye. She's seen this look before. She revolts him. He's done with her.

The rain has stopped. The sirens near, and soon two fire trucks and an ambulance are pulling into the River Run parking lot. The flashing red lights hurt Kristy's eyes. A young EMT in her early twenties with long bangs and thick hands approaches her.

"You okay?"

Kristy nods dumbly. "I think so."

A firefighter joins them. "Can you tell me what happened?" he asks as his crew files out of the truck and detaches fat black hoses. His voice is kind.

"We were cleaning up from our annual luau, and it was dark so we used the tiki torches for light, and then the storm blew in, and . . ." Kristy is speaking loudly so that Justin and Charlie, who are within earshot, can hear the story she's weaving. Neither can lie for shit.

"Was anyone else here besides you three?"

Kristy whispers so that Charlie and Justin cannot hear her. "My sister lost everything."

"Is she here?"

Kristy shakes her head no. The firefighter has warm eyes and thick eyebrows, just like Beverly. "What's your name?"

"Paul."

Paul. That's a good, solid name.

"What do you mean about your sister? Is she here?"

"She's home."

"How did she lose everything?"

"I took it," Kristy says as matter-of-factly as she would say "Pass the salt" or "I'll have that last piece of chicken."

57

JUSTIN

Justin releases Dad from his embrace, but he stays close, unsure if his father is going to try something stupidly heroic again.

"Those tiki torches are nothing but trouble," the firefighter says after he finishes talking to Aunt Kristy.

Mom was right about the torches. It's almost as if she had a premonition that this was all going to burn down. It physically aches to think about the prideful smile Mom flashed when people asked her about the old photos of her family hanging on the wall. And it hurts even more to think about how Dad and Aunt Kristy betrayed her. Not even Mom, the best denier he knows, can pretend that this isn't going to hurt.

58

CHARLIE

Charlie, Kristy, and Justin do not leave the parking lot until the fire has been extinguished.

"Can we salvage anything in there?" Charlie asks one of the firefighters.

"I'm guessing no."

Charlie grimaces. How will he ever tell Gillian? "Can we get back into the pool?"

"Not a chance." The fireman flicks on his enormous flashlight; a power surge has knocked out the weak auxiliary lights encircling River Run. The air is damp and saturated with smoke. The fireman shines his light on one of the tiki torches on the ground.

"It's not like we weren't warned," Charlie says to no one in particular.

"Let's take a look." The fireman directs a circle of light toward the tree.

Charlie adjusts his eyes. "Oh, sweet Jesus."

The enormous oak now bridges the width of the pool, while the swing does the dead-man float in the shallow end.

Kristy motions toward the tree. And Gillian's beloved swing. "Gillian was supposed to call the arborist," she snarls.

"I don't think we can blame Gillian for this, Kristy," Charlie snaps. She's one selfish human being.

"We need to get hold of Karl." Justin texts the pool manager furiously.

"Good call." Charlie can't look at his son.

"He must have lost his cell service." Justin still isn't looking up from his phone.

"Charlie."

He flinches. "What?" He wants her to go away.

"I forgot something in there," Kristy says quietly.

"I have it." He walks to his car and retrieves the bra, which he had wrapped in a towel. She follows him, of course.

"Thank you." Her voice shakes.

"Don't mention it." *And get the fuck out of here.*

59

KRISTY

The street is pitch-black when Kristy gets home. The asphalt warms her feet as she walks up the driveway, organizing her dress on the way.

The house is too quiet. No hum of the air-conditioning or refrigerator. She pulls out her iPhone and jumps on the Channel 9 website. Derecho. They've already given it a name. The perfect and rare combination of humidity and today's astronomically high temperature conspired to create this explosion of weather. A hundred thousand homes in Northern Virginia without power. This is going to be a long outage.

She walks downstairs to the unfinished part of the basement, to the circuit breaker, and flips on the generator switch. Then she showers in the guest bathroom, lathering herself, washing away any remnant of Charlie. After she finishes, she puts on a terrycloth robe she bought for visitors last Black Friday.

Noises are coming from the guest room. What the hell?

"Mia?" Kristy opens the door just enough to make out Liam's boxy head. "Oh, great." She shuts the door.

Mia emerges, disheveled.

"Jesus, Mia."

"He was going to leave and then the storm hit."

"He can stay."

"Really?" Mia asks.

"It's not safe out there." Kristy cinches the belt on her robe and climbs the steps to her room.

Predictably, David's sound asleep in their bed. He's dozed through the luau, Gillian's hasty exit from the party, his wife fucking her brother-in-law, the historic event called a derecho, a fire, and his daughter having sex with Liam. Oh, to be David. Oh, to expend his free thoughts on golf games with his buddies, reunions with his med-school friends, and the occasional tiff with his intrusive mother, who is out of his hair for the bulk of the summer. Now Israel feels like a safer place than their community pool. Because it is.

She changes into a camisole and a matching pair of pajama shorts, combs her hair, and climbs into bed with her husband. David's skin is cool. What will she tell Mia and David about what happened at the pool? She needs to call Charlie and ask him. No, she just needs to call Charlie.

60

JUSTIN

Justin's hands are still trembling when he starts the engine. He blasts the air-conditioning and drives away from the pool, his father, Aunt Kristy, the carnage of it all. The streets are littered with enormous branches. Downed trees. No stoplights. He doesn't care. He aches for the slush. He drives to three 7-Elevens before he finds one with power. Hand on the udder, purple ice pouring into his cup, he finally exhales.

61

CHARLIE

No power. The house is pitch-black without the small lights—green from the microwave clock, blue from the Wi-Fi router, red from the smoke detector—that shine twenty-four hours a day and whose existence you forget until an outage shuts them down. He showers quickly in the dark, trying to conserve the remains of their hot water. After he finishes, he wads up his smoke-drenched clothes, stuffs them into the bathroom trash-can liner, and throws the whole mess into the garage.

He opens the door to Sebby's room. Gillian lies on her side in her party dress, Sebby's comforter bunched at her feet, her body covered by a thin white sheet. He tiptoes to the bed and peers down at her.

"I'm so glad you're safe," she says. She puts her hand on his leg. "That was some storm."

He sits down on the side of the mattress, as he did when Sebby used to suffer nightmares. "Which one?"

She rolls over and rests her weight on her elbows. "What do you mean?"

He reaches up and digs his nails into his bare scalp. "Mine. Ours. Mother Nature's."

"I'm sorry. I was being horrible." She grabs her phone from Sebby's nightstand.

Charlie puts his hand over hers. "Please, not now. No Facebook."

"Did you think I was going to post something?" she laughs.

"Kind of."

"No, I'm going to check weather.com to find out what's going on. I heard sirens."

"Please put your phone down, Gillian."

"Just a sec." Her eyes scan the screen. "Oh, my God. Did you read about this storm? It was a land hurricane!"

"Put down your phone." Charlie presses his thumb to his twitching neck vein.

"Hundred-mile-an-hour gusts. I'm not surprised. The windows rattled like chattering teeth."

Charlie waits for her to wrap her arms around the enormity of the storm, knowing that she never will.

"That's what woke me up. The winds."

"Your phone," he says as he would to one of his coaches sneaking a Snapchat during practice. "Put it down."

"You're scaring me." She lets it drop on the bed. "What?"

Charlie gropes for words. Should he stick with the story Kristy told the firefighter? Was that their official line? Or should he tell her the truth? Would they ever recover? She's ready to forgive him right now. They could go on and pretend none of this happened. Gillian is good at that. He'll pull back from the pool and pay more attention to her. He'll find a real job, pay off the growing debt he's been ignoring.

The words find him. "There was a fire at the pool."

She bolts up straight. "Is Justin okay? Was anyone hurt?"

"Justin"—he swallows—"and everyone else is fine."

"Where is he?"

"He's on his way home," Charlie lies. One problem at a time.

"What happened?" The question sounds like a statement.

"One of the tiki torches blew over." He tells her about the clubhouse and the oak tree and the swing.

She interrupts him. "Had to be Liam who relit the torches."

Cheese weenie that he is, he doesn't correct her. He'll figure a way out of this. He has to, or he'll lose everything. He probably already has.

She draws her knees to her chest while he speaks, and when he's done, she jumps out of bed and returns to their room. He trails her, tripping over a sandal she's left on Sebby's floor. She shoves her foot into the other sandal and brushes by him on her way down the stairs, one foot bare. He follows her. "Come on, Gil. It's late."

She ignores him as she walks out the front door, down the steps, and into the van, which he's parked in the driveway since their electric garage door likely won't be working for days. She moves with the same urgency as when she got the call that May was in the hospital with a collapsed lung. Charlie takes the passenger seat, and she doesn't ask him any more questions as they drive the few blocks to the pool. The firemen have finally left by the time their car bumps down the road to the lot, swerving twice to avoid hitting big branches. He isn't even sure she's aware that he's sitting beside her until they reach the parking lot, for his third time tonight. In her one sandal, Gillian runs toward the gate to the pool, Charlie at her heels.

"Gillian, it's not a good idea to go inside."

She steps over the branches, under the yellow tape, and through the gate, toward the precise spot where he and Kristy fucked.

62

GILLIAN

Gillian examines the massive fallen tree. This is her fault. She should have called the arborist, but she didn't because she didn't want him to tell her that the tree could topple.

Charlie takes her hand. "Gillian, we can't be near the pool. It's dangerous."

"I want the swing. Now."

"We can rescue it tomorrow, in the daylight," he assures her.

She walks toward the water. "No, tonight."

After twenty-two years of marriage, her husband must know that if he doesn't try to retrieve her beloved relic, she'll walk right into that pool after it. "Okay, okay. You sit here, and I'll get you the swing."

He picks up a long branch and positions himself on the ledge of the pool. He tries to thread the rope with the branch. It's too dark without the interior pool lights. With each failed attempt, he jabs at the swing harder. Finally he manages to snag the rope, lure the swing toward him with the branch, and hoist it from the pool. He turns to Gillian, who is facing him with her arms outstretched. When he presents her with the swing, she almost cries.

"Thank you." She cradles the wood plank in her arms.

He takes her hand and leads her to the gate. "Come on, let's get out of here."

She drops his hand, and he tails her as she walks to the van. She opens the back and settles the swing down as she would a baby. She turns to him. "Give me a minute, Charlie."

After Gillian lays the swing to rest, she moves on to the next task. She extracts her large backup flashlight from the emergency bin where they store a first-aid kit, bottled water, Clif Bars, and a spare blanket. Charlie never worries about such things; leave Gillian to do the fretting and planning. Nobody has paid attention to her efforts to keep them safe. Look at the stink she had to raise about those torches and the placement of the grills. She knew they were a stupid idea. Well, she's having the last laugh. Ha-ha.

How could she have slept through the storm? It looks as though a tornado hit. She shines her light on the charred clubhouse.

"Gillian, don't go in there." Charlie walks toward her.

She ignores him and makes a beeline for the clubhouse.

"Then here." He tosses her one of his flip-flops. "There's probably broken glass all over."

In one flip-flop and one sandal, Gillian shuffles toward the pool house, ducking under the hazard tape the fire team strung across the entryway. The air is so hot and smoky, she starts to wheeze. The walls and lifeguard check-in table are blanketed in a heavy layer of silky black soot. She faces the old photo wall and closes her eyes. She knows all the images by heart. Her bare toes are covered in black. She plucks photos from the wreckage. She won't leave until she finds the original picture she took of her father's famous swan dive, which makes her hurt and yearn and celebrate the innocence of the pool, as sweet as the ice cream from the truck that still arrives promptly at five, playing the same tired song. "Do your ears hang low? Do they wobble to and fro?" she sings to herself.

The photo of her father is intact, the only damage a crack in the glass. She studies it closely, remembering more things she edited out:

her mother biting her cuticles to shreds, Patrick covering his eyes with his Frisbee. She sings louder. "Can you tie 'em in a knot, can you tie 'em in a bow?"

Gillian and Patrick once shared a code of silence. They never spoke of the vodka bottles in the trash or the nights their father didn't come home or the bloated dead Sebastian the police found near a culvert in McLean, less than five miles from their house. May pawned her wedding diamond and the post-affair apology jewelry from Sebastian to hush the student teacher, a petite brunette like all the others, May included, who had jumped out of his precious Mustang while it was flying around the curves of Georgetown Pike. May also took care of the hospital bill for the young woman's shoulder surgery and sent her a bouquet of stargazer lilies, and the woman felt so sorry for the perfectly imperfect Norton family that she wrote May a condolence note.

Gillian and Patrick would still be close today if he hadn't started dissecting their childhood. Analysis paralysis. Life is meant to be lived.

"One more little look," she says aloud in the tone that soothes her clients. "Then you put it away someplace safe." She walks back into the hot night air, climbs into the van, and wraps the framed photo in the blanket, wedging it between the swing and the emergency bin, comfortably out of reach. "All safe," she whispers to herself.

63

KRISTY

Kristy does not sleep the night of the derecho. She counts David's breaths in multiples of ten while replaying her sex with Charlie. She's certain that he's never had sex with Gillian with such violence, and this gives her more pleasure than if she'd orgasmed. Maybe she should post something on Facebook. "Road rash. Ouchie, ouchie." #hotderechosex. She's a monster.

Oh, shit, and then there's Justin. She and Charlie have scarred him. She feels ill. And Mia and Liam downstairs. David would be furious that she let Liam spend the night. She has to handle this properly. She doesn't want to give Mia any hang-ups about sex. Doesn't want to make her feel dirty. Flo had never wanted Kristy to be too anything. Too sexy. Too smart. Too fancy. Too pretty. Too visible. She made it easy for Kristy to walk away from home and disappear into David's family as if she were never a Frick at all.

All spinning thoughts, though, lead back to Charlie. How about if she calls him up and they make a deal? They can have sex four more times and then quit each other. Four. That's it. Fantasizing about four more times with Charlie is like sipping the first glass of wine or dropping the first f-bomb after Lent. She can't stop, doesn't want to. She can make him choose her. For God's sake, hasn't Gillian been given enough?

David wakes up to the buzz of their noisy and expensive generator.

"Did the A/C break?" He puts on his glasses and glances at the blank clock on the television. "No power?"

"There was a huge storm last night," Kristy says. "They're calling it a derecho."

"During the luau?"

"No. It hit afterwards."

Kristy repeats the story she gave the fireman, explaining how the storm blew in while she and Charlie were cleaning up from the party. She describes the tiki torches and the leis and the clubhouse and the oak tree and the swing.

He listens with his doctor's attentiveness. "Thank God nobody got hurt."

She allows herself to fall into him.

"Wow," he murmurs into her hair. "The swing? The clubhouse?"

Kristy shakes her head yes, her hair brushing against his chest.

"How's Gillian?"

"I don't know."

"You mean she wasn't there?"

"It's a long story. And there's something else I have to tell you."

"What else could there possibly be?"

Mia interrupts them by knocking on their bedroom door.

"Come in," David calls.

Kristy looks at Mia, and the expression on her daughter's face signals that Liam has gone home. Well, at least this is one thing she won't have to tell David, just yet.

"Some night, huh, Mi?" David asks.

"I can't believe you slept through the whole thing, Dad."

Kristy pats his shoulder. "He sure did."

"Mom and I didn't," Mia says.

"You two should have woken me up." He extends his free arm to Mia. "Come here."

Kristy brushes her lips against his cheek.

He picks up his phone and checks the Channel 9 website. "Deh-RAY-choh. That's how you say it." He reads on. "Eighty-mile-an-hour winds!!"

"I read a hundred," Mia chimes in.

"Yes, they were strong." Kristy shivers at the image of the tree falling into the pool.

David holds her tighter and continues reading. "This baby traveled across the country, all the way from the Midwest."

"OMG." Mia picks her head up from her own phone. "Epic."

"Ladies, this is the definition of a perfect storm." David reads on about the science of the storm, the precision with which the variables have to collude to make a derecho hit.

Perfect storm indeed. Had Charlie been out the night the committee met to pick a new coach or had the pipe not burst in her father's basement or . . . she never would have relapsed. She'd still be Krillian.

"I'm so glad you two are okay." David's voice oozes the love and concern he gives freely to his needy patients; he can parcel out a little more for his family.

"Thousands of homes have lost power, like all over the place," Mia reports.

"Power outages are the perfect antidote for the sentiment that life is passing you by too quickly." David repeats one of his favorite sayings.

"We won't feel it," Kristy says. She and David debated the extravagance of a generator, but he reminded her that as an obstetrician he needs a place where he can sleep and eat, or he'll be no good to his patients. Babies' lives are at stake.

"Let's go and take a look." David releases Mia and Kristy and swings his legs over the side of the bed. They all dress and meet up outside. It's six o'clock in the morning and the thermometer reads ninety degrees.

"It's going to hit a hundred again today," Mia announces.

"Heat wave from hell." Kristy fans herself.

"What a mess." David takes in the fat branches strewn all over the front lawn, their mailbox ripped from the ground, and the street littered with tree limbs and trash blown from bins and bags: empty tampon boxes, yogurt containers, banana peels. Across the street, a sixty-foot pine tree was cleaved right down the middle, one of the halves crushing their neighbor's Subaru.

Mia's car is parked horizontally in the driveway. David looks at her. "Mia, were you drinking last night?"

Kristy butts in. "No, that was me." She had been willing to dismiss the no-drinking-and-driving, not-even-a-drop, no-exceptions-ever edict she's been beating into her kids' heads since they were old enough to say the word "car."

"Good modeling," David admonishes her.

"I'm so sorry," she murmurs, knowing damned well that she'd make the exact same decision again if it meant seeing Charlie alone.

"Wait, breaking news." Mia studies her phone. "I just got a text from Coach Charlie. Today's meet is off."

Kristy flinches at the mention of Charlie's name.

"Oh, here's another one from Karl." Mia reads the message. "Until further notice, River Run is closed for business, no power, no pump."

"Who is Karl?" asks David.

"The pool manager," Kristy and Mia answer in unison.

"All lifeguards and coaches need to report to River Run to help clean up as soon as possible," Mia reads on. "That's me."

"Okay, let's call Hanson's people to get this lawn taken care of." David heads back toward the house, stepping over the windblown garbage.

Kristy collects the refuse and stuffs it into their trash bin. After all these years, she still can't get used to the idea of calling other people to do anything. Travis mows lawns, cleans up debris, and fixes broken mailboxes, and Kristy's cousins are the kind of people David calls to tend to their house. They work for gas stations and lawn services and live in duplexes and townhouses in zip codes David has never heard of.

When she goes inside, David is preparing coffee with his generator-powered espresso machine. For once, he isn't on call. "We're out of milk."

"We have some in the basement fridge." She flies downstairs to the guest room and yanks the sheets off the bed. The room smells like sex. She doesn't want to think about it. She retrieves a fresh set of sheets from the linen closet and makes the bed. Mid-hospital corner, she spots a wad of slimy clear plastic. She picks it up with a tissue and flushes it down the toilet.

At least the girl had the sense to use a condom. Lord knows where that Liam has been. Kristy understands his appeal, although she would never have gone for someone so obviously handsome. Before snatching a gallon of milk from the fridge, she checks behind the fluffy pillows on the three sofas in their large rec room for other signs of Liam and Mia.

David is waiting for her at the top of the steps, and she hands him the carton of milk.

He strokes her breast. "Do you want to have hot sex?"

Her skin is one raw nerve ending; she takes his hand and leads him to their bedroom.

"Let me lock the door," he says.

"I have a present for you." She strips naked and lies on the sheets.

"Happy Hanukkah to me." He kneels on the floor, squeezes her ass, and pulls her toward him. She closes her eyes and pretends that these hands and this tongue belong to Charlie Cloud. After they finish, they lie side by side, sweating.

David kisses her ribs. "That was really hot."

"Hmmm . . ." She wonders what Charlie's doing right now. Picturing him at the pool, she romanticizes the nobility of his picking up trash that David will always leave for someone else to clear. Despite what they've done to Justin, she still wants Charlie. She's like a drunk throwing up from alcohol poisoning but still craving more gin. She takes David's hand and guides it back between her legs.

"We should lose power more often," he says with a wink in his voice.

"No talking." She closes her eyes again.

Fortunately, Mia has the good sense to come home from cleaning up the pool without Liam. Kristy's removing the laundry from the dryer when Mia comes to find her.

"I could have done that, Mom." She takes one of the fitted sheets and tries to fold it.

"Here, let me show you how." Kristy stuffs her right hand into the corner of the sheet. "Now fold in half and tuck in the corners."

Mia's mesmerized. "You're really good at this."

"Lots of practice." Kristy continues to drape and fold, the mountain-fresh scent of her fabric softener soothing her nerves.

"I know, from when you worked in a nursing home." Mia picks up a flat sheet. "I'll do this one."

There's no good way for Kristy to tell Mia that she found a used condom under the guest bed, so she simply blurts it out.

Mia makes neat creases on the sheet with her hand. "Are you going to tell Dad?"

"I don't know. I'm worried." Kristy peels a dryer sheet from a pillowcase. "He just seems like the kind of guy—"

"Who uses girls."

"A little bit."

"He's fun, Mom."

Kristy sighs. "Make sure you keep using protection."

"Are we really going to have the STD talk now?"

"Do we need to?"

"No."

"Okay, be careful."

"Mom, are you mad?"

"I'm not mad. I just don't want you to get hurt."

"I won't."

"Sweetie, girls are wired differently than men."

"You sound like a Fifties housewife."

"I'm practical."

"Trust me, I know what I'm doing."

Kristy irons her hand over the stack of freshly washed sheets.

"Mom, don't worry, I'm going to dump Liam." Mia's voice is full of resolve.

Kristy looks at her daughter as if she were an alien. She's beautiful, even in the harsh fluorescent basement light. She's half Weinstein and half Norton, Kristy reminds herself. Who knows whether Kristy's love addiction is due to nature or nurture? It doesn't matter. In the deepest place inside her, she knows that Mia is not an addict. And she knows that her daughter, true to her word, will toss Liam aside soon. Attagirl. This new confidence in Mia and in a working generator gives her the assurance that her family will be okay, that she can take off for a little bit. She needs to put distance between herself and Charlie. And Gillian.

64

CHARLIE

Charlie scoops handfuls of twigs from the pool, relieved that Justin hasn't shown up to clean. How can he ever face him? He can't allow himself to ponder what Justin saw or how his son can survive such a betrayal. He can't face Mia either, so he sends her home, and he sends Liam home because he's a waste of space. Charlie cleans debris from the pool almost maniacally, as if he can restore River Run to the way he found it before the derecho. He didn't sleep last night, and his eyes burn and his muscles ache as he fills Hefty bags with soggy leaves, until the deck is spotless. The late-morning sun bears down on him as he contemplates the tree in the middle of the pool. Fuck.

Unfiltered water be damned, he takes off his shirt, dives into the deep end, swims over to the tree, and plunges his body underneath its girth. He places his hands on the huge trunk and bench-presses with all his strength. The oak doesn't budge. Dizzy from his exertion, he tries three more times to lift the tree.

Why didn't Gillian call the arborist? Someone could have been killed. Well, he or Kristy, but that isn't the point. God forbid Gillian loses her precious tree swing or the sun casts a slightly different shadow over the pool than it had when she was growing up. But then again, Gillian's allegiance to her Christmas lights and traditional setup for the party could have saved the pool house had she fought harder. She's been losing her fights, and all summer he's pitied and hated her for it.

He floats on his back and looks hard at the wreckage of the pool house. How could he be the slightest bit angry with Gillian? After what happened? After everything she lost? He can't shake the image of her carrying that swing from the pool, in the dark, in her sweat-stained dress and matted hair, wearing one sandal and one flip-flop. Then there's Justin's look of pain and disgust, which will be seared into Charlie's brain as long as he lives. He can remove every leaf and branch from River Run, and it won't solve anything.

He contemplates resigning. That would be the decent thing to do, but then what? Gillian will want to know why, and they'll have to find another new coach, which will stoke the robust River Run gossip mill. She'll be crushed. Devastated. But can their marriage survive this secret? Have they ever been truly honest with each other? She's always repainted their lives on Facebook, and more recently she's been leaving the mail for him to sort when new credit-card statements or overdue notices arrive. Keeping one secret makes it easy to keep another, like how much he enjoyed Kristy's attention. Past tense.

He can't think about this anymore. Not now. He has work to do. He must find a place for the team to practice and schedule a rain date for today's meet and . . .

The tasks exhaust him. All he wants to do is lie on his back and gaze up at the bright blue sky. He wants to drift in these fetid waters and forget. How has he ended up here? He could blame his father for being so hard on him and thus playing a role in his path to this ugly spot, but that's getting old. His father didn't make him fuck his wife's best friend, and in so doing destroy Justin.

"Charlie!" a male voice barks at him. He lifts his head to find the pool manager trying to get his attention.

"Get out of the pool right now," Karl shouts.

Charlie sprints to the wall, heads-up water-polo freestyle, and hops out of the water.

"You know you're not supposed to be in there when the pump is down. What the hell is wrong with you?"

"I'm not thinking."

"No, you're not."

"Apologies."

"We've got bigger fish to fry." Karl looks at the tree. "This is going to be a bear to deal with."

"I tried to move that beast myself."

"Maybe the storm made us all a little nuts." Karl pushes his shades up his pug nose.

Filthy water drips from Charlie's body, darkening the cement beneath his feet. "No understatement there."

"Well, at least your guys cleaned up well." Karl goes on to complain about the sloppy job the guards did at the other three pools he manages. "Sorry I yelled at you."

"I deserved it," Charlie says. "How long before you think we can swim again?"

"Depends on how fast Dominion Power can get to these tens of thousands of homes."

"What a shit show."

"Hey, do you have a working phone?"

Charlie shakes his head. "No juice."

Karl reaches into his bag and pulls out a legal pad. "You want to take a crack at writing the letter to the pool members? I'll take a picture of your masterpiece and send it out from my phone."

"No problem."

"Thanks. I'm going to take a reading of the pH levels." He hands Charlie the pad and takes a testing kit out of his bag.

Charlie's a good enough writer, but he's stumped. He starts moving his pen, and a gush of words comes out of him.

Dear Pool Members,

It is with great remorse that I report the happenings on the night of June 29. Though nobody could have predicted the fierce winds, the pool should have been empty. I was the one who relit the tiki torches, and I was the one who cavorted with my wife's best friend. In front of my son too. Nice, huh? Otherwise, we would still have a pool house, and I would still have a marriage, and my wife, who has done nothing but work her rear off for River Run for years, would still have her place. Everyone needs a place.

I thought this was mine. But nothing you take without asking first truly belongs to you. For the past fifteen summers, I've watched my wife during swim season. At the pool, she had an extra verve to her. She was her very best and sometimes very worst Gillian. She kept an eye on your kids and tried to make the summers magical. She and Kristy. I took that from her too.

Now nobody has a pool. Not for now, anyway. Stay tuned for updates on alternate practice sites.

With deepest regrets,

Charlie Cloud

He rips the paper from the pad and tears it to smithereens.

"Hey, Charlie. You don't have to be Shakespeare," Karl teases.

Charlie blushes. "You're right." He writes another letter, with just the facts, no contrition or goopy apologies. He keeps the real one for Karl, who's now checking his iPhone. "It's going to be at least a week until we get power back, according to Dominion."

"Oh, man." It's going to be a bitch finding a pool in Northern Virginia for the team to practice.

"Let's put the hard copy on the fence, just in case." Karl hands Charlie a piece of tape.

Charlie attaches the tape to the note. "Thanks, Karl."

"Go home and clean yourself up, Charlie."

65

KRISTY

The house is quiet. David and Mia have gone out for bagels to feed the kids who will be camping out at the Weinstein home during the power outage. Kristy ambles into her walk-in closet, opens her underwear drawer, and removes Flo's envelope with her birth certificate and the clipping. If Gillian only knew that they were sisters, that Kristy slept with Charlie. Just last month, during Gillian's annual spring closet rehab, the two sat on the floor, swaddling Kristy's sweaters in cedar-scented, moth-resistant wraps and stacking them in the cedar chest Gillian found on eBay. Kristy sucked up Gillian's love and endless instruction like they were the dregs of Nora's formula. *Kristy, kick more when you swim backstroke, Kristy, you might want to wear some pantyhose with that dress, Kristy, best not to drop the f-bomb around the River Run ladies. Kristy, Kristy, Kristy. Let me package a little bit of class for you. Surely the Container Store must carry the right vessel.* Who are the Nortons, anyway? Although she never felt anything but gratitude for Gillian's affection, now every good thing Gillian has ever done for her feels like proof that Kristy had to be taught how to comport herself like a Norton. She doesn't need hand-me-downs from Gillian's perfect little childhood. Kristy's certain that Sebastian Norton held baby Gillian against his big chest and later taught her how to write a perfect English paper or do a perfect swan dive at River Run. He probably helped five-year-old Gillian carve her name into that swing at the pool, her little fingers cupped in his large paw. Kristy's so tired of pressing her nose against the glass, watching people like Nora and Gillian soak up more than their fair share of love from a father who adores them and a mother who isn't ashamed of them.

She opens the cedar chest and removes Flo's envelope from the folds of one of her dozen cashmere cardigans. Wool makes her itch. Plus, she can well afford cashmere. She plucks her sandals and pumps from the shoe rack Gillian gave her and drops them. Next she clears the cold metal belt and scarf rod with one hand, watching silk and leather fall to the floor of her closet like rain. She mixes up the color-coded hangers. Blasphemy! She kneels amidst a blanket of clothes, winded, before collapsing onto the very spot where she and Gillian sat and sorted.

66

GILLIAN

The morning after the derecho, Gillian empties her freezer of Ziplocs containing watery dead bananas she froze to make banana bread. Last week she took advantage of a pre–July Fourth sale at the Safeway and stocked the freezer with a hundred dollars' worth of chicken breasts and hamburger patties. She'll do what she's always done during a power outage, take the meat to Kristy's and they'll arrange an impromptu barbecue. Whatever tension has existed between them will dissolve after what happened last night. Natural disasters have a way of bringing people together, Gillian always thought when she watched news stories about the survivors of Hurricane Katrina. She and Kristy will have a good cry over the River Run tragedy (Gillian can wait until then to let her tears loose) and reboot for the second part of the summer. They have to.

Gillian loads the frozen meat into recyclable grocery bags, the icy packages burning her hands. A memory surfaces like a sneeze. She was thirteen when an August storm knocked the lights out in the D.C. metro area. Her mother emptied the basement freezer. "This meat is going to go rancid if we don't get our power back soon, Gil," she said as if the preservation of the two porterhouses she held in her tiny hands was the most important thing in the world. Mr. Danforth, the chairman of the board of directors at her father's school, had made an emergency visit and was speaking in a hushed tone upstairs in the den. On the way to the bathroom, Gillian heard her father say something about "an old maid who flung herself at me," in that way he did when he stretched the truth, like the time he convinced Gillian that it was *her* fault that the vodka bottle *he'd* dropped had shattered. By the next power outage, this time a winter storm, ten more women, none of them old maids, had come forward, and Gillian swore to herself that if she ever did get married she'd find a husband who wouldn't humiliate her.

"Carry on, Gillian," her mother would have said in her firm tone, so Gillian places the bags of meat in the passenger seat and drives the two miles to Kristy's house. Normally she would let herself in through the kitchen entrance, but not today.

David answers the door, looking clean and dry, a cup of steaming coffee nestled in his hand, his *New York Times* tucked under his arm. "A little power outage isn't going to stand between David and his creature comforts," Charlie commented after the Weinsteins purchased a generator that cost a year of Sebby's Hofstra tuition.

She has to hand it to David for kissing her sweaty cheek, but in his line of work he's used to seeing and smelling women at their worst. "Let me take those for you." He ushers her through the Gillian-organized mudroom, into the Gillian-organized kitchen. The dishwasher is humming, and Mia, Amber, and a few other lifeguards are playing a heated game of Apples to Apples, their phones and chargers plugged into outlets throughout the kitchen, a basket of bagels and a large half-eaten box of Dunkin' donuts on the table. Justin should be here too, but he's been acting funny all day, even given the pool tragedy. Maybe he's sick? She'll take his temperature when she gets home.

"Hi, guys," Gillian says, hoping that the drama of the storm will erase their memories of her anger last night. Where's Kristy?

Mia looks up from her game. "I'm really sorry about the pool."

The rest of the kids look at Gillian as if she were standing in a funeral receiving line.

"Nobody was hurt, and that's the most important thing." Gillian manages to sound upbeat.

"Where's Justin?" Mia asks. "We've been texting him."

"Holed up in his room."

"That's a bummer. Let me try him again." Mia texts with one hand.

Still no Kristy. "Thanks, Mia."

"Let me go get Kristy for you." David calls to her for the second time and then excuses himself to find her.

Kristy comes up from the basement, a stack of laundry in her arms. She looks drawn, but fresh, clean. "Hi." She doesn't put down the towels and T-shirts or invite Gillian to sit and visit.

"I thought we could grill tonight. Do a little power-outage party!"

Kristy glances toward the bags on the counter as if Gillian's mere presence has put her out.

Mia cups her mouth with her hands, creating a fake megaphone. "Go, Krillian!"

"Oh, Mia." Gillian winks at her.

"It would be awesome. We could watch the Olympic trials." Mia looks up the schedule on her phone. "Missy Franklin is swimming tonight!"

Kristy looks beleaguered. "Sorry, not tonight, people."

"Come on, Mom. It's part of the whole experience." Mia moves her arms into the shape of a circle.

The kids at the table all look at Kristy.

Kristy reveals no emotion, good or bad. "Your grandpa's knee is acting up. He needs some love."

Kristy is lying again. Gillian has witnessed her give off what Kristy herself calls the "You're about as welcome as a case of scabies" vibe to her in-laws on an occasion or two. Now it's directed toward Gillian. Again. She's clearly not going to put down the basket of laundry or invite Gillian into the den to mourn the loss of River Run as they've known it. Gillian studies her more carefully. This Kristy is beyond distracted or rude; an aura of that new disquieting energy seeps out of her every pore. The tension between Krillian is palpable. Gillian feels Mia's eyes on them.

"Give my best to Travis, Kristy."

Kristy finally puts down the basket and walks past Gillian to the back door. Gillian follows.

"I'll store the meat for you," Kristy offers grudgingly.

For right now this is all Kristy has for her, Gillian thinks as she leaves the cool house.

"Please tell Justin we're waiting for him," Mia calls after Gillian, so kindly that she feels something deep inside her break, like one of the branches of the fallen oak.

67

JUSTIN

Justin has lost his will to move. He curls up in the fetal position under his damp sheets on the top floor of the house. He hasn't drunk anything since last night's Slurpee. Mia texts him about five times to come to her house and hang out and take advantage of their power, but he ignores her. He only has enough juice in his phone to make one call.

Sebby picks up on the first ring. "What's up with that storm? Shit, you good?"

"Not really."

Sebby pauses. "I talked to Mom, and she said that everything was fine."

Justin cackles. "You realize how ridiculous you sound." Subtext: When was anything *not* fine with Mom?

Sebby doesn't laugh. "You're right."

"I don't have much battery left here, so listen up." Justin tells the story cold.

"Okay, you need to get the *hell* out of the house, so this is what you're going to do." Sebby calmly instructs him to pack an overnight bag and ride his bike to Bob & Edith's diner, where Uncle Patrick will be waiting for him. "And you're going to tell Dad to tell Mom that you're staying with the Johnsons because they have a generator."

Justin nods even though Sebby can't see him.

"Hang tight, little brother."

Justin stuffs a small backpack with a few pairs of shorts, underwear, T-shirts, toothbrush, and his charger. He texts Dad and sneaks out of the house before Mom gets home.

Bob & Edith's is teeming with rank customers who've lost power and the contents of their refrigerators. Uncle Patrick waves to Justin from a booth at the far end of the diner. He stands up when Justin approaches, and they hug it out. The first thing Justin notices about his uncle is that his irises look outrageously blue against the sober, crisp whites of his eyes. Uncle Patrick is twice the width of Justin, but who isn't? He sports a faded T-shirt with some aerospace company's logo on the front. Blond strands stripe his full head of gray hair, and his enormous hands are veiny and freckled. He looks older than Mom.

"Nice and cool in here, huh?" Uncle Patrick motions Justin to sit. "You hungry?"

Justin hasn't eaten since before the luau. "I guess I am."

A heavy-lidded woman who looks like she's been waiting tables for a long time approaches them. "What'll it be, boys?"

"Order whatever you want. My treat," Uncle Patrick says the way he used to when he took Justin and Sebby on an outing. This Uncle Patrick is different, though, more mellow or something.

"Thank you so much, Uncle Patrick. I'd like an order of blueberry hotcakes with a side of scrapple."

"Scrapple?" She winks. "My kind of guy. Anything to drink?"

"Coke, please," he says. "And a glass of water."

Uncle Patrick orders a hamburger with mayo and pickles and a cup of black coffee, and then, they check each other out for a few seconds. Uncle Patrick breaks their silence. "You look more and more like your mother. My mother too."

"And Elizabeth McGovern, right?"

Uncle Patrick gives a closed-mouth chuckle.

"Sebby looks like you," Justin says. "And, um, Sebastian Norton."

Uncle Patrick strokes the side of his cheek. "I suppose, yes."

The waitress comes with their beverages, and Justin thanks her and downs the entire glass of water in one gulp. If he were a dog, his nose would be dust-dry right now. Uncle Patrick pushes his water toward Justin, and after Justin guzzles it, he starts to feel a little better.

"I'm sorry about, you know, everything that happened last night." Uncle Patrick unwraps his silverware from his napkin. "Sebby told me."

"I don't want you to think badly of my dad," Justin says.

"I'm not here to judge."

The waitress comes by with more water. "Drink up. It's hot as Hades out there."

Justin waits until she walks away. "So, Uncle Patrick. Are you bummed about what happened to River Run?"

He shrugs. "It's complicated."

Justin feels like he did when Mom told him the Easter Bunny wasn't real. "But your dad, I mean my grandfather or whatever, was a total god."

Uncle Patrick looks down at his lap and closes his eyes for a second as if he's about to say grace.

"According to Mom, and some of the old-timers too," Justin says.

"Don't kid yourself. Your mom had it rough."

Justin clings to the lore. "Come on. The swan dive? The races Sebastian Norton won against the lifeguards? The games he invented for the kids? We still play—"

"Sharks and Manta Rays." Uncle Patrick looks wistful.

"Awesome game."

"I know. Justin, your grandfather was absolutely that person, that handsome legend with the crazy charisma."

"And?"

Uncle Patrick takes two long sips of coffee. "He was also a mean drunk."

Justin studies the ice cubes in his glass as if they're a crystal ball.

He's looking for his grandfather, the headmaster, the rock star, the math genius, the mean drunk. Uncle Patrick doesn't say anything. He simply waits.

"Does Sebby know about all this?" Justin thinks back to the time Sebby stopped wanting to master the Sebastian Norton swan dive, and he knows the answer to his question, and that what Uncle Patrick has told him is true.

"Yes."

"How did you two become so close?"

"He found me."

The waitress returns with their plates. No chitchat, though. A real pro, she likely senses when her customers are engaged in the kind of talk you don't interrupt.

Justin loses his appetite. "After the time my mom made him swim the IM in the dark?"

Uncle Patrick removes the top of the ketchup bottle. "Later, in college. But I know about that IM thing too."

Justin plays with his straw. "That was way fucked up."

"Cut your mom some slack." Uncle Patrick's tone is gently reproachful. "You haven't walked in her shoes."

Justin takes a bite of scrapple. Despite his nausea, the greasy salt activates his taste buds, and he finishes the food. And the Coke. And then he feels sick all over again. He folds up his dirty napkin. "Please tell me about my grandparents. I want to know everything you told Sebby."

Uncle Patrick swallows the last bite of his burger. Then he talks. The customers are boisterous, but Justin isn't sure he could have gone through with this conversation without the ambient noise. He wants to know about the good parts of Sebastian and May, starting at River Run, and Uncle Patrick tells him how people young and old vied for Sebastian's attention because of the way he made them feel. Mom has that quality too. Selected to serve as the youngest headmaster in the history of his first school, Sebastian was the golden boy. Everyone loved May too. She was Southern, smart, and demure, and looked exactly like Mom (and Justin). But she was too weak to protect herself or her children from Sebastian's ugliness.

Twenty years ago, Uncle Patrick fell off the wagon hard, and he brought the sad story of Sebastian Norton to one of his therapists at Hazelden (funded by Mom). The therapist dismissed the family Sebastian lore. May had always told Patrick that Sebastian started drinking because he got in over his head at work, that he had been promoted too early, had married into a family of old money (long since squandered by May's alcoholic older brother), and was thus insecure. But that wasn't the full truth. Once, when Sebastian smacked the crap out of Patrick, he said that it was nothing compared to the beatings his father had dished out, and that Patrick was a coddled little mama's boy. Sebastian's father was an alcoholic, like Sebastian, like Sebastian's son.

Uncle Patrick pauses after his story and sips his coffee. "Like Sebby too."

"Sebby?"

"He came to me after his freshman year of college."

"He didn't drink that much."

"With his permission, I will tell you that he did."

Justin feels weak. "Do my parents know?"

Uncle Patrick shakes his head no.

"Are you like his AA sponsor or something?"

Uncle Patrick smiles. "Or something."

"Shouldn't Mom know what you did for Sebby?"

Uncle Patrick tells Justin that he worried that Mom would deny away Sebby's problem, which would screw up Sebby's sobriety. Gillian's way of coping with Sebastian was to make excuses for him. Sure, Gillian would hide in the basement with Patrick when Sebastian's storms erupted. Focus on the positive, Patrick, she'd say the next day while she tilted his head back and squeezed droppers of Visine into his eyes to cover a night of crying. "When we talk about our childhood, your mom refuses to admit that Sebastian drank or got nasty or cheated on our mom. Talking to her makes me feel like I'm looking into a funhouse mirror."

Justin understands exactly what Uncle Patrick means, like when Mom posted a picture with a chirpy comment about the dinner with the O'Learys when it was a total shit show. He can think of a million other examples. "Who decided that you should stop coming around?"

Uncle Patrick fiddles with his fork. "It was mutual. I couldn't get better without being honest about my family history."

"I don't even know what to say."

They finish up their water, and as promised, Uncle Patrick takes care of the check.

KRISTY

It's kind of cute that Mia and her friends have migrated from Apples to Apples to Scrabble, but it's also sad that Justin isn't here to play. Kristy hopes he's okay. Right now she sees Gillian as a mere impediment to Charlie. She doesn't care that she's chasing away her best friend. And sister. She's like an emphysema patient sucking in nicotine through a hole in her throat.

Normally she would invite herself to play Scrabble because figuring out spelling patterns and anomalies massages her brain, but it's time to get the hell out of Arlington. She needs to think. She packs a bag and takes it out to the car before she speaks to David, who is in his study organizing the medical journals stacked up on his desk.

"We hosting a barbecue tonight?" David is an extraordinary griller, which is why he embraces the power-outage parties they've thrown for the swim team.

"Nope. My dad reinjured his knee."

David removes his glasses and looks up at her as if to say, "So what?"

"I'm going to go see him, love."

He looks dejected, as he always does when she isn't at his beck and call. "Now?"

Normally his clinginess makes her feel wanted. "Yeah, now."

"What about dinner?"

She's spoiled this man. "You can take Mia out or cook or—"

"You're right, Kristy." He gets up and takes her in his arms. "You should help Travis."

It feels good to drive, finally alone with her thoughts. What's Charlie doing right now? She fantasizes about their meeting up. "We need to talk," he'll tell her, and they'll head off to a deserted spot. It won't matter where. They'll admit how wrong this is, and then they won't be able to stop themselves from having sex again. In her car. In the middle of a blackout, with the long June sun shining through the windows and warming their fingers, cold from the A/C. Four times, she'll tell him, and then they'll be done with each other.

She taps on her Star of David. *Think about the consequences of your actions.* She tries channeling Beverly. Use your tools of the program. Make an outreach call. Go to a meeting. Write about the people you will hurt. Pray. Do service.

She makes a U-turn and drives by the pool, hoping to see Charlie's car, but the lot is empty. She drives to his house, not even deliberating for a second as she parks in the driveway. She will apologize to Gillian for her rudeness today and check in on Justin. Yes, that's why she's here. She knocks for a few minutes, but nobody answers. Her fingers tremble as she locates the Clouds' house key on her ring.

The lock is tricky, but she knows to lift and turn the key at the same time. *Count to three, Kristy. Think back to all the times you've let yourself into Gillian's house.* During a busy swim meet, she ran back to the house for Gillian's orange folder—"her life," Gillian called it. She let herself in when Gillian was recovering from her hysterectomy and couldn't handle the steps. Kristy brought meals for a week, and they watched rom-coms and movies every day. *The Princess Bride* was their favorite, partially because Kristy had a thing for Wallace Shawn. The effortless intimacy of it all: lounging on the bed with popcorn, changing Gillian's dressing, cleaning vomit from her shoes when the pain medication made her sick.

Kristy turns the key in the moody lock and lets herself into the house, its air warm and stale from lack of circulation.

"Yoo-hoo," she shouts.

Like a bloodhound who has just caught a scent of its prey, she follows a trail of Gillian's discarded clothing up the stairs, to Gillian and Charlie's bedroom. She doesn't care if Justin catches her in their house. She hears water running and continues toward the bathroom to the source of a sound that is not human, a combination of wailing and whining. The bathroom mirror reflects Charlie and Gillian in clear view. With no power, the water must be too cold to steam the shower door. They clutch each other, and Gillian sobs as if she's lost a parent, or a spouse, or a sibling.

Kristy turns on her heel and takes the stairs two at a time, her heart smashing against her breastbone. She lets herself out of the house and into her car and mows down a large branch as she speeds off. She belches up bile and swallows it back down. She isn't stupid enough to think that Charlie's going to leave Gillian for her. Still, the sight of them wrapped around each other slices her right open. Again she's on the outside peering in, her nose pressed against that clear shower door. Gillian's shower door.

Hot tears stream down Kristy's face as she drives the twenty-seven miles into her past, the little town with one public pool, pickup trucks instead of SUVs in driveways, and parents who work too many hours to have the time to plan elaborate parties with tiki torches.

She parks in front of her old house, where a blue television light shines through the living room window. She can still turn around and go back home, but she wants to see her dad. Maybe he can make her feel whole, or at least legitimate. This is all she's ever wanted from him—from anyone, really.

She knocks on his door. The television blares generic cop-show music. When he answers, she sees how awful she looks through the reflection in his eyes. He's in an old pair of jeans and one of his button-down plaid shirts, face shaved and hair combed.

"Come in, come on in, Kristy."

The house is warm, though air-conditioned, and smells like the lemony soap he uses to wash dishes. The frying pan is placed neatly in the drying rack, and a bowl of walnuts and a silver nutcracker sit on the coffee table. Not a fan of idle hands, he cracks the nuts while he watches television. This is how they discovered Mia's walnut allergy. The first time they visited Flo and Travis, she broke out in hives.

They sit together at the kitchen table.

"How's the basement?" she asks.

"All dried out." He looks at her closely. "You all right, Kris?"

She shakes her head no. "Dad, did you see the news?"

"Yes, yes, the derecho," he says, as if recalling the name of a childhood friend.

She corrects his pronunciation, mimicking David's earlier sounding of the word. "Deh-RAY-choh."

"Got it. Deh-RAY-choh. Can I get you a root beer or a glass of water?"

"I'm fine, thanks."

"Everyone okay?"

"Did you worry about us? Were you going to call?"

He sinks into his chair. "Kristy."

"It's okay." But it isn't. He would have checked in on Nora.

He raises an eyebrow. "I don't worry about you, sweetheart. David takes good care of you."

"Having money doesn't protect you from a tree falling on your head or—" She stops, because her nose is tingling and she's afraid she's about to cry.

"Did a tree fall in your neighborhood?"

"The big oak fell at the pool. Kerplunk. The tree. The swing. Right in the water."

He sits up straight. "Was anybody hurt?"

She rises to hunt down a tissue because the tears are coming. "Not the way you think."

"Here." He hands her a box of Kleenex from the counter. "What does that mean?"

She blows her nose, and he glances away, and now she feels foolish. They pretend she's not crying, because they've never made a habit of expressing big sloppy emotions. She gets up. "Forget it. I just came by because I wanted to make sure you were safe."

He walks her to the door. "Sure I can't get you something?" He's trying.

"Yeah, actually a cold root beer would go down pretty nicely right now."

She follows him back to the kitchen. He retrieves two cans of generic root beer from the fridge. He puts a few ice cubes in the glasses and pours a fresh round of nuts into the orange bowl she remembers from Flo's chicken-soup night. He sets out a blue bowl for the shells. They crack nuts and sip root beer. Kristy concentrates on digging out the fruit from each shell. For now she's sated, sitting next to the man who raised her, whom she's called Dad for all these years, whom she has, in this moment, all to herself.

"Dad, can I stay here for the night?"

On her wrist he rests his slender hand, like David's, perfect for tying sutures and fixing loose wires. "Stay as long as you like."

69

GILLIAN

Gillian and Charlie lie on their bed, wet from the shower and naked, savoring the few seconds of cool. They don't touch, don't speak. Their neighbors' generator drones through the open windows. Gillian's eyes are puffy and her head aches from sobbing, but she's glad that Justin is staying with the Johnsons. She doesn't know if she's capable of keeping her tears in the bottle now that they've escaped.

When her cell phone rings, she wraps herself in a towel and runs downstairs to answer. It's Patrick. She wants to tell her brother about the pool and saving the swing and the photo of Sebastian, because nobody in the world, not even Kristy, would understand better than Patrick what exactly River Run means to her.

"How are you doing?" Patrick asks as if he's making a condolence call.

"I'm fine." Now Patrick's sympathy annoys her.

"I'm really sorry, Gil." Patrick speaks slowly. "I saw a photo of River Run on the Channel 9 website."

"Patrick, everything is fine. We'll fix it."

"It's okay for you to be sad. I know the pool is important to you."

"It's okay for you to *not* be sad." She almost snorts thinking of Patrick, likely sipping black coffee and doing his "tenth step."

"You know what I think about when I think about you, Gil?"

She rubs her temples. "Patrick, not tonight."

"Bear with me for a second. Remember how Dad used to tease me at the dinner table?" He doesn't wait for her to answer, but she knows exactly what he means. Patrick didn't understand how to navigate Sebastian's moods, and when their father unfurled his drunk sarcastic wit on him, he'd run upstairs to Gillian's closet and curl his body into a ball next to the shoe rack Gillian built at camp that one awful summer.

"It was you, never Mom, who came to find me and tell me that everything was going to be okay." Patrick's voice is cracking.

"I didn't mean to snap at you." Gillian might resume her shower cry if she's not very careful.

"I just wanted to say thank you."

"Oh, Patrick." Her brother has been crippled by their childhood, like one of those melting frozen bananas that would have leaked all over had she not stored them in a Ziploc.

"You going to be okay, Gil?"

"Of course I am. This is what we do. Carry on."

"It's the Norton way," Patrick says, his voice so faint Gillian can barely hear him.

"Nothing wrong with that." Gillian and Patrick say a quick good-bye, and she marches upstairs, phone in hand.

"Texting with Sebby." Charlie's sitting up in bed pecking at his phone. "Everyone's safe and checking in on you."

Gillian hangs up her towel in the bathroom. "Oh, for Pete's sake, everyone is acting like we buried someone."

"We're worried, Gil."

"I'm fine." Her eyes are still swollen from her big cry.

"Oh, and Shannon has texted twice too."

"Well, that's very nice of everyone to worry, and I'll text Shannon and absolve her of her guilt." Gillian twists her hair in a bun. "But enough of all this. We have work to do."

"Work?"

"Yes! We must find a pool to practice in and reschedule today's meet, for starters."

Charlie's shoulders relax or slump or something in between as he makes room for her on the bed.

Gillian sits next to him. "Onward!"

70

KRISTY

"Good night, Dad." Kristy gives Travis a little wave. "Thanks for letting me stay."

He sweeps his hand across his body and toward the stairs. "A solid night's sleep will do you good."

She hesitates before she enters her old bedroom. She opens the door and takes in the room: the two single beds, the old lamp, and her prized possession, the small desk Travis bought at a yard sale and painted white. Kristy sits down on her bed, on a juice stain on the floral quilt, no doubt the product of one of her nieces' or nephews' overnights with Travis. Mia and Isaac have never spent the night here. Since Kristy left home, she hasn't stayed overnight either, not even during the last days of Flo's life, though she managed her mother's hospice care and communicated with the doctors; for those few final months she and Travis were a team. The night Flo's will was read, David came home early from the hospital and caught Kristy staring down a bottle of rum. "You're still nursing, love," he gently scolded, and then Mia, not even one, woke up almost on cue. When Mia's little pink mouth attached to her nipple, Kristy let down a rush of milk and tears. The next day she left Mia with a babysitter and scrubbed the remnants of Flo's illness from the upstairs bedrooms. That was the last time she climbed the steps to the second floor of her childhood home.

She uses the bathroom she once shared with Travis, Flo, and Nora. She combs her hair with Travis's metal comb.

Kristy can't sleep, so she checks Facebook on her phone, looking for updates from Gillian. Nothing. She wants to call Charlie so badly. Instead, she slips on the backless sundress she's packed, in case she meets up with Charlie, and sneaks out of the house. She drives to her old watering hole and sidles up to the far end of the bar.

"Mai tai, please," she says to the bartender, scanning the room until she spots a thirty-something man with radically asymmetrical features. She gazes at him until he looks at her, and then she holds him in her eyes for nearly a minute. One of her most successful moves by far.

He comes over and takes a seat next to her. "So what's a pretty woman like you doing in a dump like this?"

She waves her wedding ring in his face and gulps down half her drink.

"That's some rock you've got there, lady."

"You got that right, mister."

"I like a woman with some sass."

"I got sass."

"What's your name?"

"Candy."

"Well, Candy, I'm Austin."

She glances at the bartender. It takes her thirty seconds to figure out which cocktail waitress he's fucking. The redhead. She knows the looks, the way they brush against each other when they think nobody's paying attention. Kristy is paying attention. She bets that Red is the bartender's girl on the side. Kristy can spot that girl. That girl was pockmarked or plain during the time when boys and girls started pairing off. That girl developed early and offered her breasts to the boys who were pairing off with girls with self-respect. That girl bloomed late and then revenge-shat on the boys, or their prototypes, who didn't look at her during the time when girls and boys were pairing off. That girl has a dad who doesn't see her because he's drunk, distracted, or depressed, or otherwise occupied with the kid who shares his blood. That girl has a mom who is ashamed of her. That girl will take attention any way she can get it.

"Take a picture, it lasts longer, Candy." He nudges her with his elbow.

She turns her full attention to Austin, blocking out Charlie holding Gillian howling in the shower, Travis's reliable knack for giving her just short of what she needs despite her efforts and his, and Sebastian Norton, who hadn't a clue she existed. She was invisible, just the way Flo wanted it. She steals a look in the mirror to check her reflection. She looks old and beat, but over the years she's learned that blond hair and a decent pair of boobs can erase a whole lot of flaws.

"Are you okay?" Austin looks a little freaked out.

"No. I'm far from okay, but I'm okay." It's her job to be okay for David and the kids.

"Okay." They find this hysterically funny. They laugh hard for a few minutes, and then she places her hand on the back of his neck and draws him toward her for a kiss. She likes that he tastes like cigarettes and whiskey. She presses her body into his, and soon they're making out like two teenagers, which evolves into dry-humping pretty quickly. When she opens her eyes, she catches the bartender stuffing down a smirk. She remembers the contempt on Charlie's face when he looked at her during the fire. She pushes Austin away, unzips her purse, plucks a twenty from her wallet, and tosses the bill on the bar.

"Ciao, Austin." She yanks her arm from his meaty hand. "And ciao to you too, honey," she says to the barkeep.

The heat and alcohol are wearing on her. All she wants to do is rest for a few minutes, take a little nap, and she'll be good to go. She drives the car around back, where soon the bartender will bring the redhead for a quickie, the kind of anonymous space her workmates used to fuck her. She leans her head against the seat and closes her eyes. Finally she can sleep.

71

JUSTIN

Uncle Patrick's townhouse is clean and cool and only ten or so miles from the Clouds' home. Mom never said that Uncle Patrick lived far away, she never said much about him at all, so Justin assumed he'd moved to a different part of the state. Hell, Justin could have been riding his bike here all these years.

"How come you didn't lose your power?" he asks his uncle.

"Fluke, but I'm not going to question my good luck." Patrick motions Justin to follow him upstairs.

Justin sleeps deeply on the pullout couch in Uncle Patrick's office. His uncle is some kind of computer whiz who works as an IT consultant for months at a time. His desk is spotless, and there's only one picture on the wall, Uncle Patrick holding a marlin. No family. No kids. No photo of Sebastian Norton. No swan dive.

The smell of coffee wafts up to Justin's room. It feels good to catch some z's, but now it's time for him to get up and face the shit that is his life.

"Good morning, Uncle Patrick."

"You slept well." He hands Justin a cup of coffee.

Justin rubs the back of his neck with his hand. "I did. Thanks for putting me up."

"Eggs?"

"That would be great, thanks so much." Justin takes a sip of coffee. "Rocket fuel."

"Should have warned ya." Uncle Patrick cracks an egg.

"I hate to say it, but now I'm thinking that my grandfather was kind of a douche."

Uncle Patrick cracks another egg and then gives Justin his full attention. "Go on."

Justin's embarrassed. "I'm sorry, that wasn't respectful."

"Honesty is important too." Uncle Patrick leans on the counter. "No denying that he loved us fiercely."

"But?"

While Patrick scrambles Justin's eggs and makes toast, he tells a story about the time he tried out for his middle-school baseball team and the hours Sebastian spent trying to teach him how to throw a curveball. Sebastian gave Patrick his old mitt, which he used for the tryouts. Patrick had a mediocre arm, but he made the team because his technique was stellar, thanks to his father. Sebastian also coached third base, sometimes too enthusiastically, but only Patrick could tell if he'd been drinking before the games.

Justin has never seen Mom drunk, but when Uncle Patrick tells this story, he gets exactly why she similarly stepped over the line when she made Sebby swim in the dark. She's too much sometimes. Maybe she's been channeling her father. Even so, she doesn't deserve what Dad has done to her.

"I'm not too happy with my dad right now." Justin butters his toast.

"I don't blame you." Patrick sighs. "But trust me, your dad is nothing like Sebastian Norton."

72

GILLIAN

Gillian feels like a veritable Laura Ingalls Wilder when she wakes up on the second day of the power outage. There's food and ice to be gathered, towels to be hung out to dry in the sunlight. Exhilarating! Without any cable, they'll play games or read every word of the Sunday *Times*. For today she and Charlie will forget all about River Run and the swim team. She can't bring herself to talk to him about the fire. The very thought of asking her running list of questions makes her tired and worried that she'll break down in tears again. Today they won't talk about Kristy either.

Thanks to Gillian's relationships with her fellow team reps in the league, practice and meet rescheduling has been taken care of. Starting tomorrow, Charlie and his coaching staff will run practice at 6:30 p.m. at a pool a few miles away, not ideal, but they won't even miss a day of training. Yesterday's meet is rescheduled for Thursday night, and tomorrow Gillian will bop on over to her new client's house, located in a development that's fully powered. Oh, what bliss!

Charlie stirs. He kicks off the sheet and turns to her. "Do you want to go to church?"

"This heat wave has no end in sight, according to the Channel 9 website." Gillian giggles. "What some people won't do for a little A/C!"

"Maybe." Charlie looks glum.

"I didn't mean to make fun of you, but why the sudden spiritual call?" Gillian asks.

"We used to take the kids when they were little. I liked that."

"I miss them."

"Justin will be home soon." Charlie rolls over. "When the power comes back."

"Okay, church it is."

"Thank you." Charlie presses his lips to her forehead. "And thanks for helping out with the scheduling too."

"You're welcome, and I like the idea of going to church."

She showers quickly and dresses in a tailored but casual floral skirt and fitted tank top from Anthropologie, her favorite store. She towels the moisture out of her hair and ties it back.

"You look nice," Charlie says. "Give me a second, I'll be right out."

She waits on the porch for him. The temperature is already in the low nineties, but the air feels fresher than in her stuffy basement. She focuses on nothing but the sounds of the cicadas, as if they belong to a channel she can crank up to drown out the obnoxious whir of her neighbor's generator.

She feels Charlie's presence. He's looking at her with an odd intensity, the way you would gaze at a spouse who has just received news of a military deployment or a scary diagnosis.

"You look troubled, Charlie."

He wraps his arms around her, and she buries her face in his warm shoulder. After a few seconds she can barely breathe, but the hug feels good. "Maybe we need more derechos," she says into his damp polo shirt.

He releases her. "No, I don't think so."

She weaves her fingers through his. "Let's go."

Pastor Alan makes a joke about how it took an act of God to finally pack the church. Gillian's scalp perspires, further dampening her hair. Charlie holds her hand and guides her to two seats in the last pew.

Gillian made a big fuss over their boys' confirmations. Her father had taken Gillian and Patrick to church every Sunday, no matter how hung over he was or how cruel he'd been to them hours before entering the sanctuary. Most of the student body from his school attended their church, and Gillian knew to smile and sing the hymns loudly, and she relished doing so because it made her parents proud. Her mother dressed herself and Gillian extra carefully. They were a nice-looking family. Perfect. Afterwards, they'd go to IHOP for breakfast. If her father was trying to stay sober, he'd order a stack of chocolate chip pancakes with gobs of whipped cream, and if he was drinking, he'd pick at a soft-boiled egg, and if the egg wasn't prepared to his satisfaction, he'd say a pleasant thank-you to the waitress but they'd hear about it when they got in the car.

Gillian looks around the church and recognizes the parents of Seby's and Justin's friends, people with whom their lives have been knitted via sports and carpools. She was keenly aware of which spouses traveled for work and couldn't be counted on to drive, which parents got a little too into it at their kids' meets, and which children poked around getting dressed in the locker room, oblivious to their drivers' revving engines and tight pickup schedules. She knew how these moms dinnered their kids: fresh-cooked, Trader Joe's frozen, takeout, drive-thru, or combinations thereof. She knew how clean they kept their cars and their children. Carpooling displayed the crumbs and wrappers and detritus of everyday life. May had never carpooled. She never wanted anyone's children driving with Sebastian, yet only now does Gillian wonder how May allowed her children to drive with their drunk father. This is the kind of memory that Patrick griped about when he was in rehab.

Gillian chimes in loudly for the Lord's Prayer. She'd stopped praying the night her father broke the blue plate. After the service, they file out into the impossibly steamy hallway. She doesn't want to make small talk with their friends. They'll ask: What happened at River Run? They won't believe her if she says she really doesn't know. They'll ask: What are the kids doing this summer? And she'll respond with: How was Rehoboth? Bethany? Costa Rica? And why bother asking these questions? She's seen their vacation photos posted on Facebook.

"Let's go, Charlie," she says.

"Do you want to grab something to eat?"

"Maybe a bagel." She hates going out for breakfast.

They drive to Bruegger's, order two coffees and two plain bagels with light plain cream cheese and tomatoes, and violate Gillian's no-eating-in-the-car rule. "Our car is going to become our second home," Charlie says as he reaches into the bag and hands her a bagel and napkins, which they spread out on their laps.

Both tear open the paper and bite hard. "Darn it," Gillian says as tomato splatters on her top. The dough tastes like cardboard and the cream cheese is cloying. She wraps up the bagel and takes a swig of coffee.

"Wanna go to a movie?" Charlie asks.

Gillian wipes a glob of cream cheese from his chin. "Sure."

73

CHARLIE

Charlie doesn't look up the movie showings and times on his phone; he drives Gillian right downtown to an artsy theater near the Verizon Center. By chance, they arrive in time for the start of *The Best Exotic Marigold Hotel*, a movie about a bunch of retired Brits who try to find their bliss in Jaipur. He purchases a bucket of popcorn and a large Diet Coke, and they split both.

Charlie likes sitting in the dark with Gillian, having her nearby but not having to talk to her or hide from her. He could never have predicted her response to the clubhouse fire. After she howled in the shower, a sound that will forever ring in his ears, something inside her shifted. Even in her resolute cheerfulness she's far away from him, and the further she drifts, the more he wants to hang on to her. His neediness anchors them. It always has.

Justin is still allegedly camped out at his friend's house, although Patrick was decent enough to text Charlie and let him know that Justin has been bunking with him and needs a little space. Charlie's glad that Justin sought Patrick out, another secret he will keep from Gillian. He needs time to figure out how he'll begin to mend their relationship, if that's even possible. He burps up this morning's bagel.

Gillian loves any movie starring Maggie Smith or Judi Dench. An Anglophile, she read Jane Austen's oeuvre twice in college. Charlie is transported to loud and vivid Jaipur. He imagines himself and Gillian growing as tired and regretful as this wind-worn crew, and then his entire future flashes before him in that dark, drafty, crowded theater. Where will his coaching lead him? Maybe he'll start his own swim program or build his own pool or a dome over one of the summer outdoor pools. The D.C. area is notoriously short on pool space. He could create an empire! Launch his own Marigold adventure! Train the future Michael Phelps! He'll partner with Gillian, and maybe Justin after he graduates. He steals a few glances at her profile. She's beautiful: her strong jawline, the spray of freckles that travels down her neck. He wants her. She turns to him and smiles, and he sees the love and trust in her eyes.

He wants to grow old with Gillian. He rests his head on her shoulder, and she strokes his stubbly scalp. He has relied on her compass for most of his adult life, but he doesn't want to go back to who they were, to her directing his life, to the phoniness of her constant Facebook spinning, to the unpleasantness she organizes into the finest storage bins. Charlie let emotional clutter accumulate until he stopped noticing it, like the leaky faucet he no longer heard drip. And what about Kristy? She brought out something animal in him, a selfish ferocity he never knew existed. Kristy terrifies him.

He puts Gillian's hand in his lap.

"Later, sweetie. This is really good."

Kristy would swallow him whole. He knows that. She is sexy as hell, but she's an octopus he'd have to pull off himself one tentacle at a time. And he'll never be able to look at her without thinking about what Justin saw. They shattered his son's world.

The movie's resolution is beautiful, all secrets laid out; the only hope for these folks is to live out their lives with honesty. He knows this to be true. He and Gillian can run from church to theater to other air-conditioned venues, but it won't change anything. Eventually the power will return and they'll have to go back to their lives and sweep up the ashes.

Gillian never cries in public, but she bawls through the final scene. Charlie offers her his bare arm to wipe her nose.

"No thanks, I'll use this." She reaches into the tub of popcorn and blows into a wadded-up oily napkin.

"What got to you?" Charlie asks.

"Everything. Nothing. I'm out of sorts."

"Hard not to be."

She asks him, casually, "Do you want to get a hotel room?"

"Are you kidding?"

"There's a Hilton down the street. It's not the Marigold, but it will do."

Gillian worked for the Hilton when they started dating, and they made a habit of using her employee discount to check into various hotels in town. They sat in their underwear, watching movies and munching on M&M's from the minibar, and had sex. Lots of sex.

"Let's do it, Gil."

She takes his hand, and they walk toward the hotel.

Her phone buzzes through her purse and she checks it. "Sebby," she mouths to Charlie.

He listens to her side of the conversation. "Honey, please don't worry. You couldn't have done anything." . . . "You're breaking up." . . . "I love you a lot." She tosses the phone back into her purse and wraps her arms around Charlie.

Hearing Sebby and Gillian talk about the pool has formed a lump in his throat. Sebby had forgiven her for that night. Would Justin ever be able to look at Charlie again?

They walk the rest of the way to the hotel holding hands. The lobby's packed, but the check-in line moves quickly. A young man greets them. They look at each other because his electric smile reminds them of the actor who played the young hotel manager from the movie. Must be fate.

Charlie pulls out his wallet, and when he plunks down his brand-new 0% interest Wells Fargo card, Gillian looks away. "We'd like a room, please."

The clerk types on his computer, the keys crackling as he moves his fingers. "We have one room left in the entire hotel, but it's the Presidential Suite."

"We'll take it," Charlie says without asking the price.

The clerk swipes his card, generates a receipt and two room keys, and directs them to the proper elevator.

Gillian whistles. "This is so decadent."

"When's the last time we went away together?" he asks.

"We need to get away."

"Even if we're not really getting away."

The elevator is filled with a family with two young kids, all dressed in T-shirts with logos of the White House stamped on their chests. The dad dons a Mets cap and the mom slings a tote bag over her shoulder. Charlie and Gillian used to take the boys to New York for quick weekend trips before they grew too busy with their activities.

"We should take the kids to India," Charlie says as they exit the elevator.

"I can't believe you said that. I was thinking the very same thing."

They light up with the spark of a new idea as they walk down the hall to their room. Charlie unlocks and opens the door. "Gillian, look!"

"It's palatial!" Gillian hops up on the bed. "This looks like a supersized king."

It's wonderful and horrible for Charlie to hear Gillian laugh, knowing that he's holding a stick of dynamite that could keep her from laughing for a very long time.

The room resembles a large apartment; the carpet is white and the couches a brownish-black leather, and the kitchen is stocked with sodas, microwave popcorn, and single-serving bags of designer chips and cookies. Gillian checks out the bathroom, which is the size of their bedroom, and comes out with a bottle of hair gel. "I'm going to make good use of this. I'm all frizzed out."

He kisses her along her hairline. "You're lovely."

"Oh, Charlie."

"I'm serious." He covers his face with her hair.

She kicks off her shoes and pounces on the giant bed, covered with a crisp white down comforter. Charlie joins her, wanting more than anything to lie with his wife in this anonymous space forever. He's floating. Gillian sidles up to him and caresses his chest under his shirt. He unbuttons her skirt carefully and inches it down over her hips. He knows her body well. She reaches for his belt buckle, and the entire time he's moving inside her his thoughts unspool. He thinks of Kristy's brokenness, and of what must be broken in him to want her. But he can't bear to think about Gillian, who is ready to begin their very own Marigold adventure, right here, miles away from the River Run pool. He releases himself into his wife, tumbling hard onto her body.

74

KRISTY

Power outage, day three. Kristy is hung over from her night of drinking. The alcohol was meant to numb the fantasies about Charlie that assail her with impunity. Her mouth tastes like dirty socks. She calls their landline. "Hi, you've reached the Weinsteins, we're on the other line right now . . ." Kristy recorded that message three years ago. Their old phone had died, and she and Isaac picked up a new one at the mall while they were shopping for yet another new pair of sneakers for her mid-growth-spurt son, who afterwards downed two Chick-fil-A chicken deluxe sandwiches and an order of fries. After they got home, Isaac set up the phone for her and tried to make her laugh by dancing the Macarena while she recorded the message, her voice oozing joy. Now she waits for the beep and leaves her message. "Hi, hons. Grandpa is doing much better. I should be home tomorrow or the next day. Call me. Love you."

Sunlight drenches the faded shades, its force indicating that she's slept through most of the day. She shields her eyes with the inside of one crooked elbow and checks Gillian's Facebook page with her free hand. Gillian's finally posted. Last night, while Kristy was downing mai tais with Austin, she and Charlie were enjoying an outing in D.C. Are they back home yet? So far, Kristy's refrained from texting or phoning Charlie, and his unavailability is making her feel even more on edge.

She needs to get out of this house. Travis is giving her space to come and go as she pleases, which leaves her free to wander about Manassas.

Except that she isn't free at all. Every fifteen minutes or less, she checks Gillian's Facebook page for more updates. When are they going to be home? Charlie emails about practice that afternoon at some pool in McLean, so he'll have to come home then. What if he and Gillian set up camp in that hotel for the rest of the power outage? Kristy climbs out of her skin.

Travis has left her a note saying that he's gone to the grocery to pick up a few things, and she wants to get the hell out of here before he returns. As she picks up her keys, the old family phone rings, and she answers it.

"Kristy? Is that you?" Nora's Southern accent has grown more pronounced.

"Hi, Nora."

"You're visiting Dad?"

She considers saying something snarky like "Yes, he actually has two daughters," but she stops herself. She's always expressed her resentment toward Nora more passive-aggressively, like sending her hand-me-downs Nora could never afford or planning family trips when she knew Nora would be visiting. "Yes. We've been spending a lot of time together."

"I'm so glad to hear that." Nora sounds genuinely happy.

So much for making Nora feel jealous. Nora will never feel envious of Travis's attention. She had his affection from day one. "Thanks."

"How are you doing?" Nora sounds like she doesn't want to let Kristy off the phone. Now she has two half-sisters that she wants to ignore.

"Kristy?" Nora asks timidly.

"Yeah?"

"Will you be around the last week of August?"

Kristy twirls the phone cord around her finger. Has Travis told Nora about Sebastian? Likely not. "Um . . ."

"It's okay if you aren't." Nora's voice sounds tight and sad.

Kristy pictures herself standing in her sister's kitchen, which she has never seen, next to a fridge blanketed with photos of Kristy's grown nieces and nephews, whose weddings she blew off. She imagines Nora's little face, a carbon copy of Flo's with Travis's froggy eyes, her hair wavy like Flo's and dyed red with an at-home coloring kit.

"You still there, Kristy?"

The phone cord is leaving red indentations on Kristy's pointer finger. "It's been a long time, Nora."

Nora swallows. "Fifteen years."

Yeah, fifteen years since you stuck me with caring for the woman who thought of me as an unsightly blemish. "I can't do this right now."

"I'm not going anywhere."

Then where the hell were you when I was changing Mom's diaper? "Okay, I'll tell Travis you called."

"I mean, I'm not going anywhere until August." Nora clears her throat. "And then I'm coming up your way."

"I got that, Nora."

Kristy says a quick goodbye, hangs up the phone, and bolts out of the house.

Kristy is ravenous. McDonald's. The grease will soak up the alcohol in her bloodstream. Halfway through her Quarter Pounder, she's full, so she dumps the rest in the trash. Next up: Marshalls. She loads her cart: two clingy jersey dresses, white jeans, two tank tops, and a simple sundress, only because it costs five dollars. High-heeled sandals call to her, and she adds a pair in white and black. Back in the car, she takes off her shirt and Gillian's sacred bra and changes into her new white jeans, black tank top, silver hoops, and sandals. It's only a short drive back to the bar.

"Hit me up, Red," she calls out to the waitress from last night, who is now bartending.

"Nice hoops, chica." She pours Kristy a shot of tequila and sets it down in front of her. "A little something for you while I make the mai tais. On me."

"You're trouble." Kristy downs the drink. "Chica."

Red's the kind of woman Kristy used to pick for a friend. When she did her fourth step character defect inventory with Beverly all those years ago, she learned that she'd only ever had friends who were addicts of some sort, until Gillian (if you didn't count River Run as an addiction, which it is). She confided in them about her latest man, reliving every word of affection, every touch, every phone call, every sign that she was loved, and in the retelling she copped as big a hit as she did when she was actually engaging with the man. She was Monica Lewinsky confiding in Linda Tripp. Beverly warned her that you can't truly rely on an addict friend unless they're in recovery, and even then you can lose them to a relapse any second. But Kristy would sniff out an addict in a crowded room because there was no one else on the whole planet who would understand her as deeply, wholly.

Red returns with two mai tais, and Kristy swats away thoughts of Beverly. And Nora.

She checks her phone for the ninety-seventh time today. No word from Charlie. David's on call. She's been texting regularly with David and Mia, who writes that Amber has been spending the night at their house because her family still doesn't have power. Kristy guesses that Mia is actually home alone with Liam, having sex. All rules are suspended during heat waves and power outages. Moms let their toddlers eat ice cream for breakfast, and high-school girls sleep in guest bedrooms with their boyfriends. Welcome to Power Outage Land.

Austin is back, but she isn't going to let him feel her up today. She's too tired. She plunks down a wad of cash. "Sleepy time," she says to Red, and heads outside to her car.

Two hours later, Kristy awakens from her power nap, her chin covered in drool. It's almost six. Time to check her phone. Gillian has posted a picture of Charlie standing on a pool deck talking to his swimmers bunched up in one lane. "Thank you, gracious hosts!" #squatters #derechodestruction. Charlie's finishing up practice about now. Kristy debates driving to the borrowed pool to see him. No, let Charlie come to her. They need to talk about what happened, about what to do about telling Gillian. False. Bullshit. She wants to see him, and that's the beginning, middle, and end of the story. "Meet me here," she texts, and gives him the address of the bar.

"I'll see what I can do," Charlie texts back.

This isn't what she wants. "It's really important, Charlie."

"I'll try."

She fires back. "It's about Gillian." Once they're together, she'll make him forget about her sister.

The barely audible ping on her phone makes Kristy damned near giddy. Charlie's coming. She better hit the ladies' room and freshen up.

75

CHARLIE

Charlie doesn't have to lie to Gillian about going to see Kristy, because Gillian's busy giving one of her "Let Go or Be Dragged" talks to a women's group in a fully powered community room in an Alexandria housing development. Gillian would be six degrees of mortified if she knew that Patrick has been counseling Justin after her son saw his dad banging his mom's best friend. For now, though, he needs to untangle this knot one thread at a time. What does Kristy have to tell him about Gillian? Charlie feels like he did when his mother told him that his father found one of Charlie's joints in the watering can out in the garage. It was agony waiting for his dad to come home from work and punish him, which he did by calling him a lowlife loser and grounding him for a month.

Before he takes off for the bar, he stares himself down in the rearview mirror. "You are a lowlife loser," he says. He hasn't eaten anything all day, and his mouth tastes sour as hell. The roads are so empty that he makes it to Manassas in twenty-five minutes.

The bar is small and smoky, its walls filled with photos of drunk-happy patrons. Two neon Budweiser signs illuminate the dark space. It smells like a frat house, but it's air-conditioned, and that's not nothing. Kristy is sitting at the bar, deep in conversation with a redhead, three empty shot glasses in front of her. Great, she's drunk.

"Hey, Charlie!!" She spots him while sitting with her back to him, like she has radar installed in her body. She's wearing an outfit that leaves nothing to the imagination. The tight jeans and high heels make her look like a caricature of herself.

"Let's go sit at a table," she slurs. "More privacy."

The redhead asks Charlie if he wants anything.

"Just a Coke, please."

"Party pooper," Kristy giggles. "Put that on my tab."

He waits for his soda and plunks a five-dollar bill on the bar. "I've got this."

"Follow me." She leads him to a small two-top and sits next to him. Tonight he finds her perfume noxious.

"I'm sorry about the luau," he says. "You know, about everything."

"It's not your fault."

"I lit the match, Kristy." His lower lip trembles.

She puts her fingers on his lip.

Charlie gently removes her hand. "Kristy, we need to tell Gillian what we did."

"You mean she hasn't asked who lit the tiki torches?"

"That's not what I meant. But no, she hasn't asked about the torches."

Kristy pouts. "I don't want to talk about Gillian."

"That's why I'm here."

She looks as though he's slapped her.

"You know, your text?"

She snakes her fingers up Charlie's thigh, under his shorts.

"Kristy, no."

"Please, Charlie. I figured it all out." She envelops his hands in hers.

"Figured out what?"

"We'll have sex four times, total, counting tonight, and then we'll stop."

He looks straight ahead, clenching his jaw. "I don't think so."

"Why don't you think so? You don't like my idea?" She's begging.

"Kristy, do you have something to tell me about Gillian?"

"Yes, I do."

"Can you please tell me, then?" He wants this to end. Now.

"Drive me to my dad's, and I'll tell you," she says, and struts up to the bar to settle her tab.

What choice does he have?

76

KRISTY

Lightning bugs cluster in a small formation, and Kristy tries to catch one and hold it in her hand.

Charlie opens the door for Kristy. "Look, I need to scoot back home after I drop you off."

They, the men, never have time for her. "It's only a mile from here."

Charlie takes the wheel and blasts the air. She's only ridden in his car a few times. Gillian always complains about Charlie's sloppy car, but it's spotless except for a few PowerBar wrappers in the well between the two front seats.

"Take a right at the stop sign." She gives him a few more directions, but otherwise they drive the few minutes to Travis's house without talking. He parks in front.

Kristy touches his scalp the way she did that first time.

"Please stop," he snaps.

She withdraws her hand and puts it back in her lap. She hates herself right now.

"I'm going to go. It doesn't look like you have anything to tell me about Gillian."

"Oh, yes I do, Charlie. Yes, I do." It comes to her. They will bond over her Sebastian secret. She will cry. He will hold her.

"Then just tell me and let's be done with it."

"Brace yourself, Charlie." He won't be so cranky after he hears her news.

"I'm ready for it. Hit me," he says sarcastically.

"Fasten your seat belt, Charlie." She takes a big breath and exhales. "Your wife is my sister. How 'bout that?"

"Come on." He looks at her with disgust. "What are you talking about?"

"I'm talking about Sebastian the legend's dalliance with my mother."

"That's pretty farfetched, Kristy."

"Do you want me to take you inside so you can ask Travis?" Kristy lays out the whole story for Charlie while he listens, slack-jawed. After she finishes, he shifts in his seat and focuses his gaze out the window, to the rows of houses that look exactly like hers.

Kristy can't take the silence anymore. "Did you hear me?"

"Every word." He is still looking out the window.

She folds her arms across her shoulders. "And?"

"I actually half believe you."

"I look like them." Kristy reaches over and turns Charlie's head toward her. "Patrick and Sebastian."

He studies her face. "Jesus Christ. You do."

"I'm like them." She stares at her hands, safely folded in her lap. "You know what I mean."

"Yeah." Her secret isn't going to tie them together. Charlie looks more distant and miserable than ever.

"Now you know." She instructs her tears to run wild, but they're not readily available.

Charlie looks sad. "Kristy, do you have someone to call? Maybe David?"

"I'll figure it out." Before he can ask her to leave, she climbs out of his car and starts walking toward the house.

"Kristy?" he calls after her.

If he asks her to get back in the car and go someplace with him, any place, she will. She turns around. "What?"

"I'm just really sorry this all happened."

"Me too." Now she doesn't want him to see her cry at all. She scurries into the house.

"Hi, Dad."

Travis sits at the kitchen table rereading the sports section of the *Post.* After the many nights spent in the cars of other women's men, she always came home to a dark house. But here's Travis, sitting in the brightly lit kitchen and asking her if she's hungry.

"I could eat a little something."

"How about a piece of toast? I've got some good jam." He folds up his newspaper.

"That sounds perfect, Dad."

"Grape." He winks.

She never knew he was aware of her favorite flavor. He gets up, removes two slices of white bread from the bag, and toasts them for her. He rests his chin in his palm and watches her slather the jelly on the browned bread. After she's gobbled down both slices, he softly asks, "You still hungry?"

The kind lilt in his voice makes her eyes well up. "I'm full, thanks."

"You know, when you were small, you wanted a big sister badly."

Kristy picks at her toast crumbs. She's not used to his speaking so directly, and the intimacy embarrasses her.

"You had a doll that you named RhondaMay." Travis's lips curl with amusement.

"You remember RhondaMay?"

"Funniest-looking doll I ever saw."

They laugh.

"Maybe because Nora colored in one of her teeth with a black marker." Kristy sighs.

"You have another sister now."

"And I'm as envious of her as I was of Nora."

"Honey, why are you so angry with Nora?"

"Why are you not? Weren't you at all hurt that she didn't show up when Mom was dying?" There, she said it.

Travis places a hand on her wrist. His skin is wrinkly and dry, like a lizard's. "She's not as strong as you are."

"I think you're letting her off the hook."

"She couldn't face it. Losing your mom."

Suddenly Kristy gets it. Nora suffered a different loss than Kristy did, because Flo had mothered Nora with pride and an open heart.

The dam bursts, and tears flood down her cheeks. She can't stop sobbing. She's been horrible to Gillian, who mothered her more than any other human being ever has. She practically lit the match to Gillian's sacred clubhouse. She was riddled with rage toward Sebastian for not acknowledging her existence. Who cared if he didn't even know she'd been born? In the photos Gillian shoved down the throat of every River Run member and guest, he looked handsome and dazzling. She still longs for this dead womanizer even as Travis, who has done nothing but show her kindness, holds out a paper dinner napkin.

"Dad, I'm not going to have a second sister for much longer." She blows her nose with the napkin.

"Do you want to talk about it?" Travis has never uttered these words to her.

"Charlie." No explanation necessary. Her cheeks burn.

Travis pats her shoulder stiffly. "Oh, Kris."

"What should I do?" She wipes away her tears and crumples the napkin. She half wants Travis to tell her how to win Charlie back. Despite everything, or more likely *because of* everything, she still wants him. Badly.

"No more secrets, sweetheart."

She rises and pours herself a cup of Travis's stale morning coffee.

Her father gets up and slides his arm around her shoulder, but this time, maybe for the first time ever, with ease. "I'm going to brew you a fresh pot."

77

GILLIAN

Gillian's phone rings as she navigates the maze of the parking lot at the planned community in Alexandria, looking for her van. It's Sebby checking in again. She wishes Justin would come home, although who can blame him for wanting to stay with the Johnsons?

"How was your presentation?" Sebby asks.

"Oh, your mother was a big hit." Gillian finally spots her car.

"The River Run kids are posting pictures of the clubhouse on Instagram. The whole thing is so creepy." Street noises compete with Sebby's voice.

"Well, we'll get it all taken care of. Pronto." Gillian starts the car.

"Do you want me to come home?"

Sebby's earnestness makes her tear up. "Oh, no. Don't do that. No use all of us sitting in a dark, hot house together."

"Are you sure?"

"We're all doing just fine. Tell me about you."

For the entire drive back to Arlington, Sebby fills her in on the latest about his roommate and his internship and how his boss is kind of a jerk but he likes Sebby a lot. This makes Gillian happy; folks generally warm to Justin, but Sebby has a bit of an edge.

"How's Dad?" Sebby asks.

"He's doing well, you know, busy figuring things out now that the pool is closed for a bit."

Sebby promises to phone again tomorrow, and after they hang up, Gillian has no defense against the fear and ache Sebby has always evoked in her. At his sixth-grade graduation celebration, he threw up from drinking nine cans of Mountain Dew. She knew back then to keep an eye on him, but instead she chased him away. Or did she chase him away because she couldn't bear watching him eye Charlie's occasional beer at dinner or the wine they opened for company? Because he was becoming Patrick and Sebastian Norton? She could barely tolerate him during winter break his freshman year at Hofstra. He stayed out until all hours, and in the morning his room stank of vodka. She'd know that smell anywhere. When he made a big fuss about having "a cocktail" before they ate Christmas dinner, Gillian instinctively forced the family to pose for a group photo before Sebby got drunk. But then something happened before he came home that summer, and he morphed back into the son she loved, but even better.

Home.

Odd. No Charlie. Gillian checks her phone. Nothing. Where is he? She wishes he would text. That pit swells quickly inside her, nudging open her internal memory storage unit, a vessel with a cracked airproof lid. Her memories arrive as the rudest and most unwelcome houseguests, blasting her back to the worst night of her life.

Gillian was the one who identified Sebastian's body. May found her at Fran's house, where she was observing her twenty-first birthday with the most recent permutation of the River Rats. Gillian had actually had two celebratory margaritas, so May drove them to the hospital, and before walking inside they held each other, both shivering in the warm September night. None of the familiar nurses Sebastian had charmed during prior episodes were on duty. A doctor with a practiced sympathetic smile escorted Gillian and her mother to a private room where Sebastian lay under a sheet. When May hesitated at the door, Gillian put her hand on her mother's child-sized wrist and said, "Stay here." May looked relieved. The room smelled like her drunk father: vodka,

Brut, and body odor. And the acrid scent of death. Gillian, not the doctor, pulled back the sheet. Sebastian's whitish-blond hair was matted, his eyes bruised and swollen, his cheeks bloated from the booze. Although he looked like he was sleeping with his mouth open, like he did after a bender, this felt different. His tortured spirit had left his body. Finally. Gillian kissed his gray forehead and said goodbye to this version of Sebastian, forever. After the funeral, she recast him as Sebastian the swan-diver.

Charlie isn't Sebastian, she reminds herself. Charlie is reliable and kind and loyal. He doesn't drink or fool around. He might have grown a little financially irresponsible, maybe too carried away with his coaching and his midlife crisis, but he's rock solid. That was why she picked him.

The pit is now cutting off the air supply from her lungs to her other organs. She gasps for breath.

78

JUSTIN

Justin had every intention of going home after the first night of the power outage, but talking with Uncle Patrick makes him feel better. Worse too, but mainly better. He craves more space from his parents, the pool, everything.

Now it's time to go home. He writes Uncle Patrick a note, rides his bike to the 7-Eleven, and takes his place in a long line of adults and kids splattering perfectly good Slurpee nectar all over the floor. Amateurs.

He feels a pang of guilt that he has been enjoying the luxuries of electricity while everyone else suffers. This is the fourth day of the heat wave, and grocery stores and even the 7-Eleven have run out of ice. People are camping out in their cars, charging their phones and pressing their faces against the air vents.

He pays for his drink and is sitting outside on the bike rack, sipping slowly, letting the chill travel through his blood, when Dad drives up.

Mia had texted him to ask if he was still not feeling well (he had lied to Mia and Liam about a stomach bug). She said Dad was so distracted that she and Liam practically had to run the workout. Now he's climbing out of his car and heading toward Justin, walking like the ever-besieged Candace on *Phineas and Ferb.* One of his swimmers turned him on to the show.

"We need ice," Dad says.

Justin points to the sign on the door: NO ICE.

"Bummer."

Justin takes a gulp of his Slurpee.

"Can I ask you something, Justin?"

He can't make eye contact with his father. "Yeah."

"What's the deal with the Slurpees?"

Nobody has ever asked Justin about his Slurpees before. Mom warned him of the red dye that would ravage his brain, and Liam teased him, but neither asked him why he loved the drink. "Long story."

"I've got time," Dad says sheepishly.

"Tiff and I used to drink these together."

"Used to?"

"She dumped me."

"I thought you two were just spending the summer apart. I'm sorry."

"For a guy named Dill." Justin's chest tightens at the mention of his name.

"Harper Lee or Claussen?"

"That's what I asked. Harper Lee."

"Got it."

"She's 'on holiday' with Dill's family in Iceland. Well, now they're in London." It feels good to be pissed at someone else besides Dad and to recruit Dad to the cause.

Dad looks even sadder.

"I follow her on Instagram."

"Well, don't let social media fool you. She's probably having a horrible time."

Dad's clearly referring to Mom's "Fakebooking" habit, but Justin doesn't want to open up that conversation, so he tells Charlie that he misses Tiff every second of every day and the only time he feels alive is when he's coaching the kids.

"Me too," Dad says.

"Seriously?"

"I think so."

Justin takes the final sip of his Slurpee, thinking that this is the kind of conversation he would have with Tiff. Real. Honest. "I have a grape-colored 7-Eleven tattoo on my ass."

"Me too," Dad deadpans, and they both laugh.

Dad shifts his weight from one foot to the other. "Justin, about the luau—"

Justin cuts him off. "None of my business."

Dad clenches his jaw. "I'm sorry you had to see that."

Justin might never be able to block out the look of shame that still lingers on his father's face and, even worse, the desperation of Aunt Kristy. "Me too."

"I'm even sorrier that it happened." He clears his throat as if he's going to say more.

"Dad." Justin holds up his hand. "I can't talk about this with you."

Dad's eyes well up and he raises his palms to cover his face. Justin has never seen his father cry, but he isn't going to comfort him. He doesn't want to know why his father pulled such a dick move. He doesn't care about his male menopause. After hearing the real deal about Mom's childhood, a tsunami of love for her washed over him.

"I'll see you back at the house." Justin throws his cup in the overflowing trash can. "I've got my bike."

It's time to go home.

79

CHARLIE

Charlie enters the airless house, flashlight in hand. "Gil?"

"Down here," she calls from the basement.

He shines the thin beam on each step down the stairs, holding the railing for support. Three track lights illuminate the unfinished room where they keep their large freezer. Backlit by a smaller fourth flashlight she's placed in the bottom of the freezer, Gillian faces him in her running bra, shorts, and rubber gloves. She looks devastated. Gillian never looks troubled, even when she is. Her body glistens, and she's holding an antibacterial wipe plucked from the Costco-sized package at her feet.

"You're home." She returns to her scrubbing.

"Gillian," he says. "Please stop for a second."

She unbends her body, her arms dangling at her sides. He looks her over from head to toe, and she lets him. He searches for signs of Kristy, but Gillian is all May Norton.

"What?" Gillian wipes her brow with her forearm.

He wants to hold her so badly. Does she even know that her father cheated on her mother? She only discussed her father's drinking once, when Patrick needed them to pay for his treatment.

"This is the best time to attack the freezer." Gillian waves a wipe in the air. He doesn't know anyone who cleans as meticulously as Gillian Norton Cloud. "It's so empty!"

"You sure that can't wait until morning?" He's dripping buckets just looking at her.

She digs the wipe into the far corner of the freezer. "No."

"Are you upset with me?" The room is spinning. What if she's found out?

"Nope. Just done with this power outage."

His whole body loosens. "You sure?"

"Why didn't you answer your phone?" She's still talking to him with her head in the freezer.

"I'm so sorry. I was out of juice."

She finally puts down her wipe and walks over to him and hugs him hard. "I was worried."

"Oh, Gil. I didn't mean to make you worry." She reeks of disinfectant.

"Too hot to hug." She releases him.

"How was your presentation?"

"Air-conditioned." She fans herself. "Did you have any luck with the ice?"

"No, drove ten miles out of town. Everyone is out." Why is he telling such a stupid lie?

"Hmmm . . . We have a meeting tomorrow with the insurance adjuster at the pool. Can you meet us at three?"

"Sure, and I have good news for you," Charlie says.

"We could use some good news."

"Justin texted that he's coming home." He doesn't want to tell her that he ran into him a few minutes ago, best to tell another lie. "Before my phone died." He's a shitty liar.

"When?"

"Tonight."

"That *is* good news."

She returns to the freezer, handing him a pair of gloves. "Let's finish up, then."

He puts on the gloves, bends over, and musters Gillian's vigor to abrade the spotless freezer.

80

KRISTY

Power outage, day four. Heat wave, day five. Kristy sits primly on the floral bedspread of her youth, dressed in the skort Travis laundered for her, her new clothes folded neatly in a Marshalls bag she will not bring home. The sun's starting to make an appearance, and the house is still, save for the cuckoo clock clucking away in the hall.

Travis is puttering around in the kitchen. The longer she stays in her room, the harder it will be to ask him to drive her to the bar for her car. Oh, God. Charlie. How did she get back here again? Flo was right all along. Kristy is a slut.

"Morning, Kris."

She busies herself pouring a glass of juice so she won't have to look at him. "Morning."

"I have to run an errand. Do you want me to drop you off at your car?" Travis sounds as if he's rehearsed this line. Gracious man.

"Thank you." She takes a sip of juice. "There was a strange noise coming from under the car yesterday."

"We'll have a look-see."

"I should probably go home," Kristy says. "After that."

"You can always come here if you need to, Kris."

She finishes her juice to keep from crying again and goes upstairs to retrieve her bag. Travis locks up, and the two of them walk out to his car. Kristy cranks WTOP during their short drive to the bar so they won't have to talk. "Still five hundred thousand homes without power across the DMV," the reporter announces.

"Helluva mess." That was how Travis described the flood in his basement, which seems like a century ago.

"Yeah, helluva mess," Kristy says.

After they park in the lot behind the bar, Travis takes out his old creeper, and with the ease of a much younger man he lowers himself onto the narrow plank and scoots under the car. She used to keep him company while he worked on their various Fords. He only bought American.

"Sorry to make you do this," she says to his legs. He rolls out from under her SUV as he used to do if she said something smart or funny. That was her favorite part.

"Happy to help." He disappears again. "Aahh. Here's the trouble. You ran over a piece of someone's tire rim that embedded itself in your undercarriage."

"I knew you'd figure it out." Kristy plants herself in a circle of shade while Travis fixes the problem. When he rolls back out on the creeper, she says goodbye, her heart full of gratitude and love.

"Come here, Kris." Travis leans up and kisses her forehead.

"Thanks for everything, Daddy."

Before she starts the engine, she calls Beverly.

81

JUSTIN

Mia surprises Justin by showing up in the early afternoon with a grocery bag she's filled with a homemade tuna sandwich, a bottle of ice-cold milk, and freshly baked chocolate chip cookies.

"You rock, Mia Weinstein." He takes the milk bottle and presses it against his face like his high-school Spanish teacher did when she started to sweat out of nowhere.

"Don't forget these." She sticks her arm in the bag and hands him two leftover sticks of beef jerky. "For protein."

"Grandpa Frick!" Justin makes the thumbs-up sign.

"My mom's taking care of him right now."

"What happened?"

"Apparently he hurt his knee."

"That's too bad." But maybe it isn't a bad thing that Mia's mom is away. Justin doesn't want to think about Aunt Kristy or Dad. For now he wants to scarf down his tuna sandwich. He's starving.

"Anyway, the jerky is for later. You know, if you don't get power for a while, which you might not. Dominion is saying this is going to be a long outage because there are so many trees down."

"Thanks, Scoop." Mia is constantly updating everyone, which he's always thought hilarious, even when she was younger and kind of a brat sometimes.

"Please. It's all over the national news. And the heat wave." She reads from her phone. "Dude. They're predicting eleven days in a row over ninety-five."

"Not good." He digs Mia, not like a girlfriend or anything, more like a sister. "You want to hang out in this sweatbox?"

His parents said they'd be out for a while, and he's been sitting in the basement most of the morning, trying to read.

"Yeah." She puts her hands in the back pockets of her jean shorts.

"Let's go downstairs. Coolest spot in the house."

She tags after him like a puppy, and they sit on the sheet his mother spread out on the floor. There's nothing worse than sweaty legs sticking to the carpet. Itches like hell.

"Liam didn't want to come with you today?" He laughs.

"I'm so over that."

Justin hides his smile in a bite of his sandwich.

"He's a douche, as you said." She finishes her cookie with gusto and takes a swig from his bottle of milk.

"So why did you have a thing for him anyway?"

She hands him back the bottle. "Because we got some stupid young-love paper plate award at the banquet about five years ago, and the idea stuck in my head."

"Lame." Justin downs the rest of his sandwich.

She glances up at the Ikea shelf in the corner. "You have Blokus?"

"You want to play?"

"I rule at this game." She hoists herself up from the floor and removes the box.

"Okay, I get red."

They play four rounds, and Mia wins three. Both of them are sweating their asses off, and Justin apologizes for the heat.

"This is really fun, Justin," she says simply.

"Getting my ass kicked by you is really fun, I agree."

"Math brain." She taps her head without apology.

"It's really gross in here."

"Do you want to go get a Slurpee?"

"Actually?"

"Justin. This isn't an essay question," Mia teases.

"Let's go."

They clean up the lunch remains and the game, and Justin leaves the house, the air outside only slightly warmer than in his basement. They take Mia's car and blast the A/C.

Mia's playlist is cool. "You like Vampire Weekend?"

"Liam hates them." Mia smiles mischievously.

Justin turns up the volume on "Campus."

When they pass River Run pool, Justin checks the parking lot by force of habit. Neither comment on Mom's car. He has an inkling that soon Dad and Aunt Kristy will show up. He texts Uncle Patrick to give him a heads-up on what might go down at the pool, and Patrick advises him to stay away.

"So pumped about that Slurpee, Mia."

Justin and Mia drive on, the cool air on their faces, their palms thumping their bare knees to the beat of the music.

82

GILLIAN

Gillian arrives at River Run an hour before she's scheduled to meet Charlie, Karl, and the insurance adjuster. She needs a minute alone, to think. No amount of last night's scrubbing or spooning Charlie did anything to dissolve the pit yawning inside of her. She's a nervous Nellie, one of May's favorite expressions.

She lets herself into the pool and examines the fallen oak. How many times had she put "call the arborist" on her to-do list? How many times had she made excuses not to call, to let another season pass? Someone could have been killed, and the blood would have been on her hands.

"Hey." Charlie walks through the gate Gillian has unlocked. He's lost his new swagger, and he looks almost green. She studies him more closely. His expression reminds her of Sebby's after he'd done something bad. She goes over to him, cups his chin in her hand, and peers into his eyes. They are radiating remorse.

"Where were you, Charlie?"

"I found us some ice!" He can't look at her. "At the Safeway off of—"

"What were you doing the night of the fire?"

"I was here," he answers so softly she can barely hear him.

"Here?" She coughs out the word.

He can't look her in the eye.

"Charlie, what on earth did you do?"

His body sways, and when he licks his lips she can hear that his mouth is bone-dry.

Her brain catches up with what her gut has known since the night of the derecho. Her body goes cold. Dead-cold. He's strayed. She feels it, smells it.

83

CHARLIE

Charlie feels fluish.

"Charlie, look me in the eye." Gillian is speaking in that horrid fake-calm tone.

He leans against the hot metal ladder of the closest guard stand.

"I want you to tell me every detail about that night." She's still using that voice.

He turns around. "After you went to bed, I started watching an episode of *Breaking Bad*."

"You can skip that part."

"But I don't want to skip that part." He puts his hands on his hips. "It was the part when Walter and Jesse try to kill a fly."

"A terminally ill chemistry teacher isn't central to the story."

Maybe Walter White's decision to go rogue motivated Charlie, maybe this is the key element of the story.

"Come on, Charlie. Walk me through this." She strides over to the pool and snaps her fingers at him to come, as though he's a dog.

Charlie will not be her bitch. "Gillian, this is my story, and if you want to hear it, you will have to let me tell it my way."

"Are you kidding me?" Her voice scales to an unrecognizable pitch.

"Yes, I was a shitheel, but it's still *my* story." He can imagine her turning this incident into one of her Facebook posts. #charlieaffair #bucketlist.

She sneers at him. "Okay, tell *your* story *your* way, Charlie."

He walks over to the shed. "Here is where I retrieved the tiki torches." He picks one up and stuffs it under his arm. "Now I'm going to take you to the spots where I put them. Follow me." He speed-walks to the fallen tree. "I put one here." He marches on to the grills. "Two here, spitting distance from the spilled lighter fluid and the highly flammable leis." He proceeds to a small patch of dirt near the row of lounge chairs closest to the pool. "Can we stop this nonsense now?"

"I want to know."

"Okay, so I lit the match. It was me. I did it."

"Go on."

"And the wind came in like a motherfucker and blew a torch over to the leis."

A look of recognition shades her face. "Uh-huh."

He bows his head, and when he raises it he feels faint. "And there was lighter fluid on the grass, and the leis caught on fire."

"Yeah, I knew that part." Her eyes go dead.

"Okay, so now you know." He might very well pass out.

She's quiet for a few minutes. He puts his hands over his ears to block out the cicadas, whose whining is dancing on his jangled nerve endings.

"Who were you with?" she asks with no affect.

He needs to sit down.

"Who?" she barks.

Blood pulses so relentlessly he can hear it thump in his ears.

"It had to be Kristy, Charlie."

Hearing her say these words is a kick in the balls. "What?"

"You heard me." She glowers.

"Yes." He tries to swallow, but his mouth is dry as sandpaper.

"Good on you, Charlie."

"Can we stop now?"

Her skin turns white under her freckles. "Confess."

"I confess." His voice is scratchy.

She waves a hand in the air. "Am I allowed to tell you that I really hate your story?"

"I hate it too. But there's more." Gillian needs to know that Kristy is her sister.

"GO!" She whisper-screams. "Get out."

Charlie starts to talk, but the rest of the story belongs to Kristy. He brushes his lips against Gillian's face. She smells like Gillian and smoke.

"Get away from me, Charlie."

Before he leaves the pool, he considers telling her that he loves her and that he can't imagine a life without her, and this is true. It is also true that they can no longer sanitize their lives or stow away their histories in Container Store merchandise.

84

GILLIAN

Charlie and Kristy. Charlie and Kristy sitting in a tree. K-i-s-s-i-n-g. Which one of them would take home her heart and stick it on the wall, like the buck's head hanging over Charlie's family's fireplace? Gillian's body shakes as she texts Kristy and asks her to meet her at the pool.

"Hello there, Gillian." Karl, the pool manager, startles her.

She can't muster up her fancy smile right now. "I'm sorry about the tree. I screwed up."

"I don't want you to worry about that."

Gillian puts on her sunglasses.

"Listen, the adjuster called. He's overbooked with the storm and all, so we'll have to reschedule for later this week." Karl wipes a line of sweat from his neck.

"That's fine," she says absently.

"You got any plans for the Fourth?"

"No."

"Still going to be a hot mess around here."

"It's a hot mess, all right."

"I'll leave you be. Just don't go in the water."

"Don't worry. Who would be that reckless?"

"You'd be surprised," Karl answers.

Gillian doesn't respond. The Fourth of July. She looks around the ravaged pool, imagining May and Patrick at their usual stations: May pouring cups of Hawaiian Punch for the kids and Patrick playing soccer or basketball outside the pool gate. The diving board is still intact, but there is no Sebastian to dazzle them.

She picks a lounge chair far away from the clubhouse, sits down, and waits. And wonders. Did May torture herself by imagining Sebastian having sex? By wondering if his latest conquest was on top or bottom? Did May share a meal or a cold drink or a PTA committee meeting with Sebastian's latest woman? Drive the woman's daughter home from a Girl Scout troop meeting? Did it hurt more when it was a stranger, or a friend? Did she let Sebastian tell his own story his own way when he got caught? Did it break her inside when Gillian and Patrick discovered Sebastian's cheating?

Gillian is calm-crazy. May modeled the Norton way, how to act as if your soul were not Rome, burning, burning, burning.

85

KRISTY

Beverly warns Kristy against meeting Gillian at the pool. According to Beverly, Kristy is way too fragile for a confrontation. Maybe after she's worked the steps she'll be ready to make her amends, which should start with David.

Even after the mass destruction she's caused, Kristy hopes that Charlie will be waiting with Gillian at River Run. When Mia took the mandatory health class at school, she described a movie she watched about a heroin addict who gets clean and then as soon as she's released from rehab she shoots heroin into her neck. Any equanimity Kristy felt from talking to Beverly and hugging Travis goodbye has vanished.

Kristy unzips her purse to check for the envelope with her birth certificate and the weathered photo of Sebastian. On her way into the pool, she sees Gillian. She can tell that Gillian has found out about what happened the night of the derecho by the way she's sitting, rocking back and forth like she has the stomach flu and is trying not to vomit. When Gillian spots Kristy, she springs up and walks over to the clubhouse. Kristy is frightened of this Gillian, as she knows she should be.

"Gil, what are you doing?"

"Just want to take a look, see if anything can be salvaged."

"I'm not sure that's a great idea." But Kristy follows her anyway, blowing by the yellow tape and the sign that reads "Do Not Enter." The air bleeds smoke.

As soon as Kristy walks into the pool house, Gillian shuts the door and butts her body against it. "We're going to talk in here, in this stinky, hot ruin." Her eyes are wild.

Kristy had expected Gillian to enter into crazy Facebooking mode, denying all knowledge of her husband sleeping with her best friend. This is a Gillian she has never experienced. "I'm sorry."

"Sorry for what?"

"Everything." There's no oxygen in the room.

"Oh, where shall we start? Sorry for being such a bitch this summer? For making me feel like a pariah in my own community?" Gillian's body jounces with pent-up rage.

Beverly was right. Coming to the pool was a truly rotten idea. "Yes."

"I BROUGHT YOU HERE."

Tears stream down Kristy's face. "I know, I know."

"Nobody even liked you. They thought you were aloof and shallow, what with your . . ." Gillian pats her hips.

Kristy wipes her cheek with her palm.

"And fake boobs." Spittle pools in the corner of Gillian's mouth. "I'm the one who persuaded everyone to give you a chance, to invite you to their parties. And what do you do?"

"I don't know what to say."

"How about, Gosh, Gillian, I'm so sorry for fucking your husband."

"I'm . . ." she whimpers.

Gillian sets her jaw. "I'm not going to comfort you."

Kristy tries to sniff up the mucus that is dripping down her top lip. "I know."

Gillian reaches down to the floor of the clubhouse and scoops up a handful of ashes. She rips off Kristy's sunglasses while Kristy stands still as a mannequin. Gillian rubs the soot all over Kristy's face. "Choke on this," she says.

Kristy coughs, but she doesn't wipe the soot away. She deserves this. She's a piece of shit.

"And by the way, I want my bra back." Gillian storms off, opening the door and slamming it behind her.

Kristy chases after her and grasps her wrist so hard that she leaves red fingermarks on Gillian's skin. Gillian yanks her arm away and walks around the back of the pool, behind the diving board, along the grass. She's so agile in her rage that Kristy has to take off her sandals to keep up.

"Wait, Gillian."

Gillian walks faster.

"Stop."

Gillian whirls on her. "Did you hate me that much?"

Kristy is winded. "Yes, Gillian. I hated you that much."

"What?" Gillian's mouth gapes open. "What?"

"I said, Yes, Gillian, I hated you that much, maybe even more." Kristy wipes soot from her forehead with the back of her hand.

"Why? What the heck is wrong with you, Kristy?"

"Look, you can divorce Charlie, but you'll never ever be able to get rid of me."

"Watch me." Gillian continues toward the pool exit.

"Gillian!" Kristy screeches.

"I'm done with you," Gillian yells over her shoulder.

"Stop. Walking." Kristy prays with everything she has that Gillian will turn around. Smoke-smelling sweat bleeds down her face and into her eyes, so she pinches them shut and takes stock of all that she has ruined. Gillian's love. Steady and undying. A sister's love. Please turn around, Gillian. Please turn around. Please, Gillian, please.

"I'm your sister." Kristy does not scream.

Gillian stops moving. Please, Gillian. Come back to me. And by some miracle, she does.

"You." Gillian thumps her finger against Kristy's chest. "Are not my sister."

"Yes, I am."

"You're not even my friend."

"Just hold on." Kristy removes her dusty purse from her shoulder and unzips the pocket with the envelope. "I found this in my dad's basement."

"What is it?" Gillian snarls.

"Look."

Gillian glances at the envelope. "Go on."

Kristy relays the story as she did to Beverly, quickly, as if she might not have the courage to continue if she pauses. If she doesn't tell the full story, it will get trapped inside of her forever. "So that's it. We're sisters."

Gillian breaks into a cackle.

Kristy has never heard such a sound come from Gillian, from anyone. "This is funny to you, Gillian?"

She cackles harder, but her face is pained.

"Gillian!"

Gillian takes a step toward Kristy. Her breath smells like the fasters at the end of Yom Kippur. "You took everything that was mine because you wanted a father like *Sebastian Norton*?"

"I don't know what I wanted." Kristy reaches for Gillian, who brushes her hand away.

"You're an idiot." Gillian's voice hardens to granite.

"What do you mean? Sebastian Norton was a River Run legend." Kristy mimes a swan dive. Of course she knows that Sebastian got into some trouble, but she has always seen their father through Gillian's version of him.

"Sucker." Gillian is standing way too close to Kristy.

"What are you talking about?"

Gillian puts her hands on her hips. "He was a drunk and a lech."

Kristy has never heard Gillian utter a bad word about Sebastian. "You loved him."

She takes a breath. "Sebastian Norton was a bad dog."

Kristy still wants to claim him.

"I'd have killed to have a father like Travis." Gillian backs up, takes her phone out of her pocket, and snaps a photo of Kristy.

"Come on, stop it, Gil."

"Here." She waves the image under Kristy's nose. "Look closely, Kristy."

Kristy studies her ash-streaked face and swollen eyes.

"Don't you get it?" Gillian's voice is shrill.

"Get what?" Kristy pushes the phone away from her face.

Gillian looks at Kristy like she's nothing. "You *are* Sebastian Norton."

86

GILLIAN

A rush of heat explodes up Gillian's body. She can't get away from Kristy fast enough. She takes huge strides but doesn't get far, because she steps on something sharp that sends a searing bolt of pain through her foot and up her leg. "Damn." She sits down on the grass across from the diving board and examines the shard of glass that has pierced her arch.

"What happened?" Kristy's voice penetrates Gillian, through her ears, to her brain, down to her shattered heart.

"My foot." Her toes throb.

Kristy hovers over her. It's cloudy now. The sun no longer blinds Gillian as she studies Kristy: the shock of blond hair, the dark skin, the way she turns heads every time she enters the pool. Her eyes travel to Kristy's flat arches that match her own, and Sebastian's.

"Give me your car keys, Gillian."

"I think I've given you enough." She wants Kristy to leave the pool. Her pool.

"For your first-aid kit."

"It's unlocked." Gillian clutches her foot, cataloguing the lies Kristy has told her, admonishing herself for choosing to buy them. Kristy lies just like Sebastian. One point for nature over nurture.

Kristy returns to her with the kit. "Give me your foot," she orders.

Gillian doesn't want Kristy touching her, but she decides she can endure it.

"This is going to hurt."

What could hurt worse than what Kristy has done? "Just get it over with."

Kristy sanitizes her hands before expertly tweezing the shard out in one quick motion.

"Ouch!"

"Sorry. This is going to sting." Kristy pulls the bottle of antiseptic out of the first-aid kit and sprays the cut.

Gillian's eyes water from the pain. Kristy rips the wrapper from a gauze pad and bandages Gillian's foot.

"Thank you," Gillian says grudgingly.

Kristy takes a larger piece of gauze and wipes the soot from her face.

"Just so you know," Gillian mutters, "I'm not sorry I did that to your face."

Kristy shrugs. "I don't blame you."

"I'm dizzy." Gillian buries her head between her knees and counts the blades of grass beneath her. When she lifts up her head, Kristy is playing with the shard of glass that razored Gillian's foot.

"You're not going to do something stupid with that glass, are you?" Gillian remembers Sebastian's threats.

"Of course not."

"Just give me that." Gillian snatches the glass from Kristy.

"Corona."

Gillian says, to no one, "Sebastian only drank Budweiser."

"I can stay with you."

"You're just the tonic I need right now." Gillian does not recognize the bitter shell coating her voice.

"I'm going to go, then."

"Please do."

As Gillian watches Kristy walk away, she considers chasing after her and demanding that she take a paternity test. All Kristy has to do is spit in a cup, and Gillian will know if she's tethered to this backstabber for life. She feels the answer, though. It's obvious. She allows herself to remember the rotten Sebastian, the dread she felt when he made eye contact with a woman, be it her piano teacher or a neighbor. The woman didn't have to be pretty or single or old enough to drink in the Commonwealth of Virginia. He would hold her eyes with his for that extra second or two, the way Kristy did with the manager at the Starbucks after she scalded Gillian's thighs, the way she caught Kristy eyeing Charlie at the luau. Kristy shouldn't think she's special; there are likely more Sebastian spawn living in the D.C. metro area.

Well, Gillian finally got her wish, a sister who would care about the pool, who would serve as her wingman. Be careful what you wish for.

87

KRISTY

Kristy doesn't know where to go after she leaves the pool, so she drives to the Safeway lot to grab a few minutes to collect herself. Mia is probably home, and Kristy will frighten her if she shows up in this state. She dials Beverly. No answer. Fuck. Okay, think, Kristy. What would Beverly tell you to do? Find a meeting. She's bookmarked the SLAA site. No meetings right now. She dials Beverly again. No answer. Well, it has only been thirty seconds.

The one thing that might bring her a second of relief is a smidgeon of warmth from Charlie. She conjures the image of his desire for her the night of the luau. He wanted her, until he didn't. She has to call him. It's only right for her to give him a heads-up about what just happened at the pool. He doesn't pick up. "Charlie, please call me. I just had it out with Gillian." She hopes he'll respond like he did when he drove to the bar.

What if he calls back? Asks to see her? She must look like hell right now. She takes the bag she packed to go to Travis's house into a Chipotle bathroom. The mirror is hostile to her. "Crap." A trail of soot rims her hairline and burrows between the creases on her neck. Two teenagers with long silky hair and faded jean shorts riding up their asses look away as if she's standing there naked. She smiles sweetly at them as they exit the bathroom with smug smiles plastered on their mugs. As she rinses off her face, black water swirls around the drain. With her wet hands, she slicks back her hair. The paper towel dispenser's empty, so she holds her face under the air dryer. Her clothes are filthy, so she avails herself of the handicapped stall and strips down. She rifles through her bag for a clean pair of panties and her cotton sundress, and then she brushes her teeth and rolls deodorant under her arms. She still smells bad, but spraying perfume will only make it worse. She returns to the mirror. Better. She glances at the heap of clothes on the stall floor and stuffs them into the slender trash can attached to the wall. As she exits the restaurant, bag in hand, she can hear the old familiar sound of girls whispering behind her back. She stops and gives them her best stink eye. "Power outage, girls. We do what has to be done."

Safely back in her steamy car, she checks her messages. No return calls from Charlie or Beverly. She tries them again. And again. Then she contemplates her next move. She can't face her family. Not yet. Where else can she go? She needs to find *someone* who will understand what's going on. Bingo! She Googles Patrick Sebastian Norton. He lives in Alexandria? She looks him up on WhitePages.com. Holy crap, he's only ten minutes from here.

She only met Patrick once, years ago, at Sebby's laser tag birthday party. She was so preoccupied chasing after Isaac that she didn't notice Patrick's drinking, although she vaguely remembers Charlie politely asking him to leave, maybe even calling him a cab. After the party, Gillian railed on her brother and the failure of his twelve-step malarkey. Kristy clearly recalls thinking three things: one, anyone else would have used the word "bullshit" instead of "malarkey" in this context; two, Gillian would never have fully accepted the dark addict in Kristy, nor would David; and three, Kristy better keep her shit together.

She enters Patrick's address into her GPS and drives right to his condo complex. Still nothing from Charlie or Beverly. She isn't even nervous as she knocks firmly on the bright red door to his townhouse. What more could she lose?

Her heart's too tired to race when she hears footsteps on the other side of the door. It opens, and there stands her brother. She takes him in, his broad shoulders, the graying blond hair, the narrow hips. His bright blue eyes, the color and shape of Gillian's and Justin's.

She extends her hand. "I'm Kristy Weinstein, Gillian's friend."

"I know." He scrutinizes her like she's a raccoon raiding his trash can. "About you and Charlie."

"You know?"

"Justin told me."

Gillian would have a fit if she knew that Justin and Patrick were in touch. "Can I please come in?"

He moves to the side of the doorframe and lets her into the foyer. The condo is sparse and clean. "I don't want to be rude, but why are you here?"

Best to act fast. Right now Patrick is looking at her like she's the woman who has just destroyed his family. "Because I'm your sister."

They face one another. Kristy holds up her hand and after a few seconds he presses his large paw against it. The tips of his fingers eclipse hers. When they look up from their hands, Kristy sees recognition in his eyes. In her whole life she's never felt this current with Nora. Or Gillian.

"Come in." He leads her to his cool kitchen, where the early-evening sun stripes his body and illuminates the gold in his hair.

"Why are you here right now?" This time his tone is gentle.

She blows the dog whistle that will connect them eternally. "Because my sponsor is unavailable."

His face looks like a tire that someone has pumped full of compassion. "Okay. Have you had anything to drink?"

"Not my vice."

He nods. "I see."

"Charlie's my substance."

"At least Sebastian was kind enough to split his addictions between the two of us." Patrick runs his hands through his hair.

"Guess so."

"How did none of us notice the resemblance?" He looks at her again. "It's eerie."

"If you know what to look for."

"So, what are you going to do?" he asks.

"Try to stop calling Charlie."

"That's not going to be easy."

Her limbs go flappy. A living member of her own family understands her. Finally. "You got that right."

"We have so much to talk about."

"On the other hand, we've heard each other's stories again and again in the rooms."

"Yeah," he says. "We have."

"I'm hungry."

He sets a plate in front of her and retrieves a jar of peanut butter and a box of Ritz crackers from the pantry.

"You got a spoon?"

He hands her a soup spoon from the drying rack. When she opens the jar, she notices the oval-shaped divots in the thick paste. "David hates when I eat peanut butter out of the jar."

He smiles. "Maybe something good can come from all this."

"Something already has." She sighs and scoops a big wad of Jif.

"No double-dipping," he says, and they laugh together, as if sharing an old family joke.

88

JUSTIN

The air in the house smells like wet carpet. He waits for his mom at the kitchen table. The room is dark, save for a few lit candles. When the car door slams, every muscle in his body tenses.

He barely recognizes the woman who comes through the back door. His mom's arms are caked in soot, and her hair is flying every which way out of her ponytail. Her foot is bandaged, and she's limping. "What happened?"

"Long story. I'm okay." She doesn't take off her shoes or ask for Dad before she slumps into a chair next to Justin. How could his father have done this to her? To their family? And with her best friend? He can feel Mom reading his thoughts.

"Oh, Justin." Even in the soft light, he sees the blood rush up her neck to her cheeks.

"I'm so sorry." Justin blinks away the image of Aunt Kristy with her dress on backwards.

"I'm not sure how much you know, sweetheart."

"Mom—"

"Please let me finish." She puts one of her dirty hands on his forearm. "Because there's one fact that won't go away."

He places his free hand over hers. What else is there to say?

"Do you mind, honey, pouring your old mom a glass of water?"

"Of course." He brings the water, sets it on the table, and sits back down next to her. "You don't have to tell me if you don't want to."

"No, you have to know this."

He's scared. "Okay."

She takes a big sip of water. "Aunt Kristy is actually my sister."

It's weird, but her voice lightens for a second when she says the words. He feels as though she just told him that the earth is flat. "I don't understand."

"Justin, your grandfather was a complicated man."

"I know, Mom." She looks tiny to him. "Are you okay?"

"I should be asking you that, dear. I'm the mom."

He's so pissed at Dad right now. Justin hopes he won't come home from wherever he is. He sits with Mom in the dusk. He'll stay as long as she needs him. "Do you want to play a game of gin rummy?"

"Sounds fun, but I better shower before it gets too dark." She tousles his hair before hobbling through the kitchen, shedding dirty footprints on the tile.

Justin lies on his bed, listening for Dad to open the back door, for him to climb the steps to the second floor, for his parents to start fighting. Silence. He wants them all back as they were before his father took this stupid coaching job. He feels like an old man. He falls into a deep, sweaty sleep.

89

GILLIAN

Gillian wakes up the next morning, her foot sore and her body achy. Happy Fourth of July to me. She weighs her options. She can pretend yesterday never happened, like her mother would have done. The pool is closed, but they can make a new tradition, maybe hit the Arlington parade, or grill up some hamburgers to repay the Johnsons for hosting Justin at the beach and during the first few days of the power outage. Not a chance. She can't imagine celebrating the Fourth of July anywhere besides River Run. And she can't go back there. The mess of Kristy and Charlie and the pool is too slippery to grab hold of and tuck inside a bin. The heft of what she's lost drills down on her.

Gillian can handle things differently than May did. She knows what she must do. She throws on a pair of capris, arranges her hair into a messy bun, pads downstairs to her office, and writes Justin a quick note. And then she gasses up her car and speeds north on I-95. When she hits Baltimore, she stops driving. Baltimore is the perfect spot to hide, and she checks into a Marriott festooned with red, white, and blue balloons. To think that only days earlier, she and Charlie were engaging in their Marigold adventure.

It occurs to her to find the hotel gym. Inside the nice-sized facility, she kicks off her sandals and jumps on a bike, using the ball of her foot to pedal. The movement makes her arch hurt, but she doesn't care. She hasn't had anything to eat since yesterday morning, and she feels weak but strong too as she moves her legs at a steady clip. After her heart starts pumping, she sets the bike to the hardest incline. Her thigh muscles burn as she begins the climb.

A fit young mom in a tank top embroidered with an American flag enters the gym with her workout bag. Out of reflex, Gillian takes a gander inside and notices the crumpled-up shorts, a Lulu hat, and loose toiletries, clues that she could use Gillian's services. Normally Gillian would engage this woman, but she's exhausted. She guiltily thinks of her junkerboo clients. Who is Gillian to teach people how to stuff their bad memories into tidy bins? Lulu takes the next bike. Gillian feels the woman's eyes on her bare feet and linen capris. *Stop staring.* She would never say such a thing. May never allowed this type of talk. Her mother smiled when one of Sebastian's conquests, the mother of Patrick's best friend, sat next to them at the movie *Sounder*; she even offered the woman a tissue when Sounder ran away. Nortons weren't allowed to cry excessively either, so Gillian swallowed her tears over the loss of the hound.

If Kristy were to sit down next to her right this instant, Gillian wouldn't make a scene. The barrel of Kristy tears Gillian has swallowed might not even spill over. Kristy has always felt familiar to her, in that reckless, needy, all-or-nothing, compulsive Sebastian way. Sebastian was either on a bender or on a sanctimonious health kick. Kristy is either depriving herself of carbs or erasing the effects of a pecan pie misadventure with two spin classes and a hike. Kristy coupons, and she stocked her basement storage unit with cases of red wine, Crest, and Pirate's Booty when the kids were young. Sebastian and Kristy cut their parents out of their lives and tried to reinvent themselves, the vines of their rootlessness choking their unlucky targets, David and May.

Gillian is returning to a place she indeed recognizes, and it isn't fair. She worked tirelessly to prevent this very thing from happening. She picked a husband with moderate appetites, someone who would never land himself in the hospital or jail or dead-drunk on a dark road with a woman half his age. She picked a house near the River Run pool so they could spend their summers where Sebastian had been his best, where the photos and the endless flow of comments about her handsome father made her forget the mean drunk. She even picked a new sibling who would buy into all of it, who would need her in a way that Patrick no longer did, thanks to his program.

She is panting now, and the damp linen sticks to her bike seat.

Nobody works as hard as Gillian Cloud to make sure that everything's perfect. They all joke about her Facebooking, but they'll be happy one day to have a document of the life she created for them. She stands up on the bike to move her legs faster. She can no longer focus her eyes on the odometer in front of her. Pressing on the ball of her foot throws her off balance, and soon she's falling.

Thump.

She breaks her fall with her bad ankle. Pain scurries up from her slivered arch all the way to her hip until she feels nauseous. The Lulu rushes to her aid.

"That was quite a fall! Are you hurt?"

"More embarrassed than hurt." And that's saying something.

The Lulu extends her hand, and Gillian takes it. Her arch throbs in the way that her ankle did the day she lifeguarded her father at River Run, the pain as fresh as the day she first injured herself.

90

CHARLIE

Gillian returns from Baltimore changed. She's only been gone two days, but she exudes a steely reserve he's never seen before. He doesn't dare touch her. He sleeps in Sebby's room without her having to ask. Between Justin's long unquestioned absences and the void of Gillian's relentless optimism, the Cloud house feels like a mausoleum.

A week after the derecho, the power finally returns. Yet the heat wave continues for another four days, and most people have come unglued from sweating and eating fast food or cans of tuna and beans from their pantries and wearing dirty underwear.

And then there's the matter of Kristy, who's phoned him a dozen times since Gillian found out about them. She calls under the guise of checking in on Gillian, but the desperation in her voice enervates him. His sister-in-law is a vulture who swooped down on the entire Cloud family and left its carcass on the deck of the pool.

Karl has in fact managed to remove the big oak tree, and River Run is back in business, sans the pool house. Despite the porta-potties, it feels good to have the team back at the pool for their first post-derecho practice, kind of like sleeping in your own bed after a long camping trip. Charlie's all business. Mia and Liam are no longer speaking, which makes things easier for everyone. Charlie can talk freely with Justin about the relay carnival lineup without worrying about hurting Gillian. That's pretty much all he and Justin can talk about, though.

A few days before the next meet, Charlie approaches Shannon and asks if she'll take over for Kristy as automation rep.

"I'd be glad to, Charlie." She adjusts her sunglasses. "Look, I've wanted to tell you again how so sorry I am about the tiki torches."

"It was a fluke thing." He doesn't mean to sound harsh, but he wants to clip this conversation. "It wasn't your fault."

"All-righty, then." Shannon claps her hands together. "Happy to do automation. Anything you need."

They manage without a team rep, because Gillian has trained her people well.

The swimmers are clearing out, but Charlie isn't ready to face Gillian. He settles into a lounge chair, the relay carnival lineup on his lap. He can't concentrate, and his eyes travel to the charred and gutted clubhouse, which is in his direct line of vision.

Justin surprises him by sitting down one chair over. "It's totally weird without Mom here."

"It is." Charlie knows what he means. He feels Gillian more in her absence than he did when she was reigning over the Manta Rays. His shame over what he's done to his wife and son devours him. He wishes Justin would say more, but Charlie won't push.

He gazes across the pool at Shannon chatting lightly with one of the newer swim moms. The freedom he felt when he started coaching fills him, the same liberation he felt when he left his job last winter, when he decided to remake his life. He attracted Manta Ray families who wanted something new. Charlie set his marriage on fire too. Now in planning to rebuild the clubhouse, and maybe his marriage along with it, problems with the foundation have surfaced and will be addressed. He once read about how the Aborigines burn their fields to prepare the soil for understory plants. Maybe the razing of the clubhouse will make way for something healthier to flourish.

MAY 2013

91

GILLIAN

Gillian only agrees to attend the ribbon-cutting ceremony for the new clubhouse because it seems important to Justin and Sebby, both home for Memorial Day weekend. Gillian has ghosted River Run as Kristy ghosted her last summer. She hasn't seen or spoken to Kristy since she attacked her with the ashes. Even driving by the pool parking lot hurts. The only happy recollections she has of her childhood were from her time at River Run. Now her only family memories are of the scary times when the Nortons were not at the pool. When these long-buried thoughts of Sebastian grab her by the throat, she calls Patrick to apologize again for "gaslighting you about our childhood." And she asks her brother for more stories about Sebastian's history, hat in hand. Patrick knows a handful of tales about their grandfather's drunken rages and Sebastian seeking refuge from the whippings with his aunt. She forces herself to listen to every detail.

The summer after Sebastian died, Gillian returned to the pool to help coach the Manta Rays. In retrospect, the River Run community likely knew that Sebastian had been drunk when he crashed his beloved Mustang, but nobody knew about the girl in the car. In death, Sebastian morphed into who he was when he was healthy, as the dead often do. And by the time Gillian returned to River Run with Charlie and the boys, only a handful of old-timers were left, and they were more than happy to indulge the mythology Gillian created about her father. It was simple to find a new batch of River Rats and start anew.

Shortly after the derecho, Charlie asked Gillian whether she minded if he headed the construction of the new pool house, and he attacked his first-ever real estate project with ferocity. She said no, because she'd come to the hard truth that neither the pool nor Charlie belonged to her. They never had.

She watches Charlie create a business plan for placing winter domes over outdoor community pools in order to accommodate the large numbers of Northern Virginia swimmers. His energy buoys her, but she never offers to help. She's busy too, though. She's taken on a host of new clients, but on the advice of her new therapist she no longer facilitates their stowing away their painful memories.

A month ago, Charlie moved back into their bedroom, but she can't make love to him. Not yet.

KRISTY

Kristy and Beverly engage in long talks about whether she should attend the River Run clubhouse ribbon-cutting ceremony. She's now truly in recovery, but only because she does everything Beverly tells her to: goes to meetings twice a week, texts or speaks with Beverly every day, journals, adds two shifts to her hotline gig, and anonymously donates her savings from her nursing job to the River Run construction fund as an amend. She meets Travis for lunch once every two weeks or so, and when Nora visited last August, Kristy invited her out for Mexican food, and over chips and guac, Nora's favorite, made an amend for years of trying to make Nora feel small.

Most importantly, she deletes Charlie's contact information from her phone and stops herself from showing up at his gym. It takes much longer to stop replaying the time when he looked at her with lust. That memory is like crack. After the high of conjuring Charlie's face, she feels riddled with shame. Kristy and Beverly decide that she will not make an amend to David, but rather do a living amend, which means no Charlie. Kristy tells David, Mia, and Isaac about Sebastian, not because she's ready but because she doesn't want them to find out from someone else. She tells them that she needs some time away from the Clouds to process this new development, and they seem to understand. But Kristy knows that her presence today at the ribbon-cutting ceremony at River Run, a legacy now shared by Isaac and Mia, means something to them.

93

JUSTIN

On the morning of the ribbon-cutting, Justin and Sebby decorate the pool with streamers and balloons. They camp out in the freshly minted guard station and help this year's crop of lifeguards check in members. They keep one eye on the entrance to the parking lot, waiting for Mom or their honest-to-God Aunt Kristy to appear. Neither shows up for the actual ribbon-cutting, organized by Mrs. O'Leary.

"Your mom might not make it today, guys," Charlie says to them after the ceremony, his arms brimming with cases of Pepsi.

Justin knows better.

Last week he was waist-deep in the pool, helping a swimmer master the dolphin kick, when he thought he saw Mom standing outside the fence. But then she was gone, and he wondered if he was seeing things. Nobody mentions her name. Ever. And even though Mia is coaching, Aunt Kristy has all but vaporized, as if she went up in smoke along with the clubhouse.

Justin lugs the remaining cases of soda to the pavilion and dumps the cans into a dusty bucket of ice. It's a scorcher today, but not as humid as it was during last summer's heat wave. Justin rewinds the weeks leading up to the storm, imagining scenarios in which he could have stopped what happened that night. He frequently asks people what they were doing the night of the derecho in the hope that their stories will obliterate his own memory. Every Washingtonian, it seems, has a derecho story. First they speak of the trees, the way their limbs danced or their trunks heaved themselves onto roofs and parked cars. Then they curse Dominion Energy and tell tales of sleeping in their basements, taking cold showers, camping out in malls, and the crazy shit they extracted from their freezers and barbecued before it rotted. No phones. No power. No rules. Surreal.

Justin's derecho story trumps them all, hands down. Every time. He takes a small chunk of ice from the bucket and presses it into Sebby's back. Sebby thwacks him on the head. They play a game of Scrabble on their phones and wait.

"Hey . . ." Justin nudges Sebby. "Look."

Sebby turns toward the parking lot.

Mom is walking toward them, her arms swaying freely against her sides.

94

GILLIAN

Justin and Sebby are sitting at the new check-in gate together, shirtless and tanned, clearly waiting for her to arrive. Justin is clicking a pen (property of River Run) impatiently. The sight of Sebby, a miniature version of both Patrick and Sebastian, takes her breath away. She would have come earlier, but she was waiting for Charlie to leave the pool first. It was too soon for her to see him there.

"Look at you two. Are you the welcoming committee?" Gillian tugs at the bill of Sebby's visor.

They smile at her the way they used to when she picked them up from preschool and they screamed out, "You're here!" and jumped into her arms. The clubhouse smells like sawdust and wet paint. The urge to hurt Kristy has subsided, but like the pain in her ankle, it shows up if she forgets about it for too long.

"Do you want me to give you a tour?" Justin offers.

Gillian's not certain that she's ready to experience the new-and-improved River Run facility, but she can't say no to Justin.

"Room for one more?"

Gillian recognizes Kristy's voice immediately. She doesn't trust herself to make eye contact with her. "Lead the way, Justin."

Justin is too enthusiastic when he shows them the new structure. The building no longer looks like someone's home with the sounds and scents of ghosts trapped in the walls. It's simply a pool house with a terrace and a snack bar and a trophy case. The walls are heavily windowed, affording little room to hang photos.

"It's lovely," Kristy says.

"Hmmm . . ." Gillian isn't ready to face Kristy, so she walks out to the terrace and then the pool, relieved to hear Kristy's footsteps behind her. She keeps walking, past two families packing up their picnic basket to go home, past the stump of the big oak tree, past Riley O'Leary, who is playing her last game of Sharks and Manta Rays, past Karl talking to a lifeguard, and to the diving board. Gillian stops. *Mis-ter. Nor-ton. Mis-ter. Nor-ton.* She can almost hear the chant.

Gillian feels Kristy standing behind her, and she finally faces her sister. Kristy's eyes look rehab-sad, Sebastian Norton rehab-sad, and a softening begins to take root inside her. For Kristy and their dad. She looks harder into Kristy's eyes, her father's eyes, deep brown pools. She makes herself see what she stored away: Kristy cleaning Gillian's angry purple wound after her hysterectomy; Kristy shimmying up against Charlie hours before they set fire to the pool house; the hungry grown woman who was always slurping down milk and coffee. She sees Sebastian's drunk father chasing him around the dinner table with a butcher knife and Sebastian patiently teaching her long division.

Gillian looks around to where Sebastian sat before his swan dive, and now she can't help but see the empty Budweiser bottles that she edited out of the photo. She excised the scary pieces of her father. That's not love. Sebastian Norton was damaged and desperate for shelter, from his father, from his past, and from himself. And to love a person is to accept their ugliness and beauty.

"Hey, Gil." Patrick, sober, lean, and neatly dressed in a pair of khaki shorts and a polo shirt, approaches her, and she sees the nervous little blond boy who, like her, kept vigil over Sebastian, ready to duck and cover at the first sign of his wrath. Patrick takes his place on the other side of Gillian.

Gillian holds out her hands, and Kristy and Patrick each take one. She looks to the left and then to the right. The sun casts a warm gold on her siblings' light hair. The Norton children. As Gillian's and Kristy's kids walk over to them, she prays for the first time since that night in the hospital. She prays that Kristy and Patrick and Sebby will stay in recovery, she prays that Sebastian's grandchildren and great-grandchildren will roam free, far from his demons. And she prays that they will know to find love and comfort in good places. That's what she prays for the hardest.

The Norton children and grandchildren form a loose human chain alongside the pool.

Kristy loops her pinkie through Gillian's, and Gillian holds on tight.

95

JUSTIN

Justin feels a thin steel wire connecting each Norton descendant, stringing them together as if they are the green and white disks spanning a lane line. Someone is missing. He tears himself away from the family and walks briskly to the shiny new diving board. He climbs up the ladder, two rungs at a time. When he reaches the top, he walks with great purpose to the end of the plank.

He stands still for a few seconds.

He jumps, once, twice, three times, and on the fourth bounce he raises his hands over his head and explodes into the air. He flies into the cloudless sky, over the placid water. Mom, Uncle Patrick, Aunt Kristy, Sebby, Mia, and Isaac crane their necks to watch him, cupping their brows to shield their eyes from the orange sun. He flings his arms wide, completely vulnerable to that magnetic force that terrified him last summer. Nothing. Only the warm breeze created by his own movement. On his descent, he spots his family dropping their hands from their foreheads, part wave, part salute to the ghost of Sebastian Norton. And Justin continues his dive into the River Run pool, like a swan.

THE END

ACKNOWLEDGMENTS

My heart is full of gratitude for the many people who helped *Swimming with Ghosts* make its way into the world. I'll start with my agent, Jill Marr, for her enduring friendship and guidance, the Turner/Keylight team including Todd Bottorff for publishing my book, Ryan Smernoff for his enthusiasm, stellar editorial skills, and for grasping the guts and heart of the novel, and the Turner marketing crew and Michelle Blankenship for their efforts to spread the word far and wide.

Big thanks to my readers for their encouragement and insights: Melissa Goldman Davidson, David Groff, Tara Ison, Anna Rojas White. And to Tracy Kroloff, beta reader extraordinaire, and Jamie Holland, an early, middle, and final reader who offered rounds of brilliant notes. Thank you, Shannon O'Neill, for excellent editorial advice and the pep talk that spared this book from the paper shredder; Katy Reilly, Lisa Sorkin, and Beth Bautista, for game-changing feedback on a late draft of the novel, and Joy Johannessen, whose blue pen marks I revere.

Hugs to my crew of believers: Amy Simmons, Dara Feldman, Mark Thalman, my beloved coven/dream mappers, Colleen Dunn Bates, and Andrea Bayewitz.

Love to the Whitman, NCAP, and ASA swim moms and dads who became dear friends over the course of more than a decade of carpools and chlorine. Thanks to the Bannockburn Dolphins for years of poolside zaniness and spirit, and especially to my partner in crime,

Kate Wassiliew, who always brings the fun, and the wisdom too. Deep gratitude to Cathy Bernasek and Mike Moriarty for the scoop on the Northern Virginia Swim League and invaluable fact checking and to Melissa Mathis Olson for her smart read and for scouting out the Northern Virginia community pools, houses, and donut shops that helped me conjure the *Swimming with Ghosts* world.

My various writing communities feed my soul: the Glen Echo Workshops, New Directions, the Johns Hopkins MA in Writing Program, the DMV Women Writers; and beloved uber leaders who taught me the value of such literary kinship, the late Faye Moskowitz, Mary Kay Zuravleff, and Jean Graubart.

The characters in *Swimming with Ghosts* appeared in three short stories. Thank you, Donna Oetzel, for egging me on with your smart feedback on "Whoopie Pies"; Susan Coll for a beautiful friendship and for selecting "Take Your Mark" for *District Lines* and Lisa Couturier for nominating the piece for a Pushcart Prize; Trish Murphy for publishing "Brain Freeze" in *Superstition Review* and John Penovich for engineering the audio version of the story, and Caroline Bock for including "I Am Your Mask" in the Washington Writers' Publishing House anthology *This Is What America Looks Like.*

Big thanks to Anne Lamott for her work, support, and for teaching me the perfect prayer for all occasions and to every person and every book, of which there were many, that provided me with experience, strength, and hope and a deeper understanding of the complexities of addiction.

Extra special helping of love to Beth Lynch for her belief in parking karma, in me, and in our ability to transcend our most devastating personal histories, one breath at a time.

I wish my mom, Lotta Brafman, were alive to see this book come to fruition, and I wish we could have talked about all that I learned while writing it. She was a world-class kveller, as is my father, Stuart Brafman, a natural storyteller who modeled both hard work and vision. Thanks to my brother, Lester Brafman, who always has my back. And loads of gratitude to my Helfs: Gabriela, for her pitch-perfect ear and ginormous heart; Gideon, for reading the whole novel aloud to me when I needed to hear it and for touching me with his songs, and to Tom, my first reader, my love.

BOOK GROUP QUESTIONS

1. Why does Gillian hold on so fiercely to the River Run pool and its traditions?
2. Kristy and Gillian were drawn together like magnets when they met at the playground when their children were young. Do two people have to share a bloodline to experience such an instant and familiar intimacy?
3. Discuss the specific loss of a friend breakup.
4. How have Sebastian Norton and his legacy of addiction influenced his three children's lives differently? How have his grandchildren, particularly Sebby and Justin, been affected by his alcoholism? Discuss Patrick's sobriety and his role in Sebby's and Justin's lives.
5. How might Kristy's life have been different had she grown up with Sebastian instead of Travis for a father? Why does Kristy cut herself off emotionally from Travis, Flo, and Nora? What draws her back to Travis during her most desperate moment?
6. There are crucial passages when characters are aware of the destructive nature of their choices, and they make them anyway. Why?
7. The derecho has been described as a perfect storm. What does that mean in the context of this story? What specific combination of factors conspires to set the story in motion? How do you explain Charlie's new passion for the community that Gillian holds dear? How is a derecho a metaphor for Kristy's relapse?
8. Ultimately, the derecho decimates the physical space of the River

Run pool and the internal space of the characters' lives. What will it take for them to rebuild the relationships with the people who matter to them the most? Do you think they can?

9. The ghost motif surfaces throughout the novel. How? What does it mean to ghost a loved one? To be haunted? To demystify a family ghost?
10. What does it ultimately mean to swim with ghosts? Is it possible to transcend a painful family legacy?
11. The epigraph for this novel is a quote from Toni Morrison's novel, *Song of Solomon*. "If you surrendered to the air, you could ride it" and the final image in the novel is of Justin flying through the air, mid-swan dive. What does the recurrence of the swan dive signify? Why do you think the author opens and closes the novel with the image of taking flight?

ABOUT THE AUTHOR

Michelle Brafman is the author of the novel *Washing the Dead* and *Bertrand Court: Stories*. Her essays and short stories have appeared in *Slate*, *LitHub*, *The Forward*, *Tablet*, and elsewhere. She teaches fiction writing in the Johns Hopkins University MA in Writing Program. A former swim mom and NCAA All-American freestyler, Michelle has never lived more than a mile away from a pool, lake, ocean, or river. Learn more at www.michellebrafman.com.